00 401 070 940

091
26

16

Northamptonshire

DISCARDED

Libraries

KT-371-202

THE GIRL ON THE TRAIN

Rachel catches the same commuter train every morning. She even feels she knows the people who live in one of the houses. 'Jess and Jason', she calls them. Their life – as she sees it – is perfect. If only Rachel could be that happy.
And then she sees something shocking. It's only a minute until the train moves on, but it's enough. Now everything's changed. Now Rachel has a chance to become a part of the lives she's only watched from afar. Now they'll see: she's much more than just the girl on the train...

THE GIRL ON THE TRAIN

by

Paula Hawkins

Magna Large Print Books
Long Preston, North Yorkshire,
BD23 4ND, England.

British Library Cataloguing in Publication Data.

Hawkins, Paula
    The girl on the train.

    A catalogue record of this book is
    available from the British Library

    ISBN 978-0-7505-4223-4

First published in Great Britain in 2015 by Doubleday
an imprint of Transworld Publishers

Copyright © Paula Hawkins 2015

Cover illustration by arrangement with Arcangel Images

Paula Hawkins has asserted her right under the Copyright, Designs
and Patents Act, 1988 to be identified as the author of this work.

Published in Large Print 2016 by arrangement with
Transworld Publishers

All Rights reserved. No part of this publication may be reproduced,
stored in a retrieval system, or transmitted in any form or by any
means, electronic, mechanical, photocopying, recording or otherwise
without the prior permission of the Copyright owner.

Northamptonshire
Libraries

Magna Large Print is an imprint of Library Magna Books Ltd.

Printed and bound in Great Britain by
T.J. (International) Ltd., Cornwall, PL28 8RW

This book is a work of fiction and
any resemblance to actual persons,
living or dead, is purely coincidental.

For Kate

She's buried beneath a silver birch tree, down towards the old train tracks, her grave marked with a cairn. Not more than a little pile of stones, really. I didn't want to draw attention to her resting place, but I couldn't leave her without remembrance. She'll sleep peacefully there, no one to disturb her, no sounds but birdsong and the rumble of passing trains.

One for sorrow, two for joy, three for a girl. Three for a girl. I'm stuck on three, I just can't get any further. My head is thick with sounds, my mouth thick with blood. Three for a girl. I can hear the magpies, they're laughing, mocking me, a raucous cackling. A tiding. Bad tidings. I can see them now, black against the sun. Not the birds, something else. Someone's coming. Someone is speaking to me. *Now look. Now look what you made me do.*

RACHEL

Morning

There is a pile of clothing on the side of the train tracks. Light-blue cloth – a shirt, perhaps – jumbled up with something dirty white. It's probably rubbish, part of a load fly-tipped into the scrubby little wood up the bank. It could have been left behind by the engineers who work this part of the track, they're here often enough. Or it could be something else. My mother used to tell me that I had an overactive imagination; Tom said that too. I can't help it, I catch sight of these discarded scraps, a dirty T-shirt or a lonesome shoe, and all I can think of is the other shoe, and the feet that fitted into them.

The train jolts and scrapes and screeches back into motion, the little pile of clothes disappears from view and we trundle on towards London, moving at a brisk jogger's pace. Someone in the seat behind me gives a sigh of helpless irritation; the 8.04 slow train from Ashbury to Euston can test the patience of the most seasoned commuter. The journey is supposed to take fifty-four minutes, but it rarely does: this section of the track is ancient, decrepit, beset with signalling problems and never-ending engineering works.

The train crawls along; it judders past warehouses and water towers, bridges and sheds, past modest Victorian houses, their backs turned squarely to the track.

My head leaning against the carriage window, I watch these houses roll past me like a tracking shot in a film. I see them as others do not; even their owners probably don't see them from this perspective. Twice a day, I am offered a view into other lives, just for a moment. There's something comforting about the sight of strangers safe at home.

Someone's phone is ringing, an incongruously joyful and upbeat song. They're slow to answer, it jingles on and on around me. I can feel my fellow commuters shift in their seats, rustle their newspapers, tap at their computers. The train lurches and sways around the bend, slowing as it approaches a red signal. I try not to look up, I try to read the free newspaper I was handed on my way into the station, but the words blur in front of my eyes, nothing holds my interest. In my head I can still see that little pile of clothes lying at the edge of the track, abandoned.

Evening

The pre-mixed gin and tonic fizzes up over the lip of the can as I bring it to my mouth and sip. Tangy and cold, the taste of my first ever holiday with Tom, a fishing village on the Basque coast in 2005. In the mornings we'd swim the half-mile to the little island in the bay, make love on secret hidden beaches; in the afternoons we'd sit at a bar drinking strong, bitter gin and tonics, watching swarms of beach footballers playing chaotic 25-a-side games on the low-tide sands.

I take another sip, and another; the can's already half empty but it's OK, I have three more in the plastic bag at my feet. It's Friday, so I don't have to feel guilty about drinking on the train. TGIF. The fun starts here.

It's going to be a lovely weekend, that's what they're telling us. Beautiful sunshine, cloudless skies. In the old days we might have driven to Corly Wood with a picnic and the papers, spent all afternoon lying on a blanket in dappled sunlight, drinking wine.

We might have barbecued out back with friends, or gone to The Rose and sat in the beer garden, faces flushing with sun and alcohol as the afternoon went on, weaving home, arm in arm, falling asleep on the sofa.

Beautiful sunshine, cloudless skies, no one to play with, nothing to do. Living like this, the way I'm living at the moment, is harder in the summer when there is so much daylight, so little cover of darkness, when everyone is out and about, being flagrantly, aggressively happy. It's exhausting, and it makes you feel bad if you're not joining in.

The weekend stretches out ahead of me, forty-eight empty hours to fill. I lift the can to my mouth again, but there's not a drop left.

Monday, 8 July 2013

Morning

It's a relief to be back on the 8.04. It's not that I can't wait to get into London to start my week – I don't particularly want to be in London at all. I just want to lean back in the soft, sagging velour seat, feel the warmth of the sunshine streaming through the window, feel the carriage rock back and forth and back and forth, the comforting rhythm of wheels on tracks. I'd rather be here, looking out at the houses beside the track, than almost anywhere else.

There's a faulty signal on this line, about half-way through my journey. I assume it must be faulty, in any case, because it's almost always red; we stop there most days, sometimes just for a few seconds, sometimes for minutes on end. If I sit in carriage D, which I usually do, and the train stops at this signal, which it almost always does, I have a perfect view into my favourite track-side house: number fifteen.

Number fifteen is much like the other houses along this stretch of track: a Victorian semi, two storeys high, overlooking a narrow, well-tended garden which runs around twenty feet down to-wards some fencing, beyond which lie a few metres of no man's land before you get to the railway track. I know this house by heart. I know every brick, I know the colour of the curtains in the upstairs bedroom (beige, with a dark-blue print), I know that the paint is peeling off the bathroom window frame and that there are four

16

tiles missing from a section of the roof over on the right-hand side.

I know that on warm summer evenings, the occupants of this house, Jason and Jess, sometimes climb out of the large sash window to sit on the makeshift terrace on top of the kitchen-extension roof. They are a perfect, golden couple. He is dark haired and well built, strong, protective, kind. He has a great laugh. She is one of those tiny bird-women, a beauty, pale-skinned with blonde hair cropped short. She has the bone structure to carry that kind of thing off, sharp cheekbones dappled with a sprinkling of freckles, a fine jaw.

While we're stuck at the red signal, I look for them. Jess is often out there in the mornings, especially in the summer, drinking her coffee. Sometimes, when I see her there, I feel as though she sees me too, I feel as though she looks right back at me, and I want to wave. I'm too self-conscious. I don't see Jason quite so much, he's away a lot with work. But even if they're not there, I think about what they might be up to. Maybe this morning they've both got the day off and she's lying in bed while he makes breakfast, or maybe they've gone for a run together, be-cause that's the sort of thing they do. (Tom and I used to run together on Sundays, me going at slightly above my normal pace, him at about half his, just so we could run side by side.) Maybe Jess is upstairs in the spare room, painting, or maybe they're in the shower together, her hands pressed against the tiles, his hands on her hips.

Evening

Turning slightly towards the window, my back to the rest of the carriage, I open one of the little bottles of Chenin Blanc I purchased from the Whistlestop at Euston. It's not cold, but it'll do. I pour some into a plastic cup, screw the top back on and slip the bottle into my handbag. It's less acceptable to drink on the train on a Monday, unless you're drinking with company, which I am not.

There are familiar faces on these trains, people I see every week, going to and fro. I recognize them and they probably recognize me. I don't know whether they see me, though, for what I really am.

It's a glorious evening, warm but not too close, the sun starting its lazy descent, shadows lengthening and the light just beginning to burnish the trees with gold. The train is rattling along, we whip past Jason and Jess's place, they pass in a blur of evening sunshine. Sometimes, not often, I can see them from this side of the track. If there's no train going in the opposite direction, and if we're travelling slowly enough, I can sometimes catch a glimpse of them out on their terrace. If not – like today – I can imagine them. Jess will be sitting with her feet up on the table out on the terrace, a glass of wine in her hand, Jason standing behind her, his hands on her shoulders. I can imagine the feel of his hands, the weight of them, reassuring and protective. Sometimes I catch myself trying to remember the last time I had meaningful physical contact with another person, just a hug or a heartfelt squeeze of my hand, and my heart twitches.

18

Tuesday, 9 July 2013

Morning

The pile of clothes from last week is still there, and it looks dustier and more forlorn than it did a few days ago. I read somewhere that a train can rip the clothes right off you when it hits. It's not that unusual, death by train. Two to three hundred a year, they say, so at least one every couple of days. I'm not sure how many of those are accidental. I look carefully, as the train rolls slowly past, for blood on the clothes, but I can't see any.

The train stops at the signal as usual. I can see Jess standing on the patio in front of the French doors. She's wearing a bright print dress, her feet are bare. She's looking over her shoulder, back into the house; she's probably talking to Jason, who'll be making breakfast. I keep my eyes fixed on Jess, on her home, as the train starts to inch forward. I don't want to see the other houses; I particularly don't want to see the one four doors down, the one which used to be mine.

I lived at number twenty-three Blenheim Road for five years, blissfully happy and utterly wretched. I can't look at it now. That was my first home. Not my parents' place, not a flatshare with other students, my first home. I can't bear to look at it. Well, I can, I do, I want to, I don't want to, I try not to. Every day I tell myself not to look, and every day I look. I can't help myself, even though there is nothing I want to see there, even though

19

anything I do see will hurt me. Even though I remember so clearly how it felt that time I looked up and noticed that the cream linen blind in the upstairs bedroom was gone, replaced by something in soft baby pink; even though I still remember the pain I felt when I saw Anna watering the rose bushes near the fence, her T-shirt stretched tight over her bulging belly, and I bit my lip so hard it bled.

I close my eyes tightly and count to ten, fifteen, twenty. There, it's gone now, nothing to see. We roll into Witney station and out again, the train starting to pick up pace as suburbia melts into grimy north London, terraced houses replaced by tagged bridges and empty buildings with broken windows. The closer we get to Euston the more anxious I feel; pressure builds, how will today be? There's a filthy, low-slung concrete building on the right-hand side of the track about five hundred metres before we get into Euston. On its side, someone has painted: LIFE IS NOT A PARA-GRAPH. I think about the bundle of clothes on the side of the track and I feel as though my throat is closing up. Life is not a paragraph and death is no parenthesis.

Evening

The train I take in the evening, the 17.56, is slightly slower than the morning one – it takes one hour and one minute, a full seven minutes longer than the morning train despite not stopping at any extra stations. I don't mind, because just as I'm in no great hurry to get into London in the morning, I'm in no hurry to get back to Ashbury in the evening either. Not just because it's Ashbury, although the place itself is bad enough, a 1960s new town, spreading like a tumour over the heart of Buckinghamshire. No better or worse than a dozen other towns like it, a centre filled with cafés and mobile-phone shops and branches of JD Sports, surrounded by a band of suburbia and beyond that the realm of the multiplex cinema and out-of-town Tesco. I live in a smart(ish), new(ish) block situated at the point where the commercial heart of the place starts to bleed into the residential outskirts, but it is not my home. My home is the Victorian semi on the tracks, the one I part-owned. In Ashbury I am not a homeowner, not even a tenant – I'm a lodger, occupant of the small second bedroom in Cathy's bland and inoffensive duplex, subject to her grace and favour.

Cathy and I were friends at university. Half-friends, really, we were never that close. She lived across the hall from me in my first year and we were doing the same course, so we were natural allies in those first few daunting weeks, before we met people with whom we had more in common. We didn't see much of each other after the first year and barely at all after college, except for the occasional wedding. But in my hour of need she happened to have a spare room going and it made sense. I was so sure that it would only be for a couple of months, six at the most, and I didn't know what else to do. I'd never lived by myself, I'd gone from parents to flatmates to Tom, I found the idea overwhelming, so I said

21

yes. And that was nearly two years ago.

It's not *awful*. Cathy's a nice person, in a forceful sort of way. She makes you notice her niceness. Her niceness is writ large, it is her defining quality and she needs it acknowledged, often, daily almost, which can be tiring. But it's not so bad, I can think of worse traits in a flatmate. No, it's not Cathy, it's not even Ashbury that bothers me most about my new situation (I still think of it as new, although it's been two years). It's the loss of control. In Cathy's flat I always feel like a guest at the very outer limit of their welcome. I feel it in the kitchen, where we jostle for space when cooking our evening meals. I feel it when I sit beside her on the sofa, the remote control firmly within her grasp. The only space which feels like mine is my tiny bedroom, into which a double bed and a desk have been crammed, with barely enough space to walk between them. It's comfortable enough, but it isn't a place you want to be, so instead I linger in the living room or at the kitchen table, ill at ease and powerless. I have lost control over everything, even the places in my head.

Wednesday, 10 July 2013

Morning

The heat is building. It's barely half past eight and already the day is close, the air heavy with moisture. I could wish for a storm, but the sky is an insolent blank, pale, watery blue. I wipe away the sweat on my top lip. I wish I'd remembered to

22

buy a bottle of water.

I can't see Jason and Jess this morning, and my sense of disappointment is acute. Silly, I know. I scrutinize the house, but there's nothing to see. The curtains are open downstairs but the French doors are closed, sunlight reflecting off the glass. The sash window upstairs is closed, too. Jason may be away working. He's a doctor, I think, probably for one of those overseas organizations. He's constantly on call, a bag packed on top of the wardrobe; there's an earthquake in Iran or a tsunami in Asia and he drops everything, he grabs his bag and he's at Heathrow within a matter of hours, ready to fly out and save lives.

Jess, with her bold prints and her Converse trainers and her beauty, her attitude, works in the fashion industry. Or perhaps in the music business, or in advertising – she might be a stylist or a photographer. She's a good painter, too, plenty of artistic flair. I can see her now, in the spare room upstairs, music blaring, window open, a brush in her hand, an enormous canvas leaning against the wall. She'll be there until midnight; Jason knows not to bother her when she's working.

I can't really see her, of course. I don't know if she paints, or whether Jason has a great laugh, or whether Jess has beautiful cheekbones. I can't see her bone structure from here and I've never heard Jason's voice. I've never seen them up close, they didn't live at that house when I lived down the road. They moved in after I left two years ago, I don't know when exactly. I suppose I started noticing them about a year ago, and gradually, as the months went past, they became important to me.

I don't know their names either, so I had to name them myself. Jason, because he's handsome in a British film star kind of way, not a Depp or a Pitt, but a Firth, or a Jason Isaacs. And Jess just goes with Jason, and it goes with her. It fits her, pretty and carefree as she is. They're a match, they're a set. They're happy, I can tell. They're what I used to be, they're Tom and me, five years ago. They're what I lost, they're everything I want to be.

Evening

My shirt, uncomfortably tight, buttons straining across my chest, is pit stained, damp patches clammy beneath my arms. My eyes and throat itch. This evening I don't want the journey to stretch out; I long to get home, to undress and get into the shower, to be where no one can look at me. I look at the man in the seat opposite mine. He is about my age, early to mid-thirties, with dark hair, greying at the temples. Sallow skin. He's wearing a suit, but he's taken the jacket off and slung it on the seat next to him. He has a MacBook, paper thin, open in front of him. He's a slow typist. He's wearing a silver watch with a large face on his right wrist – it looks expensive, a Breitling maybe. He's chewing the inside of his cheek. Perhaps he's nervous. Or just thinking deeply. Writing an important email to a colleague at the office in New York, or a carefully worded break-up message to his girlfriend. He looks up suddenly and meets my eye; his glance travels over me, over the little bottle of wine on the table in front of me. He looks away. There's something about the set of his mouth which suggests distaste. He finds me distasteful.

I am not the girl I used to be. I am no longer desirable, I'm off-putting in some way. It's not just that I've put on weight, or that my face is puffy from the drinking and the lack of sleep; it's as if people can see the damage written all over me, they can see it in my face, the way I hold myself, the way I move.

One night last week, when I left my room to get myself a glass of water, I overheard Cathy talking to Damien, her boyfriend, in the living room. I stood in the hallway and listened. 'She's lonely,' Cathy was saying, 'I really worry about her. It doesn't help, her being alone all the time.' Then she said, 'Isn't there someone from work, maybe, or the rugby club?' and Damien said, 'For Rachel? Not being funny, Cath, but I'm not sure I know anyone that desperate.'

Thursday, 11 July 2013

Morning

I'm picking at the plaster on my forefinger. It's damp, it got wet when I was washing out my coffee mug this morning; it feels clammy, dirty, though it was clean on this morning. I don't want to take it off because the cut is deep. Cathy was out when I got home, so I went to the off-licence and bought two bottles of wine. I drank the first one and then I thought I'd take advantage of the fact that she was out and cook myself a steak, make a red-onion relish, have it with a green salad. A good, healthy meal. I sliced through the top of my finger while chopping the onions. I must have gone to the bathroom to clean it up and gone to lie down for a while and just forgotten all about the kitchen, because I woke up around ten and I could hear Cathy and Damien talking and he was saying how disgusting it was that I would leave the place like that. Cathy came upstairs to see me, she knocked softly on my door and opened it a fraction. She cocked her head to one side and asked if I was OK. I apologized without being sure what I was apologizing for. She said it was all right, but would I mind cleaning up a bit? There was blood on the chopping board, the room smelled of raw meat, the steak was still sitting out on the counter top, turning grey. Damien didn't even say hello, he just shook his head when he saw me and went upstairs to Cathy's bedroom.

After they'd both gone to bed I remembered that I hadn't drunk the second bottle, so I opened that. I sat on the sofa and watched television with the sound turned down really low so they wouldn't hear it. I can't remember what I was watching, but at some point I must have felt lonely, or happy, or something, because I wanted to talk to someone. The need for contact must have been overwhelming and there was no one I could call except for Tom.

There's no one I want to talk to except for Tom.

The call log on my phone says I rang four times: at 11.02, 11.12, 11.54, 12.09. Judging from the length of the calls, I left two messages. He may even have picked up, but I don't remember talking to him. I remember leaving the first message; I think I just asked him to call me. That may be what I said in both of them, which isn't too bad.

The train shudders to a standstill at the red signal and I look up.

Jess is sitting on her patio, drinking a cup of coffee. She has her feet up against the table and her head back, sunning herself. Behind her, I think I can see a shadow, someone moving: Jason. I long to see him, to catch a glimpse of his handsome face. I want him to come outside, to stand behind her, the way he does, to kiss the top of her head.

He doesn't come out, and her head falls forward. There is something about the way she is moving today that seems different; she is heavier, weighed down. I will him to come out to her, but the train jolts and slogs forward and still there is no sign of him; she's alone. And now, without thinking, I find myself looking directly into my house, and I can't look away. The French doors are flung open, light streaming into the kitchen. I can't tell, I really can't, whether I'm seeing this or imagining it – is she there, at the sink, washing up? Is there a little girl sitting in one of those bouncy baby chairs, up there on the kitchen table?

I close my eyes and let the darkness grow and spread until it morphs from a feeling of sadness into something worse: a memory, a flashback. I didn't just ask him to call me back. I remember now, I was crying. I told him that I still loved him, that I always would. *Please, Tom, please, I need to talk to you. I miss you.* No no no no no no no.

I have to accept it, there's no point trying to push it away. I'm going to feel terrible all day, it's going to come in waves – stronger then weaker then stronger again – that twist in the pit of my stomach, the anguish of shame, the heat coming to my face, my eyes squeezed tight as though I could make it all disappear. And I'll be telling myself all day, it's not the worst thing, is it? It's not the worst thing I've ever done, it's not as if I fell over in public, or yelled at a stranger in the street. It's not as if I humiliated my husband at a summer barbecue by shouting abuse at the wife of one of his friends. It's not as if we got into a fight one night at home and I went for him with a golf club, taking a chunk out of the plaster in the hallway outside the bedroom. It's not like going back to work after a three-hour lunch and staggering through the office, everyone looking, Martin Miles taking me to one side, *I think you should probably go home, Rachel.* I once read a book by a former alcoholic where she described giving oral sex to two different men, men she'd just met in a res-taurant on a busy London high street. I read it and I thought, I'm not *that* bad. This is where the bar is set.

Evening

I have been thinking about Jess all day, unable to focus on anything but what I saw this morning. What was it that made me think that something

28

was wrong? I couldn't possibly see her expression at that distance, but I felt when I was looking at her that she was alone. More than alone – lonely. Perhaps she was – perhaps he's away, gone to one of those hot countries he jets off to to save lives. And she misses him, and she worries, although she knows he has to go.

Of course she misses him, just as I do. He is kind and strong, everything a husband should be. And they are a partnership. I can see it, I know how they are. His strength, that protectiveness he radiates, it doesn't mean she's weak. She's strong in other ways; she makes intellectual leaps that leave him open-mouthed in admiration. She can cut to the nub of a problem, dissect and analyse it in the time it takes other people to say good morning. At parties, he often holds her hand, even though they've been together years. They respect each other, they don't put each other down.

I feel exhausted this evening. I am sober, stone cold. Some days I feel so bad that I have to drink; some days I feel so bad that I can't. Today, the thought of alcohol turns my stomach. But sobriety on the evening train is a challenge, particularly now, in this heat. A film of sweat covers every inch of my skin, the inside of my mouth prickles, my eyes itch, mascara rubbed into their corners.

My phone buzzes in my handbag, making me jump. Two girls sitting across the carriage look at me and then at each other, with a sly exchange of smiles. I don't know what they think of me, but I know it isn't good. My heart is pounding in my chest as I reach for the phone. I know this will be nothing good either: it will be Cathy, perhaps, asking me ever so nicely to maybe give the booze a rest this evening? Or my mother, telling me that she'll be in London next week, she'll drop by the office, we can go for lunch. I look at the screen. It's Tom. I hesitate for just a second and then I answer it.

'Rachel?'

For the first five years I knew him, I was never Rachel, always Rach. Sometimes Shelley, because he knew I hated it and it made him laugh to watch me twitch with irritation and then giggle because I couldn't help but join in when he was laughing. 'Rachel, it's me.' His voice is leaden, he sounds worn out. 'Listen, you have to stop this, OK?' I don't say anything. The train is slowing and we are almost opposite the house, my old house. I want to say to him, *Come outside, go and stand on the lawn. Let me see you.* 'Please, Rachel, you can't call me like this all the time. You've got to sort yourself out.' There is a lump in my throat as hard as a pebble, smooth and obstinate. I cannot swallow. I cannot speak. 'Rachel? Are you there? I know things aren't good with you, and I'm sorry for you, I really am, but... I can't help you, and these constant calls are really upsetting Anna. OK? I can't help you any more. Go to AA or something. Please, Rachel. Go to an AA meeting after work today.'

I pull the filthy plaster off the end of my finger and look at the pale, wrinkled flesh beneath, dried blood caked at the edge of my fingernail. I press the thumbnail of my right hand into the centre of the cut and feel it open up, the pain sharp and hot.

I catch my breath. Blood starts to ooze from the wound. The girls on the other side of the carriage are watching me, their faces blank.

MEGAN

One year earlier

Wednesday, 16 May 2012

Morning

I can hear the train coming; I know its rhythm by heart. It picks up speed as it accelerates out of Northcote station and then, after rattling round the bend, it starts to slow down, from a rattle to a rumble, and then sometimes a screech of brakes as it stops at the signal a couple of hundred yards from the house. My coffee is cold on the table, but I'm too deliciously warm and lazy to bother getting up to make myself another cup.

Sometimes I don't even watch the trains go past, I just listen. Sitting here in the morning, eyes closed and the hot sun orange on my eyelids, I could be anywhere. I could be in the south of Spain, at the beach; I could be in Italy, the Cinque Terre, all those pretty coloured houses and the trains ferrying the tourists back and forth. I could be back in Holkham with the screech of gulls in my ears and salt on my tongue and a ghost train passing on the rusted track half a mile away.

The train isn't stopping today, it trundles slowly past. I can hear the wheels clacking over the points, I can almost feel it rocking. I can't see the faces of the passengers and I know they're just commuters heading to Euston to sit behind desks, but I can dream: of more exotic journeys, of adventures at the end of the line and beyond. In my head, I keep travelling back to Holkham; it's odd that I still think of it, on mornings like this, with such affection, such longing, but I do. The wind in the grass, the big slate sky over the dunes, the house infested with mice and falling down, full of candles and dirt and music. It's like a dream to me now.

I feel my heart beating just a little too fast.

I can hear his footfall on the stairs, he calls my name.

'You want another coffee, Megs?'

The spell is broken, I'm awake.

Evening

I'm cool from the breeze and warm from the two fingers of vodka in my Martini. I'm out on the terrace, waiting for Scott to come home. I'm going to persuade him to take me out to dinner at the Italian on Kingly Road. We haven't been out for bloody ages.

I haven't got much done today. I was supposed to sort out my application for the fabrics course at St Martins; I did start it, I was working downstairs in the kitchen when I heard a woman screaming, making a horrible noise, I thought someone was being murdered. I ran outside into the garden, but I couldn't see anything.

I could still hear her though, it was nasty, it went right through me, her voice really shrill and desperate. 'What are you doing? What are you doing with her? Give her to me, give her to me.' It seemed to go on and on, though it probably only lasted a few seconds.

I ran upstairs and climbed out on to the terrace and I could see, through the trees, two women down by the fence, a few gardens over. One of them was crying – maybe they both were – and there was a child bawling its head off too.

I thought about calling the police, but it all seemed to calm down then. The woman who'd been screaming ran into the house, carrying the baby. The other one stayed out there. She ran up towards the house, she stumbled and got to her feet and then just sort of wandered round the garden in circles. Really weird. God knows what was going on. But it's the most excitement I've had in weeks.

My days feel empty now I don't have the gallery to go to any longer. I really miss it. I miss talking to the artists. I even miss dealing with all those tedious yummy mummies who used to drop by, Starbucks in hand, to gawk at the pictures, telling their friends that little Jessie did better pictures than that at nursery school.

Sometimes I feel like seeing if I can track down anybody from the old days, but then I think, what would I talk to them about now? They wouldn't even recognize Megan the happily married sub-urbanite. In any case, I can't risk looking backwards, it's always a bad idea. I'll wait until the summer is over, then I'll look for work. It seems like a shame to waste these long summer days. I'll find something, here or elsewhere, I know I will.

Tuesday, 14 August 2012

Morning

I find myself standing in front of my wardrobe, staring for the hundredth time at a rack of pretty clothes, the perfect wardrobe for the manager of a small but cutting-edge art gallery. Nothing in it says 'nanny'. God, even the word makes me want to gag. I put on jeans and a T-shirt, scrape my hair back. I don't even bother putting on any make-up. There's no point, is there, prettying myself up to spend all day with a baby?

I flounce downstairs, half spoiling for a fight. Scott's making coffee in the kitchen. He turns to me with a grin and my mood lifts instantly. I re-arrange my pout to a smile. He hands me a coffee and kisses me.

There's no sense blaming him for this, it was my idea. I volunteered to do it, to become a childminder for the people down the road. At the time, I thought it might be fun. Completely in-sane, really, I must have been mad. Bored, mad, curious. I wanted to see. I think I got the idea after I heard her yelling out in the garden and I wanted to know what was going on. Not that I've asked, of course. You can't really, can you?

Scott encouraged me – he was over the moon

when I suggested it. He thinks spending time around babies will make me broody. In fact, it's doing exactly the opposite; when I leave their house I run home, can't wait to strip my clothes off and get into the shower and wash the baby smell off me.

I long for my days at the gallery; prettied up, hair done, talking to adults about art or films or nothing at all. Nothing at all would be a step up from my conversations with Anna. God, she's dull! You get the feeling that she probably had something to say for herself once upon a time, but now everything is about the child: is she warm enough? Is she too warm? How much milk did she take? And she's always *there,* so most of the time I feel like a spare part. My job is to watch the child while Anna rests, to give her a break. A break from what, exactly? She's weirdly nervous, too. I'm constantly aware of her, hovering, twitching. She flinches every time a train passes, jumps when the phone rings. They're just so fragile, aren't they? she says, and I can't disagree with that.

I leave the house and walk, leaden-legged, the fifty yards along Blenheim Road to their house. No skip in my step. Today, she doesn't open the door, it's him, the husband. Tom, suited and booted, off to work. He looks handsome in his suit – not Scott handsome, he's smaller and paler, and his eyes are a little too close together when you see him up close – but he's not bad. He flashes me his wide, Tom Cruise smile, and then he's gone, and it's just me and her and the baby.

35

Afternoon

I quit!

I feel so much better, as if anything is possible. I'm free!

I'm sitting on the terrace, waiting for the rain. The sky is black above me, swallows looping and diving, the air thick with moisture. Scott will be home in an hour or so and I'll have to tell him. He'll only be pissed off for a minute or two, I'll make it up to him. And I won't just be sitting around the house all day: I've been making plans. I could do a photography course, or set up a market stall, sell jewellery. I could learn to cook.

I had a teacher at school who told me once that I was a mistress of self-reinvention. I didn't know what he was on about at the time, I thought he was trying it on, but I've since come to like the idea. Runaway, lover, wife, waitress, gallery manager, nanny, and a few more in between. So who do I want to be tomorrow?

I didn't really mean to quit, the words just came out. We were sitting there, around the kitchen table, Anna with the baby on her lap, and Tom had popped back to pick something up, so he was there too, drinking a cup of coffee, and it just seemed ridiculous, there was absolutely no point in me being there. Worse than that, I felt uncomfortable, as if I was intruding.

'I've found another job,' I said, without really thinking about it. 'So I'm not going to be able to do this any longer.' Anna gave me a look – I don't think she believed me. She just said, 'Oh, that's a shame,' and I could tell she didn't mean it. She looked relieved. She didn't even ask me what the job was, which was a relief, because I hadn't thought up a convincing lie.

Tom looked mildly surprised. He said, 'We'll miss you,' but that's a lie, too.

The only person who'll really be disappointed is Scott, so I have to think of something to tell him. Maybe I'll tell him Tom was hitting on me. That'll put an end to it.

Thursday, 20 September 2012

Morning

It's just after seven, it's chilly out here now, but it's so beautiful like this, all these strips of garden side by side, green and cold and waiting for fingers of sunshine to creep up from the tracks and make them all come alive. I've been up for hours; I can't sleep. I haven't slept in days. I hate this, hate insomnia more than anything, just lying there, brain going round, tick, tick, tick, tick. I itch all over. I want to shave my head.

I want to run. I want to take a road trip, in a convertible, with the top down. I want to drive to the coast – any coast. I want to walk on a beach. Me and my big brother were going to be road trippers. We had such plans, Ben and I. Well, they were Ben's plans mostly – he was such a dreamer. We were going to ride motorbikes from Paris to the Côte d'Azur, or all the way down the Pacific coast of the USA, from Seattle to Los Angeles; we were going to follow in Che Guevara's tracks from Buenos Aires to Caracas. Maybe if I'd done all that, I wouldn't have ended up here, not knowing what to do next. Or maybe, if I'd done all that, I'd have ended up exactly where I am and I would be perfectly contented. But I didn't do all that, of course, because Ben never got as far as Paris, he never even made it as far as Cambridge. He died on the A10, his skull crushed beneath the wheels of an articulated lorry.

I miss him every day. More than anyone, I think. He's the big hole in my life, in the middle of my soul. Or maybe he was just the beginning of it. I don't know. I don't even know whether all this is really about Ben, or whether it's about everything that happened after that, and everything that's happened since. All I know is, one minute I'm ticking along fine and life is sweet and I want for nothing, and the next, I can't wait to get away, I'm all over the place, slipping and sliding again.

So, I'm going to see a therapist! Which could be weird, but it could be a laugh, too. I've always thought that it might be fun to be Catholic, to be able to go to the confessional and unburden yourself and have someone tell you that they forgive you, to take all the sin away, wipe the slate clean.

This is not quite the same thing, of course. I'm a bit nervous, but I haven't been able to get to sleep lately, and Scott's been on my case to go. I told him, I find it difficult enough talking to people I *know* about this stuff – I can barely even talk to you about it. He said, that's the point, you can say anything to strangers. But that isn't completely true. You can't just say *anything*. Poor Scott. He doesn't know the half of it. He loves me so much it makes me ache. I don't know how he does it. I would drive me mad.

But I have to do *something* and at least this feels like action. All those plans I had – photography courses and cookery classes – when it comes down to it, they feel a bit pointless, as if I'm playing at real life instead of actually living it. I need to find something that I *must* do, something undeniable. I can't do this, I can't just be a wife. I don't understand how anyone does it – there is literally nothing to do but wait. Wait for a man to come home and love you. Either that, or look around for something to distract you.

Evening

I've been kept waiting. The appointment was for half an hour ago, and I'm still here, sitting in the reception room flicking through *Vogue*, thinking about getting up and walking out. I know doctors' appointments run over, but therapists'? Films have always led me to believe that they kick you out the moment your fifty minutes are up. I suppose Hollywood isn't really talking about the kind of therapist you get referred to on the NHS.

I'm just about to go up to the receptionist and tell her that I've waited long enough, I'm leaving, when the doctor's office door swings open and this very tall, lanky man emerges, looking apologetic and holding out his hand to me.

'Mrs Hipwell, I am so sorry to have kept you

waiting,' he says, and I just smile at him and tell him it's all right, and I feel, in this moment, that it will be all right, because I've only been in his company for a minute or two and already I feel soothed.

I think it's the voice. Soft and low. Slightly accented, which I was expecting, because his name is Dr Kamal Abdic. I guess he must be mid-thirties, although he looks very young with his incredible dark honey skin. He has hands I could imagine on me, long and delicate fingers, I can almost feel them on my body.

We don't talk about anything substantial, it's just the introductory session, the getting-to-know-you stuff; he asks me what the trouble is and I tell him about the panic attacks, the insomnia, the fact that I lie awake at night too frightened to fall asleep. He wants me to talk a bit more about that, but I'm not ready yet. He asks me whether I take drugs, drink alcohol. I tell him I have other vices these days, and I catch his eye and I think he knows what I mean. Then I feel as if I ought to be taking this a bit more seriously, so I tell him about the gallery closing and that I feel at a loose end all the time, my lack of direction, the fact that I spend too much time in my head. He doesn't talk much, just the occasional prompt, but I want to hear him speak, so as I'm leaving I ask him where he's from.

'Maidstone,' he says, 'in Kent. But I moved to Corly a few years back.' He knows that wasn't what I was asking; he gives me a wolfish smile.

Scott is waiting for me when I get home, he thrusts a drink into my hand, he wants to know all about it. I say it was OK. He asks me about the therapist: did I like him, did he seem nice? OK, I say again, because I don't want to sound too enthusiastic. He asks me whether we talked about Ben. Scott thinks everything is about Ben. He may be right. He may know me better than I think he does.

Tuesday, 25 September 2012

Morning

I woke early this morning, but I did sleep for a few hours, which is an improvement on last week. I felt almost refreshed when I got out of bed, so instead of sitting on the terrace I decided to go for a walk.

I've been shutting myself away, almost without realizing it. The only places I seem to go these days are to the shops, my pilates classes and the therapist. Occasionally to Tara's. The rest of the time, I'm at home. It's no wonder I get restless.

I walk out of the house, turn right and then left on to Kingly Road. Past the pub – the Rose. We used to go there all the time; I can't remember why we stopped. I never liked it all that much, too many couples just the right side of forty drinking too much and casting around for something better, wondering if they'd have the courage. Perhaps that's why we stopped going, because I didn't like it. Past the pub, past the shops. I don't want to go far, just a little circuit, to stretch my legs.

It's nice being out early, before the school run,

41

before the commute gets going; the streets are empty and clean, the day full of possibility. I turn left again, I walk down to the little playground, the only rather poor excuse for green space we have. It's empty now, but in a few hours it will be swarming with toddlers, mothers and au pairs. Half the pilates girls will be here, head to toe in Sweaty Betty, competitively stretching, manicured hands wrapped around their Starbucks.

I carry on past the park and down towards Roseberry Avenue. If I turned right here I'd go up past my gallery – what was my gallery, now a vacant shop window – but I don't want to, because that still hurts a little. I tried so hard to make a success of it. Wrong place, wrong time – no call for art in suburbia, not in this economy. Instead, I turn right, past the Tesco Express, past the other pub, the one where people from the estate go, and back towards home. I can feel butterflies now, I'm starting to get nervous. I'm afraid of bumping into the Watsons, because it's always awkward when I see them; it's patently obvious that I don't have a new job, that I lied because I didn't want to carry on working for them.

Or rather, it's awkward when I see *her*. Tom just ignores me. But Anna seems to take things personally. She obviously thinks that my short-lived career as a nanny came to an end because of her or because of her child. It actually wasn't about *her child* at all, although the fact that the child never stops whinging did make her hard to love. It's all so much more complicated, but of course I can't explain that to her. Anyway. That's one of the reasons I've been shutting myself away, I suppose,

42

because I don't want to see the Watsons. Part of me hopes they'll just move. I know she doesn't like being here: she hates that house, hates living among his ex-wife's things, hates the trains.

I stop at the corner and peer into the underpass. That smell of cold and damp always sends a little shiver down my spine, it's like turning over a rock to see what's underneath: moss and worms and earth. It reminds me of playing in the garden as a child, looking for frogs by the pond with Ben. I walk on. The street is clear – no sign of Tom or Anna – and the part of me that can't resist a bit of drama is actually quite disappointed.

Evening

Scott's just called to say he has to work late, which is not the news I wanted to hear. I'm feeling edgy, have been all day. Can't keep still. I need him to come home and calm me down, and now it's going to be hours before he gets here and my brain is going to keep racing round and round and round and I know I've got a sleepless night coming.

I can't just sit here, watching the trains, I'm too jittery, my heartbeat feels like a flutter in my chest, like a bird trying to get out of a cage. I slip my flip-flops on and go downstairs, out of the front door and on to Blenheim Road. It's around seven thirty – a few stragglers on their way home from work. There's no one else around, though you can hear the cries of kids playing in their back gardens, taking advantage of the last of the summer sunshine, before they get called in for dinner.

I walk down the road, towards the station. I stop for a moment outside number twenty-three and think about ringing the doorbell. What would I say? Ran out of sugar? Just fancied a chat? Their blinds are half open but I can't see anyone inside.

I carry on, towards the corner, and without really thinking about it, I continue down into the underpass. I'm about halfway through when the train runs overhead, and it's glorious: it's like an earthquake, you can feel it right in the centre of your body, stirring up the blood. I look down and notice that there's something on the floor, a hair band, purple, stretched, well used. Dropped by a runner, probably, but something about it gives me the creeps and I want to get out of there quickly, back into the sunshine.

On the way back down the road, he passes me in his car, our eyes meet for just a second and he smiles at me.

RACHEL

Friday, 12 July 2013

Morning

I am exhausted, my head thick with sleep. When I drink, I hardly sleep at all. I pass out cold for an hour or two, then I wake, sick with fear, sick with myself. If I have a day when I don't drink, that

44

night I fall into the heaviest of slumbers, a deep unconsciousness, and in the morning I cannot wake properly, I cannot shake sleep, it stays with me for hours, sometimes all day long.

There is just a handful of people in my carriage today, none in my immediate vicinity. There is no one watching me, so I lean my head against the window and close my eyes.

The screech of the train's brakes wakes me. We're at the signal. At this time of morning, at this time of year, the sun shines directly on to the back of the trackside houses, flooding them with light. I can almost feel it, the warmth of that morning sunshine on my face and arms as I sit at the breakfast table, Tom opposite me, my bare feet resting on top of his because they're always so much warmer than mine, my eyes cast down at the newspaper. I can feel him smiling at me, the blush spreading from my chest to my neck, the way it always did when he looked at me a certain way.

I blink hard and Tom's gone. We're still at the signal. I can see Jess in her garden, and behind her a man walking out of the house. He's carrying something – a mug of coffee, perhaps – and I look at him and realize that it isn't Jason. This man is taller, slender, darker. He's a family friend; he's her brother or Jason's brother. He bends down, placing the mugs on the metal table on their patio. He's a cousin from Australia, staying for a couple of weeks; he's Jason's oldest friend, best man at their wedding. Jess walks towards him, she puts her hands around his waist and she kisses him, long and deep. The train moves.

I can't believe it. I snatch air into my lungs, I

realize that I've been holding my breath. Why would she do that? Jason loves her, I can see it, they're happy. I can't believe she would do that to him, he doesn't deserve that. I feel a real sense of disappointment, I feel as though *I* have been cheated. A familiar ache fills my chest. I have felt this way before. On a larger scale, to a more intense degree, of course, but I remember the quality of the pain. You don't forget it.

I found out the way everyone seems to find out these days: an electronic slip. Sometimes it's a text or a voicemail message; in my case it was an e-mail, the modern-day lipstick on the collar. It was an accident, really, I wasn't snooping. I wasn't supposed to go near Tom's computer, because he was worried I would delete something important by mistake, or click on something I shouldn't and let in a virus or a Trojan or something.

'Technology's not really your strong point, is it, Rach?' he said after the time I managed to delete all the contacts in his email address book by mistake. So I wasn't supposed to touch it. But I was actually doing a good thing, I was trying to make amends for being a bit miserable and difficult, I was planning a special fourth-anniversary getaway, a trip to remind us how we used to be. I wanted it to be a surprise, so I had to check his work schedule secretly, I had to look.

I wasn't snooping, I wasn't trying to catch him out or anything, I knew better than that. I didn't want to be one of those awful suspicious wives who go through their husband's pockets. Once, I answered his phone when he was in the shower and he got quite upset and accused me of not trusting him. I felt awful because he seemed so hurt.

I needed to look at his work schedule, and he'd left his laptop on, because he'd run out late for a meeting. It was the perfect opportunity, so I had a look at his calendar, noted down some dates. When I closed down the browser window with his calendar in it, there was his email account, logged in, laid bare. There was a message at the top from aboyd@cinnamon.com. I clicked. XXXXX. That was it, just a line of Xs. I thought it was spam at first, until I realized that they were kisses.

It was a reply to a message he'd sent a few hours before, just after seven, when I was still slumbering in our bed.

I fell asleep last night thinking of you, I was dreaming about kissing your mouth, your breasts, the inside of your thighs. I woke this morning with my head full of you, desperate to touch you. Don't expect me to be sane, I can't be, not with you.

I read through his messages: there were dozens, hidden in a folder entitled 'Admin'. I discovered that her name was Anna Boyd, and that my husband was in love with her. He told her so, often. He told her that he'd never felt like this before, that he couldn't wait to be with her, that it wouldn't be long until they could be together.

I don't have words to describe what I felt that day, but now, sitting on the train, I am furious, nails digging into my palms, tears stinging my eyes. I feel a flash of intense anger. I feel as though something has been taken away from *me*. How

47

could she? How could Jess do this? What is wrong with her? Look at the life they have, look how beautiful it is! I have never understood how people can blithely disregard the damage they do by following their hearts. Who was it said that following your heart is a good thing? It is pure egotism, a selfishness to conquer all. Hatred floods me. If I saw that woman now, if I saw Jess, I would spit in her face. I would scratch her eyes out.

Evening

There's been a problem on the line. The 17.56 fast train to Stoke has been cancelled, so its passengers have invaded my train and it's standing room only in the carriage. I, fortunately, have a seat, but by the aisle, not next to the window, and there are bodies pressed against my shoulder, my knee, invading my space. I have an urge to push back, to get up and shove. The heat has been building all day, closing in on me, I feel as though I'm breathing through a mask. Every single window has been opened and yet, even while we're moving, the carriage feels airless, a locked metal box. I cannot get enough oxygen into my lungs. I feel sick. I can't stop replaying the scene in the coffee shop this morning, I can't stop feeling as though I'm still there, I can't stop seeing the looks on their faces.

I blame Jess. I was obsessing this morning about Jess and Jason, about what she'd done and how he would feel, about the confrontation they'd have when he found out and when his world, like mine, was ripped apart. I was walking around in a daze, not concentrating on where I was going. Without thinking, I went into the coffee shop that everyone from Huntingdon Whiteley uses. I was through the door before I saw them, and by the time I did it was too late to turn back; they were looking at me, eyes widening for a fraction of a second before they remembered to fix smiles on their faces. Martin Miles with Sasha and Harriet, a triumvirate of awkwardness, beckoning, waving me over.

'Rachel!' Martin said, arms outstretched, pulling me into a hug. I wasn't expecting it, my hands were caught between us, fumbling against his body. Sasha and Harriet smiled, they gave me tentative air kisses, trying not to get too close. 'What are you doing here?'

For a long, long moment, I went blank. I looked at the floor, I could feel myself colouring and, realizing it was making it worse, I gave a false laugh and said, 'Interview. Interview.'

'Oh.' Martin failed to hide his surprise, while Sasha and Harriet nodded and smiled. 'Who's that with?'

I couldn't remember the name of a single public relations firm. Not one. I couldn't think of a property company either, let alone one which might realistically be hiring. I just stood there, rubbing my lower lip with my forefinger, shaking my head, and eventually Martin said, 'Top secret, is it? Some firms are weird like that, aren't they? Don't want you saying anything until the contracts are signed and it's all official.' It was bullshit and he knew it, he did it to save me and nobody bought it, but everyone pretended they did and nodded along. Harriet and Sasha were looking over my shoulder at the door, they were embarrassed for me, they wanted a way out.

'I'd better go and order my coffee,' I said. 'Don't want to be late.'

Martin put his hand on my forearm and said, 'It's great to see you, Rachel.' His pity was almost palpable. I'd never realized, not until the last year or two of my life, how shaming it is to be pitied.

The plan had been to go to Holborn Library on Theobalds Road, but I couldn't face it, so I went to Regent's Park instead. I walked to the very far end, next to the zoo. I sat down in the shade beneath a sycamore tree, thinking of the unfilled hours ahead, replaying the conversation in the coffee shop, remembering the look on Martin's face when he said goodbye to me.

I must have been there for less than half an hour when my mobile rang. It was Tom again, calling from the home phone. I tried to picture him, working at his laptop in our sunny kitchen, but the image was spoilt by encroachments from his new life. She would be there somewhere, in the background, making tea or feeding the little girl, her shadow falling over him. I let the call go to voice-mail. I put the phone back into my bag and tried to ignore it. I didn't want to hear any more, not today; today was already awful enough and it was not yet ten thirty in the morning. I held out for about three minutes before I retrieved the phone and dialled into voicemail. I braced myself for the agony of hearing his voice – that voice which used to speak to me with laughter and light and now is used only to admonish or console or pity – but it wasn't him.

'Rachel, it's Anna.' I hung up.

I couldn't breathe and I couldn't stop my brain from racing or my skin from itching, so I got to my feet and walked to the corner shop on Titchfield Street and bought four gin and tonics in cans, then went back to my spot in the park. I opened the first one and drank it as fast as I could, and then opened the second. I turned my back to the path so that I couldn't see the runners and the mothers with buggies and the tourists, and if I couldn't see them, I could pretend like a child that they couldn't see me. I called my voicemail again.

'Rachel, it's Anna.' Long pause. 'I need to talk to you about the phone calls.' Another long pause – she's talking to me and doing something else, multi-tasking, the way busy wives and mothers do, tidying up, loading the washing machine. 'Look, I know you're having a tough time,' she says, as though she has nothing to do with my pain, 'but you can't call us at night all the time.' Her tone is clipped, irritable. 'It's bad enough that you wake us when you call, but you wake Evie, too, and that's just not acceptable. We're struggling to get her to sleep through at the moment.' *We're struggling to get her to sleep through.* We. Us. Our little family. With our problems and our routines. Fucking bitch. She's a cuckoo, laying her egg in my nest. She has taken everything from me. She has taken everything and now she calls me to tell me that my distress is inconvenient for her?

I finish the second can and make a start on the third. The blissful rush of alcohol hitting my bloodstream lasts only a few minutes and then I

51

feel sick. I'm going too fast, even for me, I need to slow down; if I don't slow down something bad is going to happen. I'm going to do something I will regret. I'm going to call her back, I'm going to tell her I don't care about her and I don't care about her family and I don't care if her child never gets a good night's sleep for the rest of its life. I'm going to tell her that the line he used with her – *don't expect me to be sane* – he used it with me, too, when we were first together; he wrote it in a letter to me, declaring his undying passion. It's not even his line: he stole it from Henry Miller. Everything she has is secondhand. I want to know how that makes her feel. I want to call her back and ask her, what does it feel like, Anna, to live in my house, surrounded by the furniture I bought, to sleep in the bed that I shared with him for years, to feed your child at the kitchen table he fucked me on?

I still find it extraordinary that they chose to stay there, in that house, in *my* house. I couldn't believe it when he told me. I loved that house. I was the one who insisted we buy it, despite its location. I liked being down there on the tracks, I liked watching the trains go by, I enjoyed the sound of them, not the scream of an inter-city express but the old-fashioned trundling of ancient rolling stock. Tom told me, it won't always be like this, they'll eventually upgrade the line and then it will be fast trains screaming past, but I couldn't believe it would ever actually happen. I would have stayed there, I would have bought him out if I'd had the money. I didn't, though, and we couldn't find a buyer at a decent price when we divorced, so instead he said he'd buy me out and stay on until he got the right price for it. But he never found the right buyer, instead he moved her in, and she loved the house like I did, and they decided to stay. She must be very secure in herself, I suppose, in them, for it not to bother her, to walk where another woman has walked before. She obviously doesn't think of me as a threat. I think about Ted Hughes, moving Assia Wevill into the home he'd shared with Plath, of her wearing Sylvia's clothes, brushing her hair with the same brush. I want to ring Anna up and remind her that Assia ended up with her head in the oven, just like Sylvia did.

I must have fallen asleep, the gin and the hot sun lulling me. I woke with a start, scrabbling around desperately for my handbag. It was still there. My skin was prickling, I was alive with ants, they were in my hair and on my neck and chest and I leaped to my feet, clawing them away. Two teenage boys, kicking a football back and forth twenty yards away, stopped to watch, bent double with laughter.

The train stops. We are almost opposite Jess and Jason's house, but I can't see across the carriage and the tracks, there are too many people in the way. I wonder whether they are there, whether he knows, whether he's left, or whether he's still living a life he's yet to discover is a lie.

Saturday, 13 July 2013

Morning

I know without looking at a clock that it is some-

53

where between seven forty-five and eight fifteen. I know, from the quality of the light, from the sounds of the street outside my window, from the sound of Cathy vacuuming the hallway right outside my room. Cathy gets up early to clean the house every Saturday, no matter what. It could be her birthday, it could be the morning of the Rapture – Cathy will get up early on Saturday to clean. She says it's cathartic, it sets her up for a good weekend, and because she cleans the house aerobically, it means she doesn't have to go to the gym.

It doesn't really bother me, this early-morning vacuuming, because I wouldn't be asleep anyway. I cannot sleep in the mornings; I cannot snooze peacefully until midday. I wake abruptly, my breath jagged and heart racing, my mouth stale, and I know immediately that's it. I'm awake. The more I want to be oblivious, the less I can be. Life and light will not let me be. I lie there, listening to the sound of Cathy's urgent, cheerful busyness, and I think about the clothes on the side of the railway line and about Jess kissing her lover in the morning sunshine.

The day stretches out in front of me, not a minute of it filled.

I could go to the farmers' market on the Broad; I could buy venison and pancetta and spend the day cooking.

I could sit on the sofa with a cup of tea and *Saturday Kitchen* on TV.

I could go to the gym.

I could rewrite my CV.

I could wait for Cathy to leave the house, go to

54

the off-licence and buy two bottles of Sauvignon Blanc.

In another life, I woke early, too, the sound of the 8.04 rumbling past; I opened my eyes and listened to the rain against the window. I felt him behind me, sleepy, warm, hard. Afterwards, he went to get the papers and I made scrambled eggs, we sat in the kitchen drinking tea, we went to the pub for a late lunch, we fell asleep, tangled up together in front of the TV. I imagine it's different for him now, no lazy Saturday sex or scrambled eggs, instead a different sort of joy, a little girl tucked up between him and his wife, babbling away. She'll be just learning to talk now, all Dada and Mama and a secret language incomprehensible to anyone but a parent.

The pain is solid and heavy, it sits in the middle of my chest. I cannot wait for Cathy to leave the house.

Evening

I am going to see Jason.

I spent all day in my bedroom, waiting for Cathy to go out, so that I could have a drink. She didn't. She sat steadfast and unmoveable in the living room, 'just catching up on a bit of admin'. By late afternoon I couldn't stand the confinement or the boredom any longer, so I told her I was going out for a walk. I went to the Wheatsheaf, the big, anonymous pub just off the High Street, and I drank three large glasses of wine. I had two shots of Jack Daniel's. Then I walked to the station, bought a couple of cans of gin and tonic and got on to the train.

I am going to see Jason.

I'm not going to *visit* him, I'm not going to turn up at his house and knock on the door. Nothing like that. Nothing crazy. I just want to go past the house, roll by on the train. I've nothing else to do, and I don't feel like going home. I just want to see him. I want to see them.

This isn't a good idea. I know it's not a good idea.

But what harm can it do?

I'll go to Euston, I'll turn around, I'll come back. (I like trains, and what's wrong with that? Trains are wonderful.)

Before, when I was still myself, I used to dream of taking romantic train journeys with Tom. (The Bergen Line for our fifth anniversary, the Blue Train for his fortieth.)

Hang on, we're going to pass them now.

The light is bright, but I can't see all that well. (Vision doubling. Close one eye. Better.)

There they are! Is that him? They're standing on the terrace. Aren't they? Is that Jason? Is that Jess?

I want to be closer, I can't see. I want to be closer to them.

I'm not going to Euston. I'm going to get off at Witney. (I shouldn't get off at Witney, it's too dangerous, what if Tom or Anna sees me?)

I'm going to get off at Witney.

This is not a good idea.

This is a very bad idea.

There's a man on the opposite side of the train, sandy blond hair veering towards ginger. He's smiling at me. I want to say something to him, but the words keep evaporating, vanishing off my tongue before I have the chance to say them. I can taste them, but I can't tell if they are sweet or sour.

Is he smiling at me, or is he sneering? I can't tell.

Sunday, 14 July 2013

Morning

My heartbeat feels as though it is in the base of my throat, uncomfortable and loud. My mouth is dry, it hurts to swallow. I roll on to my side, my face turned to the window. The curtains are drawn, but what light there is hurts my eyes. I bring my hand up to my face; I press my fingers against my eyelids, trying to rub away the ache. My fingernails are filthy.

Something is wrong. For a second, I feel as though I'm falling, as though the bed has disappeared from beneath my body. Last night. Something happened. The breath comes sharply into my lungs and I sit up, too quickly, heart racing, head throbbing.

I wait for the memory to come. Sometimes it takes a while. Sometimes it's there in front of my eyes in seconds. Sometimes it doesn't come at all.

Something happened, something bad. There was an argument. Voices were raised. Fists? I don't know, I don't remember. I went to the pub, I got on to the train, I was at the station, I was on the street. Blenheim Road. I went to Blenheim Road.

It comes over me like a wave, black dread.

Something happened, I know it did. I can't picture it, but I can feel it. The inside of my mouth hurts, as though I've bitten my cheek, there's a metallic tang of blood on my tongue. I feel nauseated, dizzy. I run my hands through my hair, over my scalp. I flinch. There's a lump, painful and tender, on the right side of my head. My hair is matted with blood.

I stumbled, that's it. On the stairs, at Witney station. Did I hit my head? I remember being on the train, but after that there is a gulf of blackness, a void. I'm breathing deeply, trying to slow my heart rate, to quell the panic rising in my chest. Think. What did I do? I went to the pub, I got on the train. There was a man there – I remember now, reddish hair. He smiled at me. I think he talked to me, but I can't remember what he said. There's something more to him, more to the memory of him, but I can't reach it, can't find it in the black.

I'm frightened, but I'm not sure what I'm afraid of, which just exacerbates the fear. I don't even know whether there's anything to be frightened of. I look around the room. My phone is not on the bedside table. My handbag is not on the floor, it's not hanging over the back of the chair where I usually leave it. I must have had it, though, because I'm in the house, which means I have my keys.

I get out of bed. I'm naked. I catch sight of myself in the full-length mirror on the wardrobe. My hands are trembling. Mascara is smeared over my cheekbones and I have a cut on my lower lip. There are bruises on my legs. I feel sick. I sit back down on the bed and put my head between my knees, waiting for the wave of nausea to pass. I get to my feet, grab my dressing gown and open the bedroom door just a crack. The flat is quiet. For some reason I am certain Cathy isn't here. Did she tell me that she was staying at Damien's? I feel as though she did, though I can't remember when. Before I went out? Or did I speak to her later? I walk as quietly as I can out into the hallway. I can see that Cathy's bedroom door is open. I peer into her room. Her bed is made. It's possible she has already got up and made it, but I don't think she stayed here last night, which is a source of some relief. If she isn't here, she didn't see or hear me come in last night, which means that she doesn't know how bad I was. This shouldn't matter, but it does: the sense of shame I feel about an incident is proportionate not just to the gravity of the situation, but also to the number of people who have witnessed it.

At the top of the stairs I feel dizzy again, and grip the banister tightly. It is one of my great fears (along with bleeding into my belly when my liver finally packs up) that I will fall down the stairs and break my neck. Thinking about this makes me feel ill again. I want to lie down, but I need to find my bag, check my phone. I at least need to know that I haven't lost my credit cards, I need to know who I called and when. My handbag has been dumped in the hallway, just inside the front door. My jeans and underwear sit next to it in a crumpled pile; I can smell the urine from the bottom of the stairs. I grab my bag to look for my phone – it's in there, thank God, along with a bunch of scrunched-up twenties and a bloodstained Kleenex. The nausea comes over me again, stronger this time; I can taste the bile in the back of my throat and I run, but I don't make it to the bathroom, I vomit on the carpet halfway up the stairs.

I have to lie down. If I don't lie down, I'm going to pass out, I'm going to fall. I'll clean up later.

Upstairs, I plug in my phone and lie down on the bed. I raise my limbs, gently, gingerly, to inspect them. There are bruises on my legs, above the knees, standard drink-related stuff, the sort of bruises you get from walking into things. My upper arms bear more worrying marks, dark, oval impressions that look like fingerprints. This is not necessarily sinister, I have had them before, usually from when I've fallen and someone has helped me up. The crack on my head feels bad, but it could be from something as innocuous as getting into a car. I might have taken a taxi home.

I pick up my phone. There are two messages. The first is from Cathy, received just after five, asking where I've got to. She's going to Damien's for the night, she'll see me tomorrow. She hopes I'm not drinking on my own. The second is from Tom, received at ten fifteen. I almost drop the phone in fright as I hear his voice; he's shouting.

'Jesus Christ, Rachel, what the hell is wrong with you? I have had enough of this, all right? I've just spent the best part of an hour driving around looking for you. You've really frightened Anna, you know that? She thought you were going to ... she thought... It's all I could do to get her not to ring

60

the police. Leave us alone. Stop calling me, stop hanging around, just leave us alone. I don't want to speak to you. Do you understand me? I don't want to speak to you, I don't want to see you, I don't want you anywhere near my family. You can ruin your own life if you want to, but you're not ruining mine. Not any more. I'm not going to protect you any longer, understand? Just stay away from us.'

I don't know what I've done. What did I do? Between five o'clock and ten fifteen, what was I doing? Why was Tom looking for me? What did I do to Anna? I pull the duvet over my head, I close my eyes tightly. I imagine myself going to the house, walking along the little pathway between their garden and the neighbour's garden, climbing over the fence. I think about sliding open the glass doors, stealthily creeping into the kitchen. Anna's sitting at the table. I grab her from behind, I wind my hand into her long blonde hair, I jerk her head backwards, I pull her to the floor and I smash her head against the cool blue tiles.

Evening

Someone is shouting. From the angle of the light streaming in through my bedroom window I can tell I have been sleeping a long time; it must be late afternoon, early evening. My head hurts. There's blood on my pillow. I can hear someone yelling downstairs.

'I do not believe this! For God's sake! Rachel! RACHEL!'

I fell asleep. Oh Jesus, and I didn't clear up the vomit on the stairs. And my clothes in the hallway. Oh God, oh God.

I pull on a pair of tracksuit bottoms and a T-shirt. Cathy is standing right outside my bedroom door when I open it. She looks horrified when she sees me.

'What on earth happened to you?' she says, then raises her hand. 'Actually, Rachel, I'm sorry, but I just don't want to know. I cannot have this in my house. I cannot have...' She tails off, but she's looking back down the hall, towards the stairs.

'I'm sorry,' I say. 'I'm so sorry, I was just really ill and I meant to clear it up...'

'You weren't ill, were you? You were drunk. You were hung-over. I'm sorry, Rachel. I just can't have this. I cannot live like this. You have to go, OK? I'll give you four weeks to find somewhere else, but then you have to go.' She turns around and walks towards her bedroom. 'And for the love of God, will you clean up that mess?' She slams her bedroom door behind her.

After I've finished cleaning up, I go back to my room. Cathy's bedroom door is still closed, but I can feel her quiet rage radiating through it. I can't blame her. I'd be furious if I came home to piss-soaked knickers and a puddle of vomit on the stairs. I sit down on the bed and flip open my lap-top, log into my email account and start to compose a note to my mother. I think, finally, the time has come. I have to ask her for help. If I moved home, I wouldn't be able to go on like this, I would have to change, I would have to get better. I can't think of the words, though, I can't think of a way to explain this to her. I can picture her face as she reads my plea for help, the sour disappointment, the exasperation. I can almost hear her sigh.

My phone beeps. There's a message on it, received hours ago. It's Tom again. I don't want to hear what he has to say, but I have to, I can't ignore him. My heartbeat quickens as I dial into my voicemail, bracing myself for the worst.

'Rachel, will you phone me back?' He doesn't sound so angry any longer and my heartbeat slows a little. 'I want to make sure you got home all right. You were in some state last night.' A long, heartfelt sigh. 'Look. I'm sorry that I yelled last night, that things got a bit ... overheated. I do feel sorry for you, Rachel, I really do, but this has just got to stop.'

I play the message a second time, listening to the kindness in his voice and the tears come. It's a long time before I stop crying, before I'm able to compose a text message to him saying, I'm very sorry, I'm at home now. I can't say anything else because I don't know what exactly it is I'm sorry for. I don't know what I did to Anna, how I frightened her. I don't honestly care that much, but I do care about making Tom unhappy. After everything he's been through, he deserves to be happy. I will never begrudge him happiness, I only wish it could be with me.

I lie down on the bed and crawl under the duvet. I want to know what happened; I wish I knew what I had to be sorry for. I try desperately to make sense of an elusive fragment of memory. I feel certain that I was in an argument, or that I witnessed an argument. Was that with Anna? My fingers go to the wound on my head, to the cut on my lip. I can almost see it, I can almost hear the words, but it shifts away from me again. I just can't get a handle on it. Every time I think I'm about to seize the moment, it drifts back into the shadow, just beyond my reach.

MEGAN

Tuesday, 2 October 2012

Morning

It's going to rain soon, I can feel it coming. My teeth are chattering in my head, the tips of my fingers are white with a tinge of blue. I'm not going inside. I like it out here, it's cathartic, cleansing, like an ice bath. Scott will come and haul me inside soon anyway, he'll wrap me in blankets, like a child.

I had a panic attack on the way home last night. There was a motorbike, revving its engine over and over and over, and a red car driving slowly past, like a kerb crawler, and two women with buggies blocking my path. I couldn't get past them on the pavement, so I went into the street and was almost hit by a car coming in the opposite direction, which I hadn't even seen. The driver leaned on the horn and yelled something at me. I couldn't catch my breath, my heart was racing, I felt that lurch in my stomach, like when you've taken a pill and you're just about to come up, that punch of adrenaline that makes you feel sick and excited and scared all at once.

I ran home and through the house and down to the tracks, then I sat down there, waiting for the train to come, to rattle through me and take away the other noises. I waited for Scott to come and calm me down, but he wasn't at home. I tried to climb over the fence, I wanted to sit on the other side for a while, where no one else goes. I cut my hand, so I went inside, and then Scott came back and asked me what had happened. I said I was doing the washing-up and dropped a glass. He didn't believe me, he got very upset.

I got up in the night, left Scott sleeping and sneaked down to the terrace. I dialled his number and listened to his voice when he picked up, at first soft with sleep, and then louder, wary, worried, exasperated. I hung up and waited to see if he'd call back. I hadn't disguised my number, so I thought he might. He didn't, so I called again, and again, and again. I got voicemail then, bland and businesslike, promising to call me back at his earliest convenience. I thought about calling the practice, bringing forward my next appointment, but I don't think even their automated system works in the middle of the night, so I went back to bed. I didn't sleep at all.

I might go to Corly Wood this morning to take some photographs; it'll be misty and dark and atmospheric in there, I should be able to get some good stuff. I was thinking about maybe making little cards, seeing if I could sell them in the gift shop on Kingly Road. Scott keeps saying that I don't need to worry about working, that I should just rest. Like an invalid! The last thing I need is rest. I need to find something to fill my days. I know what's going to happen if I don't.

Evening

Dr Abdic – Kamal, as I have been invited to call him – suggested in this afternoon's session that I start keeping a diary. I almost said, I can't do that, I can't trust my husband not to read it. I didn't, because that would feel horribly disloyal to Scott. But it's true. I could never write down the things I actually feel or think or do. Case in point: when I came home this evening, my laptop was warm. He knows how to delete browser histories and whatever, he can cover his tracks perfectly well, but I know that I turned the computer off before I left. He's been reading my emails again.

I don't really mind, there's nothing to read in there. (A lot of spam emails from recruitment companies and Jenny from pilates asking me if I want to join her Thursday-night supper club, where she and her friends take turns cooking each other dinner. I'd rather die.) I don't mind, because it reassures him that there's nothing going on, that I'm not up to anything. And that's good for me – it's good for us – even if it isn't true. And I can't really be angry with him, because he has good reason to be suspicious. I've given him cause in the past and probably will again. I am not a model wife. I can't be. No matter how much I love him, it won't be enough.

Morning

I slept for five hours last night, which is longer than I have done in ages, and the weird thing is, I was so wired when I got home yesterday evening I thought I'd be bouncing off the walls for hours. I told myself that I wouldn't do it again, not after last time, but then I saw him and I wanted him and I thought, why not? I don't see why I should have to restrict myself, lots of people don't. Men don't. I don't want to hurt anybody, but you have to be true to yourself, don't you? That's all I'm doing, being true to my real self, the self nobody knows – not Scott, not Kamal, no one.

After my pilates class last night I asked Tara if she wanted to go to the cinema with me one night next week, then if she'd cover for me.

'If he calls, can you just say I'm with you, that I'm in the loo and I'll ring him straight back? Then you call me, and I call him, and it's all cool.'

She smiled and shrugged and said, 'All right,' she didn't even ask where I was going or who with. She really wants to be my friend.

I met him at the Swan in Corly, he'd got us a room. We have to be careful, we can't get caught. It would be bad for him, life-wrecking. It would be a disaster for me, too. I don't even want to think about what Scott would do.

He wanted me to talk afterwards, about what

happened when I was young, living in Norwich. I'd hinted at it before, but last night he wanted the details. I told him things, but not the truth. I lied, made stuff up, told him all the sordid things he wanted to hear. It was fun. I don't feel bad about lying, I doubt whether he believed most of it anyway. I'm pretty sure he lies, too.

He lay on the bed, watching me as I got dressed. He said, 'This can't happen again, Megan. You know it can't. We can't keep doing this.' And he was right, I know we can't. We shouldn't, we ought not to, but we will. It won't be the last time. He won't say no to me. I was thinking about it on the way home, and that's the thing I like most about it, having power over someone. That's the intoxicating thing.

Evening

I'm in the kitchen, opening a bottle of wine, when Scott comes up behind me and puts his hands on my shoulders and squeezes and says, 'How did it go, with the therapist?' I tell him it was fine, that we're making progress. He's used now to not getting any details out of me. Then: 'Did you have fun with Tara last night?'

I can't tell, because my back's to him, whether he's really asking or whether he suspects something. I can't detect anything in his voice.

'She's really nice,' I say. 'You and she'd get on. We're going to the cinema next week, actually. Maybe I should bring her round for something to eat after?'

'Am I not invited to the cinema?' he asks.

'You're very welcome,' I say, and I turn to him and kiss him on the mouth, 'but she wants to see that thing with Sandra Bullock, so...'

'Say no more! Bring her round for dinner afterwards, then,' he says, his hands pressing gently on my lower back.

I pour the wine and we go outside. We sit side by side on the edge of the patio, our toes in the grass.

'Is she married?' he asks me.

'Tara? No. Single.'

'No boyfriend?'

'Don't think so.'

'Girlfriend?' he asks, eyebrow raised, and I laugh. 'How old is she then?'

'I don't know,' I say. 'Around forty.'

'Oh. And she's all alone. That's a bit sad.'

'Mmm. I think she might be lonely.'

'They always go for you, the lonely ones, don't they? They make a beeline straight for you.'

'Do they?'

'She doesn't have kids, then?' he asks, and I don't know if I'm imagining it, but the second the subject of children comes up, I can hear an edge in his voice and I can feel the argument coming and I just don't want it, can't deal with it, so I get to my feet and I tell him to bring the wine glasses, because we're going to the bedroom.

He follows me and I take off my clothes as I'm going up the stairs, and when we get there, when he pushes me down on the bed, I'm not even thinking about him, but it doesn't matter because he doesn't know that. I'm good enough to make him believe that it's all about him.

RACHEL

Monday, 15 July 2013

Morning

Cathy called me back just as I was leaving the flat this morning and gave me a stiff little hug. I thought she was going to tell me that she wasn't kicking me out after all, but instead she slipped a typewritten note into my hand, giving me formal notice of my eviction, including a departure date. She couldn't meet my eye. I felt sorry for her, I honestly did, though not quite as sorry as for myself. She gave me a sad smile and said, 'I hate to do this to you, Rachel, I honestly do.' The whole thing felt very awkward. We were standing in the hallway, which, despite my best efforts with the bleach, still smelled a bit of sick. I felt like crying, but I didn't want to make her feel worse than she already did, so I just smiled cheerily and said, 'Not at all, it's honestly no problem,' as though she'd just asked me to do her a small favour.

On the train, the tears come, and I don't care if people are watching me; for all they know, my dog might have been run over. I might have been diagnosed with a terminal illness. I might be a barren, divorced, soon-to-be-homeless alcoholic.

It's ridiculous, when I think about it. How did I find myself here? I wonder where it started, my

70

decline; I wonder at what point I could have halted it. Where did I take the wrong turn? Not when I met Tom, who saved me from grief, after Dad died. Not when we married, carefree, drenched in bliss, on an oddly wintry May day seven years ago. I was happy, solvent, successful. Not when we moved into number twenty-three, a roomier, lovelier house than I'd imagined I'd live in at the tender age of twenty-six. I remember those first days so clearly, walking around, shoe-less, feeling the warmth of wooden floorboards underfoot, relishing the space, the emptiness of all those rooms waiting to be filled. Tom and I, making plans: what we'd plant in the garden, what we'd hang on the walls, what colour to paint the spare room – already, even then, in my head, the baby's room.

Maybe it was then. Maybe that was the moment when things started to go wrong, the moment when I imagined us no longer a couple, but a family; and after that, once I had that picture in my head, just the two of us could never be enough. Was it then that Tom started to look at me differently, his disappointment mirroring my own? After all he gave up for me, for the two of us to be together, I let him think that he wasn't enough.

I let the tears flow as far as Northcote, then I pull myself together, wipe my eyes and start writing a list of things to do today on the back of Cathy's eviction letter:

Holborn Library
Email Mum
Email Martin, reference???

71

Find out about AA meetings – central
    London/Ashbury
Tell Cathy about job?

When the train stops at the signal, I look up and see Jason standing on the terrace, looking down at the track. I feel as though he's looking right at me, and I get the oddest sensation – I feel as though he's looked at me like that before; I feel as though he's really seen me. I imagine him smiling at me, and for some reason I feel afraid.

He turns away and the train moves on.

Evening

I'm sitting in A&E at University College Hospital. I was knocked down by a taxi while crossing Gray's Inn Road. I was sober as a judge, I'd just like to point out, although I was in a bit of a state, distracted, panicky almost. I'm having an inch-long cut above my right eye stitched up by an extremely handsome junior doctor who is disappointingly brusque and businesslike. When he's finished stitching, he notices the bump on my head.

'It's not new,' I tell him.

'It looks pretty new,' he says.

'Well, not new today.'

'Been in the wars, have we?'

'I bumped it, getting into a car.'

He examines my head for a good few seconds and then says, 'Is that so?' He stands back and looks me in the eye. 'It doesn't look like it. It looks more like someone's hit you with something,' he says, and I go cold. I have a memory of ducking down to avoid a blow, raising my hands. Is that a real memory? The doctor approaches again and peers more closely at the wound. 'Something sharp, serrated maybe...'

'No,' I say. 'It was a car. I bumped it getting into a car.' I'm trying to convince myself as much as him.

'OK.' He smiles at me then and steps back again, crouching down a little so that our eyes are level. 'Are you all right...' he consults his notes, 'Rachel?'

'Yes.'

He looks at me for a long time; he doesn't believe me. He's concerned. Perhaps he thinks I'm a battered wife. 'Right. I'm going to clean this up for you, because it looks a bit nasty. Is there someone I can call for you? Your husband?'

'I'm divorced,' I tell him.

'Someone else then?' He doesn't care that I'm divorced.

'My friend, please, she'll be worried about me.' I give him Cathy's name and number. Cathy won't be worried at all – I'm not even late home yet – but I'm hoping that the news that I've been hit by a taxi might make her take pity on me and forgive me for what happened yesterday. She'll probably think the reason I got knocked down is because I was drunk. I wonder if I can ask the doctor to do a blood test or something, so that I can provide her with proof of my sobriety. I smile up at him, but he isn't looking at me, he's making notes. It's a ridiculous idea anyway.

It was my fault, the taxi driver wasn't to blame.

I stepped right out – ran right out, actually – in front of the cab. I don't know where I thought I was running to. I wasn't thinking at all, I suppose, at least not about myself. I was thinking about Jess. Who isn't Jess, she's Megan Hipwell, and she's missing.

I'd been in the library on Theobalds Road. I'd just emailed my mother (I didn't tell her anything of significance, it was a sort of test-the-waters email, to gauge how maternal she's feeling towards me at the moment) via my Yahoo account. On Yahoo's front page there are news stories, tailored to your postcode or whatever – God only knows how they know my postcode, but they do. And there was a picture of her, Jess, *my* Jess, the perfect blonde, next to a headline which read CONCERN FOR MISSING WITNEY WOMAN.

At first I wasn't sure. It looked like her, she looked exactly the way she looks in my head, but I doubted myself. Then I read the story and I saw the street name and I knew.

Buckinghamshire Police are becoming increasingly concerned for the welfare of a missing twenty-nine-year-old woman, Megan Hipwell, of Blenheim Road, Witney. Ms Hipwell was last seen by her husband, Scott Hipwell, on Saturday night when she left the couple's home to visit a friend at around seven o'clock. Her disappearance is 'completely out of character', Mr Hipwell said. Ms Hipwell was wearing jeans and a red T-shirt. She is five foot four, slim, with blonde hair and blue eyes. Anyone with information regarding Ms Hipwell is requested to contact Buckinghamshire Police.

She's missing. Jess is missing. Megan is missing. Since Saturday. I googled her – the story appeared in the *Witney Argus,* but with no further details. I thought about seeing Jason – Scott – this morning, standing on the terrace, looking at me, smiling at me. I grabbed my bag and got to my feet and ran out of the library into the road, right into the path of a black cab.

'Rachel? Rachel?' The good-looking doctor is trying to get my attention. 'Your friend is here to pick you up.'

MEGAN

Thursday, 10 January 2013

Morning

Sometimes I don't want to go anywhere, I think I'll be happy if I never have to set foot outside the house again. I don't even miss working. I just want to remain safe and warm in my haven with Scott, undisturbed.

It helps that it's dark and cold and the weather is filthy. It helps that it hasn't stopped raining for weeks – freezing, driving, bitter rain accompanied by gales howling through the trees, so loud they drown out the sound of the train. I can't hear it on the tracks, enticing me, tempting me to journey elsewhere.

Today, I don't want to go anywhere, I don't want

to run away, I don't even want to go down the road. I want to stay here, holed up with my husband, watching TV and eating ice cream, after calling him to come home from work early so we can have sex in the middle of the afternoon.

I will have to go out later, of course, because it's my day for Kamal. I've been talking to him lately about Scott, about all the things I've done wrong, my failure as a wife. Kamal says I have to find a way of making myself happy, I have to stop looking for happiness elsewhere. It's true, I do, I know I do, and then I'm in the moment and I just think, fuck it, life's too short.

I think about that time when we went on a family holiday to Santa Margherita in the Easter school holidays. I'd just turned fifteen and I met this guy on the beach, much older than I was – thirties, probably, possibly even early forties – and he invited me to go sailing the next day. Ben was with me and he was invited too, but – ever the protective big brother – he said we shouldn't go because he didn't trust the guy, he thought he was a sleazy creep. Which, of course, he was. But I was furious, because when were we ever going to get the chance to sail around the Ligurian Sea on some bloke's private yacht? Ben told me we'd have lots of opportunities like that, that our lives would be full of adventure. In the end we didn't go, and that summer Ben lost control of his motorbike on the A10, and he and I never got to go sailing.

I miss the way we were when we were together, Ben and I. We were fearless.

I've told Kamal all about Ben, but we're getting closer to the other stuff now, the truth, the whole truth – what happened with Mac, the before, the after. It's safe with Kamal, he can't ever tell anyone because of patient confidentiality.

But even if he could tell someone, I don't think he would. I trust him, I really do. It's funny, but the thing that's been holding me back from telling him everything is not the fear of what he'd do with it, it's not the fear of judgement, it's Scott. It feels like I'm betraying Scott if I tell Kamal something I can't tell him. When you think about all the other stuff I've done, the other betrayals, this should be peanuts, but it isn't. Somehow this feels worse, because this is real life, this is the heart of me, and I don't share it with him.

I'm still holding back, because obviously I can't say everything I'm feeling. I know that's the point of therapy, but I just can't. I have to keep things vague, jumble up all the men, the lovers and the exes, but I tell myself that's OK, because it doesn't matter who they are. It matters how they make me feel. Stifled, restless, hungry. Why can't I just get what I want? Why can't they give it to me?

Well, sometimes they do. Sometimes all I need is Scott. If I can just learn how to hold on to this feeling, this one I'm having now – if I could just discover how to focus on this happiness, enjoy the moment, not wonder about where the next high is coming from – then everything will be all right.

Evening

I have to focus, when I'm with Kamal. It's difficult not to let my mind wander, when he looks at

77

me with those leonine eyes, when he folds his hands together on his lap, long legs crossed at the knee. It's hard not to think of the things we could do together.

I have to focus. We've been talking about what happened after Ben's funeral, after I ran off. I was in Ipswich for a while; not long. I met Mac there, the first time. He was working in a pub or something. He picked me up on his way home. He felt sorry for me.

'He didn't even want ... you know.' I start laughing. 'We got back to his flat and I asked for the money, and he looked at me like I was mad. I told him I was old enough, but he didn't believe me. And he waited, he did, until my sixteenth birthday. He'd moved, by then, to this old house near Holkham. An old stone cottage at the end of a lane leading nowhere, with a bit of land around it, about half a mile from the beach. There was an old railway track running along one side of the property. At night I'd lie awake – I was always buzzing then, we were smoking a lot – and I used to imagine I could hear the trains, I used to be so sure I'd get up and go outside and look for the lights.'

Kamal shifts in his chair, he nods, slowly. He doesn't say anything. This means I'm to go on, I'm to keep talking.

'I was actually really happy there, with Mac. I lived with him for God, it was about three years, I think, in the end. I was ... nineteen when I left. Yeah. Nineteen.'

'Why did you leave, if you were happy there?' he asks me. We're there now, we got there quicker than I thought we would. I haven't had time to go through it all, to build up to it. I can't do it. It's too soon.

'Mac left me. He broke my heart,' I say, which is the truth, but also a lie. I'm not ready to tell the whole truth yet.

Scott isn't home when I get back, so I get my laptop out and google him, for the first time ever. For the first time in a decade, I look for Mac. I can't find him, though. There are hundreds of Craig McKenzies in the world, and none of them seems to be mine.

Friday, 8 February 2013

Morning

I'm walking in the woods. I've been out since before it got light, it's barely dawn now, deathly quiet except for the occasional outburst of chatter from the magpies in the trees above my head. I can feel them watching me, beady-eyed, calculating. A tiding of magpies. One for sorrow, two for joy, three for a girl, four for a boy, five for silver, six for gold, seven for a secret never to be told.

I've got a few of those.

Scott is away, on a course somewhere in Sussex. He left yesterday morning and he's not back until tonight. I can do whatever I want.

Before he left, I told Scott I was going to the cinema with Tara after my session. I told him my phone would be off, and I spoke to her, too. I warned her that he might ring, that he might check up on me. She asked me, this time, what I was up to. I just winked and smiled and she laughed. I think she might be lonely, that her life could do with a bit of intrigue.

In my session with Kamal, we were talking about Scott, about the thing with the laptop. It happened about a week ago. I'd been looking for Mac – I'd done several searches, I just wanted to find out where he was, what he was up to. There are pictures of almost everyone on the internet these days, and I wanted to see his face. I couldn't find him. I went to bed early that night. Scott stayed up watching TV, and I'd forgotten to delete my browser history. Stupid mistake – it's usually the last thing I do before I shut down my computer, no matter what I've been looking at. I know Scott has ways of finding what I've been up to anyway, being the techie he is, but it takes a lot longer, so most of the time he doesn't bother.

In any case, I forgot. And the next day, we got into a fight. One of the bruising ones. He wanted to know who Craig was, how long I'd been seeing him, where we met, what he did for me that Scott didn't do. Stupidly, I told Scott that he was a friend from my past, which only made it worse. Kamal asked me if I was afraid of Scott, and I got really pissed off.

'He's my husband,' I snapped. 'Of course I'm not afraid of him.'

Kamal looked quite shocked. I actually shocked myself. I hadn't anticipated the force of my anger, the depth of my protectiveness towards Scott. It was a surprise to me, too.

'There are many women who are frightened of their husbands, I'm afraid, Megan.' I tried to say something, but he held up his hand to silence me. 'The behaviour you're describing – reading your emails, going through your internet browser history – you describe all this as though it is commonplace, as though it is normal. It isn't, Megan. It isn't normal to invade someone's privacy to that degree. It's what is often seen as a form of emotional abuse.'

I laughed then, because it sounded so melodramatic. 'It isn't abuse,' I told him. 'Not if you don't mind. And I don't. I don't mind.'

He smiled at me then, a rather sad smile. 'Don't you think you should?' he asked.

I shrugged. 'Perhaps I should, but the fact is, I don't. He's jealous, he's possessive. That's the way he is. It doesn't stop me loving him, and some battles aren't worth fighting. I'm careful – usually. I cover my tracks, so it isn't usually an issue.'

He gave a little shake of the head, almost imperceptible.

'I didn't think you were here to judge me.' I said.

When the session ended, I asked him if he wanted to have a drink with me. He said no, he couldn't, it wouldn't be appropriate. So I followed him home. He lives in a flat just down the road from the practice. I knocked on his door, and when he opened it, I asked, 'Is this appropriate?' I slipped my hand around the back of his neck, stood on tiptoe and kissed him on the mouth.

'Megan,' he said, voice like velvet. 'Don't. I can't do this. Don't.'

It was exquisite, that push and pull, desire and restraint. I didn't want to let the feeling go, I

81

wanted so badly to be able to hold on to it.

I got up in the early hours of the morning, head spinning, full of stories. I couldn't just lie there, awake, alone, my mind ticking over all those opportunities which I could take or leave, so I got up and got dressed and started walking. Found myself here. I've been walking around and playing things back in my head – he said, she said, temptation, release; if only I could settle on something, choose to stick, not twist. What if the thing I'm looking for can never be found? What if it just isn't possible?

The air is cold in my lungs, the tips of my fingers are turning blue. Part of me just wants to lie down here, among the leaves, let the cold take me. I can't. It's time to go.

It's almost nine by the time I get back to Blenheim Road and as I turn the corner I see her, coming towards me, pushing the buggy in front of her. The child, for once, is silent. She looks at me and nods and gives me one of those weak smiles, which I don't return. Usually, I would pretend to be nice, but this morning I feel real, like myself. I feel high, almost like I'm tripping, and I couldn't fake nice if I tried.

Afternoon

I fell asleep in the afternoon. I woke feverish, panicky. Guilty. I do feel guilty. Just not guilty enough.

I thought about him leaving in the middle of the night, telling me, once again, that this was the last time, the very last time, we can't do this again. He was getting dressed, pulling on his jeans. I was lying on the bed and I laughed, because that's what he said last time, and the time before, and the time before that. He shot me a look. I don't know how to describe it, it wasn't anger, exactly, not contempt – it was a warning.

I feel uneasy. I walk around the house; I can't settle, I feel as though someone else has been here while I was sleeping. There's nothing out of place, but the house feels different, as though things have been touched, subtly shifted out of place, and as I walk around I feel as though there's someone else here, always just out of my line of sight. I check the French doors to the garden three times, but they're locked. I can't wait for Scott to get home. I need him.

RACHEL

Tuesday, 16 July 2013

Morning

I'm on the 8.04, but I'm not going into London. I'm going to Witney instead. I'm hoping that being there will jog my memory, that I'll get to the station and I'll see everything clearly, I'll know. I don't hold out much hope, but there is nothing else I can do. I can't call Tom. I'm too ashamed, and in any case, he's made it clear. He wants nothing more to do with me.

Megan is still missing; she's been gone more than sixty hours now and the story is becoming national news. It was on the BBC website and MailOnline this morning; there were a few snippets mentioning it on other sites, too.

I printed out both the BBC and *Mail* stories; I have them with me. From them I have gleaned the following:

Megan and Scott argued on Saturday evening. A neighbour reported hearing raised voices. Scott admitted that they argued, and said that he believed his wife had gone to spend the night with a friend, Tara Epstein, who lives in Corly.

Megan never got to Tara's house. Tara says the last time she saw Megan was on Friday afternoon at their pilates class. (I knew Megan would do pilates.) According to Ms Epstein, 'She seemed fine, normal. She was in a good mood, she was talking about doing something special for her thirtieth birthday next month.'

Megan was seen by one witness walking to-wards Witney train station at around seven fifteen on Saturday evening.

Megan has no family in the area. Both her parents are deceased.

Megan is unemployed. She used to run a small art gallery in Witney, but it closed down in April last year. (I knew Megan would be arty.)

Scott is a self-employed IT consultant. (I can't bloody believe Scott is an IT consultant.)

Megan and Scott have been married for three years; they have been living in the house on Blenheim Road since January 2012.

According to the *Daily Mail,* their house is worth £400,000.

Reading this, I know that things look bad for Scott. Not just because of the argument, either; it's just the way things are: when something bad happens to a woman, the police look at the husband or the boyfriend first. However, in this case, the police don't have all the facts. They're only looking at the husband, presumably because they don't know about the boyfriend.

It could be that I am the only person who knows that the boyfriend exists.

I scrabble around in my bag for a scrap of paper. On the back of a card slip for two bottles of wine, I write down a list of most likely possible explanations for the disappearance of Megan Hipwell:

1. She has run off with her boyfriend, who from here on in I will refer to as B.
2. B has harmed her.
3. Scott has harmed her.
4. She has simply left her husband and gone to live elsewhere.
5. Someone other than B or Scott has harmed her.

I think the first possibility is most likely, and four is a strong contender, too, because Megan is an independent, wilful woman, I'm sure of it. And if she were having an affair, she might need to get away to clear her head, mightn't she? Five does not seem especially likely, since murder by a stranger isn't all that common.

The bump on my head is throbbing, and I can't

stop thinking about the argument I saw, or imagined, or dreamed about, on Saturday night. As we pass Megan and Scott's house, I look up. I can hear the blood pulsing in my head. I feel excited. I feel afraid. The windows of number fifteen, reflecting morning sunshine, look like sightless eyes.

Evening

I'm just settling into my seat when my phone rings. It's Cathy. I let it go to voicemail.

She leaves a message: 'Hi Rachel, just phoning to make sure you're OK.' She's worried about me, because of the thing with the taxi. 'I just wanted to say that I'm sorry, you know, about the other day, what I said about moving out. I shouldn't have. I overreacted. You can stay as long as you want to.' There's a long pause and then she says, 'Give me a ring, OK? And come straight home, Rach, don't go to the pub.'

I don't intend to. I wanted a drink at lunchtime; I was desperate for one after what happened in Witney this morning. I didn't have one though, because I had to keep a clear head. It's been a long time since I've had anything worth keeping a clear head for.

It was so strange, this morning, my trip to Witney. I felt as though I hadn't been there in ages, although of course it's only been a few days. It may as well have been a completely different place, though, a different station in a different town. I was a different person to the one who went there on Saturday night. Today I was stiff

86

and sober, hyper-aware of the noise and the light and fear of discovery.

I was trespassing. That's what it felt like this morning, because it's their territory now, it's Tom and Anna's and Scott and Megan's. I'm the outsider, I don't belong there, and yet everything is so familiar to me. Down the concrete steps at the station, right past the newspaper kiosk into Roseberry Avenue, half a block to the end of the T-junction, to the right the archway leading to a dank pedestrian underpass beneath the track, and to the left Blenheim Road, narrow and tree-lined, flanked with its handsome Victorian terraces. It feels like coming home: not just any home but a childhood home, a place left behind a lifetime ago; it's the familiarity of walking up stairs and knowing exactly which one is going to creak.

The familiarity isn't just in my head, it's in my bones; it's muscle memory. This morning, as I walked past the blackened tunnel mouth, the entrance to the underpass, my pace quickened. I didn't have to think about it because I always walk a little faster on that section. Every night, coming home, especially in winter, I used to pick up the pace, glancing quickly to the right, just to make sure. There was never anyone there – not on any of those nights and not today – and yet I stopped dead as I looked into the darkness this morning, because I could suddenly see myself. I could see myself a few metres in, slumped against the wall, my head in my hands, and both head and hands smeared with blood.

My heart thudding in my chest, I stood there, morning commuters stepping around me as they continued on their way to the station, one or two turning to look at me as they passed, as I stood stock still. I didn't know – don't know – if it was real. Why would I have gone into the underpass? What reason would I have had to go down there, where it's dark and damp and stinks of piss?

I turned around and headed back to the station. I didn't want to be there any longer; I didn't want to go to Scott and Megan's front door. I wanted to get away from there. Something bad happened there, I know it did.

I paid for my ticket and walked quickly up the station steps to the other side of the platform, and as I did it came to me again in a flash: not the underpass this time, but the steps; stumbling on the steps and a man taking my arm, helping me up. The man from the train, with the reddish hair. I could see him, a vague picture but no dialogue. I could remember laughing – at myself, or at something he said. He was nice to me, I'm sure of it. Almost sure. Something bad happened, but I don't think it had anything to do with him.

I got on the train and went into London. I went to the library and sat at a computer terminal, looking for stories about Megan. There was a short piece on the *Telegraph* website which said that 'a man in his thirties is helping police with their enquiries.' Scott, presumably. I can't believe he would have hurt her. I know that he wouldn't. I've seen them together; I *know* what they're like together. They gave a Crimestoppers number too, which you can ring if you have information. I'm going to call it on the way home, from a pay phone. I'm going to tell them about B, about what

I saw.

My phone rings just as we're getting into Ashbury. It's Cathy again. Poor girl, she really is worried about me.

'Rach? Are you on the train? Are you on your way home?' She sounds anxious.

'Yes, I'm on my way,' I tell her. 'I'll be fifteen minutes'

'The police are here, Rachel,' she says, and my entire body goes cold. 'They want to talk to you.'

Wednesday, 17 July 2013

Morning

Megan is still missing, and I have lied – repeatedly – to the police.

I was in a panic by the time I got back to the flat last night. I tried to convince myself that they'd come to see me about my accident with the taxi, but that didn't make sense. I'd spoken to police at the scene – it was clearly my fault. It had to be something to do with Saturday night. I must have done something. I must have committed some terrible act and blacked it out.

I know it sounds unlikely. What could I have done? Gone to Blenheim Road, attacked Megan Hipwell, disposed of her body somewhere and then forgotten all about it? It sounds ridiculous.

It *is* ridiculous. But I know something happened on Saturday. I knew it when I looked into that dark tunnel under the railway line, my blood turning to ice water in my veins.

Blackouts happen, and it isn't just a matter of being a bit hazy about getting home from the club or forgetting what it was that was so funny when you were chatting in the pub. It's different. Total black; hours lost, never to be retrieved.

Tom bought me a book about it. Not very romantic, but he was tired of listening to me tell him how sorry I was in the morning when I didn't even know what I was sorry for. I think he wanted me to see the damage I was doing, the kind of things I might be capable of. It was written by a doctor, but I've no idea whether it was accurate: the author claimed that blacking out wasn't simply a matter of forgetting what had happened, but having no memories to forget in the first place. His theory was that you get into a state where your brain no longer makes short-term memories. And while you're there, in deepest black, you don't be-have as you usually would, because you're simply reacting to the very last thing that you *think* hap-pened, because – since you aren't making mem-ories – you might not actually know what the last thing that happened really was. He had anecdotes, too, cautionary tales for the blacked-out drinker: there was a guy in New Jersey who got drunk at a fourth of July party. Afterwards, he got into his car, drove several miles in the wrong direction on the motorway and ploughed into a van carrying seven people. The van burst into flames and six people died. The drunk guy was fine. They always are. He had no memory of getting into his car.

There was another man, in New York this time, who left a bar, drove to the house he'd grown up in, stabbed its occupants to death, took off all his clothes, got back into his car, drove home and went to bed. He got up the next morning feeling terrible, wondering where his clothes were and how he'd got home, but it wasn't until the police came to get him that he discovered he had brutally slain two people for no apparent reason whatsoever.

So, it sounds ridiculous, but it's not impossible, and by the time I got home last night I had convinced myself that I was in some way involved in Megan's disappearance.

The police officers were sitting on the sofa in the living room, a forty-something man in plain clothes and a younger one in uniform with acne on his neck. Cathy was standing next to the window, wringing her hands. She looked terrified. The policemen got up. The plain-clothes one, very tall and slightly stooped, shook my hand and introduced himself as Detective Inspector Gaskill. He told me the PC's name as well, but I don't remember it. I wasn't concentrating. I was barely breathing.

'What's this about?' I barked at them. 'Has something happened? Is it my mother? Is it Tom?'

'Everyone's all right, Ms Watson, we just need to talk to you about what you did on Saturday evening,' Gaskill said. It's the sort of thing they say on television; it didn't seem real. They want to know what I did on Saturday evening. What the fuck did I do on Saturday evening?

'I need to sit down,' I said, and the detective motioned for me to take his place on the sofa, next to Neck Acne. Cathy was shifting from one foot to another, chewing on her lower lip. She looked frantic.

'Are you all right, Ms Watson?' Gaskill asked me. He motioned to the cut above my eye.

'I was knocked down by a taxi,' I said. 'Yesterday afternoon, in London. I went to the hospital. You can check.'

'OK,' he said, with a slight shake of his head. 'So, Saturday evening?'

'I went to Witney,' I said, trying to keep the waver out of my voice.

'To do what?'

Neck Acne had a notebook out, pencil raised.

'I wanted to see my husband,' I said.

'Oh, Rachel,' Cathy said.

The detective ignored her. 'Your husband?' he said. 'You mean your ex-husband? Tom Watson?' Yes, I still bear his name. It was just more convenient. I didn't have to change my credit cards, email address, get a new passport, things like that.

'That's right. I wanted to see him, but then I decided that it wasn't a good idea, so I came home.'

'What time was this?' Gaskill's voice was even, his face completely blank. His lips barely moved when he spoke. I could hear the scratch of Neck Acne's pencil on paper, I could hear the blood pounding in my ears.

'It was ... um ... I think it was around six thirty. I mean, I think I got the train at around six o'clock.'

'And you came home...?'

'Maybe seven thirty?' I glanced up and caught Cathy's eye and I could see from the look on her face that she knew I was lying. 'Maybe a bit later than that. Maybe it was closer to eight. Yes, actually, I remember now – I think I got home just after eight.' I could feel the colour rising to my cheeks; if this man didn't know I was lying then he didn't deserve to be on the police force.

The detective turned around, grabbed one of the chairs pushed under the table in the corner and pulled it towards him in a swift, almost violent movement. He placed it directly opposite me, a couple of feet away. He sat down, his hands on his knees, head cocked to one side. 'OK,' he said. 'So you left at around six, meaning you'd be in Witney by six thirty. And you were back here around eight, which means you must have left Witney at around seven thirty. Does that sound about right?'

'Yes, that seems right,' I said, that wobble back in my voice, betraying me. In a second or two he was going to ask me what I'd been doing for an hour, and I had no answer to give him.

'And you didn't actually go to see your ex-husband. So what did you do during that hour in Witney?'

'I walked around for a bit.'

He waited, to see if I was going to elaborate. I thought about telling him I went to a pub, but that would be stupid – that's verifiable. He'd ask me which pub, he'd ask me whether I'd spoken to anyone. As I was thinking about what I should tell him, I realized that I hadn't actually thought to ask him to explain *why* he wanted to know where I was on Saturday evening, and that in itself must have seemed odd. That must have made me look guilty of something.

'Did you speak to anyone?' he asked me, reading my mind. 'Go into any shops, bars...?'

'I spoke to a man in the station!' I blurted this out loudly, triumphantly almost, as though it meant something. 'Why do you need to know this? What is going on?'

Detective Inspector Gaskill leaned back in the chair. 'You may have heard that a woman from Witney – a woman who lives on Blenheim Road, just a few doors along from your ex-husband – is missing. We have been going door to door, asking people if they remember seeing her that night, or if they remember seeing or hearing anything unusual. And during the course of our enquiries, your name came up.' He fell silent for a bit, letting this sink in. 'You were seen on Blenheim Road that evening, around the time that Ms Hipwell, the missing woman, left her home. Mrs Anna Watson told us that she saw you in the street, near Ms Hipwell's home, not very far from her own property. She said that you were acting strangely, and that she was worried. So worried, in fact, that she considered calling the police.'

My heart was fluttering like a trapped bird. I couldn't speak, because all I could see at that moment was myself, slouched in the underpass, blood on my hands. *Blood on my hands.* Mine, surely? It had to be mine. I looked up at Gaskill, saw his eyes on mine and knew that I had to say something quickly to stop him reading my mind. 'I didn't do anything,' I said. 'I didn't. I just... I just wanted to see my husband...'

'Your *ex*-husband,' Gaskill corrected me again. He pulled a photograph out of his jacket pocket and showed it to me. It was a picture of Megan. 'Did you see this woman on Saturday night?' he asked. I stared at it for a long time. It felt so surreal having her presented to me like that, the perfect blonde I'd watched, whose life I'd constructed and deconstructed in my head. It was a close-up head shot, a professional job. Her features were a little heavier than I'd imagined, not quite so fine as those of the Jess in my head. 'Ms Watson? Did you see her?'

I didn't know if I'd seen her. I honestly didn't know. I still don't.

'I don't think so,' I said.

'You don't think so? So you might have seen her?'

'I ... I'm not sure.'

'Had you been drinking on Saturday evening?' he asked. 'Before you went to Witney, had you been drinking?'

The heat came rushing back to my face. 'Yes,' I said.

'Mrs Watson – Anna Watson – said that she thought you were drunk when she saw you outside her home. Were you drunk?'

'No,' I said, keeping my eyes firmly on the detective so that I didn't catch Cathy's eye. 'I'd had a couple of drinks in the afternoon, but I wasn't drunk.'

Gaskill sighed. He seemed disappointed in me. He glanced over at Neck Acne, then back at me. Slowly, deliberately, he got to his feet and pushed the chair back to its position under the table. 'If you remember anything about Saturday night, anything that might be helpful to us, would you please call me?' he said, handing me a business card.

95

As Gaskill nodded sombrely at Cathy, preparing to leave, I slumped back into the sofa. I could feel my heart rate starting to slow, and then it raced again as I heard him ask me, 'You work in public relations, is that correct? Huntingdon Whitely?'

'That's right,' I said. 'Huntingdon Whitely.'

He is going to check, and he is going to know I lied. I can't let him find out for himself, I have to tell him.

So that's what I'm going to do this morning. I'm going to go round to the police station to come clean. I'm going to tell him everything: that I lost my job months ago, that I was very drunk on Saturday night and I have no idea what time I came home. I'm going to say what I should have said last night: that he's looking in the wrong direction. I'm going to tell him that I believe Megan Hipwell was having an affair.

Evening

The police think I'm a rubbernecker. They think I'm a stalker, a nut-case, mentally unstable. I should never have gone to the police station. I've made my own situation worse and I don't think I've helped Scott, which was the reason I went there in the first place. He needs my help, because it's obvious the police will suspect that he's done something to her, and I know it isn't true, because I know him. I really feel that, crazy as it sounds. I've seen the way he is with her. He couldn't hurt her.

OK, so helping Scott was not my sole reason

for going to the police. There was the matter of the lie, which needed sorting out. The lie about me working for Huntingdon Whitely.

It took me ages to get up the courage to go into the station. I was on the verge of turning back and going home a dozen times, but eventually I went in. I asked the desk sergeant if I could speak to Detective Inspector Gaskill, and he showed me to a stuffy waiting room, where I sat for over an hour until someone came to get me. By that time I was sweating and trembling like a woman on her way to the scaffold. I was shown into another room, smaller and stuffier still, windowless and airless. I was left there alone for a further ten minutes before Gaskill and a woman, also in plain clothes, turned up. Gaskill greeted me politely; he didn't seem surprised to see me. He introduced his companion as Detective Sergeant Riley. She is younger than I am, tall, slim, dark-haired, pretty in a sharp-featured, vulpine sort of way. She did not return my smile.

We all sat down and nobody said anything they just looked at me expectantly.

'I remembered the man,' I said. 'I told you there was a man at the station. I can describe him.' Riley raised her eyebrows ever so slightly and shifted in her seat. 'He was about medium height, medium build, reddish hair. I slipped on the steps and he caught my arm.' Gaskill leaned forward, his elbows on the table, hands clasped together in front of his mouth. 'He was wearing... I think he was wearing a blue shirt.'

This is not actually true. I do remember a man, and I'm pretty sure he had reddish hair, and I think that he smiled at me, or smirked at me, when I was on the train. I think that he got off at Witney, and I think he might have spoken to me. It's possible I might have slipped on the steps. I have a memory of it, but I can't tell whether the memory belongs to Saturday night, or to another time. There have been many slips, on many staircases. I have no idea what he was wearing.

The detectives were not impressed with my tale. Riley gave an almost imperceptible shake of her head. Gaskill unclasped his hands and spread them out, palms upwards, in front of him. 'OK. Is that really what you came here to tell me, Ms Watson?' he asked. There was no anger in his tone, he sounded almost encouraging. I wished that Riley would go away. I could talk to him; I could trust him.

'I don't work for Huntingdon Whitely any longer,' I said.

'Oh.' He leaned back in his seat, looking more interested.

'I left three months ago. My flatmate – well, she's my landlady really – I haven't told her. I'm trying to find another job. I didn't want her to know because I thought she would worry about the rent. I have some money. I can pay my rent, but... Anyway, I lied to you yesterday about my job and I apologize for that.'

Riley leaned forward and gave me an insincere smile. 'I see. You no longer work for Huntingdon Whitely. You don't work for anyone, is that right? You're unemployed?' I nodded. 'OK. So you're not signing on, nothing like that?'

'No.'

'And ... your flatmate, she hasn't noticed that you don't go to work every day?'

'I do. I mean, I don't go to the office, but I go into London, the way I used to, at the same time and everything, so that she... So that she won't know.' Riley glanced at Gaskill; he kept his eyes on my face, the hint of a frown between his eyes. 'It sounds odd, I know...' I said and I tailed off then, because it doesn't just sound odd, it sounds insane when you say it out loud.

'Right. So, you pretend to go to work every day?' Riley asked me, her brow knitted too, as though she were concerned about me. As though she thought I was completely deranged. I didn't speak or nod or do anything, I kept silent. 'Can I ask why you left your job, Ms Watson?'

There was no point in lying. If they hadn't intended to check out my employment record before this conversation, they bloody well would now. 'I was fired,' I said.

'You were dismissed,' Riley said, a note of satisfaction in her voice. It was obviously the answer she'd anticipated. 'Why was that?'

I gave a little sigh and appealed to Gaskill. 'Is this really important? Does it matter why I left my job?'

Gaskill didn't say anything, he was consulting some notes that Riley had pushed in front of him, but he did give the slightest shake of his head. Riley changed tack.

'Ms Watson, I wanted to ask you about Saturday night.' I glanced at Gaskill – *we've already had this conversation* – but he wasn't looking at me. 'All right,' I said. I kept raising my hand to my scalp, worrying at my injury. I couldn't stop myself.

'Tell me why you went to Blenheim Road on Saturday night. Why did you want to speak to your ex-husband?'

'I don't really think that's any of your business,' I said, and then, quickly, before she had time to say anything else, 'Would it be possible to have a glass of water?'

Gaskill got to his feet and left the room, which wasn't really the outcome I was hoping for. Riley didn't say a word; she just kept looking at me, the trace of a smile still on her lips. I couldn't hold her gaze, I looked at the table, I let my eyes wander around the room. I knew this was a tactic: she was remaining silent so that I would become so uncomfortable that I had to say something, even if I didn't really want to. 'I had some things I needed to discuss with him,' I said. 'Private matters.' I sounded pompous and ridiculous.

Riley sighed. I bit my lip, determined not to speak until Gaskill came back into the room. The moment he returned, placing a glass of cloudy water in front of me, Riley spoke.

'Private matters?' she prompted.

'That's right.'

Riley and Gaskill exchanged a look, I wasn't sure if it was irritation or amusement. I could taste the sweat on my upper lip. I took a sip of water; it tasted stale. Gaskill shuffled the papers in front of him and then pushed them aside, as though he was done with them, or as though whatever was in them didn't interest him all that much.

'Ms Watson, your ... er ... your ex-husband's current wife, Mrs Anna Watson, has raised concerns about you. She told us that you have been bothering her, bothering her husband, that you have come to the house uninvited, that on one occasion...' Gaskill glanced back at his notes, but Riley interrupted.

'On one occasion you broke into Mr and Mrs Watson's home and took their child, their newborn baby.'

A black hole opened up in the centre of the room and swallowed me. 'That is not true!' I said. 'I didn't *take*... It didn't happen like that, that's wrong. I didn't... I didn't take her.'

I got very upset then, I started to shake and cry, I said I wanted to leave. Riley pushed her chair back and got to her feet, shrugged at Gaskill and left the room. Gaskill handed me a Kleenex.

'You can leave any time you like, Ms Watson. You came here to talk to us.' He smiled at me then, an apologetic sort of smile. I liked him in that moment, I wanted to take his hand and squeeze it, but I didn't, because that would have been weird. 'I think you have more to tell me,' he said, and I liked him even more for saying *tell me* rather than *tell us*.

'Perhaps,' he said, getting to his feet and ushering me towards the door, 'you would like to take a break, stretch your legs, get yourself something to eat. Then when you're ready, come back, and you can tell me everything.'

I was planning to just forget the whole thing and go home. I was walking back towards the train station, ready to turn my back on everything. Then I thought about the train journey, about going backwards and forwards on that line, past the house – Megan and Scott's house – every day. What if they never found her? I was going to wonder forever – and I understand that this is not very likely, but even so – whether my saying something might have helped her. What if Scott was accused of harming her just because they never knew about B? What if she was at B's house right now, tied up in the basement, hurt and bleeding, or buried in the garden?

I did as Gaskill said, I bought a ham-and-cheese sandwich and a bottle of water from a corner shop and took it to Witney's only park, a rather sorry little patch of land surrounded by 1930s houses and given over almost entirely to an asphalted playground. I sat on a bench at the edge of this space, watching mothers and childminders scolding their charges for eating sand out of the pit. I used to dream of this, a few years back. I dreamed of coming here – not to eat ham-and-cheese sandwiches in between police interviews, obviously – I dreamed of coming here with my own baby. I thought about the buggy I would buy, all the time I would spend in Trotters and at the Early Learning Centre sizing up adorable outfits and educational toys. I thought about how I would sit here, bouncing my own bundle of joy on my lap.

It didn't happen. No doctor has been able to explain to me why I can't get pregnant. I'm young enough, fit enough, I wasn't drinking heavily when we were trying. My husband's sperm was active and plentiful. It just didn't happen. I didn't suffer the agony of miscarriage, I just didn't get pregnant. We did one round of IVF, which was all we could afford. It was, as everyone had warned us it would be, unpleasant and unsuccessful. Nobody warned me it would break us. But it did. Or rather, it broke me, and then I broke us.

The thing about being barren is that you're not allowed to get away from it. Not when you're in your thirties. My friends were having children, friends of friends were having children, pregnancy and birth and first birthday parties were everywhere. I was asked about it, all the time. My mother, our friends, colleagues at work. When was it going to be my turn? At some point our childlessness became an acceptable topic of Sunday-lunch conversation, not just between Tom and me, but more generally. What we were trying, what we should be doing, do you really think you should be having a second glass of wine? I was still young, there was still plenty of time, but failure cloaked me like a mantle, it overwhelmed me, dragged me under and I gave up hope. At the time, I resented the fact that it was always seen as my fault, that I was the one letting the side down. But as the speed with which he managed to impregnate Anna demonstrates, there was never any problem with Tom's virility. I was wrong to suggest that we should share the blame; it was all down to me.

Lara, my best friend since university, had two children in two years: a boy first and then a girl. I didn't like them. I didn't want to hear anything about them. I didn't want to be near them. Lara stopped speaking to me after a while. There was a girl at work who told me – casually, as though she were talking about an appendectomy or a wisdom-tooth extraction – that she'd recently had an

103

abortion, a medical one, and it was so much less traumatic than the surgical one she'd had when she was at university. I couldn't speak to her after that, I could barely look at her. Things became awkward in the office; people noticed.

Tom didn't feel the way I did. It wasn't his failure, for starters, and in any case, he didn't *need* a child like I did. He wanted to be a dad, he really did – I'm sure he daydreamed about kicking a football around in the garden with his son, or carrying his daughter on his shoulders in the park. But he thought our lives could be great without children, too. We're happy, he used to say to me, why can't we just go on being happy? He became frustrated with me. He never understood that it's possible to miss what you've never had, to mourn for it.

I felt isolated in my misery. I became lonely, so I drank a bit, and then a bit more, and then I became lonelier, because no one likes being around a drunk. I lost and I drank and I drank and I lost. I liked my job, but I didn't have a glittering career, and even if I had, let's be honest: women are still only really valued for two things – their looks and their role as mothers. I'm not beautiful, and I can't have kids, so what does that make me? Worthless.

I can't blame all this for my drinking – I can't blame my parents or my childhood, an abusive uncle or some terrible tragedy. It's my fault. I was a drinker anyway – I've always liked to drink. But I did become sadder, and sadness gets boring after a while, for the sad person and for everyone around them. And then I went from being a drinker to being a drunk, and there's nothing more boring than that.

I'm better now, about the children thing; I've got better since I've been on my own. I've had to. I've read books and articles, I've realized that I must come to terms with it. There are strategies, there is hope. If I straightened myself out and sobered up, there's a possibility that I could adopt. And I'm not thirty-four yet – it isn't over. I am better than I was a few years ago, when I used to abandon my trolley and leave the supermarket if the place was packed with mums and kids; I wouldn't have been able to come to a park like this, to sit near the playground and watch chubby toddlers rolling down the slide. There were times, at my lowest, when the hunger was at its worst, when I thought I was going to lose my mind.

Maybe I did, for a while. The day they asked me about it at the police station, I might have been mad then. Something Tom once said tipped me over, sent me sliding. Something he wrote, rather: I read it on Facebook that morning. It wasn't a shock – I knew she was having a baby, he'd told me, and I'd seen her, seen that pink blind in the nursery window. So I knew what was coming. But I thought of the baby as *her* baby. Until the day I saw the picture of him, holding his newborn girl, looking down at her and smiling, and beneath he'd written: 'So this is what all the fuss is about! Never knew love like this! Happiest day of my life!' I thought about him writing that – knowing that I would see it, that I would read those words and they would kill me, and writing it anyway. He didn't care. Parents don't care about anything but their children. They are the centre of the universe; they are all that really counts. Nobody else is important, no one else's suffering or joy matters, none of it is real.

I was angry. I was distraught. Maybe I was vengeful. Maybe I thought I'd show them that my distress was real. I don't know. I did a stupid thing.

I went back to the police station after a couple of hours. I asked if I could speak to Gaskill alone, but he said that he wanted Riley to be present. I liked him a little less after that.

'I didn't break into their home,' I said. 'I did go there, I wanted to speak to Tom. No one answered the doorbell...'

'So how did you get in?' Riley asked me.

'The door was open.'

The front door was open?'

I sighed. 'No, of course not. The sliding door at the back, the one leading into the garden'

'And how did you get into the back garden?'

'I went over the fence, I knew the way in...'

'So you climbed over the fence to gain access to your ex-husband's house?'

'Yes. We used to... There was always a spare key at the back. We had a place we hid it, in case one of us lost our keys or forgot them or something. But I wasn't breaking in – I didn't. I just wanted to talk to Tom. I thought maybe ... the bell wasn't working or something.'

'This was the middle of the day, during the week, wasn't it? Why did you think your ex-husband would be at home? Had you called to find out?' Riley asked.

'Jesus! Will you just let me speak?' I shouted, and she shook her head and gave me that smile again, as if she knew me, as if she could read me. 'I went over the fence,' I said, trying to control the volume of my voice, 'and knocked on the glass doors, which were partly open. There was no answer. I stuck my head inside and called Tom's name. Again, no answer, but I could hear a baby crying. I went inside and saw that Anna–'

'Mrs Watson?'

'Yes. Mrs Watson was on the sofa, sleeping. The baby was in the carrycot and was crying – screaming, actually, red in the face – she'd obviously been crying for a while.' As I said those words it struck me that I should have told them that I could hear the baby crying from the street and that's why I went round to the back of the house. That would have made me sound less like a maniac.

'So the baby's screaming and her mother's right there, and she doesn't wake?' Riley asks me.

'Yes.' Her elbows are on the table, her hands in front of her mouth so I can't read her expression fully, but I know she thinks I'm lying. 'I picked her up to comfort her. That's all. I picked her up to quieten her.'

'That's not all, though, is it, because when Anna woke up you weren't there, were you? You were down by the fence, by the train tracks.'

'She didn't stop crying right away,' I said. 'I was bouncing her up and down and she was still grizzling, so I walked outside with her.'

'Down to the train tracks?'

'Into the garden'

'Did you intend to harm the Watsons' child?'

I leaped to my feet then. Melodramatic, I know, but I wanted to make them see – make Gaskill see – what an outrageous suggestion that was. 'I don't have to listen to this! I came here to tell you about the man! I came here to help you! And now ... what exactly are you accusing me of? What are you accusing me of?'

Gaskill remained impassive, unimpressed. He motioned at me to sit down again. 'Ms Watson, the other ... er, Mrs Watson – Anna – mentioned you to us during the course of our enquiries about Megan Hipwell. She said that you had behaved erratically, in an unstable manner, in the past. She mentioned this incident with the child. She said that you have harassed both her and her husband, that you continue to call the house repeatedly.' He looked down at his notes for a moment. 'Almost nightly, in fact. That you refuse to accept that your marriage is over...'

'That is simply not true!' I insisted, and it wasn't – yes, I called Tom from time to time, but not every night, it was a total exaggeration. But I was getting the feeling that Gaskill wasn't on my side after all, and I was starting to feel tearful again.

'Why haven't you changed your name?' Riley asked me.

'Excuse me?'

'You still use your ex-husband's name. Why is that? If a man left me for another woman, I think I'd want to get rid of that name. I certainly wouldn't want to share my name with my replacement...'

'Well, maybe I'm not that petty.' I *am* that petty. I hate that she's Anna Watson.

'Right. And the ring – the one on a chain around your neck. Is that your wedding band?'

'No,' I lied. 'It's a … it was my grandmother's.'

'Is that right? OK. Well, I have to say that, to me, your behaviour suggests that – as Mrs Watson has implied – you are unwilling to move on, that you refuse to accept that your ex has a new family.'

'I don't see–'

'What this has to do with Megan Hipwell?' Riley finished my sentence. 'Well. The night Megan went missing, we have reports that you – an unstable woman who had been drinking heavily – were seen on the street where she lives. Bearing in mind that there are some physical similarities between Megan and Mrs Watson–'

'They don't look anything like each other!' I was outraged at the suggestion. Jess is nothing like Anna. Megan is nothing like Anna.

'They're both blonde, slim, petite, pale-skinned…'

'So I attacked Megan Hipwell thinking she was Anna? That's the most stupid thing I've ever heard,' I said. But that lump on my head was throbbing again and everything from Saturday night was still deepest black.

'Did you know that Anna Watson knows Megan Hipwell?' Caskill asked me, and I felt my jaw drop.

'I … what? No. No, they don't know each other.'

Riley smiled for a moment, then straightened her face. 'Yes they do. Megan did some childminding for the Watsons…' she glanced down at her notes, 'back in August and September last year.' I don't know what to say. I can't imagine it: Megan in my home, with *her*, with her baby.

'The cut on your lip, is that from when you got knocked down the other day?' Gaskill asked me.

'Yes. I bit it when I fell, I think.'

'Where was it, this accident?'

'It was in London, Theobalds Road. Near Holborn.'

'And what were you doing there?'

'I'm sorry?'

'Why were you in central London?'

I shrugged. 'I already told you,' I said coldly. 'My flatmate doesn't know that I've lost my job. So I go into London, as usual, and I go to libraries, to job hunt, to work on my CV.'

Riley shook her head, in disbelief perhaps, or wonder. How does anyone get to that point?

I pushed my chair back, readying myself to leave. I'd had enough of being talked down to, being made to look like a fool, like a mad woman. Time to play the trump card. 'I don't really know why we're talking about this,' I said. 'I would have thought that you would have better things to do, like investigating Megan Hipwell's disappearance, for example. I take it you've spoken to her lover?' Neither of them said anything, they just stared at me. They weren't expecting that. They didn't know about him. 'Perhaps you didn't know. Megan Hipwell was having an affair,' I said, and I started to walk to the door. Gaskill stopped me; he moved quietly and surprisingly quickly, and before I could put my hand on the door handle he was standing in front of me.

'I thought you didn't know Megan Hipwell?' he asked me.

110

'I don't,' I said, trying to get past him.

'Sit down,' he said, blocking my path.

I told them then about what I'd seen from the train, about how I often saw Megan sitting out on her terrace, sunbathing in the evenings or having coffee in the mornings. I told them about how last week I saw her with someone who clearly wasn't her husband, how I'd seen them kissing on the lawn.

'When was this?' Gaskill snapped. He seemed annoyed with me, perhaps because I should have told them this straight away, instead of wasting all day talking about myself.

'Friday. It was Friday morning.'

'So the day before she went missing, you saw her with another man?' Riley asked me, with a sigh of exasperation. She closed the file in front of her. Gaskill leaned back in his seat, studying my face. She clearly thought I was making it up; he wasn't so sure.

'Can you describe him?' Gaskill asked.

'Tall, dark–'

'Handsome?' Riley interrupted.

I puffed my cheeks out. 'Taller than Scott Hipwell. I know, because I've seen them together – Jess and – sorry, Megan and Scott Hipwell – and this man was different. Slighter, thinner, darker skinned. Possibly an Asian man,' I said.

'You could determine his ethnic group from the train?' Riley said. 'Impressive. Who is Jess, by the way?'

'I'm sorry?'

'You mentioned Jess a moment ago'

I could feel my face flushing again. I shook my

head, 'No, I didn't,' I said.

Gaskill got to his feet and held out his hand for me to shake. 'I think that's enough.' I shook his hand, ignored Riley and turned to go. 'Don't go anywhere near Blenheim Road, Ms Watson,' Gaskill said. 'Don't contact your ex-husband unless it's important, and don't go anywhere near Anna Watson or her child.'

On the train on the way home, as I dissect all the ways that today went wrong, I'm surprised by the fact that I don't feel as awful as I might do. Thinking about it, I know why that is: I didn't have a drink last night, and I have no desire to have one now. I am interested, for the first time in ages, in something other than my own misery. I have purpose. Or at least, I have a distraction.

Thursday, 18 July 2013

Morning

I bought three newspapers before getting on to the train this morning: Megan has been missing for four days and five nights and the story is getting plenty of coverage. The *Daily Mail*, predictably, has managed to find pictures of Megan in her bikini, but they've also done the most detailed profile I've seen of her so far.

Born Megan Mills in Rochester in 1983, she moved with her parents to King's Lynn in Norfolk when she was ten. She was a bright child, very outgoing, a talented artist and singer. A quote from a school friend says she was 'a good laugh, very pretty and quite wild.' Her wildness seems to have been exacerbated by the death of her brother, Ben, to whom she was very close. He was killed in a motorcycle accident when he was nineteen and she fifteen. She ran away from home three days after his funeral. She was arrested twice – once for theft and once for soliciting. Her relationship with her parents, the *Mail* informs me, broke down completely. Both her parents died a few years ago, without ever being reconciled with their daughter. (Reading this, I feel desperately sad for Megan. I realize that perhaps, after all, she isn't so different from me. She's isolated and lonely too.)

When she was sixteen, she moved in with a boyfriend who had a house near the village of Holkham in north Norfolk. The school friend says, 'He was an older guy, a musician or something. He was into drugs. We didn't see Megan much after they got together.' The boyfriend's name is not given, so presumably they haven't found him. He might not even exist. The school friend might be making this stuff up just to get her name into the papers.

They skip forward several years after that: suddenly Megan is twenty-four, living in London, working as a waitress in a north London restaurant. There she meets Scott Hipwell, an independent IT contractor who is friendly with the restaurant manager, and the two of them hit it off. After an 'intense courtship', Megan and Scott marry, when she is twenty-six and he is thirty.

There are a few other quotes, including one from Tara Epstein, the friend with whom Megan was supposed to stay on the night she disap-

113

peared. She says that Megan is 'a lovely, carefree girl' and that she seemed 'very happy'. 'Scott would not have hurt her,' Tara says. 'He loves her very much.' There isn't a thing Tara says that isn't a cliché. The quote that interests me is from one of the artists who exhibited their work in the gallery Megan used to manage, one Rajesh Gujral, who says that Megan is 'a wonderful woman, sharp, funny and beautiful, an intensely private person with a warm heart'. Sounds to me like Rajesh has got a crush. The only other quote comes from a man called David Clark, 'a former colleague' of Scott's, who says, 'Megs and Scott are a great couple. They're very happy together, very much in love.'

There are some news pieces about the investigation, too, but the statements from the police amount to less than nothing: they have spoken to 'a number of witnesses', they are 'pursuing several lines of enquiry.' The only interesting comment comes from Detective Inspector Gaskill, who confirms that two men are helping the police with their enquiries. I'm pretty sure that means they're both suspects. One will be Scott. Could the other be B. Could B be Rajesh?

I've been so engrossed in the newspapers that I haven't been paying my usual attention to the journey; it seems as though I've only just sat down when the train grinds to its customary halt opposite the red signal. There are people in Scott's garden – there are two uniformed police just outside the back door. My head swims. Have they found something? Have they found her? Is there a body buried in the garden or shoved under the floorboards? I can't stop thinking of the clothes on the side of the railway line, which is stupid, because I saw those there before Megan went missing. And in any case, if harm has been done to her, it wasn't by Scott, it can't have been. He's madly in love with her, everyone says so. The light is bad today, the weather's turned, the sky leaden, threatening. I can't see into the house, I can't see what's going on. I feel quite desperate. I cannot stand being on the outside – for better or worse, I am a part of this now. I need to know what's going on.

At least I have a plan. First, I need to find out if there's any way that I can be made to remember what happened on Saturday night. When I get to the library, I plan to do some research and find out whether hypnotherapy could make me remember; whether it is in fact possible to recover that lost time. Second – and I reckon this is important, because I don't think the police believed me when I told them about Megan's lover – I need to get in touch with Scott Hipwell. I need to tell him. He deserves to know.

Evening

The train is full of rain-soaked people, steam rising off their clothes and condensing on the windows. The fug of body odour, perfume and laundry soap hangs oppressively above bowed, damp heads. The clouds that menaced this morning did so all day, growing heavier and blacker until they burst, monsoon-like, this evening, just

115

as office workers stepped outside and the rush hour began in earnest, leaving the roads gridlocked and tube station entrances choked with people opening and closing umbrellas.

I don't have an umbrella and am soaked through; I feel as though someone has thrown a bucket of water over me. My cotton trousers cling to my thighs and my faded blue shirt has become embarrassingly transparent. I ran all the way from the library to the tube station with my handbag clutched against my chest to hide what I could. For some reason I found this funny – there is something ridiculous about being caught in the rain – and I was laughing so hard by the time I got to the top of Gray's Inn Road I could barely breathe. I can't remember the last time I laughed like that.

I'm not laughing now. As soon as I got myself a seat, I checked the latest on Megan's case on my phone, and it's the news I've been dreading. 'A thirty-five-year-old man is being questioned under caution at Witney police station regarding the disappearance of Megan Hipwell, missing from her home since Saturday evening.' That's Scott, I'm sure of it. I can only hope that he read my email before they picked him up, because questioning under caution is serious – it means they think he did it. Although, of course, *it* is yet to be defined. *It* may not have happened at all. Megan might be fine. Every now and again it does strike me that she's alive and well and sitting on a hotel balcony with a view of the sea, her feet up on the railings, a cold drink at her elbow.

The thought of her there both thrills and disappoints me, and then I feel sick for feeling disappointed. I don't wish her ill, no matter how angry I was with her for cheating on Scott, for shattering my illusions about my perfect couple. No, it's because I feel like I'm part of this mystery, I'm connected. I am no longer just a girl on the train, going back and forth without point or purpose. I want Megan to turn up safe and sound. I do. Just not quite yet.

I sent Scott an email this morning. His address was easy to find – I googled him and found www.shipwellconsulting.co.uk, the site where he advertises 'a range of consultancy, cloud and web-based services for business and non-profit organizations.' I knew it was him, because his business address is also his home address.

I sent a short message to the contact given on the site:

Dear Scott,
My name is Rachel Watson. You don't know me. I would like to talk to you about your wife. I do not have any information on her whereabouts, I don't know what has happened to her. But I believe I have information that could help you.
You may not want to talk to me, I would understand that, but if you do, email me on this address.
Yours sincerely,
Rachel

I don't know if he would have contacted me anyway – I doubt that I would, if I were in his shoes. Like the police, he'd probably just think I was a nutter, some weirdo who's read about the case in the newspaper. Now I'll never know – if he's been arrested, he may never get a chance to see the message. If he's been arrested, the only people who see it may be the police, which won't be good news for me. But I had to try.

And now I feel desperate, thwarted. I can't see through the mob of people in the carriage across to their side of the tracks – my side – and even if I could, with the rain still pouring down I wouldn't be able to see beyond the railway fence. I wonder whether evidence is being washed away, whether right at this moment vital clues are disappearing for ever: smears of blood, footprints, DNA-loaded cigarette butts. I want a drink so badly I can almost taste the wine on my tongue. I can imagine exactly what it will feel like for the alcohol to hit my bloodstream and make my head rush.

I want a drink and I don't want one, because if I don't have a drink today then it'll be three days, and I can't remember the last time I stayed off for three days in a row. There's a taste of something else in my mouth, too, an old stubbornness. There was a time when I had willpower, when I could run 10k before breakfast and subsist for weeks on 1,300 calories a day. It was one of the things Tom loved about me, he said: my stubbornness, my strength. I remember an argument, right at the end, when things were about as bad as they could be; he lost his temper with me. 'What happened to you, Rachel?' he asked me. 'When did you become so weak?'

I don't know. I don't know where that strength went, I don't remember losing it. I think that over time it got chipped away, bit by bit, by life, by the living of it.

The train comes to an abrupt halt, brakes screeching alarmingly, at the signal on the London side of Witney. The carriage is filled with murmured apologies as standing passengers stumble, bumping into each other, stepping on each other's feet. I look up and find myself looking right into the eyes of the man from Saturday night – the ginger one, the one who helped me up. He's staring right at me, his startlingly blue eyes locked on mine, and I get such a fright I drop my phone. I retrieve it from the floor and look up again, tentatively this time, not directly at him. I scan the carriage, I wipe the steamy window with my elbow and stare out, and then eventually I look back over at him and he smiles at me, his head cocked a little to one side.

I can feel my face burning. I don't know how to react to his smile, because I don't know what it means. Is it *Oh, hello, I remember you from the other night*, or is it *Ah, it's that pissed girl who fell down the stairs and talked shit at me the other night*, or is it something else? I don't know, but thinking about it now, I believe I have a snatch of soundtrack to go with the picture of me slipping on the steps: him saying, 'You all right, love?' I turn away and look out of the window again. I can feel his eyes on me; I just want to hide, to disappear. The train judders off and in seconds we're pulling into Witney station and people start jostling each other for position, folding newspapers and packing away Kindles and iPads as they prepare to disembark. I look up again and am flooded with relief – he's turned away from me, he's getting off the train.

It strikes me then that I'm being an idiot. I should get up and follow him, talk to him. He can tell me what happened, or what didn't happen; he might be able to fill in some of the blanks at least. I get to my feet. I hesitate – I know it's already too late, the doors are about to close, I'm in the middle of the carnage, I won't be able to push my way through the crowd in time. The doors beep and close. Still standing I turn and look out of the window as the train pulls away. He's standing on the edge of the platform in the rain, the man from Saturday night, watching me as I go past.

The closer I get to home the more irritated with myself I feel. I'm almost tempted to change trains at Northcote, go back to Witney and look for him. A ridiculous idea, obviously, and stupidly risky given that Gaskill warned me to stay away from the area only yesterday. But I'm feeling dispirited about ever recalling what happened on Saturday. A few hours of (admittedly hardly exhaustive) internet research this afternoon confirmed what I suspected: hypnosis is not generally useful in retrieving hours lost to blackout because, as my previous reading suggested, we do not make memories during blackout. There is nothing to remember. It is, will always be, a black hole in my timeline.

MEGAN

Thursday, 7 March 2013

Afternoon

The room is dark, the air close, sweet with the smell of us. We're at the Swan again, in the room under the eaves. It's different, though, because he's still here, watching me.

'Where do you want to go?' he asks me.

'A house on the beach on the Costa de la Luz,' I tell him.

He smiles. 'What will we do?'

I laugh. 'You mean apart from this?'

His fingers are tracing slowly over my belly. 'Apart from this.'

'We'll open a café, show art, learn to surf.'

He kisses me on the tip of my hipbone. 'What about Thailand?' he says.

I wrinkle my nose. 'Too many gap-year kids. Sicily,' I say. 'The Egadi islands. We'll open a beach bar, go fishing...'

He laughs again and then moves his body up over mine and kisses me. 'Irresistible,' he mumbles. 'You're irresistible.'

I want to laugh, I want to say it out loud: *See? I win! I told you it wasn't the last time, it's never the last time.* I bite my lip and close my eyes. I was right, I knew I was, but it won't do me any good to say

121

it. I enjoy my victory silently; I take pleasure in it almost as much as in his touch.

Afterwards, he talks to me in a way he hasn't done before.

Usually I'm the one doing all the talking, but this time he opens up. He talks about feeling empty, about the family he left behind, about the woman before me and the one before that, the one who wrecked his head and left him hollow. I don't believe in soul-mates, but there's an understanding between us which I just haven't felt before, or at least, not for a long time. It comes from shared experience, from knowing how it feels to be broken.

Hollowness: that I understand. I'm starting to believe that there isn't anything you can do to fix it. That's what I've taken from the therapy sessions: the holes in your life are permanent. You have to grow around them, like tree roots around concrete; you mould yourself through the gaps. All these things I know, but I don't say them out loud, not now.

'When will we go?' I ask him, but he doesn't answer me, and I fall asleep, and he's gone when I wake up.

Friday, 8 March 2013

Morning

Scott brings me coffee on the terrace.

'You slept last night,' he says, bending down to kiss my head. He's standing behind me, hands on my shoulders, warm and solid. I lean my head back against his body, close my eyes and listen to the train rumbling along the track until it stops just in front of the house. When we first moved here, Scott used to wave at the passengers, which always made me laugh. His grip tightens a little on my shoulders; he leans forward and kisses my neck.

'You slept,' he says again. 'You must be feeling better.'

'I am,' I say.

'Do you think it's worked, then?' he asks. 'The therapy?'

'Do I think I'm fixed, do you mean?'

'Not fixed,' he says, and I can hear the hurt in his voice. 'I didn't mean...'

'I know.' I lift my hand to his and squeeze. 'I was only joking. I think it's a process. It's not simple, you know? I don't know if there will be a time when I can say that it's worked. That I'm better.'

There's a silence, and he grips just a little harder. 'So you want to keep going?' he asks, and I tell him I do.

There was a time when I thought he could be everything, he could be enough. I thought that for years. I loved him completely. I still do. But I don't want this any longer. The only time I feel like me is on those secret, febrile afternoons like yesterday, when I come alive in all that heat and half-light. Who's to say that once I run, I'll find that isn't enough? Who's to say I won't end up feeling exactly the way I do right now – not safe, but stifled? Maybe I'll want to run again, and again, and eventually I'll end up back by those old tracks, because there's nowhere left to go. Maybe. Maybe not. You have to take the risk, don't you?

I go downstairs to say goodbye as he's heading off to work. He slips his arms around my waist and kisses the top of my head.

'Love you, Megs,' he murmurs, and I feel horrible then, like the worst person in the world. I can't wait for him to shut the door because I know I'm going to cry.

RACHEL

Friday, 19 July 2013

Morning

The 8.04 is almost deserted. The windows are open and the air is cool after yesterday's storm. Megan has been missing for around 133 hours, and I feel better than I have in months. When I looked at myself in the mirror this morning, I could see the difference in my face: my skin is clearer, my eyes brighter. I feel lighter. I'm sure I haven't actually lost an ounce, but I don't feel encumbered. I feel like myself – the myself I used to be.

There's been no word from Scott. I scoured the internet and there was no news of an arrest, either, so I imagine he just ignored my email. I'm disappointed, but I suppose it was to be expected. Gaskill rang this morning, just as I was leaving the house. He asked me whether I would be able to come by the station today. I was terrified for a moment, but then I heard him say in his quiet, mild tone that he just wanted me to look at a couple of pictures. I asked him whether Scott Hipwell had been arrested.

'No one has been arrested, Ms Watson,' he said.

'But the man, the one who's under caution...?'

'I'm not at liberty to say.'

His manner of speaking is so calming, so reassuring, it makes me like him again.

I spent yesterday evening sitting on the sofa in jogging bottoms and a T-shirt, making lists of things to do, possible strategies. For example, I could hang around Witney station at rush hour, wait until I see the red-haired man from Saturday night again. I could invite him for a drink and see where it leads, whether he saw anything, what he knows about that night. The danger is that I might see Anna or Tom, they would report me and I would get into trouble (more trouble) with the police. The other danger is that I might make myself vulnerable. I still have the trace of an argument in my head – I may have physical evidence of it on my scalp and lip. What if this is the man who hurt me? The fact that he smiled and waved doesn't mean anything, he could be a psychopath for all I know. But I can't see him as a psychopath. I can't explain it, but I warm to him.

I could contact Scott again. But I need to give him a reason to talk to me, and I'm worried that whatever I say will make me look like a mad woman. He might even think I had something to do with Megan's disappearance, he could report me to the police. I could end up in real trouble.

I could try hypnosis. I'm pretty sure it won't help me remember anything, but I'm curious about it anyway. It can't hurt, can it?

I was still sitting there making notes and going over the news stories I'd printed out when Cathy came home. She'd been to the cinema with Damien. She was obviously pleasantly surprised to find me sober, but she was wary, too, because we haven't really spoken since the police came round on Tuesday. I told her that I hadn't had a drink for three days, and she gave me a hug.

'I'm so glad you're getting yourself back to normal!' she chirruped, as though she knows what my baseline is.

'That thing with the police,' I said, 'it was a misunderstanding. There's no problem with me and Tom, and I don't know anything about that missing girl. You don't have to worry about it.' She gave me another hug and made us both a cup of tea. I thought about taking advantage of the goodwill I'd engendered and telling her about the job situation, but I didn't want to spoil her evening.

She was still in a good mood with me this morning. She hugged me again as I was getting ready to leave the house.

'I'm so pleased for you, Rach,' she said. 'Getting yourself sorted. You've had me worried.' Then she told me that she was going to spend the weekend at Damien's, and the first thing I thought was that I'm going to get home tonight and have a drink without anyone judging me.

126

Evening

The bitter tang of quinine, that's what I love about a cold gin and tonic. Tonic water should be by Schweppes and it should come out of a glass bottle, not a plastic one. These pre-mixed things aren't right at all, but needs must. I know I shouldn't be doing this, but I've been building up to it all day. It's not just the anticipation of solitude though, it's the excitement, the adrenaline. I'm buzzing, my skin is tingling. I've had a good day.

I spent an hour alone with Detective Inspector Gaskill this morning. I was taken in to see him straight away when I arrived at the station. We sat in his office, not in the interview room this time. He offered me coffee and when I accepted I was surprised to find that he got up and made it for me himself. He had a kettle and some Nescafé on top of a fridge in the corner of the office. He apologized for not having sugar.

I liked being in his company. I liked watching his hands move – he isn't expressive, but he moves things around a lot. I hadn't noticed this before because in the interview room there wasn't much for him to move around. Here in his office he constantly altered the position of his coffee mug, his stapler, a jar of pens, he shuffled papers into neater piles. He has large hands and long fingers with neatly manicured nails. No rings.

It felt different this morning. I didn't feel like a suspect, someone he was trying to catch out. I felt useful. I felt most useful when he took one of his folders and laid it in front of me, showing me

127

a series of photographs. Scott Hipwell, three men I'd never seen before, and then B.

I wasn't sure at first. I stared at the picture, trying to conjure up the image of the man I saw with her that day, his head bent as he stooped to embrace her.

'That's him,' I said. 'I think that's him.'

'You're not sure?'

'I think that's him.'

He withdrew the picture and scrutinized it himself for a moment. 'You saw them kissing, that's what you said? Last Friday, was it? A week ago?'

'Yes, that's right. Friday morning. They were outside, in the garden.'

'And there's no way you could have misinterpreted what you saw? It wasn't a hug, say, or a ... a platonic kind of kiss?'

'No, it wasn't. It was a proper kiss. It was ... romantic.' I thought I saw his lips flicker then, as though he were about to smile.

'Who is he?' I asked Gaskill. 'Is he... Do you think she's with him?' He didn't reply, just shook his head a little. 'Is this... Have I helped? Have I been helpful at all?'

'Yes, Ms Watson. You've been helpful. Thank you for coming in.'

We shook hands and for a second he placed his left hand on my right shoulder lightly, and I wanted to turn and kiss it. It's been a while since anyone touched me with anything approaching tenderness. Well, apart from Cathy.

Gaskill ushered me out of the door and into the main, open-plan part of the office. There were perhaps a dozen police officers in there. One or two shot me sideways glances, there might have been a flicker of interest or disdain, I couldn't be sure. We walked through the office and into the corridor and then I saw him walking towards me, with Riley at his side: Scott Hipwell. He was coming through the main entrance. His head was down but I knew right away that it was him. He looked up and nodded an acknowledgement to Gaskill, then he glanced at me. For just a second our eyes met and I could swear that he recognized me. I thought of that morning when I saw him on the terrace, when he was looking down at the track, when I could feel him looking at me. We passed each other in the corridor. He was so close to me I could have touched him – he was beautiful in the flesh, hollowed out and coiled like a spring, nervous energy radiating off him. As I got to the main hallway I turned to look at him, sure I could feel his eyes on me, but when I looked back it was Riley who was watching me.

I took the train into London and went to the library. I read every article I could find about the case, but learned nothing more. I looked for hypnotherapists in Ashbury, but didn't take it any further – it's expensive and it's unclear whether it actually helps with memory recovery. But reading the stories of those who claimed that they had recovered memories through hypnotherapy, I realized that I was more afraid of success than failure. I'm afraid not just of what I might learn about that Saturday night, but so much more. I'm not sure I could bear to relive the stupid, awful things I've done, to hear the words I said in spite, to remember the look on Tom's face as I said them. I'm too afraid to venture into that darkness.

I thought about sending Scott another email, but there's really no need. The morning's meeting with Detective Inspector Gaskill proved to me that the police are taking me seriously. I have no further role to play, I have to accept that now. And I can feel at least that I may have helped, because I cannot believe it could be a coincidence that Megan disappeared the day after I saw her with that man.

With a joyful click, fizz, I open the second can of G&T and realize, with a rush, that I haven't thought about Tom all day. Until now, anyway. I've been thinking about Scott, about Gaskill, about B, about the man on the train. Tom has been relegated to fifth place. I sip my drink and feel that at last I have something to celebrate. I know that I'm going to be better, that I'm going to be happy. It won't be long.

Saturday, 20 July 2013

Morning

I never learn. I wake with a crushing sensation of wrongness, of shame, and I know immediately that I've done something stupid. I go through my awful, achingly familiar ritual of trying to remember exactly what I did. I sent an email. That's what it was.

At some point last night, Tom got promoted back up the list of men I think about, and I sent him an email. My laptop is on the floor next to my bed; it sits there, a squat, accusatory presence. I step over it as I get up to go to the bathroom. I drink water directly from the tap, giving myself a cursory glance in the mirror.

I don't look well. Still, three days off isn't bad, and I'll start again today. I stand in the shower for ages, gradually reducing the water temperature, making it cooler and cooler until it's properly cold. You can't step directly into a cold stream of water, it's too shocking, too brutal, but if you get there gradually, you hardly notice it; it's like boiling a frog in reverse. The cool water soothes my skin; it dulls the burning pain of the cuts on my head and above my eye.

I take my laptop downstairs and make a cup of tea. There's a chance, a faint one, that I wrote an email to Tom and didn't send it. I take a deep breath and open my Gmail account. I'm relieved to see I have no messages. But when I click on the Sent folder, there it is: I have written to him, he just hasn't replied. Yet. The email was sent just after eleven last night; I'd been drinking for a good few hours by then. That adrenaline and booze buzz I had earlier on would have been long gone. I click on the message.

Could you please tell your wife to stop lying to the police about me? Pretty low, don't you think, trying to get me into trouble? Telling police I'm obsessed with her and her ugly brat? She needs to get over herself. Tell her to leave me the fuck alone.

I close my eyes and snap the laptop shut. I am cringing literally, my entire body folding into

131

itself. I want to be smaller; I want to disappear. I'm frightened, too, because if Tom decides to show this to the police, I could be in real trouble. If Anna is collecting evidence that I am vindictive and obsessive, this could be a key piece in her dossier. And why did I mention the little girl? What sort of person does that? What sort of person thinks like that? I don't bear her any ill will – I couldn't think badly of a child, any child, and especially not Tom's child. I don't understand myself; I don't understand the person I've become. God, he must hate me. *I* hate me – that version of me anyway, the version who wrote that email last night. She doesn't even feel like me, because I am not like that. I am not hateful.

Am I? I try not to think of the worst days, but the memories crowd into my head at times like this. Another fight, towards the end: waking post-party, post-blackout, Tom telling me how I'd been the night before, embarrassing him again, insulting the wife of a colleague of his, shouting at her for flirting with my husband. 'I don't want to go anywhere with you any more,' he told me. 'You ask me why I never invite friends round, why I don't like going to the pub with you any more. You honestly want to know why? It's because of you. Because I'm ashamed of you.'

I pick up my handbag and my keys. I'm going to the Londis down the road. I don't care that it's not yet nine o'clock in the morning I'm frightened and I don't want to have to think. If I take some painkillers and have a drink now, I can put myself out, I can sleep all day. I'll face it later. I get to the front door, my hand poised above the handle, then

I stop. I could apologize. If I apologize right now, I might be able to salvage something. I might be able to persuade him not to show the message to Anna or to the police. It wouldn't be the first time he'd protected me from her.

That day last summer, when I went to Tom and Anna's, it didn't happen exactly the way I told the police it had. I didn't ring the doorbell, for starters. I wasn't sure what I wanted – I'm still not sure what I intended. I did go down the pathway and over the fence. It was quiet, I couldn't hear anything. I went up to the sliding doors and looked in. It's true that Anna was sleeping on the sofa. I didn't call out, to her or to Tom. I didn't want to wake her. The baby wasn't crying, she was fast asleep in her carrycot, at her mother's side. I picked her up and took her outside, as quickly as I could. I remember running with her towards the fence, the baby starting to wake and to grizzle a little. I don't know what I thought I was doing. I wasn't going to hurt her. I got to the fence, holding her tightly against my chest. She was crying properly now, starting to scream. I was bouncing her and shushing her and then I heard another noise, a train coming, and I turned my back to the fence and I saw her – Anna – hurtling towards me, her mouth open like a gaping wound, her lips moving but I couldn't hear what she was saying.

She took the child from me and I tried to run away, but I tripped and fell. She was standing over me, screaming at me, she told me to stay put or she'd call the police. She rang Tom and he came home and sat with her in the living room. She was crying hysterically, she still wanted to phone the police, she wanted to have me arrested for kidnapping. Tom calmed her down, he begged her to let it go, to let me go. He saved me from her. Afterwards he drove me home, and when he dropped me off he took my hand. I thought it was a gesture of kindness, of reassurance, but he squeezed tighter and tighter and tighter until I cried out, and his face was red when he told me that he would kill me if I ever did anything to harm his daughter.

I don't know what I intended to do that day. I still don't. At the door, I hesitate, my fingers grasped around the handle. I bite down hard on my lip. I know that if I start drinking now, I will feel better for an hour or two and worse for six or seven. I let go of the handle and walk back into the living room, and I open my laptop again. I have to apologize, I have to beg forgiveness. I log back into my email account and see that I have one new message. It isn't from Tom. It's from Scott Hipwell.

Dear Rachel,
Thank you for contacting me. I don't remember Megan mentioning you to me, but she had a lot of gallery regulars – I'm not very good with names. I would like to talk to you about what you know. Please telephone me on 07583 123657 as soon as possible.
Regards,
Scott Hipwell.

For an instant, I imagine that he's sent the email to the wrong address. This message is intended for someone else. It's just the briefest of moments, and then I remember. I remember. Sitting on the sofa, halfway through the second bottle, I realized that I didn't want my part to be over. I wanted to be at the heart of it.

So I wrote to him.

I scroll down from his email to mine.

Dear Scott,
Sorry for contacting you again, but I feel it's important that we talk. I'm not sure if Megan ever mentioned me to you – I'm a friend from the gallery – I used to live in Witney. I think I have information that would interest you. Please email me back on this address.
Rachel Watson.

I can feel the heat come to my face, my stomach a pit of acid. Yesterday – sensible, clear-headed, right-thinking – I decided I must accept that my part in this story was over. But my better angels lost again, defeated by drink, by the person I am when I drink. Drunk Rachel sees no consequences, she is either excessively expansive and optimistic or wrapped up in hate. She has no past, no future. She exists purely in the moment. Drunk Rachel – wanting to be part of the story, needing a way to persuade Scott to talk to her – she lied. *I* lied.

I want to drag knives over my skin, just so that I can feel something other than shame, but I'm not even brave enough to do that. I start writing to Tom, writing and deleting, writing and deleting, trying to find ways to ask forgiveness for the things I said last night. If I had to write down every transgression for which I should apologize to Tom, I could fill a book.

Evening

A week ago, almost exactly a week ago, Megan Hipwell walked out of number fifteen, Blenheim Road and disappeared. No one has seen her since. Neither her phone nor her bank cards have been used since Saturday either. When I read that in a news story earlier today, I started to cry. I am ashamed now of the secret thoughts I had. Megan is not a mystery to be solved, she is not a figure who wanders into the tracking shot at the beginning of a film, beautiful, ethereal, insubstantial. She is not a cipher. She is real.

I am on the train, and I'm going to her home. I'm going to meet her husband.

I had to phone him. The damage was done. I couldn't just ignore the email – he would tell the police. Wouldn't he? I would, in his position, if a stranger contacted me, claiming to have information, and then disappeared. He might have called the police already; they might be waiting for me when I get there.

Sitting here, in my usual seat, though not on my usual day, I feel as though I am driving off a cliff. It felt the same this morning when I dialled his number, like falling through the dark, not knowing when you're going to hit the ground. He spoke to me in a low voice, as though there were someone else in the room, someone he didn't want to overhear.

'Can we talk in person?' he asked.

'I ... no. I don't think so...'

'Please?'

I hesitated just for a moment, and then I agreed.

'Could you come to the house? Not now, my ... there are people here. This evening?' He gave me the address, which I pretended to note down.

'Thank you for contacting me,' he said, and he hung up.

I knew as I was agreeing that it wasn't a good idea. What I know about Scott, from the papers, is almost nothing. What I know from my own observations, I don't *really* know. I don't know anything about Scott. I know things about Jason – who, I have to keep reminding myself, doesn't exist. All I know for sure – for absolutely certain – is that Scott's wife has been missing for a week. I know that he is probably a suspect. And I know, because I saw that kiss, that he has a motive to kill her. Of course, he might not know that he has a motive, but... Oh, I've tied myself up in knots thinking about it, but how could I pass up the opportunity to approach that house, the one I've observed a hundred times from the trackside, from the street? To walk up to his front door, to go inside, to sit in his kitchen, on his terrace, where they sat, where I watched them?

It was too tempting. Now I sit on the train, my arms wrapped around myself, hands jammed against my sides to stop them from trembling, like an excited child caught up in an adventure. I was so glad to have a purpose that I stopped thinking about the reality. I stopped thinking about Megan.

I'm thinking about her now. I have to convince

Scott that I knew her – a little, not a lot. That way, he'll believe me when I tell him that I saw her with another man. If I admit to lying right away, he'll never trust me. So I try to imagine what it would have been like to drop by the gallery chat with her over a coffee. Does she drink coffee? We would talk about art, perhaps, or yoga, or our husbands. I don't know anything about art, I've never done yoga. I don't have a husband. And she betrayed hers.

I think of the things her real friends said about her: *wonderful, funny, beautiful, warm-hearted. Loved.* She made a mistake. It happens. We are none of us perfect.

ANNA

Saturday, 20 July 2013

Morning

Evie wakes just before six. I get out of bed, slip into the nursery and pick her up. I feed her and take her back to bed with me.

When I wake again, Tom's not at my side, but I can hear his footfalls on the stairs. He's singing, low and tuneless, *Happy birthday to you, happy birthday to you...* I hadn't even thought about it earlier, I'd completely forgotten; I didn't think of anything but fetching my little girl and getting back to bed. Now I'm giggling before I'm even properly awake. I open my eyes and Evie's smiling too, and when I look up, Tom's standing at the foot of the bed, holding a tray. He's wearing my Orla Kiely apron and nothing else.

'Breakfast in bed, birthday girl,' he says. He places the tray at the end of the bed and scoots round to kiss me.

I open my presents. I have a pretty silver bracelet with onyx inlay from Evie, and a black silk teddy and matching knickers from Tom, and I can't stop smiling. He climbs back into bed and we lie with Evie between us. She has her fingers curled tightly around his forefinger and I have hold of her perfect pink foot, and I feel as though fireworks are going off in my chest. It's impossible, this much love.

A while later, when Evie gets bored of lying there, I get her up and we go downstairs and leave Tom to snooze. He deserves it. I potter round, tidying up a bit. I drink my coffee outside on the patio, watching the half-empty trains rattle past, and think about lunch. It's hot – too hot for a roast, but I'll do one anyway, because Tom loves roast beef and we can have ice cream afterwards to cool us down. I just need to pop out to get that Merlot he likes, so I get Evie ready, strap her in the buggy and we stroll down to the shops.

Everyone told me I was insane to agree to move into Tom's house. But then everyone thought I was insane to get involved with a married man, let alone a married man whose wife was highly unstable, and I've proved them wrong on that one. No matter how much trouble she causes, Tom and Evie are worth it. But they were right about the

139

house. On days like today, with the sun shining, when you walk down our little street – tree-lined and tidy, not quite a cul-de-sac, but with the same sense of community – it could be perfect. Its pavements are busy with mothers just like me, with dogs on leads and toddlers on scooters. It could be ideal. It could be, if you weren't able to hear the screeching brakes of the trains. It could be, so long as you didn't turn around and look back down towards number fifteen.

When I get back, Tom is sitting at the dining-room table looking at something on the computer. He's wearing shorts but no shirt; I can see the muscles moving under his skin when he moves. It still gives me butterflies to look at him. I say hello, but he's in a world of his own and when I run my fingertips over his shoulder he jumps. The laptop snaps shut.

'Hey,' he says, getting to his feet. He's smiling but he looks tired, worried. He takes Evie from me without looking me in the eye.

'What?' I ask. 'What is it?'

'Nothing,' he says, and he turns away towards the window, bouncing Evie on his hip.

'Tom, what?'

'It's nothing.' He turns back and gives me a look and I know what he's going to say before he says it. 'Rachel. Another email.' He shakes his head and he looks so wounded, so upset, and I hate it, I can't bear it. Sometimes I want to kill that woman.

'What's she said?'

He just shakes his head again. 'It doesn't matter. It's just ... the usual. Bullshit.'

'I'm sorry,' I say, and I don't ask what bullshit

exactly, because I know he won't want to tell me. He hates upsetting me with this stuff.

'It's OK. It's nothing. Just the usual pissed non-sense.'

'God, is she ever going to go away? Is she ever going to just let us be happy?'

He comes over to me and, with our daughter between us, kisses me. 'We *are* happy,' he says. 'We are.'

Evening

We *are* happy. We had lunch and lay out on the lawn, and then when it got too hot we came inside and ate ice cream while Tom watched the Grand Prix. Evie and I made playdough, and she ate quite a bit of that, too. I think about what's going on down the road and I think about how lucky I am, how I got everything that I wanted. When I look at Tom, I thank God that he found me, too, that I was there to rescue him from that woman. She'd have driven him mad in the end, I really think that – she'd have ground him down, she'd have made him into something he's not.

Tom's taken Evie upstairs to give her a bath. I can hear her squealing with delight from here and I'm smiling again – the smile has barely fallen from my lips all day. I do the washing-up, tidy up the living room, think about dinner. Something light. It's funny, because a few years ago I would have hated the idea of staying in and cooking on my birthday, but now it's perfect, it's the way it should be. Just the three of us.

I pick up Evie's toys, scattered around the living-room floor, and return them to their trunk. I'm looking forward to putting her down early tonight, to slipping into that teddy Tom bought me. It won't be dark for hours yet, but I light the candles on the mantelpiece and open the second bottle of Merlot to let it breathe. I'm just leaning over the sofa to pull the curtains shut when I see a woman, her head bent to her chest, scuttling along the pavement on the opposite side of the street. She doesn't look up, but it's her, I'm sure of it. I lean further forward, my heart hammering in my chest, trying to get a better look, but the angle's wrong and I can't see her now.

I turn, ready to bolt out of the front door to chase her down the street, but Tom's standing there in the doorway, Evie wrapped in a towel in his arms.

'Are you OK?' he asks. 'What's wrong?'

'Nothing,' I say, stuffing my hands into my pockets so that he can't see them shaking. 'Nothing's wrong. Nothing at all.'

RACHEL

Sunday, 21 July 2013

Morning

I wake with my head full of him. It doesn't seem real, none of it does. My skin prickles. I would dearly love to have a drink, but I can't. I need to keep a clear head. For Megan. For Scott.

I made an effort yesterday. I washed my hair and put some make-up on. I wore the only jeans I still fit into, with a cotton print blouse and sandals with a low heel. I looked OK. I kept telling myself that it was ridiculous to care about my appearance, because the last thing Scott was going to be thinking about was what I looked like, but I couldn't help myself. It was the first time I was ever going to be around him, it mattered to me. Much more than it should.

I took the train, leaving Ashbury around six thirty, and I was in Witney just after seven. I took that walk along Roseberry Avenue, past the underpass. I didn't look this time, couldn't bear to. I hurried past number twenty-three, Tom and Anna's place, chin to chest and sunglasses on, praying they wouldn't see me. It was quiet, no one around, a couple of cars driving carefully down the centre of the road between ranks of parked vehicles. It's a sleepy little street, tidy and affluent, with lots of young families; they're all having their dinner around seven o'clock, or sitting on the sofa, mum and dad with the little ones squeezed between them, watching *X-Factor.*

From number twenty-three to number fifteen can't be more than fifty or sixty paces, but that journey stretched out, it seemed to take an age; my legs were leaden, my footing unsteady, as though I were drunk, as though I might just slip off the pavement.

Scott opened the door almost before I'd finished knocking my trembling hand still raised as he appeared in the doorway, looming ahead of me, filling the space.

'Rachel?' he asked, looking down at me, unsmiling. I nodded. He offered his hand and I took it. He gestured for me to enter the house, but for a moment I didn't move. I was afraid of him. Up close he is physically intimidating, tall and broad-shouldered, his arms and chest well defined. His hands are huge. It crossed my mind that he could crush me – my neck, my ribcage – without much effort.

I moved past him into the hallway, my arm brushing against his as I did, and felt a flush rising to my face. He smelled of old sweat, and his dark hair was matted against his head as though he hadn't showered in a while.

It was in the living room that the déjà vu hit me, so strong it was almost frightening. I recognized the fireplace flanked by alcoves on the far wall, the way the light streamed in from the street through slanted blinds; I knew that when I turned to my left there would be glass and green and beyond that the railway line. I turned and there was the kitchen table, the French doors behind it and the lush patch of lawn. I knew this house. I felt dizzy, I wanted to sit down; I thought about that black hole last Saturday night, all those lost hours.

It didn't mean anything, of course. I know that house, but not because I've been there. I know it because it's exactly the same as number twenty-three: a hallway leads to the stairs, and on the right-hand side is the living room, knocked through into the kitchen. The patio and the garden are familiar to me because I've seen them from the train. I didn't go upstairs, but I know that if I had, there would have been a landing with a large sash window on it, and that if you climbed through that window you would find yourself on the makeshift roof terrace. I know that there will be two bedrooms, the master with two large windows looking out on to the street and a smaller room at the back, overlooking the garden. Just because I know that house inside and out does not mean that I've been there before.

Still, I was trembling when Scott showed me into the kitchen. He offered me a cup of tea. I sat down at the kitchen table while he boiled the kettle, dropped a teabag into a mug and slopped boiling water over the counter, muttering to himself under his breath. There was a sharp smell of antiseptic in the room, but Scott himself was a mess, a sweat patch on the back of his T-shirt, his jeans hanging loose on his hips as though they were too big for him. I wondered when was the last time he had eaten.

He placed the mug of tea in front of me and sat on the opposite side of the kitchen table, his hands folded in front of him. The silence stretched out, filling the space between us, the whole room; it rang in my ears, and I felt hot and uncomfortable, my mind suddenly blank. I didn't know what I was doing there. Why on earth had I come? In the distance, I heard a low rumbling – the train was coming. It felt comforting, that old sound.

'You're a friend of Megan's?' he said at last.

Hearing her name from his lips brought a lump to my throat. I stared down at the table, my hands wrapped tightly around the mug.

'Yes,' I said. 'I know her ... a little. From the gallery.'

He looked at me, waiting, expectant. I could see the muscle flex in his jaw as he clenched his teeth. I searched for words that wouldn't come. I should have prepared better.

'Have you had any news?' I asked. His gaze held mine and for a second I felt afraid. I'd said the wrong thing; it was none of my business whether there was any news. He would be angry, he'd ask me to leave.

'No,' he said. 'What was it that you wanted to tell me?'

The train rolled slowly past and I looked out towards the tracks. I felt dizzy, as though I were having an out-of-body experience, as though I were looking out at myself.

'You said in your email that you wanted to tell me something about Megan.' The pitch of his voice raised a little.

I took a deep breath. I felt awful. I was acutely

aware that what I was about to say was going to make everything worse, was going to hurt him.

'I saw her with someone,' I said. I just blurted it out, blunt and loud with no build-up, no context.

He stared at me. 'When? You saw her on Saturday night? Have you told the police?'

'No, it was Friday morning,' I said, and his shoulders slumped.

'But ... she was fine on Friday. Why is that important?' That pulse in his jaw went again, he was becoming angry. 'You saw her with ... you saw her with who? With a man?'

'Yes, I–'

'What did he look like?' He got to his feet, his body blocking the light. 'Have you told the police?' he asked again.

'I did, but I'm not sure they took me very seriously,' I said.

'Why?'

'I just... I don't know... I thought you should know.'

He leaned forward, his hands on the table, clenched into fists.

'What are you saying? You saw her where? What was she doing?'

Another deep breath. 'She was ... out on your lawn,' I said. 'Just there,' I pointed out to the garden. 'She... I saw her from the train.' The look of incredulity on his face was unmistakeable. 'I take the train into London from Ashbury every day. I go right past here. I saw her, she was with someone. And it ... it wasn't you.'

'How do you know?... Friday morning? Friday

– the day before she went missing?'

'Yes.'

'I wasn't here.' he said. 'I was away. I was at a conference in Birmingham, I got back on Friday evening.' Spots of colour appeared high on his cheeks, his scepticism giving way to something else. 'So you saw her, on the lawn, with someone? And...'

'She kissed him,' I said. I had to get it out eventually. I had to tell him. 'They were kissing.'

He straightened up, his hands, still balled into fists, hanging at his sides. The spots of colour on his cheeks grew darker, angrier.

'I'm sorry,' I said. 'I'm so sorry. I know this is a terrible thing to hear...'

He held up his hand, waved me away. Contemptuous. He wasn't interested in my sympathy.

I know how that feels. Sitting there, I remembered with almost perfect clarity how it felt when I sat in my own kitchen, five doors down, while Lara, my former best friend, sat opposite me, her fat toddler squirming on her lap. I remember her telling me how sorry she was that my marriage was over, I remember losing my temper at her platitudes. She knew nothing of my pain. I told her to piss off and she told me not to speak like that in front of her child. I haven't seen her since.

'What did he look like, this man you – saw her with?' Scott asked. He was standing with his back to me, looking out on to the lawn.

'He was tall – taller than you, maybe. Dark-skinned. I think he might have been Asian. Indian – something like that.'

'And they were kissing, out here in the garden?'

'Yes.'

He gave a long sigh. 'Jesus, I need a drink.' He turned to face me. 'Would you like a beer?'

I did, I wanted a drink desperately, but I said no. I watched as he fetched himself a bottle from the fridge, opened it, took a long slug. I could almost feel the cold liquid sliding down my throat as I watched him; my hand ached for want of a glass. Scott leaned against the counter, his head bent almost to his chest.

I felt wretched then. I wasn't helping, I had just made him feel worse, increased his pain. I was intruding on his grief, it was wrong. I should never have gone to see him. I should never have lied. Obviously, I should never have lied.

I was just getting to my feet when he spoke. 'It could... I don't know. It might be a good thing, mightn't it? It could mean that she's all right. She's just...' He gave a hollow little laugh. 'She's just run off with someone.' He brushed a tear from his cheek with the back of his hand and my heart screwed up into a tight little ball. 'But the thing is, I can't believe she wouldn't call.' He looked at me as though I held the answers, as though I would know. 'Surely she would call me, wouldn't she? She would know how panicked ... how desperate I would be. She's not vindictive like that, is she?'

He was talking to me like someone he could trust – like Megan's friend – and I knew that it was wrong, but it felt good. He took another swig of his beer and turned towards the garden. I followed his gaze to a little pile of stones against the fence, a rockery long since started and never finished. He raised the bottle halfway to his lips again, and then he stopped. He turned to face me.

'You saw Megan from the train?' he asked. 'So you were ... just looking out of the window and there she was, a woman you happen to know?' The atmosphere in the room had changed. He wasn't sure any more, whether I was an ally, whether I was to be trusted. Doubt passed over his face like a shadow.

'Yes, I ... I know where she lives,' I said, and I regretted the words the moment they came out of my mouth. 'Where *you* live, I mean. I've been here before. A long time ago. So sometimes I'd look out for her when I went past.' He was staring at me; I could feel the heat rising to my face. 'She was often out there.'

He placed his empty bottle down on the counter, took a couple of steps towards me and sat down in the seat nearest to me, at the table.

'So you knew Megan well then? I mean, well enough to come round to the house?'

I could feel the blood pulsing in my neck, sweat at the base of my spine, the sickening rush of adrenaline. I shouldn't have said that, shouldn't have complicated the lie.

'It was just one time, but I ... I know where the house is because I used to live nearby.' He raised his eyebrows at me. 'Down the road. Number twenty-three.'

He nodded slowly. 'Watson,' he said. 'So you're, what, Tom's ex-wife?'

'Yes. I moved out a couple of years ago,'

'But you still visited Megan's gallery?'

'Sometimes.'

'And when you saw her, what did you... Did she talk about personal things, about me?' His voice was husky. 'About anyone else?'

I shook my head. 'No, no. It was usually just ... passing the time, you know.' There was a long silence. The heat in the room seemed to build suddenly, the smell of antiseptic rising from every surface. I felt faint. To my right there was a side table adorned with photographs in frames. Megan smiled out at me, cheerfully accusing.

'I should go now,' I said. 'I've taken up enough of your time.' I started to get up, but he reached an arm out and placed his hand on my wrist, his eyes never leaving my face.

'Don't go just yet,' he said softly. I didn't stand up, but I withdrew my hand from beneath his; it felt uncomfortably as though I were being restrained. 'This man,' he said. 'This man you saw her with – do you think you'd recognize him again? If you saw him?'

I couldn't say that I already *had* identified the man to the police. My whole rationale for approaching him had been that the police hadn't taken my story seriously. If I admitted the truth, the trust would be gone. So I lied again.

'I'm not sure,' I said. 'But I think I might.' I waited a moment, and then I went on. 'In the newspapers, there was a quote from a friend of Megan's. His name was Rajesh. I was wondering if–'

Scott was already shaking his head. 'Rajesh Gujral? I can't see it. He's one of the artists who used to exhibit at the gallery. He's a nice enough guy, but... He's married, he's got kids.' As if that

151

meant something. 'Wait a second,' he said, getting to his feet. 'I think there might be a picture of him somewhere.'

He disappeared upstairs. I felt my shoulders drop and realized that I'd been sitting rigid with tension since I arrived. I looked over at the photographs again: Megan in a sundress on a beach; a close-up of her face, her eyes a startling blue. Just Megan. No pictures of the two of them together.

Scott reappeared, holding a pamphlet which he presented to me. It was a leaflet, advertising a show at the gallery. He turned it over. 'There,' he said, 'that's Rajesh.'

The man was standing next to a colourful abstract painting: he was older, bearded, short, stocky. It wasn't the man I had seen, the man I had identified to the police. 'It's not him,' I said. Scott stood at my side, staring down at the pamphlet, before abruptly turning and marching out of the room and up the stairs again. A few moments later, he came back with a laptop and sat down at the kitchen table.

'I think...' he said, opening the machine and turning it on, 'I think I might...' He fell silent and I watched him, his face a picture of concentration, the muscle in his jaw locked. 'Megan was seeing a therapist,' he told me. 'His name is ... Abdic. Kamal Abdic. He's not Asian, he's from Serbia, or Bosnia, somewhere like that. He's dark-skinned though. He could pass for Indian from a distance.' He tapped away at the computer. 'There's a website, I think. I'm sure there is. I think there's a picture...'

He spun the laptop round so that I could see

the screen. I leaned forward to get a closer look. 'That's him,' I said. 'That's definitely him.'

Scott snapped the laptop shut. For a long time, he didn't say anything. He sat with his elbows on the table, his forehead resting on his fingertips, his arms trembling.

'She was having anxiety attacks.' he said at last. 'Trouble sleeping, things like that. It started last year some time. I don't remember when exactly.' He talked without looking at me, as though he were talking to himself, as though he'd forgotten I was there at all. 'I was the one who suggested she talk to someone. I was the one who encouraged her to go, because I didn't seem to be able to help her.' His voice cracked a little then. 'I couldn't help her. And she told me that she'd had similar problems in the past and that eventually they'd go away, but I made her ... I *persuaded* her to go to the doctor. That guy was recommended to her.' He gave a little cough to clear his throat. 'The therapy seemed to be helping. She was happier.' He gave a short, sad laugh. 'Now I know why.'

I reached out my hand to give him a pat on the arm, a gesture of comfort. Abruptly, he drew away and got to his feet. 'You should go,' he said brusquely. 'My mother will be here soon – she won't leave me alone for more than an hour or two.' At the door, just as I was leaving, he caught hold of my arm.

'Have I seen you somewhere before?' he asked.

For a moment, I thought about saying, You might have done. *You might have seen me at the police station, or here on the street. I was here on Saturday night.* I shook my head. 'No, I don't think so.'

I walked away towards the train station as quickly as I could. About halfway along the street, I turned to look back. He was still standing there in the doorway, watching me.

Evening

I've been checking my email obsessively, but I've heard nothing from Tom. How much better life must have been for jealous drunks before emails and texts and mobile phones, before all this electronica and the traces it leaves.

There was almost nothing in the papers about Megan today. They're moving on already, the front pages devoted to the political crisis in Turkey, the four-year-old girl mauled by dogs in Wigan, the England football team's humiliating loss to Montenegro. Megan is being forgotten, and she's only been gone a week.

Cathy invited me out to lunch. She was at a loose end because Damien has gone to visit his mother in Birmingham. She wasn't invited. They've been seeing each other for almost two years now, and she still hasn't met his mother. We went to Giraffe on the High Street, a place I loathe. Seated in the centre of a room heaving with shrieking under-fives, Cathy quizzed me about what I'd been up to. She was curious about where I was last night.

'Have you met someone?' she asked me, her eyes alight with hope. It was quite touching really.

I almost said yes, because it was the truth, but lying was easier. I told her I'd been to an AA meeting in Witney.

'Oh,' she said, embarrassed, dipping her eyes to her limp Greek salad. 'I thought you'd maybe had a little slip. On Friday.'

'Yes. It won't be plain sailing Cathy,' I said, and I felt awful, because I think she really cares whether I get sober or not. 'But I'm doing my best.'

'If you need me to, you know, come with you...'

'Not at this stage,' I said. 'But thank you.'

'Well, maybe we could do something else together, like go to the gym?' she asked.

I laughed, but when I realized she was being serious I said I'd think about it.

She's just left – Damien rang to say he was back from his mother's, so she's gone round to his place. I thought about saying something to her – why do you go running to him whenever he calls? But I'm really not in a great position to give relationship advice – or any advice, come to that – and in any case I feel like a drink. (I've been thinking about it ever since we sat down in Giraffe and the spotty waiter asked if we'd like a glass of wine and Cathy said 'No, thank you' very firmly.) So I wave her off and feel the little anticipatory tingle run over my skin and I push away the good thoughts *(Don't do this, you're doing really well)*. I'm just putting my shoes on to go to the off-licence and my phone rings. Tom. It'll be Tom. I grab the phone from my bag and look at the screen and my heart bangs like a drum.

'Hi.' There is silence, so I ask, 'Is everything OK?'

After a little pause Scott says, 'Yeah, fine. I'm OK. I just called to say thank you, for yesterday.

For taking the time to let me know.'

'Oh, that's all right. You didn't need–'

'Am I disturbing you?'

'No. It's fine.' There is silence on the end of the line, so I say again, 'It's fine. Have you ... has something happened? Did you speak to the police?'

'The family liaison officer was here this afternoon,' he says. My heart rate quickens. 'Detective Sergeant Riley. I mentioned Kamal Abdic to her. Told her that he might be worth speaking to.'

'You said ... you told her that you'd spoken to me?' My mouth is completely dry.

'No, I didn't. I thought perhaps... I don't know. I thought it would be better if I came up with the name myself. I said ... it's a lie, I know, but I said that I'd been racking my brains to think of anything significant, and that I thought it might be worth speaking to her therapist. I said that I'd had some concerns about their relationship in the past.'

I can breathe again. 'What did she say?' I ask him.

'She said they had already spoken to him, but that they would do again. She asked me lots of questions about why I hadn't mentioned him before. She's... I don't know. I don't trust her. She's supposed to be on my side, but all the time I feel like she's snooping, like she's trying to trip me up.'

I'm stupidly pleased that he doesn't like her either; another thing we have in common, another thread to bind us.

'I just wanted to say thank you, anyway. For

coming forward. It was actually … it sounds odd, but it was good to talk to someone … someone I'm not close to. I felt as though I could think more rationally. After you left, I kept thinking about the first time Megan went to see him – Abdic – about the way she was when she came back. There was something about her, a lightness.' He exhales loudly. 'I don't know. Maybe I'm imgining it.'

I have the same feeling I did yesterday – that he's no longer really talking to me, he's just talking. I've become a sounding board, and I'm glad of it. I'm glad to be of use to him.

'I've spent the whole day going through Megan's things again,' he says. 'I've already searched our room, the whole house, half a dozen times, looking for something, anything that would give me an indication as to where she could be. Something from him, perhaps. But there's nothing. No e-mails, no letters, nothing. I thought about trying to contact him, but the practice is closed today and I can't find a mobile number.'

'Is that a good idea, do you think?' I ask. 'I mean, do you not think you should just leave him to the police?' I don't want to say it out loud, but we must both be thinking it: he's dangerous. Or at least, he could be dangerous.

'I don't know, I just don't know.' There's a desperate edge to his voice that's painful to hear, but I have no comfort to offer. I can hear his breathing on the other end of the line; it sounds short, quickened, as though he's afraid. I want to ask him if he has someone there with him, but I can't: it would sound wrong, forward.

'I saw your ex today,' he says, and I can feel the hairs on my arms stand up.

'Oh?'

'Yes, I went out for the papers and saw him in the street. He asked me if I was all right, whether there was any news.'

'Oh,' I repeat, because it's all I can say, words won't form. I don't want him to speak to Tom. Tom knows that I don't know Megan Hipwell. Tom knows that I was on Blenheim Road the night she disappeared.

'I didn't mention you. I didn't ... you know. I wasn't sure if I should have mentioned that I'd met you.'

'No, I don't think you should have. I don't know. It might be awkward.'

'All right,' he says.

After that, there's a long silence. I'm waiting for my heartbeat to slow. I think he's going to ring off, but then he says, 'Did she really never talk about me?'

'Of course ... of course she did,' I say. 'I mean, we didn't talk all that often, but–'

'But you came to the house. Megan hardly ever invites people round. She's really private, protective of her own space.'

I'm searching for a reason. I wish I had never told him I'd been to the house.

'I just came round to borrow a book.'

'Really?' He doesn't believe me. She's not a reader. I think of the house – there were no books on the shelves there. 'What sort of things did she say? About me?'

'Well, she was very happy,' I say. 'With you, I

158

mean. Your relationship.' As I'm saying this I realize how odd it sounds, but I can't be specific, and so I try to save myself. 'To be honest with you, I was having a really hard time in my marriage, so I think it was a kind of compare and contrast thing. She lit up when she spoke about you.' What an awful cliché.

'Did she?' He doesn't seem to notice, there's a note of wistfulness in his voice. 'That's so good to hear.' He pauses, and I can hear his breathing, quick and shallow, on the other end of the line. 'We had ... we had a terrible argument,' he says. 'The night she left. I hate the idea that she was angry with me when...' he tails off.

'I'm sure she wasn't angry with you for long,' I say. 'Couples fight. Couples fight all the time.'

'But this was bad, it was terrible, and I can't... I feel like I can't tell anyone, because if I did they would look at me like I was guilty.'

There's a different quality to his voice now: haunted, saturated with guilt.

'I don't remember how it started,' he says, and immediately I don't believe him, but then I think about all the arguments I've forgotten, and I bite my tongue. 'It got very heated. I was very... I was unkind to her. I was a bastard. A complete bastard. She was upset. She went upstairs and put some things in a bag. I don't know what exactly, but I noticed later that her toothbrush was gone, so I knew she wasn't planning on coming home. I assumed ... I thought she must have gone to Tara's for the night. That happened once before. Just one time. It wasn't like this happened all the time.

'I didn't even go after her,' he says, and it hits

me yet again that he's not really talking to me, he's confessing. He's on one side of the confessional and I'm on the other, faceless, unseen. 'I just let her go.'

'That was on Saturday night?'

'Yes. That was the last time I saw her.'

There was a witness who saw her – or saw 'a woman fitting her description' – walking towards Witney station at around quarter past seven, I know that from the newspaper reports. That was the final sighting. No one remembered seeing her on the platform, or on the train. There is no CCTV at Witney, and she wasn't picked up on the CCTV at Corly, although the reports said that this didn't prove she wasn't there, because there are 'significant blindspots' at that station.

'What time was it when you tried to contact her?' I ask him. Another long silence.

'I ... I went to the pub. The Rose, you know, just around the corner, on Kingly Road? I needed to cool down, to get things straight in my head. I had a couple of pints, then I went back home. That was just before ten. I think I was hoping that she'd have had time to calm down and that she'd be back. But she wasn't.'

'So it was around ten o'clock when you tried to call her?'

'No.' His voice is little more than a whisper now. 'I didn't. I drank a couple more beers at home, I watched some TV. Then I went to bed.'

I think about all the arguments I had with Tom, all the terrible things I said after I'd had too much, all the storming out into the street, shouting at him, telling him I never wanted to see him

160

again. He always rang me, he always talked me down, coaxed me home.

'I just imagined she'd be sitting in Tara's kitchen, you know, talking about what a shit I am. So I left it.'

He left it. It sounds callous and uncaring, and I'm not surprised he hasn't told this story to anyone else. I am surprised that he's telling anyone at all. This is not the Scott I imagined, the Scott I knew, the one who stood behind Megan on the terrace, his big hands on her bony shoulders, ready to protect her from anything.

I'm ready to hang up the phone, but Scott keeps talking. 'I woke up early. There were no messages on my phone. I didn't panic – I assumed she was with Tara and that she was still angry with me. I rang her then and got her voicemail, but I still didn't panic. I thought she was probably still asleep, or just ignoring me. I couldn't find Tara's number, but I had her address – it was on a business card on Megan's desk. So I got up and I drove round there.'

I wonder, if he wasn't worried, why he felt he needed to go round to Tara's house, but I don't interrupt. I let him talk.

'I got to Tara's place a little after nine. It took her a while to come to the door, but when she did, she looked really surprised to see me. It was obvious that I was the last person she expected to see on her doorstep at that time of the morning, and that's when I knew... That's when I knew that Megan wasn't there. And I started to think... I started...' The words catch and I feel wretched for doubting him.

161

'She told me the last time she'd seen Megan was at their pilates class on Friday night. That's when I started to panic.'

After I hang up the phone, I think about how, if you didn't know him, if you hadn't seen how he was with her, as I have, a lot of what he'd said would not ring quite true.

Monday, 22 July 2013

Morning

I feel quite befuddled. I slept soundly but dreamily and this morning I am struggling to wake up properly. The hot weather has returned and the carriage is stifling today, despite being only half full. I was late getting up this morning and didn't have time to pick up a newspaper or to check the news on the internet before I left the house, so I am trying to get the BBC site on my phone, but for some reason it is taking forever to load. At Northcote a man with an iPad gets on and takes the seat next to me. He has no problems at all getting the news up, he goes straight to the *Daily Telegraph* site and there it is, in big, bold letters, the third story: MAN ARRESTED IN CONNECTION WITH MEGAN HIPWELL DISAPPEARANCE.

I get such a fright that I forget myself and lean right over to get a better look. He looks up at me, affronted, almost startled.

'I'm sorry,' I say. 'I know her. The missing woman. I know her.'

162

'Oh, how awful,' he says. He's a middle-aged man, well spoken and well dressed. 'Would you like to read the story?'

'Please. I can't get anything to come up on my phone.'

He smiles kindly and hands me the tablet. I touch the headline and the story comes up.

A man in his thirties has been arrested in connection with the disappearance of Megan Hipwell, twenty-nine, the Witney woman who has been missing since Saturday 13 July. Police were not able to confirm whether the man arrested is Megan Hipwell's husband, Scott Hipwell, who was questioned under caution on Friday. In a statement this morning a police spokesman said: We can confirm that we have arrested a man in connection with Megan's disappearance. He has not yet been charged with an offence. The search for Megan continues, and we are searching an address which we believe may be a crime scene.

We are passing the house now; for once, the train has not stopped at the signal. I whip my head around, but I'm too late. It's gone. My hands are trembling as I hand the iPad back to its owner. He shakes his head sadly. 'I'm very sorry,' he says.

'She isn't dead,' I say. My voice is a croak and even I don't believe me. Tears are stinging the back of my eyes. I was in his house. I was there. I sat across the table from him, I looked into his eyes, I felt something. I think about those huge hands and about how, if he could crush me, he could destroy her – tiny, fragile Megan.

The brakes screech as we approach Witney

163

station and I leap to my feet.

'I have to go,' I tell the man next to me, who looks a little surprised but nods sagely.

'Good luck,' he says.

I run along the platform and down the stairs. I'm going against the flow of people, and am almost at the bottom of the stairs when I stumble and a man says, 'Watch it!' I don't glance up at him because I'm looking at the edge of the concrete step, the second to last one. There's a smear of blood on it. I wonder how long it's been there. Could it be a week old? Could it be my blood? Hers? Is her blood in the house, I wonder, is that why they've arrested him? I try to picture the kitchen, the living room. The smell: very clean, antiseptic. Was that bleach? I don't know, I can't remember now, all I can remember clearly is the sweat on his back and the beer on his breath.

I run past the underpass, stumbling at the corner of Blenheim Road. I'm holding my breath as I hurry along the pavement, head down, too afraid to look up, but when I do there's nothing to see. There are no vans parked outside Scott's house, no police cars. Could they have finished searching the house already? If they had found something they would still be there, surely; it must take hours, going over everything, processing the evidence. I quicken my pace. When I get to his house I stop, take a deep breath. The curtains are drawn, upstairs and down. The curtains in the neighbour's window twitch. I'm being watched. I step into the doorway, my hand raised. I shouldn't be here. I don't know what I'm doing here. I just wanted to see. I wanted to *know*. I'm caught, for a

164

moment, between going against my every instinct and knocking on that door, and turning away. I turn to leave, and it's at that moment that the door opens.

Before I have time to move, his hand shoots out, he grabs my forearm and pulls me towards him. His mouth is a grim line, his eyes wild. He is desperate. Flooded with dread and adrenaline, I see darkness coming. I open my mouth to cry out, but I'm too late, he yanks me into the house and slams the door behind me.

MEGAN

Thursday, 21 March 2013

Morning

I don't lose. He should know this about me. I don't lose games like this.

The screen on my phone is blank. Stubbornly, insolently blank. No text messages, no missed calls. Every time I look at it, it feels like I've been slapped, and I get angrier and angrier. What happened to me in that hotel room? What was I thinking? That we made a connection, that there was something real between us? He has no intention of going anywhere with me. But I believed him for a second – more than a second – and that's what really pisses me off. I was ridiculous, credulous. He was laughing at me, all along.

If he thinks I'm going to sit around crying over him, he's got another thing coming. I can live without him, I can do without him just fine – but I don't like to lose. It's not like me. None of this is like me. I don't get rejected. I'm the one who walks away.

I'm driving myself insane, I can't help it. I can't stop going back to that afternoon at the hotel and going over and over what he said, the way he made me feel.

Bastard.

If he thinks I will just disappear, go quietly, he's mistaken. If he doesn't pick up soon, I'm going to stop calling his mobile and call him at home. I'm not just going to be ignored.

At breakfast, Scott asks me to cancel my therapy session. I don't say anything. I pretend I haven't heard him.

'Dave's asked us round to dinner,' he says. 'We haven't been over there for ages. Can you re-arrange your session?'

His tone is light, as though this is a casual request, but I can feel him watching me, his eyes on my face. We're on the edge of an argument and I have to be careful.

'I can't, Scott, it's too late,' I say. 'Why don't you ask Dave and Karen to come here on Saturday instead?' Just the thought of entertaining Dave and Karen at the weekend is wearing, but I'm going to have to compromise.

'It's not too late,' he says, putting his coffee cup down on the table in front of me. He rests his hand on my shoulder for just a moment, says, 'Cancel it, OK?' and walks out of the room.

The second the front door closes, I pick up the coffee cup and hurl it against the wall.

Evening

I could tell myself that it's not really a rejection. I could try to persuade myself that he's just trying to do the right thing, morally and professionally. But I know that isn't true. Or at least, it's not the whole truth, because if you want someone badly enough, morals (and certainly professionalism) don't come into it. You'll do anything to have them. He just doesn't want me badly enough.

I ignored Scott's calls all afternoon, I turned up to my session late, and walked straight into his office without a word to the receptionist. He was sitting at his desk, writing something. He glanced up at me when I walked in, didn't smile, then looked back down at his papers. I stood in front of his desk, waiting for him to look at me. It felt like forever before he did.

'Are you OK?' he asked eventually. He smiled at me then. 'You're late.'

The breath was catching in my throat, I couldn't speak. I walked around the desk and leaned against it, my leg brushing against his thigh. He drew back a little.

'Megan,' he said, 'are you all right?'

I shook my head. I put my hand out to him, and he took it.

'Megan,' he said again, shaking his head.

I didn't say anything.

'You can't... You should sit down,' he said.

'Let's talk.'

I shook my head.

'Megan.'

Every time he said my name he made it worse.

He got to his feet and circled the desk, walking away from me. He stood in the middle of the room.

'Come on,' he said, his voice businesslike – brusque, even. 'Sit down.'

I followed him into the middle of the room, put one hand on his waist, the other against his chest. He held me by my wrists and moved away from me.

'Don't, Megan. You can't ... we can't...' He turned away.

'Kamal,' I said, my voice catching. I hated the sound of it. 'Please.'

'This ... here. It's not appropriate. It's normal, believe me, but...'

I told him then that I wanted to be with him.

'It's transference, Megan,' he said. 'It happens from time to time. It happens to me, too. I really should have introduced this topic last time. I'm sorry.'

I wanted to scream then. He made it sound so banal, so bloodless, so common.

'Are you telling me you feel nothing?' I asked him. 'You're saying I'm imagining all this?'

He shook his head. 'You have to understand, Megan, I shouldn't have let things get this far.'

I moved closer to him, put my hands on his hips and turned him around. He took hold of my arms again, his long fingers locked around my wrists. 'I could lose my job,' he said, and then I really lost my temper.

I pulled away, angry, violently. He tried to hold me, but he couldn't. I was yelling at him, telling him I didn't give a shit about his *job*. He was trying to quieten me – worried, I assume, about what the receptionist thought, what the other patients thought. He grabbed hold of my shoulders, his thumbs digging into the flesh at the top of my arms, and told me to calm down, to stop behaving like a child. He shook me, hard; I thought for a moment he was going to slap my face.

I kissed him on the mouth, I bit his lower lip as hard as I could; I could taste his blood in my mouth. He pushed me away.

I plotted revenge on my way home. I was thinking of all the things I could do to him. I could get him fired, or worse. I won't though, because I like him too much. I don't want to hurt him. I'm not even that upset about the rejection any more. What bothers me most is that I haven't got to the end of my story, and I can't start over with someone else, it's too hard.

I don't want to go home now, because I don't know how I'm going to be able to explain the bruises on my arms.

RACHEL

Monday, 22 July 2013

Evening

And now I wait. It's agonizing, the not knowing, the slowness with which everything is bound to move. But there's nothing more to do.

I was right, this morning, when I felt that dread. I just didn't know what I had to be afraid of.

Not Scott. When he pulled me inside he must have seen the terror in my eyes, because almost immediately he let go of me. Wild-eyed and dishevelled, he seemed to shrink back from the light, and closed the door behind us. 'What are you doing here? There are photographers, journalists everywhere. I can't have people coming to the door. Hanging around. They'll say things... They'll try – they'll try anything, to get pictures, to get...'

'There's no one out there,' I said, though to be honest I hadn't really looked. There might have been people sitting in cars, waiting for something to happen.

'What are you doing here?' he demanded again.

'I heard ... it was on the news. I just wanted ... is it him? Have they arrested him?'

He nodded. 'Yes, early this morning. The family liaison person was here. She came to tell me. But she couldn't ... they won't tell me why. They must have found something, but they won't tell me what. It's not her, though. I know that they haven't found her.'

He sits down on the stairs and wraps his arms around himself. His whole body is trembling.

'I can't stand it. I can't stand waiting for the phone to ring. When the phone rings, what will it be? Will it be the worst news? Will it be...' He tails off, then looks up as though he's seeing me for the first time. 'Why did you come?'

'I wanted... I thought you wouldn't want to be alone.'

He looked at me as though I was insane. 'I'm not alone,' he said. He got up and pushed past me into the living room. For a moment, I just stood there. I didn't know whether to follow him or to leave, but then he called out, 'Do you want a coffee?'

There was a woman outside on the lawn, smoking. Tall, with salt and pepper hair, she was smartly dressed in black trousers and white blouse done up to the throat. She was pacing up and down the patio, but as soon as she caught sight of me, she stopped, flicked her cigarette on to the paving stones and crushed it beneath her toe.

'Police?' she asked me doubtfully, as she entered the kitchen.

'No, I'm–'

'This is Rachel Watson, Mum,' Scott said. 'The woman who contacted me about Abdic.'

She nodded slowly, as though Scott's explanation didn't really help her; she took me in, her gaze sweeping rapidly over me from head to toe and back again. 'Oh.'

'I just, er...' I didn't have a justifiable reason for being there. I couldn't say, could I, *I just wanted to know. I wanted to see.*

'Well, Scott is very grateful to you for coming forward. We're obviously waiting now to find out what exactly is going on.' She stepped towards me, took me by the elbow and turned me gently towards the front door. I glanced at Scott, but he wasn't looking at me; his gaze was fixed somewhere out of the window, across the tracks.

'Thank you for stopping by, Mrs Watson. We really are very grateful to you.'

I found myself on the doorstep, the front door closed firmly behind me, and when I looked up I saw them: Tom, pushing a buggy, and Anna at his side. They stopped dead when they saw me. Anna raised her hand to her mouth and swooped down to grab her child. The lioness protecting her cub. I wanted to laugh at her, to tell her, I'm not here for you, I couldn't be less interested in your daughter.

I'm cast out. Scott's mother made that clear. I'm cast out and I'm disappointed, but it shouldn't matter, because they have Kamal Abdic. They've got him, and I helped. I did something right. They've got him, and it can't be long now before they find Megan and bring her home.

ANNA

Monday, 22 July 2013

Morning

Tom woke me up early with a kiss and a cheeky grin. He has a late meeting this morning, so he suggested we take Evie around the corner for breakfast. It's a place where we used to meet when we first started seeing each other. We'd sit in the window – she was at work in London so there was no danger of her walking past and noticing us. But there was that thrill, even so – perhaps she'd come home early for some reason: perhaps she'd be feeling ill, or have forgotten some vital papers. I dreamed of it. I willed her to come along one day, to see him with me, to know in an instant that he was no longer hers. It's hard to believe now that there was once a time when I wanted her to appear.

Since Megan went missing I've avoided walking this way whenever possible – it gives me the creeps passing that house – but to get to the café it's the only route. Tom walks a little way ahead of me, pushing the buggy; he's singing something to Evie, making her laugh. I love it when we're out like this, the three of us. I can see the way people look at us; I can see them thinking, *What a beautiful family*. It makes me proud – prouder

173

than I've ever been of anything in my life.

So I'm sailing along in my bubble of happiness, and we're almost at number fifteen when the door opens. For a moment I think I'm hallucinating, because *she* walks out. Rachel. She comes out of the front door and stands there for a second, sees us and stops dead. It's horrible. She gives us the strangest smile, a grimace almost, and I can't help myself, I lunge forward and grab Evie out of her buggy, startling her in the process. She starts to cry.

Rachel walks quickly away from us, towards the station.

Tom calls after her, 'Rachel! What are you doing here? Rachel!' But she keeps going, faster and faster until she's almost running, and the two of us just stand there, then Tom turns to me and with one glance at the expression on my face says, 'Come on. Let's just go home.'

Evening

We found out when we got home that they've arrested someone in connection with Megan Hipwell's disappearance. Some guy I'd never heard of, a therapist she'd been seeing. It was a relief, I suppose, because I'd been imagining all sorts of awful things.

'I told you it wouldn't be a stranger,' Tom said. 'It never is, is it? In any case, we don't even know what's happened. She's probably fine. She's probably run off with someone.'

'So why have they arrested that man then?'

174

He shrugged. He was distracted, pulling on his jacket, straightening his tie, getting ready to go and meet the day's last client.

'What are we going to do?' I asked him.

'Do?' He looked at me blankly.

'About her. Rachel. Why was she here? Why was she at the Hipwells' house? Do you think ... do you think she was trying to get into our garden – you know, going through the neighbours' gardens?'

Tom gave a grim laugh. 'I doubt it. Come on, this is Rachel we're talking about. She wouldn't be able to haul her fat arse over all those fences. I've no idea what she was doing there. Maybe she was pissed, went to the wrong door?'

'In other words, she meant to come round here?'

He shook his head. 'I don't know. Look, don't worry about it, OK? Keep the doors locked. I'll give her a ring and find out what she's up to.'

'I think we should call the police.'

'And say what? She hasn't actually done anything–'

'She hasn't done anything *lately* – unless you count the fact that she was here the night Megan Hipwell disappeared,' I said. 'We should have told the police about her ages ago.'

'Anna, come on.' He slipped his arms around my waist. 'I hardly think Rachel has anything to do with Megan Hipwell going missing. But I'll talk to her, OK?'

'But you said after last time–'

'I know,' he said softly. 'I know what I said.' He kissed me, slipped his hand into the waistband of my jeans. 'Let's not get the police involved unless

175

we really need to.'

I think we do need to. I can't stop thinking about that smile she gave us, that sneer. It was almost triumphant. We need to get away from here. We need to get away from *her*.

RACHEL

Tuesday, 23 July 2013

Morning

It takes me a while to realize what I'm feeling when I wake. There's a rush of elation, tempered with something else: a nameless dread. I know we're close to finding the truth. I just can't help feeling that the truth is going to be terrible.

I sit up in bed and grab my laptop, turn it on and wait impatiently for it to boot up, then log on to the internet. The whole process seems interminable. I can hear Cathy moving around the house, washing up her breakfast things, running upstairs to brush her teeth. She hovers for a few moments outside my door. I imagine her knuckles raised, ready to rap. She thinks better of it and runs back down the stairs.

The BBC news page comes up. The headline is about benefit cuts, the second story about yet another 1970s television star accused of sexual indiscretions. Nothing about Megan; nothing about Kamal. I'm disappointed. I know that the police have twenty-four hours to charge a suspect, and they've had that now. In some circumstances, they can hold someone for an extra twelve hours, though.

I know all this because I spent yesterday doing my research. After I was shown out of Scott's house, I came back here, turned on the television and spent most of the day watching the news, reading articles online. Waiting.

By midday, the police had named their suspect. On the news, they talked about 'evidence discovered at Dr Abdic's home and in his car', but they didn't say what. Blood, perhaps? Her phone, as yet undiscovered? Clothes, a bag, her toothbrush? They kept showing pictures of Kamal, close-ups of his dark, handsome face. The picture they use isn't a mugshot, it's a candid shot: he's on holiday somewhere, not quite smiling, but almost. He looks too soft, too beautiful to be a killer, but appearances can be deceptive – they say Ted Bundy looked like Cary Grant.

I waited all day for more news, for the charges to be made public: kidnap, assault, or worse. I waited to hear where she is, where he's been keeping her. They showed pictures of Blenheim Road, the station, Scott's front door. Commentators mused on the likely implications of the fact that neither Megan's phone nor her bank cards had been used for more than a week.

Tom called more than once. I didn't pick up. I know what he wants. He wants to ask why I was at Scott Hipwell's house yesterday morning. Let him wonder. It has nothing to do with him. Not everything is about him. I imagine he's calling at her behest in any case. I don't owe her any explanations.

I waited and waited, and still no charge: instead, we heard more about Kamal, the trusted mental-health professional who listened to Megan's secrets and troubles, who gained her trust and then abused it, who seduced her and then, who knows what?

I learned that he is a Muslim, a Bosniak, a survivor of the Balkans conflict who came to Britain as a fifteen-year-old refugee. No stranger to violence, he lost his father and two older brothers at Srebrenica. He has a conviction for domestic violence. The more I heard about Kamal, the more I knew that I was right: I was right to speak to the police about him, I was right to contact Scott.

I get up and pull my dressing gown around me, hurry downstairs and flick on the TV. I have no intention of going anywhere today. If Cathy comes home unexpectedly, I can tell her I'm ill. I make myself a cup of coffee and sit down in front of the television, and I wait.

Evening

I got bored around three o'clock. I got bored with hearing about benefits and seventies TV paedophiles, I got frustrated with hearing nothing about Megan, nothing about Kamal, so I went to the off-licence and bought two bottles of white wine.

I'm almost at the bottom of the first bottle when it happens. There's something else on the

178

news now, shaky camera footage taken from a half-built (or half-destroyed) building, explosions in the distance. Syria, or Egypt, maybe Sudan? I've got the sound down, I'm not really paying attention. Then I see it: the ticker running across the bottom of the screen tells me that the government is facing a challenge to legal-aid cuts and that Fernando Torres will be out for up to four weeks with a hamstring strain and that the suspect in the Megan Hipwell disappearance has been released without charge.

I put my glass down and grab the remote, clicking the volume button up, up, up. This can't be right. The war report continues, it goes on and on, my blood pressure rising with it, but eventually it ends and they go back to the studio and the newsreader says:

'Kamal Abdic, the man arrested yesterday in connection with the disappearance of Megan Hipwell, has been released without charge. Abdic, who was Mrs Hipwell's therapist, was detained yesterday, but was released this morning because police say there is insufficient evidence to charge him.'

I don't hear what she says after that. I just sit there, my eyes blurring over, a wash of noise in my ears, thinking, *they had him. They had him and they let him go.*

Upstairs, later. I've had too much to drink, I can't see the computer screen properly, everything doubles, trebles. I can read if I hold my hand over one eye. It gives me a headache. Cathy is home, she called out to me and I told her I was in bed, unwell. She knows that I'm drinking.

My belly is awash with alcohol. I feel sick. I can't think straight. Shouldn't have started drinking so early. Shouldn't have started drinking at all. I phoned Scott's number an hour ago, again a few minutes ago. Shouldn't have done that either. I just want to know, what lies has Kamal told them? What lies have they been fool enough to believe? The police have messed the whole thing up. Idiots. That Riley woman, her fault. I'm sure of it.

The newspapers haven't helped. There was no domestic violence conviction, they're saying now. That was a mistake. They're making *him* look like the victim.

Don't want to drink any more. I know that I should pour the rest down the sink, because otherwise it'll be there in the morning and I'll get up and drink it straight away, and once I've started I'll want to go on. I should pour it down the sink, but I know I'm not going to. Something to look forward to in the morning.

It's dark, and I can hear someone calling her name. A voice, low at first, but then louder. Angry, desperate, calling Megan's name. It's Scott – he's unhappy with her. He calls her again and again. It's a dream, I think. I keep trying to grasp at it, to hold on to it, but the harder I struggle, the fainter and the further away it gets.

Wednesday, 24 July 2013

Morning

I'm woken by a soft tapping at the door. Rain

batters against the windows; it's after eight but still seems dark outside. Cathy pushes the door gently open and peers into the room.

'Rachel? Are you all right?' She catches sight of the bottle next to my bed and her shoulders sag. 'Oh, Rachel.' She comes across to my bed and picks up the bottle. I'm too embarrassed to say anything. 'Are you not going into work?' she asks me. 'Did you go yesterday?'

She doesn't wait for me to answer, just turns to go, calling back as she does, 'You'll end up getting yourself sacked if you carry on like this.'

I should just say it now, she's already angry with me. I should go after her and tell her: I was sacked months ago for turning up blind drunk after a three-hour lunch with a client during which I managed to be so rude and unprofessional that I cost the firm his business. When I close my eyes, I can still remember the tail end of that lunch, the look on the waitress's face as she handed me my jacket, weaving into the office, people turning to look. Martin Miles taking me to one side. *I think it's best if you go home now, Rachel.*

There is a crack of thunder, a flash of light. I jolt upright. What was it I thought of last night? I check my little black book, but I haven't written anything down since midday yesterday: notes about Kamal – age, ethnicity, conviction for domestic violence. I pick up a pen and cross out that last point.

Downstairs, I make myself a cup of coffee and turn on the TV. The police held a press conference last night, they're showing clips from it on Sky News. Detective Inspector Gaskill's up there,

181

looking pale and gaunt and chastened. Hangdog. He never mentions Kamal's name, just says that a suspect had been detained and questioned, but has been released without charge and that the investigation is ongoing. The cameras pan away from him to Scott, sitting hunched and uncomfortable, blinking in the light of the cameras, his face a twist of anguish. It hurts my heart to see him. He speaks softly, his eyes cast down. He says that he has not given up hope, that no matter what the police say, he still clings to the idea that Megan will come home.

The words come out hollow, they ring false, but without looking into his eyes, I can't tell why. I can't tell whether he doesn't really believe she's coming home because all the faith he once possessed has been ripped away by the events of the past few days, or because he really *knows* that she's never coming home.

It comes to me, just then: the memory of calling his number yesterday. Once, twice? I run upstairs to get my phone, and find it tangled up in the bedclothes. I have three missed calls: one from Tom and two from Scott. No messages. The call from Tom was last night, as was the first call from Scott, but later, just before midnight. The second call from him was this morning a few minutes ago.

My heart lifts a little. This is good news. Despite his mother's actions, despite their clear implications *(Thank you very much for your help, now get lost)*, Scott still wants to talk to me. He needs me. I'm momentarily flooded with affection for Cathy, filled with gratitude to her for pouring the rest of the wine away. I have to keep a clear head, for

182

Scott. He needs me thinking straight.

I take a shower, get dressed and make another cup of coffee, and then I sit down in the living room, little black book at my side, and I call Scott.

'You should have told me,' he says as soon as he picks up, 'what you are.' His tone is flat, cold. My stomach is a small, hard ball. He knows. 'Detective Sergeant Riley spoke to me, after they let him go. He denied having an affair with her. And the witness who suggested that there was something going on was unreliable, she said. An alcoholic. Possibly mentally unstable. She didn't tell me the witness's name, but I take it she was talking about you?'

'But ... no,' I say. 'No. I'm not... I hadn't been drinking when I saw them. It was eight thirty in the morning.' Like that means anything. 'And they found evidence, it said so on the news. They found–'

'Insufficient evidence.'

The phone goes dead.

Friday, 26 July 2013

Morning

I am no longer travelling to my imaginary office. I have given up the pretence. I can barely be bothered to get out of bed. I think I last brushed my teeth on Wednesday. I am still feigning illness, although I'm pretty sure I'm fooling no one.

I can't face getting up, getting dressed, getting on to the train, going into London, wandering the streets. It's hard enough when the sun is shining, it's impossible in this rain. Today is the third day of cold, driving, relentless downpour.

I'm having trouble sleeping, and it's not just the drinking now, it's the nightmares. I'm trapped somewhere, and I know that someone's coming, and there's a way out, I know there is, I know that I saw it before, only I can't find my way back to it, and when he does get me, I can't scream. I try – I suck the air into my lungs and I force it out – but there's no sound, just a rasping, like a dying person fighting for air.

Sometimes, in my nightmares, I find myself in the underpass by Blenheim Road, the way back is blocked and I cannot go further because there is something there, someone waiting, and I wake in pure terror.

They're never going to find her. Every day, every hour that passes I become more certain. She will be one of those names, hers will be one of those stories: lost, missing, body never found. And Scott will not have justice, or peace. He will never have a body to grieve over; he will never know what happened to her. There will be no closure, no resolution. I lie awake thinking about it and I ache. There can be no greater agony, nothing can be more painful than the not knowing, which will never end.

I have written to him. I admitted my problem, then I lied again, saying that I had it under control, that I was seeking help. I told him that I am not mentally unstable. I no longer know whether that's true or not. I told him that I was very clear about what I saw, and that I hadn't been drinking when

184

I saw it. That, at least, is true. He hasn't replied. I didn't expect him to. I am cut off from him, shut out. The things I want to say to him, I can never say. I can't write them down, they don't sound right. I want him to know how sorry I am that it wasn't enough to point them in Kamal's direction, to say, *look, there he is.* I should have seen something. That Saturday night, I should have had my eyes open.

Evening

I am soaked through, freezing cold, the ends of my fingers blanched and wrinkled, my head throbbing from a hangover that kicked in at about half past five. Which is about right, considering I started drinking before midday. I went out to get another bottle, but I was thwarted by the ATM, which gave me the much-anticipated riposte: *There are insufficient funds in your account.*

After that, I started walking. I walked aimlessly for over an hour, through the driving rain. The pedestrianized centre of Ashbury was mine alone. I decided, somewhere along that walk, that I have to do something. I have to make amends for being insufficient.

Now, sodden and almost sober, I'm going to call Tom. I don't want to know what I did, what I said, that Saturday night, but I have to find out. It might jog something. For some reason, I am certain that there is something I'm missing, something vital. Perhaps this is just more self-deception, yet another attempt to prove to myself that I'm not worthless. But perhaps it's real.

'I've been trying to get hold of you since Monday,' Tom says when he answers the phone. 'I called your office,' he adds, and he lets that sink in.

I'm on the back foot already, embarrassed, ashamed. 'I need to talk to you,' I say, 'about Saturday night. That Saturday night.'

'What are you talking about? *I* need to talk to *you* about Monday, Rachel. What the hell were you doing at Scott Hipwell's house?'

'That's not important, Tom–'

'Yes it bloody is. What were you doing there? You do realize, don't you, that he could be... I mean, we don't know, do we? He could have done something to her. Couldn't he? To his wife.'

'He hasn't done anything to his wife,' I say confidently. 'It isn't him.'

'How the hell would you know? Rachel, what is going on?'

'I just... You have to believe me. That isn't why I called you. I needed to talk to you about that Saturday. About the message you left me. You were so angry. You said I'd scared Anna.'

'Well, you had. She saw you stumbling down the street, you shouted abuse at her. She was really freaked out, after what happened last time. With Evie.'

'Did she ... did she do something?'

'Do something?'

'To me?'

'*What?*'

'I had a cut, Tom. On my head. I was bleeding.'

'Are you accusing Anna of hurting you?' He's yelling now, he's furious. 'Seriously, Rachel. That

186

is enough! I have persuaded Anna – on more than one occasion – not to go to the police about you, but if you carry on like this – harassing us, making up stories–'

'I'm not accusing her of anything, Tom. I'm just trying to figure things out. I don't–'

'You don't remember! Of course not. Rachel doesn't remember.' He sighs wearily. 'Look. Anna saw you – you were drunk and abusive. She came home to tell me, she was upset, so I went out to look for you. You were in the street. I think you might have fallen. You were very upset. You'd cut your hand.'

'I hadn't–'

'Well, you had blood on your hand then. I don't know how it got there. I told you I'd take you home, but you wouldn't listen. You were out of control, you were making no sense. You walked off and I went to get the car, but when I came back, you'd gone. I drove up past the station but I couldn't see you. I drove around a bit more – Anna was very worried that you were hanging around somewhere, that you'd come back, that you'd try to get into the house. I was worried you'd fall, or get yourself into trouble... I drove all the way to Ashbury. I rang the bell, but you weren't at home. I called you a couple of times. I left a message. And yes, I was angry. I was really pissed off by that point.'

'I'm sorry Tom,' I say. 'I'm really sorry.'

'I know,' he says. 'You're always sorry.'

'You said that I shouted at Anna,' I say, cringing at the thought of it. 'What did I say to her?'

'I don't know,' he snaps. 'Would you like me to

187

go and get her? Perhaps you'd like to have a chat with her about it?'

'Tom...'

'Well, honestly – what does it matter now?'

'Did you see Megan Hipwell that night?'

'No.' He sounds concerned now. 'Why? Did you? You didn't do something, did you?'

'No, of course I didn't.'

He's silent for a moment. 'Well, why are you asking about this then? Rachel, if you know something...'

'I don't know anything,' I say. 'I didn't see anything.'

'Why were you at the Hipwells' house on Monday? Please tell me – so that I can put Anna's mind at ease. She's worried.'

'I had something to tell him. Something I thought might be useful.'

'You didn't see her, but you had something useful to tell him?'

I hesitate for a moment. I'm not sure how much I should tell him, whether I should keep this just for Scott. 'It's about Megan,' I say. 'She was having an affair.'

'Wait – did you know her?'

'Just a little,' I say.

'How?'

'From her gallery.'

'Oh,' he says. 'So who's the guy?'

'Her therapist,' I tell him. 'Kamal Abdic. I saw them together.'

'Really? The guy they arrested? I thought they'd let him go.'

'They have. And it's my fault, because I'm an

unreliable witness.'

Tom laughs. It's soft, friendly, he isn't mocking me. 'Rachel, come on. You did the right thing, coming forward. I'm sure it's not just about you.' In the background, I can hear the prattle of the child, and Tom says something away from the phone, something I can't hear. 'I should go,' he says. I can imagine him putting down the phone, picking up his little girl, giving her a kiss, embracing his wife. The dagger in my heart twists, round and round and round.

Monday, 29 July 2013

Morning

It's 8.07 and I'm on the train. Back to the imaginary office. Cathy was with Damien all weekend, and when I saw her last night, I didn't give her a chance to berate me. I started apologizing for my behaviour straight away, said I'd been feeling really down, but that I was pulling myself together, turning over a new leaf. She accepted, or pretended to accept, my apologies. She gave me a hug. Niceness writ large.

Megan has dropped out of the news almost completely. There was a comment piece in the *Sunday Times* about police incompetence which referred briefly to the case, an unnamed source at the Crown Prosecution Service citing it as 'one of a number of cases in which the police have made a hasty arrest on the basis of flimsy or flawed evidence.'

189

We're coming to the signal. I feel the familiar rattle and jolt, the train slows and I look up, because I have to, because I cannot bear not to, but there is never anything to see any longer. The doors are closed and the curtains drawn. There is nothing to see but rain, sheets of it, and muddy water pooling at the bottom of the garden.

On a whim, I get off the train at Witney. Tom couldn't help me, but perhaps the other man could – the red-haired man. I wait for the disembarking passengers to disappear down the steps and then I sit on the only covered bench on the platform. I might get lucky. I might see him getting on to the train. I could follow him, I could talk to him. It's the only thing I have left, my last roll of the dice. If this doesn't work, I have to let it go. I just have to let it go.

Half an hour goes by. Every time I hear footsteps on the steps, my heart rate goes up. Every time I hear the clacking of high heels, I am seized with trepidation. If Anna sees me here, I could be in trouble. Tom warned me. He's persuaded her not to get the police involved, but if I carry on...

Quarter past nine. Unless he starts work very late, I've missed him. It's raining harder now, and I can't face another aimless day in London. The only money I have is a tenner I borrowed from Cathy, and I need to make that last until I've summoned up the courage to ask my mother for a loan. I walk down the steps, intending to cross underneath to the opposite platform and go back to Ashbury, when suddenly I spot Scott hurrying out of the newsagent opposite the station entrance, his coat pulled up around his face.

I run after him and catch him at the corner, right opposite the underpass. I grab his arm and he wheels round, startled.

'Please,' I say, 'can I talk to you?'

'Jesus Christ,' he snarls at me. 'What the fuck do you want?'

I back away from him, holding my hands up. 'I'm sorry,' I say. 'I'm sorry. I just wanted to apologize, to explain…'

The downpour has become a deluge. We are the only people on the street, both of us soaked to the skin. Scott starts to laugh. He throws his hands up in the air and roars with laughter. 'Come to the house,' he says. 'We're going to drown out here.'

Scott goes upstairs to fetch me a towel while the kettle boils. The house is less tidy than it was a week ago, the disinfectant smell displaced by something earthier. A pile of newspapers sits in the corner of the living room; there are dirty mugs on the coffee table and the mantelpiece.

Scott appears at my side, proffering the towel. 'It's a tip, I know. My mother was driving me insane, cleaning, tidying up after me all the time. We had a bit of a row. She hasn't been round for a few days.' His mobile phone starts to ring, he glances at it, puts it back in his pocket. 'Speak of the Devil. She never bloody stops.'

I follow him into the kitchen.

'I'm so sorry about what happened,' I say.

He shrugs. 'I know. And it's not your fault anyway. I mean, it might've helped if you weren't…'

'If I wasn't a drunk?'

His back is turned, he's pouring the coffee.

'Well, yes. But they didn't actually have enough

191

to charge him with anything anyway.' He hands me the mug and we sit down at the table. I notice that one of the photograph frames on the sideboard has been turned face-down. Scott is still talking. 'They found things – hair, skin cells – in his house, but he doesn't deny that she went there. Well, he did deny it at first, then he admitted that she had been there.'

'Why did he lie?'

'Exactly. He admitted that she'd been to the house twice, just to talk. He won't say what about – there's the whole confidentiality thing. The hair and the skin cells were found downstairs. Nothing up in the bedroom. He swears blind they weren't having an affair. But he's a liar, so...' He passes his hand over his eyes. His face looks as though it is sinking into itself, his shoulders sag. He looks shrunken. 'There was a trace of blood on his car.'

'Oh my God.'

'Yeah. Matches her blood type. They don't know if they can get any DNA because it's such a small sample. It could be nothing, that's what they keep saying. How could it be nothing, that her blood's on his car?' He shakes his head. 'You were right. The more I hear about this guy, the more I'm sure.' He looks at me, right at me, for the first time since we got here. 'He was fucking her, and she wanted to end it, so he ... he did something. That's it. I'm sure of it.'

He's lost all hope, and I don't blame him. It's been more than two weeks and she hasn't turned on her phone, hasn't used a credit card, hasn't withdrawn money from an ATM. No one has

192

seen her. She is gone.

'He told the police that she might have run away,' Scott says.

'Dr Abdic did?'

Scott nods. 'He told the police that she was unhappy with me and she might have run off.'

'He's trying to shift suspicion, get them to think that you did something.'

'I know that. But they seem to buy everything that bastard says. That Riley woman, I can tell when she talks about him. She likes him. The poor, downtrodden refugee.' He hangs his head, wretched. 'Maybe he's right. We did have that awful fight. But I can't believe... She wasn't unhappy with me. She wasn't. She wasn't.' When he says it the third time, I wonder whether he's trying to convince himself. 'But if she was having an affair, she must have been unhappy, mustn't she?'

'Not necessarily,' I say. 'Perhaps it was one of those – what do they call it? – transference things. That's the word they use, isn't it? When a patient develops feelings – or thinks they develop feelings – for a therapist. Only the therapist is supposed to resist them, to point out that the feelings aren't real.'

His eyes are on my face, but I feel as though he isn't really listening to what I'm saying.

'What happened?' he asks. 'With you. You left your husband. Was there someone else?'

I shake my head. 'Other way round. Anna happened.'

'Sorry.' He pauses.

I know what he's going to ask, so before he can, I say, 'It started before. While we were still married. The drinking. That's what you wanted to know, isn't it?'

He nods again.

'We were trying for a baby,' I say, and my voice catches. Still, after all this time, every time I talk about it the tears come to my eyes. 'Sorry.'

'It's all right.' He gets to his feet, goes over to the sink and pours me a glass of water. He puts it on the table in front of me.

I clear my throat, try to be as matter-of-fact as possible. 'We were trying for a baby and it didn't happen. I became very depressed, and I started to drink. I was extremely difficult to live with and Tom sought solace elsewhere. And she was all too happy to provide it.'

'I'm really sorry, that's awful. I know... I wanted to have a child. Megan kept saying she wasn't ready yet.' Now it's his turn to wipe the tears away. 'It's one of the things ... we argued about it sometimes.'

'Was that what you were arguing about the day she left?'

He sighs, pushing his chair back and getting to his feet. 'No,' he says, turning away from me. 'It was something else.'

Evening

Cathy is waiting for me when I get home. She's standing in the kitchen, aggressively drinking a glass of water.

'Good day at the office?' she asks, pursing her lips. She knows.

'Cathy...'

'Damien had a meeting near Euston today. On his way out, he bumped into Martin Miles. They know each other a little, remember, from Damien's days at Laing Fund Management. Martin used to do the PR for them.'

'Cathy...'

She held her hand up, took another gulp of water. 'You haven't worked there in *months!* In months! Do you know how idiotic I feel? What an idiot Damien felt? Please, *please* tell me that you have another job that you just haven't told me about. Please tell me that you haven't been pretending to go to work. That you haven't been lying to me – day in, day out – all this time.'

'I didn't know how to tell you...'

'You didn't know how to tell me? How about: *Cathy, I got fired because I was drunk at work?* How about that?' I flinch and her face softens. 'I'm sorry, but honestly, Rachel.' She really is too nice. 'What have you been doing? Where do you go? What do you do all day?'

'I walk. Go to the library. Sometimes–'

'You go to the pub?'

'Sometimes. But–'

'Why didn't you tell me?' She approaches me, placing her hands on my shoulders. 'You should have told me.'

'I was ashamed,' I say, and I start to cry. It's awful, cringe-worthy, but I start to weep. I sob and sob, and poor Cathy holds me, strokes my hair, tells me I'll be all right, that everything will be all right. I feel wretched. I hate myself almost more than I ever have.

Later, sitting on the sofa with Cathy, drinking tea, she tells me how it's going to be. I'm going to stop drinking, I'm going to get my CV in order, I'm going to contact Martin Miles and beg for a reference. I'm going to stop wasting money going backwards and forwards to London on pointless train journeys.

'Honestly, Rachel, I don't understand how you could have kept this up for so long.'

I shrug. 'In the morning, I take the 8.04, and in the evening, I come back on the 17.56. That's my train. It's the one I take. That's the way it is.'

Thursday, 1 August 2013

Morning

There's something covering my face, I can't breathe, I'm suffocating. When I surface into wakefulness, I'm gasping for air and my chest hurts. I sit up, eyes wide, and see something moving in the corner of the room, a dense centre of blackness which keeps growing, and I almost cry out – and then I'm properly awake and there's nothing there, but I *am* sitting up in bed and my cheeks are wet with tears.

It's almost dawn, the light outside is just beginning to tinge grey, and the rain of the last several days is still battering against the window. I won't go back to sleep, not with my heart hammering in my chest so much it hurts.

I think, though I can't be sure, that there's some wine downstairs. I don't remember finishing the

196

second bottle. It'll be warm, because I can't leave it in the fridge; if I do, Cathy pours it away. She so badly wants me to get better, but so far, things are not going according to her plan. There's a little cupboard in the hallway where the gas meter is. If there was any wine left, I'll have stashed it in there.

I creep out on to the landing and tiptoe down the stairs in the half light. I flip the little cupboard open and lift out the bottle: it's disappointingly light, not much more than a glassful in there. But better than nothing. I pour it into a mug (just in case Cathy comes down – I can pretend it's tea) and put the bottle in the bin (making sure to conceal it under a milk carton and a crisp packet). In the living room, I flick on the TV, mute it straight away and sit down on the sofa.

I'm flicking through channels – it's all children's TV and infomercials until with a flash of recognition I'm looking at Corly Wood, which is just down the road from here: you can see it from the train. Corly Wood in pouring rain, the fields between the tree line and train tracks submerged.

I don't know why it takes me so long to realize what's going on. For ten seconds, fifteen, twenty, I'm looking at cars and blue and white tape and a white tent in the background, and my breath is coming shorter and shorter until I'm holding it and not breathing at all.

It's her. She's been in the wood all along, just along the railway track from here. I've been past those fields every day, morning and evening, travelling by, oblivious.

In the wood. I imagine a grave dug beneath scrubby bushes, hastily covered up. I imagine

197

worse things, impossible things – her body hanging from a rope, somewhere deep in the forest where nobody goes.

It might not even be her. It might be something else. I know it isn't something else.

There's a reporter on screen now, dark hair slick against his skull. I turn up the volume and listen to him tell me what I already know, what I can feel – that it wasn't me who couldn't breathe, it was Megan.

'That's right,' he's saying, talking to someone in the studio, his hand pressed to his ear. 'The police have now confirmed that the body of a young woman has been found submerged in flood water in a field at the bottom of Corly Wood, which is less than five miles from the home of Megan Hipwell. Mrs Hipwell, as you know, went missing in early July – the thirteenth of July, in fact – and has not been seen since. Police are saying that the body, which was discovered by dog walkers out early this morning, has yet to be formally identified; however, they do believe that this is Megan that they've found. Mrs Hipwell's husband has been informed.'

He stops speaking for a while. The news anchor is asking him a question, but I can't hear it because the blood is roaring in my ears. I bring the mug up to my lips and drink every last drop.

The reporter is talking again. 'Yes, Kay, that's right. It would appear that the body was buried here in the woods, possibly for some time, and that it has been uncovered by the heavy rains that we've had recently.'

It's worse, so much worse than I imagined. I

can see her now, her ruined face in the mud, pale arms exposed, reaching up, rising up as though she were clawing her way out of the grave. I taste hot liquid, bile and bitter wine, in my mouth, and I run upstairs to be sick.

Evening

I stayed in bed most of the day. I tried to get things straight in my head. I tried to piece together, from the memories and the flashbacks and the dreams, what happened on Saturday night. In an attempt to make sense of it, to see it clearly, I wrote it all down. The scratching of my pen on paper felt like someone whispering to me; it put me on edge, I kept feeling as though there was someone else in the flat, just on the other side of the door, and I couldn't stop imagining her.

I was almost too afraid to open the bedroom door, but when I did, there was no one there, of course. I went downstairs and turned on the television again. The same pictures were still there: the woods in the rain, police cars driving along a muddy track, that horrible white tent, all of it a grey blur, and then suddenly Megan, smiling at the camera, still beautiful, untouched. Then it's Scott, head down, fending off photographers as he tries to get through his own front door, Riley at his side. Then it's Kamal's office. No sign of him, though.

I didn't want to hear the soundtrack, but I had to turn the volume up, anything to stop the silence ringing in my ears. The police say that the woman, still not formally identified, has been dead for some time, possibly several weeks. They say the cause of death has yet to be established. They say that there is no evidence of a sexual motive for the killing.

That strikes me as a stupid thing to say. I know what they mean – they mean they don't think she was raped, which is a blessing, of course, but that doesn't mean there wasn't a sexual motive. It seems to me that Kamal wanted her and he couldn't have her, that she must have tried to end it and he couldn't stand it. That's a sexual motive, isn't it?

I can't bear to watch the news any longer, so I go back upstairs and crawl under my duvet. I empty out my handbag, looking through my notes scribbled on bits of paper, all the scraps of information I've gleaned, the memories shifting like shadows, and I wonder, why am I doing this? What purpose does it serve?

MEGAN

Thursday, 13 June 2013

Morning

I can't sleep in this heat. Invisible bugs crawl over my skin, I have a rash on my chest, I can't get comfortable. And Scott seems to radiate warmth; lying next to him is like lying next to a fire. I can't get far enough away from him, and find myself clinging to the edge of the bed, sheets thrown back. It's intolerable. I thought about going to lie down on the futon in the spare room, but he hates to wake and find me gone, it always leads to a row about something. Alternative uses for the spare room, usually, or who I was thinking about while I was lying there alone. Sometimes I want to scream at him, *Just let me go. Let me go. Let me breathe.* So I can't sleep, and I'm angry. I feel as though we're having a fight already, even though the fight's only in my imagination.

And in my head, thoughts go round and round and round.

I feel like I'm suffocating.

When did this house become so bloody small? When did my life become so boring? Is this really what I wanted? I can't remember. All I know is that a few months ago I was feeling better, and now I can't think and I can't sleep and I can't draw and the urge to run is becoming overwhelming. At night when I lie awake I can hear it, quiet but unrelenting, undeniable: a whisper in my head, *Slip away.* When I close my eyes, my head is filled with images of past and future lives, the things I dreamed I wanted, the things I had and threw away. I can't get comfortable, because every way I turn I run into dead ends: the closed gallery the houses on this road, the stifling attentions of the tedious pilates women, the track at the end of the garden with its trains, always taking someone else to somewhere else, reminding me over and over and over, a dozen times a day, that I'm staying put.

I feel as though I'm going mad.

And yet just a few months ago, I was feeling better, I was getting better. I was fine. I was sleeping. I didn't live in fear of the nightmares. I could breathe. Yes, I still wanted to run away. Sometimes. But not every day.

Talking to Kamal helped me, there's no denying that. I liked it. I liked him. He made me happier. And now all that feels so unfinished – I never got to the crux of it. That's my fault, of course, because I behaved stupidly, like a child, because I didn't like feeling rejected. I need to learn to lose a little better. I'm embarrassed now, ashamed. My face goes hot at the thought of it. I don't want that to be his final impression of me. I want him to see me again, to see me better. And I do feel that if I went to him, he would help. He's like that.

I need to get to the end of the story. I need to tell someone, just once. Say the words out loud. If it doesn't come out of me, it'll eat me up. The hole inside me, the one they left, it'll just get bigger and bigger until it consumes me.

I'm going to have to swallow my pride and my shame and go to him. He's going to have to listen. I'll make him.

Evening

Scott thinks I'm at the cinema with Tara. I've been outside Kamal's flat for fifteen minutes, psyching myself up to knock on the door. I'm so afraid of the way he's going to look at me, after last time. I have to show him that I'm sorry, so I've dressed the part: plain and simple, jeans and

T-shirt, hardly any make-up. This is not about seduction, he has to see that.

I can feel my heart starting to race as I step up to his front door and press the bell. No one comes. The lights are on, but no one comes. Perhaps he has seen me outside, lurking perhaps he's upstairs, just hoping that if he ignores me I'll go away. I won't. He doesn't know how determined I can be. Once I've made my mind up, I'm a force to be reckoned with.

I ring again, and then a third time, and finally I hear footsteps on the stairs and the door opens. He's wearing tracksuit bottoms and a white T-shirt. He's barefoot, wet-haired, his face flushed.

'Megan.' Surprised, but not angry, which is a good start. 'Are you all right? Is everything all right?'

'I'm sorry,' I say, and he steps back to let me in. I feel a rush of gratitude so strong it feels almost like love.

He shows me into the kitchen. It's a mess: washing-up piled on the counter and in the sink, empty takeaway cartons spilling out of the bin. I wonder if he's depressed. I stand in the doorway; he leans against the counter opposite me, his arms folded across his chest.

'What can I do for you?' he asks. His face is arranged into a perfectly neutral expression, his therapist's face. It makes me want to pinch him, just to make him smile.

'I have to tell you–' I start, and then I stop because I can't just plunge straight into it, I need a preamble. So I change tack. 'I wanted to apologize,' I say, 'for what happened. Last time.'

'That's OK,' he says. 'Don't worry about that. If you need to talk to someone, I can refer you to someone else, but I can't–'

'Please, Kamal.'

'Megan, I can't counsel you any longer.'

'I know. I know that. But I can't start over with someone else. I can't. We got so far. We were so close. I just have to tell you. Just once. And then I'll be gone, I promise. I won't ever bother you again.'

He cocks his head to one side. He doesn't believe me, I can tell. He thinks that if he lets me back in now, he'll never be rid of me.

'Hear me out, please. This isn't going to go on for ever, I just need someone to listen.'

'Your husband?' he asks and I shake my head.

'I can't – I can't tell him. Not after all this time. He wouldn't... He wouldn't be able to see me as me any longer. I'd be someone else to him. He wouldn't know how to forgive me. Please, Kamal. If I don't spit out the poison, I feel like I'll never sleep. As a friend, not a therapist, please listen.'

His shoulders drop a little as he turns away, and I think it's over. My heart sinks. Then he opens a cupboard and pulls out two tumblers.

'As a friend, then. Would you like some wine?'

He shows me into the living room. Dimly lit by standard lamps, it has the same air of domestic neglect as the kitchen. We sit down on opposite sides of a glass table piled high with papers, magazines and takeaway menus. My hands are locked around my glass. I take a sip. It's red but cold, dusty. I swallow, take another sip. He's waiting for me to start, but it's hard, harder than I thought it was going to be. I've kept this secret for so long – a decade, more than a third of my life. It's not that easy, letting go of it. I just know that I have to start talking. If I don't do it now, I might never have the courage to say the words out loud, I might lose them altogether, they might stick in my throat and choke me in my sleep.

'After I left Ipswich, I moved in with Mac, into his cottage outside Holkham at the end of the lane. I told you that, didn't I? It was very isolated, a couple of miles to the nearest neighbour, a couple more to the nearest shops. At the beginning, we had lots of parties, there were always a few people crashed out in the living room or sleeping in the hammock outside in the summer. But we got tired of that, and Mac fell out with everyone eventually, so people stopped coming, and it was the two of us. Days used to go by and we wouldn't see anyone. We'd do our grocery shopping at the petrol station. It's odd, thinking back on it, but I needed it then, after everything – after Ipswich and all those men, all the things I did. I liked it, just Mac and me and the old railway tracks and the grass and the dunes and the restless grey sea.'

Kamal tilts his head to one side, gives me half a smile. I feel my insides flip. 'It sounds nice. But do you think you are romanticizing? "The restless grey sea"?'

'Never mind that,' I say, waving him away. 'And no, in any case. Have you been to north Norfolk? It's not the Adriatic. It is restless, and relentlessly grey.'

He holds his hands up, smiling. 'OK.'

I feel instantly better, the tension leaching out of my neck and shoulders. I take another sip of the wine; it tastes less bitter now.

'I was happy with Mac. I know it doesn't sound like the sort of place I'd like, the sort of life I'd like, but then, after Ben's death and everything that came after, it was. Mac saved me. He took me in, he loved me, he kept me safe. And he wasn't boring. And to be perfectly honest, we were taking a lot of drugs, and it's difficult to get bored when you're off your face all the time. I was happy. I was really happy.'

Kamal nods. 'I understand, although I'm not sure that sounds like a very real kind of happiness,' he says. 'Not the sort of happiness that can endure, that can sustain you.'

I laugh. 'I was seventeen. I was with a man who excited me, who adored me. I'd got away from my parents, away from the house where everything, *everything* reminded me of my dead brother. I didn't need it to endure, or sustain. I just needed it for right then.'

'So what happened?'

It seems as though the room gets darker then. Here we are, at the thing I never say.

'I got pregnant.'

He nods, waiting for me to go on. Part of me wants him to stop me, to ask more questions, but he doesn't, he just waits. It gets darker still.

'It was too late when I realized to ... to get rid of it. Of her. It's what I would have done, had I not been so stupid, so *oblivious*. The truth is that she wasn't wanted, by either of us.'

Kamal gets to his feet, goes to the kitchen and

206

comes back with a sheet of kitchen roll for me to wipe my eyes. He hands it to me and sits down. It's a while before I go on. Kamal sits, just as he used to in our sessions, his eyes on mine, his hands folded in his lap, patient, immobile. It must take the most incredible self-control, that stillness, that passivity; it must be exhausting.

My legs are trembling, my knee jerking as though on a puppeteer's string. I get to my feet to stop it. I walk to the kitchen door and back again, scratching the palms of my hands.

We were both so stupid I tell him. We didn't really even acknowledge what was happening, we just carried on. I didn't go to see a doctor, I didn't eat the right things or take supplements, I didn't do any of the things you're supposed to. We just carried on living our lives. We didn't even acknowledge that anything had changed. I got fatter and slower and more tired, we both got irritable and fought all the time, but nothing really changed until she came.'

He lets me cry. While I do so, he moves to the chair nearest mine and sits down at my side so that his knees are almost touching my thigh. He leans forward. He doesn't touch me, but our bodies are close, I can smell his scent, clean in this dirty room, sharp and astringent.

My voice is a whisper, it doesn't feel right to say these words out loud. 'I had her at home,' I say. 'It was stupid, but I had this thing about hospitals at the time, because the last time I'd been in one was when Ben was killed. Plus I hadn't been for any of the scans. I'd been smoking, drinking a bit, I couldn't face the lectures. I couldn't face any of it. I think ... right up until the end, it just didn't seem like it was real, like it was actually going to happen.'

'Mac had this friend who was a nurse, or who'd done some nursing training or something. She came round, and it was OK. It wasn't so bad. I mean, it was horrible, of course, painful and frightening, but ... then there she was. She was very small. I don't remember exactly what her weight was. That's terrible, isn't it?' Kamal doesn't say anything, he doesn't move. 'She was lovely. She had dark eyes and blonde hair. She didn't cry a lot, she slept well, right from the very beginning. She was good. She was a good girl.' I have to stop there for a moment. 'I expected everything to be so hard, but it wasn't.'

It's darker still, I'm sure of it, but I look up and Kamal is there, his eyes on mine, his expression soft. He's listening. He wants me to tell him. My mouth is dry, so I take another sip of wine. It hurts to swallow. 'We called her Elizabeth. Libby.' It feels so strange, saying her name out loud after such a long time. 'Libby,' I say again, enjoying the feel of her name in my mouth. I want to say it over and over. Kamal reaches out at last and takes my hand in his, his thumb against my wrist, on my pulse.

'One day we had a fight, Mac and I. I don't re-member what it was about. We did that every now and again – little arguments that blew up into big ones, nothing physical, nothing bad like that, but we'd scream at each other and I'd threaten to leave, or he'd just walk out and I wouldn't see him for a couple of days.'

'It was the first time it had happened since she

208

was born – the first time he'd just gone off and left me. She was just a few months old. The roof was leaking. I remember that: the sound of water dripping into buckets in the kitchen. It was freezing cold, the wind driving off the sea; it had been raining for days. I lit a fire in the living room, but it kept going out. I was so tired. I was drinking just to warm up, but it wasn't working, so I decided to get into the bath. I took Libby in with me, put her on my chest, her head just under my chin.'

The room gets darker and darker until I'm there again, lying in the water, her body pressing against mine, a candle flickering just behind my head. I can hear it guttering, smell the wax, feel the chill of the air around my neck and shoulders. I'm heavy, my body sinking into the warmth. I'm exhausted. And then suddenly the candle is out and I'm cold. Really cold, my teeth chattering in my head, my whole body shaking. The house feels like it's shaking too, the wind screaming, tearing at the slates on the roof.

'I fell asleep,' I say, and then I can't say any more, because I can feel her again, no longer on my chest, her body wedged between my arm and the edge of the tub, her face in the water. We were both so cold.

For a moment, neither of us move. I can hardly bear to look at him, but when I do, he doesn't recoil from me. He doesn't say a word. He puts his arm around my shoulder and pulls me to him, my face against his chest. I breathe him in and I wait to feel different, to feel lighter, to feel better or worse now that there is another living soul who knows. I feel relieved, I think, because I know from his reaction that I have done the right thing. He isn't angry with me, he doesn't think I'm a monster. I am safe here, completely safe with him.

I don't know how long I stay there in his arms, but when I come back to myself, my phone is ringing. I don't answer it, but a moment later it beeps to alert me that there's a text. It's from Scott. *Where are you?* And seconds after that, the phone starts ringing again. This time it's Tara. Disentangling myself from Kamal's embrace, I answer.

'Megan, I don't know what you're up to, but you need to call Scott. He's rung here four times. I told him you'd nipped out to the offie to get some wine, but I don't think he believed me. He says you're not picking up your phone.' She sounds pissed off, and I know I should appease her, but I don't have the energy.

'OK,' I say. 'Thanks. I'll ring him now.'

'Megan–' she says, but I end the call before I can hear another word.

It's after ten. I've been here for more than two hours. I turn off my phone and turn to face Kamal.

'I don't want to go home,' I say.

He nods, but he doesn't invite me to stay. Instead he says, 'You can come back, if you like. Another time.'

I step forward, closing the gap between our bodies, stand on tiptoe and kiss his lips. He doesn't pull away from me.

RACHEL

Saturday, 3 August 2013

Morning

I dreamed last night that I was in the woods, walking by myself. It was dusk, or dawn, I'm not quite sure, but there was someone else there with me. I couldn't see them, I just knew they were there, gaining on me. I didn't want to be seen, I wanted to run away, but I couldn't, my limbs were too heavy, and when I tried to cry out I made no sound at all.

When I wake, white light slips through the slats on the blind. The rain is finally gone, its work done. The room is warm; it smells terrible, rank and sour – I've barely left it since Thursday. Outside, I can hear the vacuum purr and whine. Cathy is cleaning. She'll be going out later; when she does I can venture out. I'm not sure what I will do, I can't seem to right myself. One more day of drinking, perhaps, and then I'll get myself straight tomorrow.

My phone buzzes briefly, telling me its battery is dying. I pick it up to plug it into the charger and I notice that I have two missed calls from last night. I dial into voicemail. I have one message.

'Rachel, hi. It's Mum. Listen, I'm coming down to London tomorrow. Saturday. I've got a spot of

211

shopping to do. Could we meet up for a coffee or something? Darling, it's not a good time for you to come and stay now. There's ... well, I've got a new friend, and you know how it is in the early stages.' She titters. 'Anyway, I'm very happy to give you a loan to tide you over for a couple of weeks. We'll talk about it tomorrow. OK, darling. Bye.'

I'm going to have to be straight with her, tell her exactly how bad things are. That is not a conversation I want to have stone-cold sober. I haul myself out of bed: I can go down to the shops now and just have a couple of glasses before I go out. Take the edge off. I look at my phone again, check the missed calls. Only one is from my mother – the other is from Scott. At quarter to one in the morning. I sit there, with the phone in my hand, debating whether to call him back. Not now, too early. Perhaps later? After one glass, though, not two.

I plug the phone in to charge, pull the blind up and open the window, then go to the bathroom and run a cold shower. I scrub my skin and wash my hair and try to quieten the voice in my head which tells me it's an odd thing to do, less than forty-eight hours after your wife's body has been discovered, to ring another woman in the middle of the night.

Evening

The earth is still drying out, but the sun is almost breaking through thick white cloud. I bought myself one of those little bottles of wine – just one.

I shouldn't, but lunch with my mother would test the willpower of a lifelong teetotaller. Still, she's promised to transfer £300 into my bank account, so it wasn't a complete waste of time.

I didn't admit how bad things were. I didn't tell her I've been out of work for months, or that I was fired (she thinks her money is tiding me over until my redundancy payment arrives). I didn't tell her how bad things had got on the drinking front, and she didn't notice. Cathy did. When I saw her on my way out this morning, she gave me a look and said, 'Oh for God's sake. Already?' I have no idea how she does that, but she always knows. Even if I've only had half a glass, she takes one look at me and she knows.

'I can tell from your eyes,' she says, but when I check myself in the mirror I look exactly the same. Her patience is running out, her sympathy too. I have to stop. Only not today. I can't today. It's too hard today.

I should have been prepared for it, should have expected it, but somehow I didn't. I got on to the train and she was everywhere, her face beaming from every newspaper: beautiful, blonde, happy Megan, looking right into the camera, right at me.

Someone has left behind their copy of *The Times*, so I read their report. The formal identification came last night, the post-mortem is today. A police spokesman is quoted saying that 'Mrs Hipwell's cause of death may be difficult to establish because her body has been outside for some time, and has been submerged for several days, at least.' It's horrible to think about, with her picture right in front of me. What she looked like then, what she

213

looks like now.

There's a brief mention of Kamal, his arrest and release, and a statement from DI Gaskill, saying that they are 'pursuing a number of leads', which I imagine means they are clueless. I close the newspaper and put it on the floor at my feet. I can't bear to look at her any longer. I don't want to read those hopeless, empty words.

I lean my head against the window. Soon we'll pass number twenty-three. I glance over, just for a moment, but we're too far away on this side of the track to really see anything. I keep thinking about the day I saw Kamal, about the way he kissed her, about how angry I was and how I wanted to confront her. What would have happened if I had done? What would have happened if I'd gone round then, banged on the door and asked her what the hell she thought she was up to? Would she still be out there, on her terrace?

I close my eyes. At Northcote, someone gets on and sits down in the seat next to me. I don't open my eyes to look, but it strikes me as odd, because the train is half empty. The hairs are standing up on the back of my neck. I can smell aftershave under cigarette smoke and I know that I've smelled that scent before.

'Hello.'

I look round and recognize the man with the red hair, the one from the station, from *that* Saturday. He's smiling at me, offering his hand to shake. I'm so surprised that I take it. His palm feels hard and calloused.

'You remember me?'

'Yes,' I say, shaking my head as I'm saying it.

'Yes, a few weeks ago, at the station.'

He's nodding and smiling. 'I was a bit wasted,' he says, then laughs. 'Think you were, too, weren't you, love?'

He's younger than I'd realized, maybe late twenties. He has a nice face, not good looking, just nice. Open, a wide smile. His accent's cockney, or Estuary, something like that. He's looking at me as though he knows something about me, as though he's teasing me, as though we have an in joke. We don't. I look away from him. I ought to say something, ask him, *What did you see?*

'You doing OK?' he asks.

'Yes, I'm fine.' I'm looking out of the window again, but I can feel his eyes on me and I have the oddest urge to turn towards him, to smell the smoke on his clothes and his breath. I like the smell of cigarette smoke. Tom smoked when we first met. I used to have the odd one with him, when we were out drinking or after sex. It's erotic to me, that smell; it reminds me of being happy. I graze my teeth over my lower lip, wondering for a moment what he would do if I turned to face him and kissed his mouth. I feel his body move. He's leaning forward, bending down, he picks up the newspaper at my feet.

'Awful, innit? Poor girl. It's weird, 'cos we were there that night. It was that night, wasn't it? That she went missing.'

It's like he's read my mind, and it stuns me. I whip round to look at him. I want to see the expression in his eyes. 'I'm sorry?'

'That night when I met you on the train. That was the night that girl went missing, the one they

just found. And they're saying the last time anyone saw her was outside the station. I keep thinking, you know, that I might've seen her. Don't
remember, though. I was wasted.' He shrugs.
'You don't remember anything, do you?'

It's strange, the way I feel when he says this. I
can't remember ever feeling like this before. I can't
reply because my mind has gone somewhere else
entirely, and it's not the words he's saying, it's the
aftershave. Under the smoke, that scent – fresh,
lemony, aromatic – evokes a memory of sitting on
the train next to him, just like I am now, only we're
going the other way and someone is laughing
really loudly. He's got his hand on my arm, he's
asking if I want to go for a drink, but suddenly
something is wrong. I feel frightened, confused.
Someone is trying to hit me. I can see the fist
coming and I duck down, my hands up to protect
my head. I'm not on the train any longer, I'm in
the street. I can hear laughter again, or shouting.
I'm on the steps, I'm on the pavement, it's so con-
fusing, my heart is racing. I don't want to be anywhere near this man. I want to get away from him.

I scramble to my feet, saying 'Excuse me' loudly
so the other people in the carriage will hear, but
there's hardly anyone in here and no one looks
around. The man looks up at me, surprised, and
moves his legs to one side to let me past.

'Sorry, love,' he says. 'Didn't mean to upset you.'

I walk away from him as fast as I can, but the
train jolts and sways and I almost lose my balance.
I grab on to a seat back to stop myself from falling.
People are staring at me. I hurry through to the
next carriage and all the way through to the one

after that; I just keep going until I get to the end of the train. I feel breathless and afraid. I can't explain it, I can't remember what happened, but I can feel it, the fear and confusion. I sit down, facing in the direction I have just come from so that I'll be able to see him if he comes after me.

Pressing my palms into my eye sockets, I concentrate. I'm trying to get it back, to see what I just saw. I curse myself for drinking. If only my head was straight ... but there it is. It's dark, and there's a man walking away from me. A woman walking away from me? A woman, wearing a blue dress. It's Anna.

Blood is throbbing in my head, my heart pounding. I don't know whether what I'm seeing, feeling, is real or not, imagination or memory. I squeeze my eyes tightly shut and try to feel it again, to see it again, but it's gone.

ANNA

Saturday, 3 August 2013

Evening

Tom is meeting some of his army buddies for a drink and Evie's down for her nap. I'm sitting in the kitchen, doors and windows closed despite the heat. The rain of the past week has stopped at last; now it's stiflingly close.

I'm bored. I can't think of anything to do. I fancy

going shopping, spending a bit of money on myself, but it's hopeless with Evie. She gets irritable and I get stressed. So I'm just hanging round the house. I can't watch television or look at a newspaper. I don't want to read about it, I don't want to see Megan's face, I don't want to think about it.

How can I not think about it when we're here, just four doors away?

I rang around to see if anyone was up for a playdate, but everyone's got plans. I even called my sister, but of course you've got to book her at least a week in advance. In any case, she said she was too hungover to spend time with Evie. I felt a horrible pang of envy then, a longing for Saturdays spent lying on the sofa with the newspapers and a hazy memory of leaving the club the night before.

Stupid, really, because what I've got now is a million times better, and I made sacrifices to secure it. Now I just need to protect it. So here I sit in my sweltering house, trying not to think about Megan. I try not to think about her and I jump every time I hear a noise, I flinch when a shadow passes the window. It's intolerable.

What I can't stop thinking about is the fact that Rachel was here the night Megan went missing, stumbling around, totally pissed, and then she just *disappeared.* Tom looked for her for ages, but he couldn't find her. I can't stop wondering what she was doing.

There is no connection between Rachel and Megan Hipwell. I spoke to the police officer, Detective Sergeant Riley, about it after we saw Rachel at the Hipwells' house, and she said it was nothing to worry about. 'She's a rubbernecker,' she said. 'Lonely, a bit desperate. She just wants to be involved in something.'

She's probably right. But then I think about her coming into my house and taking my child, I remember the terror I felt when I saw her with Evie down by the fence. I think about that horrible, chilling little smile she gave me when I saw her outside the Hipwells' house. Detective Sergeant Riley doesn't know just how dangerous Rachel can be.

RACHEL

Sunday, 4 August 2013

Morning

It's different, the nightmare I wake from this morning. In it, I've done something wrong, but I don't know what it is, all I know is that it cannot be put right. All I know is that Tom hates me now, he won't talk to me any longer, and he has told everyone I know about the terrible thing I've done, and everyone has turned against me: old colleagues, my friends, even my mother. They look at me with disgust, contempt, and no one will listen to me, no one will let me tell them how sorry I am. I feel awful, desperately guilty, I just can't think what it is that I've done. I wake and I know the dream must come from an old memory, some ancient transgression – it doesn't matter which one now.

After I got off the train yesterday, I hung around outside Ashbury station for a full fifteen or twenty minutes. I watched to see if he'd got off the train with me – the red-haired man – but there was no sign of him. I kept thinking that I might have missed him, that he was there somewhere, just waiting for me to walk home so that he could follow me. I thought how desperately I would love to be able to run home and for Tom to be waiting for me. To have someone waiting for me.

I walked home via the off-licence.

The flat was empty when I got back, it had the feeling of a place just vacated, as though I'd just missed Cathy, but the note on the counter said she was going out for lunch with Damien in Henley and that she wouldn't be back until Sunday night. I felt restless, afraid. I walked from room to room, picking things up, putting them down. Something felt off, but I realized eventually that it was just me.

Still, the silence ringing in my ears sounded like voices, so I poured myself a glass of wine, and then another, and then I phoned Scott. The phone went straight to voicemail: his message from another lifetime, the voice of a busy, confident man, with a beautiful wife at home. After a few minutes, I phoned again. The phone was answered, but no one spoke.

'Hello?'

'Who is this?'

'It's Rachel,' I said. 'Rachel Watson.'

'Oh.' There was noise in the background, voices, a woman. His mother, perhaps.

'You... I missed your call,' I said.

'No ... no. Did I call you? Oh. By mistake.' He sounded flustered. 'No, just put it there,' he said, and it took me a moment to realize he wasn't talking to me.

'I'm so sorry,' I said.

'Yes,' His tone was flat and even.

'So sorry.'

Thank you.'

'Did you ... did you need to talk to me?'

'No, I must have rung you by mistake,' he said, with more conviction this time.

'Oh.' I could tell he was keen to get off the phone. I knew I should leave him to his family, his grief. I knew that I should, but I didn't. 'Do you know Anna?' I asked him. 'Anna Watson?'

'Who? You mean your ex's missus?'

'Yes.'

'No. I mean not really. Megan ... Megan did a bit of babysitting for her, last year. Why do you ask?'

I don't know why I ask. I don't know. 'Can we meet?' I asked him. 'I wanted to talk to you about something.'

'About what?' He sounded annoyed. 'It's really not a great time.'

Stung by his sarcasm, I was ready to hang up when he said, 'I've got a houseful of people here. Tomorrow? Come by the house tomorrow.'

Evening

He's cut himself shaving: there's blood on his

221

cheek and on his collar. His hair is damp and he smells of soap and aftershave. He nods at me and stands aside, gesturing for me to enter the house, but he doesn't say anything. The house is dark, stuffy, the blinds in the living room closed, the curtains drawn across the French doors leading to the garden. There are Tupperware containers on the kitchen counters.

'Everyone brings food,' Scott says. He gestures at me to sit down at the table, but he remains standing, his arms hanging limply at his sides. 'You wanted to tell me something?' He is a man on autopilot, he doesn't look me in the eye. He looks defeated.

'I wanted to ask you about Anna Watson, about whether... I don't know. What was her relationship with Megan like? Did they like each other?'

He frowns, places his hands on the back of the chair in front of him. 'No. I mean ... they didn't dislike each other. They didn't really know each other very well. They didn't have a *relationship*.' His shoulders seem to sag lower still; he's weary. 'Why are you asking me about this?'

I have to come clean. 'I saw her. I think I saw her, outside the underpass by the station. I saw her that night ... the night Megan went missing.'

He shakes his head a little, trying to comprehend what I'm telling him. 'Sorry? You saw her. You were ... where were you?'

'I was here. I was on my way to see ... to see Tom, my ex-husband, but I–'

He squeezes his eyes shut, rubs his forehead. 'Hang on a minute – you were here – and you saw Anna Watson? And? I know Anna was here.

222

She lives a few doors away. She told the police that she went to the station around seven but that she didn't recall seeing Megan.' His hands grip the chair, I can tell he is losing patience. 'What exactly are you saying?'

'I'd been drinking,' I say, my face reddening with a familiar shame. 'I don't remember exactly, but I've just got this feeling–'

Scott holds his hand up. 'Enough. I don't want to hear this. You've got some problem with your ex, your ex's new wife, that's obvious. It's got nothing to do with me, nothing to do with Megan, has it? Jesus, aren't you ashamed? Do you have any idea of what I'm going through here? Do you know that the police had me in for questioning this morning?' He's pushing down so hard on the chair I fear it's going to break, I'm steeling myself for the crack. 'And you come here with this bullshit. I'm sorry your life is a total fucking disaster, but believe me, it's a picnic compared to mine. So if you don't mind...' He jerks his head in the direction of the front door.

I get to my feet. I feel foolish, ridiculous. And I am ashamed. 'I wanted to help. I wanted–'

'You can't, all right? You can't help me. No one can help me. My wife is dead, and the police think I killed her.' His voice is rising, spots of colour appear on his cheeks. 'They think I killed her.'

'But... Kamal Abdic...'

The chair crashes against the kitchen wall with such force that one of the legs splinters away. I jump back in fright, but Scott has barely moved. His hands are back at his sides, balled into fists. I can see the veins under his skin.

'Kamal Abdic,' he says, teeth gritted, 'is no longer a suspect.' His tone is even, but he is struggling to restrain himself. I can feel the anger vibrating off him. I want to get to the front door, but he is in my way, blocking my path, blocking out what little light there was in the room.

'Do you know what he's been saying?' he asks, turning away from me to pick up the chair. Of course I don't, I think, but I realize once again that he's not really talking to me. 'Kamal's got all sorts of stories. Kamal says that Megan was unhappy, that I was a jealous, controlling husband, a – what was the word? – an *emotional abuser.*' He spits the words out in disgust. 'Kamal says Megan was afraid of me.'

'But he's–'

'He isn't the only one. That friend of hers, Tara – she says that Megan asked her to cover for her sometimes, that Megan wanted her to lie to me about where she was, what she was doing.'

He places the chair back at the table and it falls over. I take a step towards the hallway, and he looks at me then. 'I am a guilty man,' he says, his face contorted in anguish. 'I am as good as convicted.'

He kicks the broken chair aside and sits down on one of the three remaining good ones. I hover, unsure. Stick or twist? He starts to talk again, his voice so soft I can barely hear him. 'Her phone was in her pocket,' he says. I take a step closer to him. 'There was a message on it from me. The last thing I ever said to her, the last words she ever read, were *Go to hell you lying bitch.*'

His chin on his chest, his shoulders start to

shake. I am close enough to touch him. I raise my hand and, trembling, put my fingers lightly on the back of his neck. He doesn't shrug me away.

'I'm sorry,' I say, and I mean it, because although I'm shocked to hear the words, to imagine that he could speak to her like that, I know what it is to love someone and to say the most terrible things to them, in anger or anguish. 'A text message,' I say. 'It's not enough. If that's all they have...'

'It's not, though, is it?' He straightens up then, shrugging my hand away from him. I walk back around the table and sit down opposite him. He doesn't look up at me. 'I have a motive. I didn't behave... I didn't react the right way when she walked out. I didn't panic soon enough. I didn't call her soon enough.' He gives a bitter laugh. 'And there is a pattern of abusive behaviour, according to Kamal Abdic.' It's then that he looks up at me, that he sees me, that a light comes on. Hope. 'You ... you can talk to the police. You can tell them that it's a lie, that he's lying. You can at least give another side of the story, tell them that I loved her, that we were happy.'

I can feel panic rising in my chest. He thinks I can help him. He is pinning his hopes on me and all I have for him is a lie, a bloody lie.

'They won't believe me,' I say weakly. 'They don't believe me. I'm an unreliable witness.'

The silence between us swells and fills the room; a fly buzzes angrily against the French doors. Scott picks at the dried blood on his cheek, I can hear his nails scratching his skin. I push my chair back, the legs scraping on the tiles, and he looks up.

'You were here,' he says, as though the piece of

information I gave him fifteen minutes ago is only now sinking in. 'You were in Witney the night Megan went missing?'

I can barely hear him above the blood thudding in my ears. I nod.

'Why didn't you tell the police that?' he asks. I can see the muscle tic in his jaw.

'I did. I did tell them that. But I didn't have... I didn't see anything. I don't remember anything.'

He gets to his feet, walks over to the French doors and pulls back the curtain. The sunshine is momentarily blinding. Scott stands with his back to me, his arms folded.

'You were drunk,' he says matter-of-factly. 'But you *must* remember something. You must – that's why you keep coming back here, isn't it?' He turns around to face me. 'That's it, isn't it? Why you keep contacting me. You know something.' He's saying this as though it's fact: not a question, not an accusation, not a theory. 'Did you see his car?' he asks. 'Think. Blue Vauxhall Corsa. Did you see it?' I shake my head and he throws his arms up in frustration. 'Don't just dismiss it. Really think. What did you see? You saw Anna Watson, but that doesn't mean anything. You saw – come on! Who did you see?'

Blinking into the sunlight, I try desperately to piece together what I saw, but nothing comes. Nothing real, nothing helpful. Nothing I could say out loud. I was in an argument. Or perhaps I witnessed an argument. I stumbled on the station steps, a man with red hair helped me up – I think that he was kind to me, although now he makes me feel afraid. I know that I had a cut on my head,

226

another on my lip, bruises on my arms. I think I remember being in the underpass. It was dark. I was frightened, confused. I heard voices. I heard someone call Megan's name. No, that was a dream. That wasn't real. I remember blood. Blood on my head, blood on my hands. I remember Anna. I don't remember Tom. I don't remember Kamal or Scott or Megan.

He is watching me, waiting for me to say something, to offer him some crumb of comfort, but I have none.

'That night,' he says, 'that's the key time.' He sits back down at the table, closer to me now, his back to the window. There is a sheen of sweat on his forehead and his upper lip, and he shivers as though with fever. 'That's when it happened. They think that's when it happened. They can't be sure...' He tails off. 'They can't be sure. Because of the condition ... of the body.' He takes a deep breath. 'But they think it was that night. Or soon after.' He's back on autopilot, speaking to the room, not to me. I listen in silence as he tells the room that the cause of death was head trauma, her skull was fractured in several places. No sexual assault, or at least none that they could confirm, because of her condition. Her condition, which was ruined.

When he comes back to himself, back to me, there is fear in his eyes, desperation.

'If you remember anything,' he says, 'you have to help me. Please, try to remember, Rachel.' The sound of my name on his lips makes my stomach flip, and I feel wretched.

On the train, on the way home, I think about

what he said, and I wonder if it's true. Is the reason that I can't let go of this trapped inside my head? Is there some knowledge I'm desperate to impart? I know that I feel something for him, something I can't name and shouldn't feel. But is it more than that? If there's something in my head, then maybe someone can help me get it out. Someone like a psychiatrist. A therapist. Someone like Kamal Abdic.

Tuesday, 6 August 2013

Morning

I've barely slept. All night, I lay awake thinking about it, turning it over and over in my mind. Is this stupid, reckless, pointless? Is it dangerous? I don't know what I'm doing. I made an appointment yesterday morning, to see Doctor Kamal Abdic. I rang his surgery and spoke to a receptionist, and asked for him by name. I might have been imagining it, but I thought she sounded surprised. She said he could see me today at four thirty. So soon? My heart battering my ribs, my mouth dry I said that would be fine. The session costs £75. That £300 from my mother is not going to last very long.

Ever since I made the appointment, I haven't been able to think of anything else. I'm afraid, but I'm excited, too. I can't deny that there's a part of me that finds the idea of meeting Kamal thrilling. Because all this started with him: a glimpse of him and my life changed course, veered off the tracks.

The moment I saw him kiss Megan, everything changed.

And I need to see him. I need to do something, because the police are only interested in Scott. They had him in for questioning again yesterday. They won't confirm it, of course, but there's footage on the internet: Scott, walking into the police station, his mother at his side. His tie was too tight, he looked strangled.

Everyone speculates. The newspapers say that the police are being more circumspect, that they cannot afford to make another hasty arrest. There is talk of a botched investigation, suggestions that a change in personnel may be required. On the internet, the talk about Scott is horrible, the theories wild, disgusting. There are screen grabs of him giving his first tearful appeal for Megan's return, and next to them are pictures of killers who had also appeared on television, sobbing, seemingly distraught at the fate of their loved ones. It's horrific, inhuman. I can only pray that he never looks at this stuff. It would break his heart.

So, stupid and reckless I may be, but I am going to see Kamal Abdic, because unlike all the speculators, I have seen Scott. I've been close enough to touch him, I know what he is, and he isn't a murderer.

Evening

My legs are still trembling as I climb the steps to Corly station. I've been shaking like this for hours, it must be the adrenaline, my heart just

229

won't slow down. The train is packed – no chance of a seat here, it's not like getting on at Euston, so I have to stand, midway through a carriage. It's like a sweatbox. I'm trying to breathe slowly, my eyes cast down to my feet. I'm just trying to get a handle on what I'm feeling.

Exultation, fear, confusion and guilt. Mostly guilt.

It wasn't what I expected.

By the time I got to the practice, I'd worked myself up into a state of complete and utter terror: I was convinced that he was going to look at me and somehow know that I knew, that he was going to view me as a threat. I was afraid that I would say the wrong thing, that somehow I wouldn't be able to stop myself from saying Megan's name. Then I walked into a doctor's waiting room, boring and bland, and spoke to a middle-aged receptionist, who took my details without really looking at me. I sat down and picked up a copy of *Vogue* and flicked through it with trembling fingers, trying to focus my mind on the task ahead while at the same time attempting to look unremarkably bored, just like any other patient.

There were two others in there: a twenty-something man reading something on his phone and an older woman who stared glumly at her feet, not once looking up, even when her name was called by the receptionist. She just got up and shuffled off, she knew where she was going. I waited there for five minutes, ten. I could feel my breathing getting shallow. The waiting room was warm and airless, and I felt as though I couldn't get enough oxygen into my lungs. I worried that I might faint.

Then a door flew open and a man came out and before I'd even had time to see him properly, I knew that it was him. I knew the way I knew that he wasn't Scott the first time I saw him, when he was nothing but a shadow moving towards her – just an impression of tallness, of loose, languid movement. He held out his hand to me.

'Ms Watson?'

I raised my eyes to meet his and felt a jolt of electricity all the way down my spine. I put my hand into his. It was warm and dry and huge, enveloping the whole of mine.

'Please,' he said, indicating for me to follow him into his office, and I did, feeling sick, dizzy all the way. I was walking in her footsteps. She did all this. She sat opposite him in the chair he told me to sit in, he probably folded his hands just below his chin the way he did this afternoon, he probably nodded at her in the same way, saying, 'OK, what would you like to talk to me about today?'

Everything about him was warm: his hand, when I shook it; his eyes; the tone of his voice. I searched his face for clues, for signs of the vicious brute who smashed Megan's head open, for a glimpse of the traumatized refugee who'd lost his family. I could not see any. For a while, I forgot myself. I forgot to be afraid of him. I was sitting there and I wasn't panicking any longer. I swallowed hard and tried to remember what I'd to say, and I said it. I told him that for four years I'd had problems with alcohol, that my drinking had cost me my marriage and my job, it was costing me my health, obviously, and I feared it might cost me my sanity, too.

'I don't remember things,' I said. 'I black out

and I can't remember where I've been or what I've done. Sometimes I wonder if I've done or said terrible things, and I can't remember. And if ... if someone tells me something I've done, it doesn't even feel like me. It doesn't feel like it was me who was doing that thing. And it's so hard to feel responsible for something you don't remember. So I never feel bad enough. I feel bad, but the thing that I've done – it's removed from me. It's like it doesn't belong to me.'

All this came out, all this truth, I just spilled it in front of him in the first few minutes of being in his presence. I was so ready to say it, I'd been waiting to say it to someone. But it shouldn't have been him. He listened, his clear amber eyes on mine, his hands folded, motionless. He didn't look around the room or make notes. He listened. And eventually he nodded slightly and said, 'You want to take responsibility for what you have done, and you find it difficult to do that, to feel fully accountable if you cannot remember it?'

'Yes, that's it, that's exactly it.'

'So, how do we take responsibility? You can apologize – and even if you cannot remember committing your transgression, that doesn't mean that your apology, and the sentiment behind your apology, is not sincere.'

'But I want to *feel* it. I want to feel ... worse.'

It's an odd thing to say, but I think this all the time. I don't feel bad enough. I know what I'm responsible for, I know all the terrible things I've done, even if I don't remember the details – but I feel distanced from those actions. I feel them at one remove.

'You think that you should feel worse than you do? That you don't feel bad enough for your mistakes?'

'Yes.'

Kamal shook his head. 'Rachel, you have told me that you lost your marriage, you lost your job – do you not think this is punishment enough?'

I shook my head.

He leaned back a little in his chair. 'I think perhaps you are being rather hard on yourself.'

'I'm not.'

'All right. OK. Can we go back a bit? To when the problem started. You said it was ... four years ago? Can you tell me about that time?'

I resisted. I wasn't completely lulled by the warmth of his voice, by the softness of his eyes. I wasn't completely hopeless. I wasn't going to start telling him the whole truth. I wasn't going to tell him how I longed for a baby. I told him that my marriage broke down, that I was de-pressed, and that I'd always been a drinker, but that things just got out of hand.

'Your marriage broke down, so ... you left your husband, or he left you, or ... you left each other?'

'He had an affair,' I said. 'He met another woman and fell in love with her.' He nodded, wait-ing for me to go on. 'It wasn't his fault, though. It was my fault.'

'Why do you say that?'

'Well, the drinking started before...'

'So your husband's affair was not the trigger?'

'No, I'd already started, my drinking drove him away, it was why he stopped...'

Kamal waited, he didn't prompt me to go on,

233

he just let me sit there, waiting for me to say the words out loud.

'Why he stopped loving me,' I said.

I hate myself for crying in front of him. I don't understand why I couldn't keep my guard up. I shouldn't have talked about real things, I should have gone in there with some totally made-up problems, some imaginary persona. I should have been better prepared.

I hate myself for looking at him and believing, for a moment, that he felt for me. Because he looked at me as though he did, not as though he pitied me, but as though he understood me, as though I was someone he wanted to help.

'So then, Rachel, the drinking started *before* the breakdown of your marriage. Do you think you can point to an underlying cause? I mean, not everyone can. For some people, there is just a general slide into a depressive or an addicted state. Was there something specific for you? A bereavement, some other loss?'

I shook my head, shrugged. I wasn't going to tell him that. I will not tell him that.

He waited for a few moments and then glanced quickly at the clock on his desk.

'We will pick up next time, perhaps?' he said, and then he smiled and I went cold.

Everything about him is warm – his hands, his eyes, his voice – everything but the smile. You can see the killer in him when he shows his teeth. My stomach a hard ball, my pulse sky-rocketing again, I left his office without shaking his outstretched hand. I couldn't stand to touch him.

I understand, I do. I can see what Megan saw in

him, and it's not just that he's arrestingly handsome. He's also calm and reassuring, he exudes a patient kindness. Someone innocent or trusting or simply troubled might not see through all that, might not see that under all that calm he's a wolf. I understand that. For almost an hour, I was drawn in. I let myself open up to him. I forgot who he was. I betrayed Scott, and I betrayed Megan, and I feel guilty about that.

But most of all, I feel guilty because I want to go back.

Wednesday, 7 August 2013

Morning

I had it again, the dream where I've done something wrong, where everyone takes against me, sides with Tom. Where I can't explain, or even apologize, because I don't know what the thing is. In the space between dreaming and wakefulness, I think of a real argument, long ago – four years ago – after our first and only round of IVF failed, when I wanted to try again. Tom told me we didn't have the money, and I didn't question that. I knew we didn't – we'd taken on a big mortgage, he had some debts left over from a bad business deal his father had coaxed him into pursuing – I just had to deal with it. I just had to hope that one day we would have the money, and in the meantime I had to bite back the tears that came, hot and fast, every time I saw a stranger with a bump, every time I heard someone else's happy news.

It was a couple of months after we'd found out that the IVF had failed that he told me about the trip. Vegas, for four nights, to watch the big fight and let off some steam. Just him and a couple of his mates from the old days, people I'd never met. It cost a fortune, I know, because I saw the booking receipt for the flight and the room in his email inbox. I've no idea what the boxing tickets cost, but I can't imagine they were cheap. It wasn't enough to pay for a round of IVF, but it'd have been a start. We'd a horrible fight about it. I don't remember the details because I'd been drinking all afternoon, working myself up to confront him about it, so when I did it was in the worst possible way. I remember his coldness the next day, his refusal to speak about it. I remember him telling me, in disappointed tones, what I'd done and said, how I'd smashed our framed wedding photograph, how I'd screamed at him for being so selfish, how I'd called him a useless husband, a failure. I remember how much I hated myself that day.

I was wrong, of course I was, to say those things to him, but what comes to me now is that I wasn't unreasonable to be angry. I had every right to be angry, didn't I? We were trying to have a baby – shouldn't we have been prepared to make sacrifices? I would have cut off a limb if it meant I could have had a child. Couldn't he have foregone a weekend in Vegas?

I lie in bed for a bit, thinking about that, and then I get up and decide to go for a walk, because if I don't do something I'm going to want to go round to the corner shop. I haven't had a drink since Sunday and I can feel the fight going on

236

within me, the longing for a little buzz, the urge to get out of my head, smashing up against the vague feeling that something has been accomplished and that it would be a shame to throw it away now.

Ashbury isn't really a good place to walk, it's just shops and suburbs, there isn't even a decent park. I head off through the middle of town, which isn't so bad when there's no one else around. The trick is to fool yourself into thinking that you're headed somewhere: just pick a spot and set off towards it. I chose the church at the top of Pleasance Road, which is about two miles from Cathy's flat. I've been to an AA meeting there. I didn't go to the local one because I didn't want to bump into anyone I might see on the street, in the supermarket, on the train.

When I get to the church, I turn around and walk back, striding purposefully towards home, a woman with things to do, somewhere to go. Normal. I watch the people I pass – the two men running, backpacks on, training for the marathon, the young woman in a black skirt and white trainers, heels in her bag, on her way to work – and I wonder what they're hiding. Are they moving to stop drinking, running to stand still? Are they thinking about the killer they met yesterday, the one they're planning to see again?

I'm not normal.

I'm almost home when I see it. I've been lost in thought, thinking about what these sessions with Kamal are actually supposed to achieve: am I really planning to rifle through his desk drawers if he happens to leave the room? To try and trap him into saying something revealing, to lead him into dangerous territory? Chances are he's a lot cleverer than I am; chances are he'll see me coming. After all, he knows his name has been in the papers – he must be alert to the possibility of people trying to get stories on him, or information from him.

This is what I'm thinking about, head down, eyes on the pavement, as I pass the little Londis shop on the right and try not to look at it because it raises possibilities, but out of the corner of my eye I see her name. I look up and it's there, in huge letters on the front of a tabloid newspaper: WAS MEGAN A CHILD KILLER?

ANNA

Wednesday, 7 August 2013

Morning

I was with the NCT girls at Starbucks when it happened. We were sitting in our usual spot by the window, the kids were spreading Lego all over the floor, Beth was trying (yet again) to persuade me to join her book club, and then Diane showed up. She had this look on her face, the self-importance of someone who is about to deliver a piece of particularly juicy gossip. She could barely contain herself as she struggled to get her double buggy through the door.

'Anna,' she said, her face grave, 'have you seen

this?' and she held up a newspaper with the head-line WAS MEGAN A CHILD KILLER? I was speechless. I just stared at it and, ridiculously, burst into tears. Evie was horrified. She *howled*. It was awful.

I went to the loos to clean myself (and Evie) up, and when I got back they were all speaking in hushed tones. Diane glanced slyly up at me and asked, 'Are you all right, sweetie?' She was enjoying it, I could tell.

I had to leave then, I couldn't stay. They were all being terribly concerned, saying how awful it must be for me, but I could see it on their faces: thinly disguised disapproval. How could you entrust your child to that monster? You must be the worst mother in the world.

I tried to call Tom on the way home, but his phone just went straight to voicemail. I left him a message to ring me back as soon as possible – I tried to keep my voice light and even, but I was trembling, and my legs felt shaky, unsteady.

I didn't buy the paper, but I couldn't resist reading the story online. It all sounds rather vague. 'Sources close to the Hipwell investigation' claim an allegation has been made that Megan 'may have been involved in the unlawful killing of her own child' ten years ago. The 'sources' also speculate that this could be a motive for her murder. The detective in charge of the whole investigation – Gaskill, the one who came to speak to us after she went missing – made no comment.

Tom rang me back – he was in between meetings, he couldn't come home. He tried to placate me, he made all the right noises, he told me it was probably a load of rubbish anyway. 'You know you can't believe half the stuff they print in the newspapers.' I didn't make too much of a fuss, because he was the one who suggested she come and help out with Evie in the first place. He must be feeling horrible.

And he's right. It may not even be true. But who would come up with a story like that? Why would you make up a thing like that? And I can't help thinking, I *knew*. I always knew there was something off about that woman. At first I just thought she was a bit immature, but it was more than that, she was sort of *absent*. Self-involved. I'm not going to lie. I'm glad she's gone. Good riddance.

Evening

I'm upstairs, in the bedroom. Tom's watching TV with Evie. We're not talking. It's my fault. He walked in the door and I just went for him.

I was building up to it all day. I couldn't help it, couldn't hide from it, she was everywhere I looked. Here, in my house, holding my child, feeding her, changing her, playing with her while I was taking a nap. I kept thinking of all the times I left Evie alone with her and it made me sick.

And then the paranoia came, that feeling I've had almost all the time I've lived in this house, of being watched. At first, I used to put it down to the trains. All those faceless bodies staring out of the windows, staring right across at us, it gave me the creeps. It was one of the many reasons why I didn't want to move in here in the first place, but Tom wouldn't leave. He said we'd lose money on the sale.

At first the trains, and then Rachel. Rachel watching us, turning up on the street, calling us up all the time. And then even Megan, when she was here with Evie: I always felt she had half an eye on me, as though she were assessing me, assessing my parenting, judging me for not being able to cope on my own. Ridiculous, I know. Then I think about that day when Rachel came to the house and took Evie, and my whole body goes cold and I think, I'm not being ridiculous at all.

So by the time Tom came home, I was spoiling for a fight. I issued an ultimatum: we have to leave, there's no way I can stay in this house, on this road, knowing everything that has gone on here. Everywhere I look now, I have to see not only Rachel, but Megan too. I have to think about everything she touched. It's too much. I said I didn't care whether we got a good price for the house or not.

'You will care when we're forced to live in a much worse place, when we can't make our mortgage payments,' he said, perfectly reasonably. I asked whether he couldn't ask his parents to help out – they have plenty of money – but he said he wouldn't ask them, that he'd never ask them for anything again, and he got angry then, said he didn't want to talk about it any more. It's because of how his parents treated him when he left Rachel for me. I shouldn't even have mentioned them, it always pisses him off.

But I can't help it. I feel desperate, because now

every time I close my eyes I see her, sitting there at the kitchen table with Evie on her lap. She'd be playing with her and smiling and chattering but it never seemed real, it never seemed as if she really wanted to be there. She always seemed so happy to be handing Evie back to me when it was time for her to go. It was almost as though she didn't like the feel of a child in her arms.

RACHEL

Wednesday, 7 August 2013

Evening

The heat is insufferable, it builds and builds. With the apartment windows open, you can taste the carbon monoxide rising from the street below. My throat itches. I'm taking my second shower of the day when the phone rings. I let it go, and it rings again. And again. By the time I'm out, it's ringing for a fourth time, and I answer.

He sounds panicky his breath short. His voice comes to me in snatches. 'I can't go home,' he says. 'There are cameras everywhere.'

'Scott?'

'I know this is ... this is really weird, but I just need to go somewhere, somewhere they won't be waiting for me. I can't go to my mother's, my friends. I'm just ... driving around. I've been driving around since I left the police station...' There's

242

a catch in his voice. 'I just need an hour or two. To sit, to think. Without them, without the police, without people asking me fucking questions. I'm sorry, but could I come to your house?'

I say yes, of course. Not just because he sounds panicked, desperate, but because I want to see him. I want to help him. I give him the address and he says he'll be there in fifteen minutes.

The doorbell rings ten minutes later: short, sharp, urgent bursts.

'I'm sorry to do this,' he says as I open the front door. 'I didn't know where to go.' He has a hunted look to him: he's shaken, pale, his skin slick with sweat.

'It's all right,' I say, stepping aside to allow him to pass me. I show him into the living room, tell him to sit down. I fetch him a glass of water from the kitchen. He drinks it, almost in one gulp, then sits, bent over, forearms on his knees, head hanging down.

I hover, unsure whether to speak or to hold my tongue. I fetch his glass and refill it, saying nothing. Eventually, he starts to speak.

'You think the worst has happened,' he says quietly. 'I mean, you would think that, wouldn't you?' He looks up at me. 'My wife is dead, and the police think that I killed her. What could be worse than that?'

He's talking about the news, about the things they're saying about her. This tabloid story, supposedly leaked by someone in the police, about Megan's involvement in the death of a child. Murky, speculative stuff, a smear campaign on a dead woman. It's despicable.

'It isn't true though,' I say to him. 'It can't be.'

His expression is blank, uncomprehending. 'Detective Sergeant Riley told me this morning,' he says. He coughs, clears his throat. 'The news I always wanted to hear. You can't imagine,' he goes on, his voice barely more than a whisper, 'how I've longed for it. I used to daydream about it, imagine how she'd look, how she'd smile at me, shy and knowing, how she'd take my hand and press it to her lips...' He's lost, he's dreaming, I have no idea what he's talking about. 'Today,' he says, 'today I got the news that Megan was pregnant.'

He starts to cry, and I am choking too, crying for an infant who never existed, the child of a woman I never knew. But the horror of it is almost too much to bear. I cannot understand how Scott is still breathing. It should have killed him, should have sucked the life right out of him. Somehow, though, he is still here.

I can't speak, can't move. The living room is hot, airless despite the open windows. I can hear noises from the street below: a police siren, young girls shouting and laughing, bass booming from a passing car. Normal life. But in here, the world is ending. For Scott, the world is ending, and I can't speak. I stand there, mute, helpless, useless.

Until I hear footfalls on the steps outside, the familiar jangle of Cathy fishing around in her huge handbag for her house keys. It jolts me to life. I have to do something: I grab Scott's hand and he looks up at me, alarmed.

'Come with me,' I say, pulling him to his feet. He lets me drag him into the hallway and up the stairs before Cathy unlocks the door. I close the bedroom door behind us.

'My flatmate,' I say by way of explanation. 'She'd ... she might ask questions. I know that's not what you want at the moment.'

He nods. He looks around my tiny room, taking in the unmade bed, the clothes, both clean and dirty, piled on my desk chair, the blank walls, the cheap furniture. I am embarrassed. This is my life: messy, shabby, small. Unenviable. As I'm thinking this, I think how ridiculous I am, to imagine that Scott could possibly care about the state of my life at this moment.

I motion for him to sit down on the bed. He obeys, wiping his eyes with the back of his hand. He breathes out heavily.

'Can I get you something?' I ask him.

'A beer?'

'I don't keep alcohol in the house,' I say, and I can feel myself going red as I say it. Scott doesn't notice though, he doesn't even look up. 'I can make you a cup of tea?' He nods again. 'Lie down,' I say. 'Rest.' He does as he's told, kicking off his shoes and lying back on the bed, docile as a sick child.

Downstairs, while I boil the kettle I make small talk with Cathy, listening to her going on about the new place in Northcote she's discovered for lunch ('really good salads') and how annoying the new woman at work is. I smile and nod, but I'm only half hearing her. My body is braced: I'm listening out for him, for creaks or footsteps. It feels unreal to have him here, in my bed, upstairs. It makes me dizzy to think about it, as though I'm dreaming.

Cathy stops talking eventually and looks at me, her, brow furrowed. 'Are you all right?' she asks. 'You look ... kind of out of it.'

'I'm just a bit tired,' I tell her. 'I'm not feeling very well. I think I'll go to bed.'

She gives me a look. She knows I've not been drinking (she can always tell), but she probably assumes I'm about to start. I don't care, I can't think about it now; I pick up the cup of tea for Scott and tell her I'll see her in the morning.

I stop outside my bedroom door and listen. It's quiet. Carefully, I twist the doorknob and push the door open. He's lying there, in exactly the same position I left him, his hands at his sides, his eyes shut. I can hear his breathing, soft and ragged. His bulk takes up half the bed, but I'm tempted to lie down in the space next to him, to put my arm across his chest, to comfort him. Instead, I give a little cough and hold out the cup of tea.

He sits up. 'Thank you,' he says gruffly, taking the mug from me. 'Thank you for ... giving me sanctuary. It's been – I can't describe how it's been, since that story came out.'

'The one about what happened years ago?'

'Yeah, that one.'

How the tabloids got hold of that story is hotly disputed. The speculation has been rife, fingers pointed at the police, at Kamal Abdic, at Scott.

'It's a lie,' I say to him. 'Isn't it?'

'Of course it is, but it gives someone a motive, doesn't it? That's what they're saying – Megan killed her baby, which would give someone – the father of the child, presumably – a motive to kill her. Years and years later.'

'It's ridiculous.'

'But you know what everyone's saying. That I made this story up, not just to make her look like a bad person, but to shift suspicion away from me, on to some unknown person. Some guy from her past that no one even knows about.'

I sit down next to him on the bed. Our thighs almost touch.

'What are the police saying about it?'

He shrugs. 'Nothing really. They asked me what I knew about it. Did I know she'd had a child before? Did I know what happened? Did I know who the father was? I said no, it was all bullshit, she'd never been pregnant...' His voice catches again. He stops, takes a sip of the tea. 'I asked them where the story came from, how it made it into the newspapers. They said they couldn't tell me. It's from him, I assume. Abdic.' He gives a long, shuddering sigh. 'I don't understand why. I don't understand why he would say things like that about her. I don't know what he's trying to do. He's obviously fucking disturbed.'

I think of the man I met the other day: the calm demeanour, the soft voice, the warmth in the eyes. As far from disturbed as it's possible to get. That smile, though. 'It's outrageous that this has been printed. There should be rules...'

'Can't libel the dead,' he says. He falls silent for a moment, then says, 'They've assured me that they won't release the information about this ... about her pregnancy. Not yet. Perhaps not at all. But certainly not until they know for sure.'

'Until they know?'

'It's not Abdic's child,' he says.

247

'They've done DNA testing?'

He shakes his head. 'No, I just know. I can't say how, but I *know*. The baby is – was – mine'

'If he thought it was his baby, it gives him a motive, doesn't it?' He wouldn't be the first man to get rid of an unwanted child by getting rid of its mother – although I don't say that out loud. And – I don't say this either – it gives Scott a motive, too. If he thought his wife was pregnant with another man's child ... only he can't have done. His shock, his distress – it has to be real. No one is that good an actor.

Scott doesn't appear to be listening any longer. His eyes, fixed on the back of the bedroom door, are glazed over, and he seems to be sinking into the bed as though into quicksand.

'You should stay here a while,' I say to him. 'Try to sleep.'

He looks at me then, and he almost smiles. 'You don't mind?' he asks. 'It would be... I would be grateful. I find it hard to sleep at home. It's not just the people outside, the sense of people trying to get to me. It's not just that. It's her. She's everywhere, I can't stop seeing her. I go down the stairs and I don't look, I force myself not to look, but when I'm past the window, I have to go back and check that she's not out there, on the terrace.' I can feel the tears pricking my eyes as he tells me. 'She liked to sit out there, you see – on this little terrace we've got. She liked to sit out there and watch the trains.'

'I know,' I say, putting my hand on his arm. 'I used to see her there sometimes.'

'I keep hearing her voice,' he says. 'I keep hearing

her calling me. I lie in bed and I can hear her calling me from outside. I keep thinking she's out there.' He's trembling.

'Lie down,' I say, taking the mug from his hand. 'Rest.'

When I'm sure that he's fallen asleep, I lie down at his back, my face inches from his shoulderblade. I close my eyes and listen to my heart beating, the throb of blood in my neck. I inhale the sad, stale scent of him.

When I wake, hours later, he's gone.

Thursday, 8 August 2013

Morning

I feel treacherous. He left me just hours ago, and here I am, on my way to see Kamal, to meet once again the man he believes killed his wife. His child. I feel sick. I wonder whether I should have told him my plan, explained that I'm doing all this for him. Only I'm not sure that I *am* doing it just for him, and I don't really have a plan.

I will give something of myself. That's my plan for today. I will talk about something real. I will talk about wanting a child. I'll see whether that provokes something – an unnatural response, any kind of reaction. I'll see where that gets me.

It gets me nowhere.

He starts out by asking me how I'm feeling, when I last had a drink.

'Sunday,' I tell him.

'Good. That's good.' He folds his hands in his

lap. 'You look well.' He smiles, and I don't see the killer. I'm wondering now what I saw the other day. Did I imagine it?

'You asked me, last time, about how the drinking started.' He nods. 'I became depressed,' I say. 'We were trying... I was trying to get pregnant. I couldn't, and I became depressed. That's when it started.'

In no time at all, I find myself crying again. It's impossible to resist the kindness of strangers. Someone who looks at you, who doesn't know you, who tells you it's OK, whatever you did, whatever you've done: you suffered, you hurt, you deserve forgiveness. I confide in him and I forget, once again, what I'm doing here. I don't watch his face for a reaction, I don't study his eyes for some sign of guilt or suspicion. I let him comfort me.

He is kind, rational. He talks about coping strategies, he reminds me that youth is on my side.

So maybe it doesn't get me nowhere, because I leave Kamal Abdic's office feeling lighter, more hopeful. He has helped me. I sit on the train and I try to conjure up the killer I saw, but I can't see him any longer. I'm struggling to see him as a man capable of beating a woman, of crushing her skull.

A terrible, shameful image comes to me: Kamal with his delicate hands, his reassuring manner, his sibilant speech, contrasted with Scott, huge and powerful, wild, desperate. I have to remind myself that this is Scott now, not as he was. I have to keep reminding myself of what he was before all this. And then I have to admit that I don't know what Scott was before all this.

Friday, 9 August 2013

Evening

The train stops at the signal. I take a sip from the cold can of gin and tonic and look up at his house, her terrace. I was doing so well, but I need this. Dutch courage. I'm on my way to see Scott, and I'll have to run all the risks of Blenheim Road before I do: Tom, Anna, police, press. The underpass, with its half-memories of terror and blood. But he asked me to come, and I couldn't refuse him.

They found the little girl last night. What was left of her. Buried in the grounds of a farmhouse near the East Anglian coast, just where someone had told them to look. It was in the papers this morning:

Police have opened an investigation into the death of a child after they found human remains buried in the garden of a house near Holkham, north Norfolk. The discovery came after police were tipped off about a possible unlawful killing during the course of their investigation into the death of Megan Hipwell, from Witney, whose body was found in Corly Woods last week.

I phoned Scott this morning when I saw the news. He didn't answer, so I left a message, telling him I was sorry. He called back this afternoon.

'Are you all right?' I asked him.

'Not really.' His voice was thick with drink.

'I'm so sorry ... do you need anything?'

251

'I need someone who isn't going to say *I told you so.*'

'I'm sorry?'

'My mother's been here all afternoon. She knew all along, apparently – *something not right about that girl, something off, no family, no friends, came from nowhere.* Wonder why she never told me.' The sound of glass breaking, swearing.

'Are you all right?' I said again.

'Can you come here?' he asked.

'To the house?'

'Yes.'

'I ... the police, journalists... I'm not sure...'

'Please. I just want some company. Someone who knew Megs, who liked her. Someone who doesn't believe all this–'

He was drunk and I knew it and I said yes anyway.

Now, sitting on the train, I'm drinking too, and I'm thinking about what he said. *Someone who knew Megs, who liked her.* I didn't know her, and I'm not sure that I like her any more. I finish my drink as quickly as I can, and open another one.

I get off at Witney. I'm part of the Friday-evening commuter throng: just another wage slave among the hot, tired masses, looking forward to getting home and sitting outside with a cold beer, dinner with the kids, an early night. It might just be the gin, but it feels indescribably good to be swept along with the crowd, everyone phone-checking, fishing in pockets for rail passes. I'm taken back, way back to the first summer we lived on Blenheim Road, when I used to rush home from work every night, desperate to get down the steps and out of the station, half running down the street. Tom would be working from home and I'd barely be through the door before he was taking my clothes off. I find myself smiling about it even now, the anticipation of it: heat rising to my cheeks as I skipped down the road, biting my lip to stop myself from grinning, my breath quickening, thinking of him and knowing he'd be counting the minutes until I got home, too.

My head is so full of those days that I forget to worry about Tom and Anna, the police and the photographers, and before I know it I'm at Scott's door, ringing the doorbell, and the door is opening and I'm feeling excited, although I shouldn't be, but I don't feel guilty about it, because Megan isn't what I thought she was anyway. She wasn't that beautiful, carefree girl out on the terrace. She wasn't a loving wife. She wasn't even a good person. She was a liar, a cheat.

She was a killer.

MEGAN

Thursday, 20 June 2013

Evening

I'm sitting on the sofa in his living room, a glass of wine in my hand. The house is still a tip. I wonder, does he always live like this, like a teenage boy? And I think about how he lost his family when he

253

was a teenager, so maybe he does. I feel sad for him. He comes in from the kitchen and sits at my side, comfortably close. If I could, I would come here every day, just for an hour or two. I'd just sit here and drink wine, feel his hand brush against mine.

But I can't. There's a point to this, and he wants me to get to it.

'OK, Megan,' he says. 'Do you feel ready now? To finish what you were telling me before?'

I lean back a little against him, against his warm body. He lets me. I close my eyes, and it doesn't take me long to get back there, back to the bathroom. It's weird, because I've spent so long trying not to think about it, about those days, those nights, but now I can close my eyes and it's almost instant, like falling asleep, right into the middle of a dream.

It was dark and very cold. I wasn't in the bath any longer. 'I don't know exactly what happened. I remember waking up, I remember knowing that something was wrong, and then the next thing I know Mac was home. He was calling for me. I could hear him downstairs, shouting my name, but I couldn't move. I was sitting on the floor in the bathroom, she was in my arms. The rain was hammering down, the beams in the roof creaking. I was so cold. Mac came up the stairs, still calling out to me. He came to the doorway and turned on the light.' I can feel it now, the light searing my retinas, everything stark and white, horrifying.

'I remember screaming at him to turn the light off. I didn't want to see, I didn't want to look at her like that. I don't know – I don't know what happened then. He was shouting at me, he was screaming in my face. I gave her to him and ran. I ran out of the house into the rain, I ran to the beach. I don't remember what happened after that. It was a long time before he came for me. It was still raining. I was in the dunes, I think. I thought about going in the water, but I was too scared. He came for me eventually. He took me home.

'We buried her in the morning. I wrapped her in a sheet and Mac dug the grave. We put her down at the edge of the property near the disused railway line. We put stones on top to mark it. We didn't talk about it, we didn't talk about anything, and we didn't look at each other. That night, Mac went out. He said he had to meet someone. I thought maybe he was going to go to the police. I didn't know what to do. I just waited for him, for *someone* to come. He didn't come back. He never came back.'

I'm sitting in Kamal's warm living room, his warm body at my side, and I'm shivering. 'I can still feel it,' I tell him. 'At night, I can still feel it. It's the thing I dread, the thing that keeps me awake: the feeling of being alone in that house. I was so frightened – too frightened to go to sleep. I'd just walk around those dark rooms and I'd hear her crying, I'd smell her skin. I saw things. I'd wake in the night and be sure that there was someone else – something else – in the house with me. I thought I was going mad. I thought I was going to die. I thought that maybe I would just stay there, and that one day someone would find me. At least that way I wouldn't have left her.'

I sniff, leaning forward to take a Kleenex from the box on the table. Kamal's hand runs down my spine to my lower back, and rests there.

'But in the end I didn't have the courage to stay. I think I waited about ten days, and then there was nothing left to eat – not a tin of beans, nothing. I packed up my things and I left.'

'Did you see Mac again?'

'No, never. The last time I saw him was that night. He didn't kiss me or even say goodbye properly. He just said he had to go out for a bit,' I shrug. 'That was it.'

'Did you try to contact him?'

I shook my head. 'No. I was too frightened, at first. I didn't know what he would do if I did get in touch. And I didn't know where he was – he didn't even have a mobile phone. I lost touch with the people who knew him. His friends were all kind of nomadic. Hippies, travellers. A few months ago, after we talked about him, I googled him. But I couldn't find him. It's odd...'

'What is?'

'In the early days, I used to see him all the time. Like, in the street, or I'd see a man in a bar and be so sure it was him that my heart would start racing. I used to hear his voice in crowds. But that stopped, a long time ago. 'Now – I think he might be dead.'

'Why do you think that?'

'I don't know. He just ... he feels dead to me.'

Kamal sits up straighter and gently moves his body away from mine. He turns so that he's facing me.

'I think that's probably just your imagination,

256

Megan. It's normal to think you see people who have been a big part of your life after you part company with them. In the early days, I used to catch glimpses of my brothers all the time. As for him "feeling dead", that's probably just a consequence of him being gone from your life for so long. In some senses he no longer feels real to you.'

He's gone back into therapy mode now, we're not just two friends sitting on the sofa any more. I want to reach out and pull him back to me, but I don't want to cross any lines. I think about last time, when I kissed him before I left – the look on his face, longing and frustration and anger.

'I wonder if, now that we've spoken about this, now that you've told me your story, it might help for you to try to contact Mac. To give you closure, to seal that chapter in your past.'

I thought he might suggest this. 'I can't,' I say. 'I can't.'

'Just think about it for a moment.'

'I can't. What if he still hates me? What if it just brings it all back, or if he goes to the police?' What if – I can't say this out loud, can't even whisper it – what if he tells Scott what I really am?

Kamal shakes his head. 'Perhaps he doesn't hate you at all, Megan. Perhaps he never hated you. Perhaps he was afraid, too. Perhaps he feels guilty. From what you have told me, he isn't a man who behaved responsibly. He took in a very young, very vulnerable girl and left her alone when she needed support. Perhaps he knows that what happened is your shared responsibility. Perhaps that's what he ran away from.'

257

I don't know if he really believes that or if he's just trying to make me feel better. I only know that it isn't true. I can't shift the blame on to him. This is one thing I have to take as my own.

'I don't want to push you into doing something you don't want to do,' Kamal says. 'I just want you to consider the possibility that contacting Mac might help you. And it's not because I believe that you owe him anything. Do you see? I believe that he owes you. I understand your guilt, I do. But he abandoned you. You were alone, afraid, panicking, grieving. He left you on your own in that house. It's no wonder you cannot sleep. Of course the idea of sleeping frightens you: you fell asleep and something terrible happened to you. And the one person who should have helped you left you all alone.'

In the moments when Kamal is saying these things, it doesn't sound so bad. As the words slip seductively off his tongue, warm and honeyed, I can almost believe them. I can almost believe that there is a way to leave all this behind, lay it to rest, go home to Scott and live my life as normal people do, neither glancing over my shoulder nor desperately waiting for something better to come along. Is that what normal people do?

'Will you think about it?' he asks, touching my hand as he does so. I give him a bright smile and say that I will. Maybe I even mean it, I don't know. He walks me to the door, his arm around my shoulders, I want to turn and kiss him again, but I don't.

Instead I ask, 'Is this the last time I'm going to see you?' and he nods. 'Couldn't we...?'

'No, Megan. We can't. We have to do the right thing.'

I smile up at him. 'I'm not very good at that,' I say. 'Never have been.'

'You can be. You will be. Go home now. Go home to your husband.'

I stand on the pavement outside his house for a long time after he shuts the door. I feel lighter, I think, freer – but sadder too, and all of a sudden I just want to get home to Scott.

I'm just turning to walk to the station when a man comes running along the pavement, earphones on, head down. He's heading straight for me and as I step back, trying to get out of the way, I slip off the edge of the pavement and fall.

The man doesn't apologize, he doesn't even look back at me and I'm too shocked to cry out. I get to my feet and stand there, leaning against a car, trying to catch my breath. All the peace I felt in Kamal's house is suddenly shattered.

It's not until I get home that I realize I cut my hand when I fell, and at some point I must have rubbed my hand across my mouth. My lips are smeared with blood.

RACHEL

Saturday, 10 August 2013

Morning

I wake early. I can hear the recycling van trundling up the street and the soft patter of rain against the window. The blinds are half up – we forgot to close them last night. I smile to myself. I can feel him behind me, warm and sleepy, hard. I wriggle my hips, pressing against him a little closer. It won't take long for him to stir, to grab hold of me, roll me over.

'Rachel,' his voice says, 'don't.' I go cold. I'm not at home, this isn't home. This is all wrong.

I roll over. Scott is sitting up now. He swings his legs over the side of the bed, his back to me. I squeeze my eyes tightly shut and try to remember, but it's all too hazy. When I open my eyes I can think straight because this room is the one I've woken up in a thousand times or more: this is where the bed is, this is the exact aspect – if I sit up now I will be able to see the tops of the oak trees on the opposite side of the street; over there, on the left, is the en suite bathroom and to the right are the built-in wardrobes. It's exactly the same as the room I shared with Tom.

'Rachel,' he says again and I reach out to touch his back, but he stands quickly and turns to face me. He looks hollowed out, like the first time I saw him, up close in the police station – as though someone has scraped away his insides, leaving a shell. This is like the room I shared with Tom, but it is the one he shared with Megan. This room, this bed.

'I know,' I say. 'I'm sorry. I'm so sorry. This was wrong.'

'Yes, it was,' he says, his eyes not meeting mine. He goes into the bathroom and shuts the door.

I lie back and close my eyes and feel myself sink into dread, that awful gnawing in my gut. What have I done? I remember him talking a lot when I first arrived, a rush of words. He was angry – angry with his mother, who never liked Megan; angry with the newspapers for what they were writing about her, the implication that she got what was coming to her; angry with the police for botching the whole thing, for failing her, failing him. We sat in the kitchen drinking beers and I listened to him talk, and when the beers were finished we sat outside on the patio and he stopped being angry then. We drank and watched the trains go by and talked about nothing: television and work and where he went to school, just like normal people. I forgot to feel what I was supposed to be feeling, we both did, because I can remember now. I can remember him smiling at me, touching my hair.

It hits me like a wave, I can feel blood rushing to my face. I remember admitting it to myself. Thinking the thought and not dismissing it, embracing it. I wanted it. I wanted to be with Jason. I wanted to feel what Jess felt when she sat out

261

there with him, drinking wine in the evening. I forgot what I was supposed to be feeling. I ignored the fact that at the very best, Jess is nothing but a figment of my imagination, and at the worst, Jess is not nothing, she is Megan – she is dead, a body battered and left to rot. Worse than that: I didn't forget. I didn't care. I didn't care because I've started to believe what they're saying about her. Did I, for just the briefest of moments, think she got what was coming to her, too?

Scott comes out of the bathroom. He's taken a shower, washed me off his skin. He looks better for it, but he won't look me in the eye when he asks if I'd like a coffee. This isn't what I wanted: none of this is right. I don't want to do this. I don't want to lose control again.

I dress quickly and go into the bathroom, and splash cold water on my face. My mascara's run, smudged at the corners of my eyes, and my lips are dark. Bitten. My face and neck are red where his stubble has grazed my skin. I have a quick flashback to the night before, his hands on me, and my stomach flips. Feeling dizzy, I sit down on the edge of the bathtub. The bathroom is grubbier than the rest of the house: grime around the sink, toothpaste smeared on the mirror. A mug, with just one toothbrush in it. There's no perfume, no moisturizer, no make-up. I wonder if she took it when she left, or whether he's thrown it all away.

Back in the bedroom, I look around for evidence of her – a robe on the back of the door, a hairbrush on the chest of drawers, a pot of lip balm, a pair of earrings – but there's nothing. I cross the bedroom to the wardrobe and am about to open it, my hand resting on the handle, when I hear him call out, 'There's coffee here!' and I jump.

He hands me the mug without looking at my face, then turns away and stands with his back to me, his gaze fixed on the tracks or something beyond. I glance to my right and notice that the photographs are gone, all of them. There's a prickle at the back of my scalp, the hairs on my forearms raised. I sip my coffee and struggle to swallow. None of this is right.

Maybe his mother did it: cleared everything out, took the pictures away. His mother didn't like Megan, he's said that over and over. Still, who does what he did last night? Who fucks a strange woman in the marital bed when his wife has been dead less than a month? He turns then, he looks at me, and I feel as though he's read my mind because he's got a strange look on his face – contempt, or revulsion – and I'm repulsed by him, too. I put the mug down.

'I should go,' I say, and he doesn't argue.

The rain has stopped. It's bright outside and I'm squinting into hazy morning sunshine. A man approaches me – he's right up in my face the moment I'm on the pavement. I put my hands up, turn sideways and shoulder-barge him out of the way. He's saying something but I don't hear what. I keep my hands raised and my head down, so I'm barely five feet away from her when I see Anna, standing next to her car, hands on hips, watching me. When she catches my eye she shakes her head, turns away and walks quickly towards her own front door, almost but not quite breaking into a run. I stand stock still for a second, watching her slight form in black leggings and a red T-shirt. I have the keenest sense of déjà vu. I've watched her run away like this before.

It was just after I moved out. I'd come to see Tom, to pick up something I'd left behind. I don't even remember what it was, it wasn't important, I just wanted to go to the house, to see him. I think it was a Sunday, and I'd moved out on the Friday, so I'd been gone about forty-eight hours. I stood in the street and watched her carrying things from a car into the house. She was moving in, two days after I'd left, my bed not yet cold. Talk about unseemly haste. She caught sight of me and I went towards her. I have no idea what I was going to say to her – nothing rational, I'm sure. I was crying, I remember that. And she, like now, ran away. I didn't know the worst of it then – she wasn't yet showing. Thankfully. I think it might have killed me.

Standing on the platform, waiting for the train, I feel dizzy. I sit down on the bench and tell myself it's just a hangover – nothing to drink for five days and then a binge, that'll do it. But I know it's more than that. It's Anna – the sight of her and the feeling I got when I saw her walking away like that. Fear.

ANNA

Saturday, 10 August 2013

Morning

I drove to the gym in Northcote for my spin class this morning, then dropped into the Matches store on the way back and treated myself to a very cute Max Mara mini dress (Tom will forgive me once he sees me in it). I was having a perfectly lovely morning, but as I parked the car there was some sort of commotion outside the Hipwells' place – photographers are there all the time now – and there she was. Again! I could hardly believe it. Rachel, barrelling past a photographer, looking rough. I'm pretty sure she'd just left Scott's house.

I didn't even get upset. I was just astounded. And when I brought it up with Tom – calmly, matter-of-factly – he was just as baffled as I was.

'I'll get in touch with her,' he said. 'I'll find out what's going on.'

'You've tried that,' I said, as gently as I could. 'It doesn't make any difference.' I suggested that maybe it was time to take legal advice, to look into getting a restraining order or something.

'She isn't actually harassing us, though, is she?' he said. 'The phone calls have stopped, she hasn't approached us, or come to the house. Don't worry about it, darling. I'll sort it.'

He's right, of course, about the harassment thing. But I don't care. There's something up, and I'm not prepared to just ignore it. I'm tired of being told not to worry. I'm tired of being told that he'll sort things out, that he'll talk to her, that eventually she'll go away. I think the time has come to take matters into my own hands. The next time I see her, I'm calling that police officer – the woman, Detective Sergeant Riley. She seemed nice, sympathetic. I know Tom feels sorry for Rachel, but honestly I think it's time I dealt with that bitch once and for all.

RACHEL

Monday, 12 August 2013

Morning

We're in the car park at Wilton Lake. We used to come here sometimes, to go swimming on really hot days. Today we're just sitting side by side in Tom's car, windows down, letting the warm breeze in. I want to lean my head back against the headrest and close my eyes and smell the pine and listen to the birds. I want to hold his hand and stay here all day.

He called me last night and asked if we could meet. I asked if this was about the thing with Anna, seeing her on Blenheim Road. I said it had nothing to do with them – I hadn't been there to bother them. He believed me, or at least he said he did, but he still sounded wary, a little anxious. He said he needed to talk to me.

'Please, Rach,' he said, and that was it – the way he said it, just like the old days, I thought my heart would burst. 'I'll come and pick you up, OK?'

I woke up before dawn and was in the kitchen making coffee at five. I washed my hair and shaved my legs and put on make-up and changed four times. And I felt guilty. Stupid, I know, but I thought about Scott – about what we did and how it felt – and I wished I hadn't done it, because it felt like a betrayal. Of Tom. The man who left me for another woman two years ago. I can't help how I feel.

Tom arrived just before nine. I went downstairs and there he was, leaning on his car, wearing jeans and an old grey T-shirt – old enough that I can remember exactly how the fabric felt against my cheek when I lay across his chest.

'I've got the morning off work,' he said when he saw me. 'I thought we could go for a drive.'

We didn't say much on the drive to the lake. He asked me how I was, and told me I looked well. He didn't mention Anna until we were sitting there in the car park and I was thinking about holding his hand.

'Yeah, um, Anna said she saw you ... and she thought you might have been coming from Scott Hipwell's house? Is that right?' He's turned to face me, but he isn't actually looking at me. He seems almost embarrassed to be asking me the question.

267

'You don't have to worry about it,' I tell him. 'I've been seeing Scott... I mean, not like that, not *seeing* him. We've become friendly. That's all. It's difficult to explain. I've just been helping him out a bit. You know – obviously you know – that he's been going through a terrible time.'

Tom nods, but he still doesn't look at me. Instead he chews on the nail of his left forefinger, a sure sign that he's worried.

'But Rach–'

I wish he'd stop calling me that, because it makes me feel light-headed, it makes me want to smile. It's been so long since I've heard him say my name like that, and it's making me hope. Maybe things aren't going so well with Anna, maybe he remembers some of the good things about us, maybe there's a part of him that misses me.

'I'm just... I'm really concerned about this.'

He looks up at me at last, his big brown eyes lock on mine and he moves his hand a little, as if he's going to take mine, but then he thinks better of it and stops. 'I know – well, I don't really know much about it, but Scott ... I know that he seems like a perfectly decent bloke, but you can't be sure, can you?'

'You think he did it?'

He shakes his head, swallows hard. 'No, no. I'm not saying that. I know... Well, Anna says that they argued a lot. That Megan sometimes seemed a little afraid of him.'

'Anna says?' My instinct is to dismiss anything that bitch says, but I can't get away from the feeling I had when I was at Scott's house on Saturday, that something was off, something was wrong.

268

He nods. 'Megan did some babysitting for us when Evie was tiny. Jesus, I don't even like to think about that now, after what's been in the papers lately. But it goes to show, doesn't it, that you think you know someone and then...' He sighs heavily. 'I don't want anything bad to happen. To you.' He smiles at me then, gives a little shrug. 'I still care about you, Rach,' he says, and I have to look away because I don't want him to see the tears in my eyes. He knows, of course, and he puts his hand on my shoulder and says, 'I'm so sorry.'

We sit for a while in comfortable silence. I bite down hard on my lip to stop myself from crying. I don't want to make this any harder for him, I really don't.

'I'm all right, Tom. I'm getting better. I am.'

'I'm really glad to hear that. You're not–'

'Drinking? Less. It's getting better.'

'That's good. You look well. You look … pretty.' He smiles at me and I can feel myself blush. He looks away quickly. 'Are you … um … are you all right, you know, financially?'

'I'm fine.'

'Really? Are you really, Rachel? Because I don't want you to–'

'I'm OK.'

'Will you take a little? Fuck, I don't want to sound like an idiot, but will you just take a little? To tide you over?'

'Honestly, I'm OK.'

He leans across then, and I can hardly breathe, I want to touch him so badly. I want to smell his neck, bury my face in that broad, muscular gap between his shoulder blades. He opens the glove box. 'Let me just write you a cheque, just in case, you know? You don't even have to cash it.'

I start laughing. 'You still keep a cheque book in the glove box?'

He starts laughing too. 'You never know,' he says.

'You never know when you're going to have to bail out your insane ex-wife?'

He rubs his thumb over my cheekbone. I raise my hand and take his in mine and kiss his palm.

'Promise me,' he says gruffly, 'you'll stay away from Scott Hipwell. Promise me, Rach.'

'I promise,' I say, and I mean it, and I can hardly see for joy, because I realize that he's not just worried about me, he's jealous.

Tuesday, 13 August 2013

Early morning

I'm on the train, looking out at a pile of clothes on the side of the tracks. Dark-blue cloth. A dress, I think, with a black belt. I can't imagine how it ended up down there. *That* certainly wasn't left behind by the engineers. We're moving, glacially though, so I have plenty of time to look, and it seems to me that I've seen that dress before, I've seen someone wearing it. I can't remember when. It's very cold. Too cold for a dress like that. I think it might snow soon.

I'm looking forward to seeing Tom's house – my house. I know that he'll be there, sitting out-side. I know he'll be alone, waiting for me. He'll stand up when we go past, he'll wave and smile. I know all this.

First, though, we stop in front of number fifteen. Jason and Jess are there, drinking wine on the terrace, which is odd, because it isn't yet eight thirty in the morning. Jess is wearing a dress with red flowers on it, she's wearing little silver earrings with birds on them – I can see them moving back and forth as she talks. Jason is standing behind her, his hands on her shoulders. I smile at them. I want to wave, but I don't want people to think I'm weird. I just watch, and I wish that I had a glass of wine too.

We've been here for ages and the train still isn't moving. I wish we'd get going, because if we don't Tom won't be there and I'll miss him. I can see Jess's face now, more clearly than usual – it's something to do with the light, which is very bright, shining directly on her like a spotlight. Jason is still behind her, but his hands aren't on her shoulders now, they're on her neck, and she looks uncomfortable, distressed. He's choking her. I can see her face turning red. She's crying. I get to my feet, I'm banging on the window and I'm screaming at him to stop, but he can't hear me. Someone grabs my arm – the guy with the red hair. He tells me to sit down, says that we're not far from the next stop.

'It'll be too late by then,' I tell him, and he says, 'It's already too late, Rachel,' and when I look back at the terrace, Jess is on her feet and Jason has a fistful of her blonde hair and he's going to smash her skull against the wall.

Morning

It's hours since I woke, but I'm still shaky, my legs trembling as I sit down in my seat. I woke from the dream with a sense of dread, a feeling that everything I thought I knew was wrong, that everything I'd seen – of Scott, of Megan – I'd made up in my head, that none of it was real. But if my mind is playing tricks, isn't it more likely to be the dream that's illusory? Those things Tom said to me in the car, all mixed up with guilt over what happened with Scott the other night: the dream was just my brain picking all that apart.

Still that familiar sense of dread grows when the train stops at the signal, and I'm almost too afraid to look up. The window is shut, there's nothing there. It's quiet, peaceful. Or it's abandoned. Megan's chair is still out on the terrace, empty. It's warm today, but I can't stop shivering.

I have to keep in mind that the things Tom said about Scott and Megan came from Anna, and no one knows better than I do that she can't be trusted.

Dr Abdic's welcome this morning seems a little half-hearted to me. He's almost stooped over, as though he's in pain, and when he shakes my hand his grip is weaker than before. I know that Scott said they wouldn't release any information about the pregnancy, but I wonder if they've told him. I wonder if he's thinking about Megan's child.

I want to tell him about the dream, but I can't think of a way to describe it without showing my hand, so instead I ask him about recovering memories, about hypnosis.

'Well,' he says, spreading his fingers out in front of him on the desk, 'there are therapists who believe that hypnosis can be used to recover repressed memories, but it's very controversial. I don't do it, nor do I recommend it to my patients. I'm not convinced that it helps, and in some instances I think it can be harmful.' He gives me a half-smile. 'I'm sorry. I know this isn't what you want to hear. But with the mind, I think, there are no quick fixes.'

'Do you know therapists who do this kind of thing?' I ask.

He shakes his head. 'I'm sorry, but I couldn't recommend one. You have to bear in mind that subjects under hypnosis are very suggestible. The memories which are "retrieved"' – he puts air quotes around the word – 'cannot always be trusted. They are not real memories at all.'

I can't risk it. I couldn't bear to have other images in my head, yet more memories that I can't trust, memories that merge and morph and shift, fooling me into believing that what is, is not, telling me to look one way when really I should be looking another way.

'So what do you suggest, then?' I ask him. 'Is there anything I can do, to try to recover what I've lost?'

He rubs his long fingers back and forth over his lips. 'It's possible, yes. Just talking about a particular memory can help you to clarify things, going over the details in a setting in which you feel safe and relaxed...'

'Like here, for example?'

273

He smiles. 'Like here, if indeed you do feel safe and relaxed here...' His voice rises, he's asking a question that I don't answer. The smile fades. 'Focusing on senses other than sight often helps. Sounds, the feel of things ... smell is particularly important when it comes to recall. Music can be powerful, too. If you are thinking of a particular circumstance, a particular day, you might consider retracing your steps, returning to the scene of the crime, as it were.' It's a common enough expression, but the hairs on the back of my neck are standing up, my scalp tingling. 'Do you want to talk about a particular incident, Rachel?'

I do, of course, but I can't tell him that, so I tell him about that time with the golf club, when I attacked Tom after we'd had a fight.

I remember waking that morning filled with anxiety, instantly knowing that something terrible had happened. Tom wasn't in bed with me, and I felt relieved. I lay on my back, playing it over. I remembered crying and crying and telling him that I loved him. He was angry, telling me to go to bed; he didn't want to listen to it any longer.

I tried to think back to earlier in the evening, to where the argument started. We were having such a good time. I'd done grilled prawns with lots of chilli and coriander, and we were drinking this delicious Chenin Blanc that he'd been given by a grateful client. We ate outside on the patio, listening to The Killers and Kings of Leon, albums we used to play when we first got together.

I remember us laughing and kissing. I remember telling him a story about something – he didn't find it as funny as I did. I remember feeling upset. Then I remember us shouting at each other, tripping through the sliding doors as I went inside, being furious that he didn't rush to help me up.

But here's the thing: 'When I got up that morning, I went downstairs. He wouldn't talk to me, barely even looked at me. I had to beg him to tell me what it was that I'd done. I kept telling him how sorry I was. I was desperately panicky. I can't explain why, I know it makes no sense, but if you can't remember what you've done, your mind just fills in all the blanks and you think the worst possible things...'

Kamal nods. 'I can imagine. Go on.'

'So eventually, just to get me to shut up, he told me. Oh, I'd taken offence at something he'd said, and then I'd kept at it, needling and bitching, and I wouldn't let it go, and he tried to get me to stop, he tried to kiss and make up, but I wouldn't have it. And then he decided to just leave me, to go upstairs to bed, and that's when it happened. I chased him up the stairs with a golf club in my hand and tried to take his head off. I'd missed, fortunately. I just took a chunk out of the plaster in the hall.'

Kamal's expression doesn't change. He isn't shocked. He just nods. 'So, you know what happened, but you can't quite feel it, is that right? You want to be able to remember it for yourself, to see it and experience it in your own memory, so that – how did you put it? – so that it *belongs* to you? And that way, you'll feel fully responsible?'

'Well,' I shrug. 'Yes. I mean, that's partly it. But there's something more. And it happened later, much later – weeks, maybe months afterwards. I kept thinking about that night. Every time I passed that hole in the wall I thought about it. Tom said he was going to patch it up, but he didn't, and I didn't want to pester him about it. One day I was standing there – it was evening and I was coming out of the bedroom and I just stopped, because I remembered. I was on the floor, my back to the wall, sobbing and sobbing, Tom standing over me, begging me to calm down, the golf club on the carpet next to my feet, and I felt it, I felt it. I was *terrified*. The memory doesn't fit with the reality, because I don't remember anger, raging fury. I remember fear.'

Evening

I've been thinking about what Kamal said, about returning to the scene of the crime, so instead of going home I've come to Witney, and instead of scurrying past the underpass, I walk slowly and deliberately right up to its mouth. I place my hands against the cold, rough brick at the entrance and close my eyes, running my fingers over it. Nothing comes. I open my eyes and look around. The road is very quiet: just one woman walking in my direction a few hundred yards off, no one else. No cars driving past, no children shouting, only a very faint siren in the distance. The sun slides behind a cloud and I feel cold, immobilized on the threshold of the tunnel, unable to go any further. I turn to leave.

The woman I saw walking towards me a moment ago is just turning the corner; she's wearing a deep-blue trench wrapped around her. She glances up at me as she passes and it's then that it comes to me. A woman ... blue ... the quality of the light. I remember: Anna. She was wearing a blue dress with a black belt, and was walking away from me, walking fast, almost like she did the other day, only this time she *did* look back, she looked over her shoulder and then she stopped. A car pulled up next to her on the pavement – a red car. Tom's car. She leaned down to speak to him through the window and then opened the door and got in, and the car drove away.

I remember that. On that Saturday night I stood here, at the entrance to the underpass, and watched Anna getting into Tom's car. Only I can't be remembering right, because that doesn't make sense. Tom came to look for me in the car. Anna wasn't in the car with him – she was at home. That's what the police told me. It doesn't make sense, and I could scream with the frustration of it, the not knowing, the uselessness of my own brain.

I cross the street and walk along the left-hand side of Blenheim Road. I stand under the trees for a while, opposite number twenty-three. They've repainted the front door. It was dark green when I lived there; it's black now. I don't remember noticing that before. I preferred the green. I wonder what else is different inside? The baby's room, obviously, but I wonder whether they still sleep in our bed, whether she puts on her lipstick in front of the mirror that I hung. I wonder if they've repainted the kitchen, or filled in that hole in the plasterwork in the corridor upstairs.

I want to cross over and thump the knocker against the black paint. I want to talk to Tom, to ask him about the night Megan went missing. I want to ask him about yesterday, when we were in the car and I kissed his hand, I want to ask him what he felt. Instead, I just stand there for a bit, looking up at my old bedroom window until I feel tears sting the back of my eyes, and I know it's time to go.

ANNA

Tuesday, 13 August 2013

Morning

I watched Tom getting ready for work this morning, putting on his shirt and tie. He seemed a little distracted, probably running through his schedule for the day – meetings, appointments, who, what, where. I felt jealous. For the first time ever, I actually envied him the luxury of getting dressed up and leaving the house and rushing around all day, with purpose, all in the service of a pay cheque.

It's not the work I miss – I was an estate agent, not a neurosurgeon, it's not exactly a job you dream about as a child – but I did like being able to wander around the really expensive houses when the owners weren't there, running my fingers over the marble worktops, sneaking a peek into the walk-in wardrobes. I used to imagine what my life would be like if I lived like that, the kind of person I would be. I'm well aware there is no job more important than that of raising a child, but the problem is that it isn't valued. Not in the sense that counts to me at the moment, which is financial. I want us to have more money so that we can leave this house, this road. It's as simple as that.

Perhaps not quite as simple as that. After Tom left for work, I sat down at the kitchen table to do battle with Evie over breakfast. Two months ago, I swear she'd eat anything. Now, if it's not strawberry yoghurt, she's not having it. I know this is normal. I keep telling myself this while I'm trying to get egg yolk out of my hair, while I'm crawling around on the floor picking up spoons and upturned bowls. I keep telling myself, this is normal.

Still, when we were finally done and she was playing happily by herself, I let myself cry for a minute. I allow myself these tears sparingly, only ever when Tom's not here, just a few moments to let it all out. It was when I was washing my face afterwards, when I saw how tired I looked, how blotchy and bedraggled and bloody awful, that I felt it again – that need to put on a dress and high heels, to blow-dry my hair and do my make-up and walk down the street and have men turn and look at me.

I miss work, but I also miss what work meant to me, in my last year of gainful employment, when I met Tom. I miss being a mistress.

I enjoyed it. I loved it, in fact. I never felt guilty. I pretended I did. I had to, with my married girlfriends, the ones who live in terror of the pert au pair or the pretty, funny girl in the office who can talk about football and spends half her life in the gym. I had to tell them that *of course* I felt terrible about it, of course I felt bad for his wife, I never meant for any of this to happen, we fell in love, what could we do?

The truth is, I never felt bad for Rachel, even before I found out about her drinking and how difficult she was, how she was making his life a misery. She just wasn't real to me, and anyway, I was enjoying myself too much. Being the other woman is a huge turn-on, there's no point denying it: you're the one he can't help but betray his wife for, even though he loves her. That's just how irresistible you are.

I was selling a house. Number thirty-four, Cranham Street. It was proving difficult to shift, because the latest interested buyer hadn't been granted a mortgage. Something about the lender's survey. So we arranged to get an independent surveyor in, just to make sure everything was OK. The sellers had already moved on, the house was empty, so I had to be there to let him in.

It was obvious from the moment I opened the door to him that it was going to happen. I'd never done anything like that before, never even dreamed of it, but there was something in the way he looked at me, the way he smiled at me. We couldn't help ourselves – we did it there in the kitchen, up against the counter. It was insane, but that's how we were. That's what he always used to say to me. *Don't expect me to be sane, Anna. Not with you.*

I pick Evie up and we go out into the garden together. She's pushing her little trolley up and down, giggling to herself as she does it, this morning's tantrum forgotten. Every time she grins at me I feel like my heart's going to explode. No matter how much I miss working, I would miss this more. And in any case, it's never going to happen. There's no way I'll be leaving her with a childminder again, no matter how qualified or vouched for they are. I'm not leaving her with anyone else ever again, not after Megan.

Evening

Tom texted me to say he was going to be a bit late this evening, he had to take a client out for a drink. Evie and I were getting ready for our evening walk. We were in the bedroom, Tom's and mine, and I was getting her changed. The light was just gorgeous, a rich orange glow filling the house, turning suddenly blue-grey when the sun went behind a cloud. I'd had the curtains pulled halfway across to stop the room getting too hot, so I went to open them and that's when I saw Rachel, standing on the opposite side of the road, looking at our house. Then she just took off, walking back towards the station.

I'm sitting on the bed and I'm shaking with fury, digging my nails into my palms. Evie's kicking her feet in the air and I'm so bloody angry I don't want to pick her up for fear I would crush her.

He told me he'd sorted this out. He told me that he phoned her on Sunday, they talked, she admitted that she had struck up some sort of friendship with Scott Hipwell, but that she didn't

281

intend seeing him any longer, that she wouldn't be hanging around any more. Tom said she promised him, and that he believed her. Tom said she was being reasonable, she didn't seem drunk, she wasn't hysterical, she didn't make threats or beg him to go back to her. He told me he thought she was getting better.

I take a few deep breaths and pull Evie up on to my lap, I lie her back against my legs and hold her hands with mine.

'I think I've had enough of this, don't you, sweetie?'

It's just so wearing: every time I think that things are getting better, that we're finally over the Rachel Issue, there she is again. Sometimes I feel like she's never, ever going to go away.

Deep inside me, a rotten seed has been planted. When Tom tells me it's OK, everything's all right, she's not going to bother us any longer, and then she does, I can't help wondering whether he's trying as hard as he can to get rid of her, or whether there's some part of him, deep down, that likes the fact that she can't let go.

I go downstairs and scrabble around in the kitchen drawer for the card that Detective Sergeant Riley left. I dial her number quickly, before I have time to change my mind.

Wednesday, 14 August 2013

Morning

In bed, his hands on my hips, his breath hot

against my neck, his skin slick with sweat against mine, he says, 'We don't do this enough any more.'

'I know.'

'We need to make more time for ourselves.'

'We do.'

'I miss you,' he says. 'I miss this. I want more of this.'

I roll over and kiss him on the lips, my eyes tight shut, trying to suppress the guilt I feel for going to the police behind his back. 'I think we should go somewhere,' he mumbles, 'just the two of us. Get away for a bit.'

And leave Evie with who, I want to ask. Your parents, whom you don't speak to? Or my mother, who is so frail she can barely care for herself?

I don't say that, I don't say anything, I just kiss him again, more deeply. His hand slips down to the back of my thigh and he grips it, hard.

'What do you think? Where would you like to go? Mauritius? Bali?'

I laugh.

'I'm serious,' he says, pulling back from me, looking me in the eye. 'We deserve it, Anna. You deserve it. It's been a hard year, hasn't it?'

'But...'

'But what?' He flashes his perfect smile at me. 'We'll figure something out with Evie, don't worry.'

'Tom, the money'

'We'll be OK.'

'But...' I don't want to say this, but I have to. 'We don't have enough money to even consider moving house, but we do have enough money for a holiday in Mauritius or Bali?'

He puffs out his cheeks, then exhales slowly, rolling away from me. I shouldn't have said it. The baby monitor crackles into life: Evie's waking up.

'I'll get her,' he says, and gets up and leaves the room.

At breakfast, Evie is doing her thing. It's a game to her now, refusing food, shaking her head, chin up, lips firmly closed, her little fists pushing at the bowl in front of her. Tom's patience wears thin quickly.

'I don't have time for this,' he says to me. 'You'll have to do it.' He gets to his feet, holding out the spoon for me to take, the expression on his face pained. I take a deep breath.

It's OK, he's tired, he has a lot of work on, he's pissed off because I didn't enter into his holiday fantasy this morning.

But it isn't OK, because I'm tired too, and I'd like to have a conversation about money and our situation here that doesn't end with him just walking out of the room. Of course, I don't say that. Instead, I break my promise to myself and I go ahead and mention Rachel.

'She's been hanging around again,' I say, 'so whatever you said to her the other day didn't do the trick.'

He gives me a sharp look. 'What do you mean, hanging around?'

'She was here last night, standing in the street right opposite the house.'

'Was she with someone?'

'No. She was alone. Why d'you ask that?'

'Fuck's sake,' he says, and his face darkens the way it does when he's really angry. 'I told her to

284

stay away. Why didn't you say anything last night?'

'I didn't want to upset you,' I say softly, already regretting bringing this up. 'I didn't want to worry you.'

'Jesus!' he says, and he dumps his coffee cup loudly in the sink. The noise gives Evie a fright and she starts to cry. This doesn't help. 'I don't know what to tell you, I honestly don't. When I spoke to her, she was fine. She listened to what I was saying and promised not to come around here any longer. She looked fine. She looked healthy, actually – back to normal...'

'She *looked* fine?' I ask him, and before he turns his back on me I can see in his face that he knows he's been caught. 'I thought you said you spoke to her on the phone?'

He takes a deep breath, sighs heavily, then turns back to me, his face a blank. 'Yeah, well, that's what I told you, darling, because I knew you'd get upset if I saw her. So I hold my hands up – I lied. Anything for an easy life.'

'Are you kidding me?'

He smiles at me, shaking his head as he steps towards me, his hands still raised in supplication. 'I'm sorry, I'm sorry. She wanted to chat in person and I thought it might be best. I'm sorry, OK? We just talked. We met in a crappy coffee shop in Ashbury and talked for twenty minutes – half an hour, tops. OK?'

He puts his arms around me and pulls me towards his chest. I try to resist him, but he's stronger than me and anyway he smells great and I don't want a fight. I want us to be on the same side. 'I'm sorry,' he mumbles again, into my hair.

'It's all right,' I say.

I let him get away with it, because I'm dealing with this now. I spoke to Detective Sergeant Riley yesterday evening, and I knew the moment we started talking that I'd done the right thing by calling her, because when I told her that I'd seen Rachel leaving Scott Hipwell's house 'on several occasions' (a slight exaggeration), she seemed very interested. She wanted to know dates and times (I could furnish her with two; I was vague about the other incidents), if they'd had a relationship prior to Megan Hipwell's disappearance, whether I thought they were in a sexual relationship now. I have to say the thought hadn't really crossed my mind – I can't imagine him going from Megan to Rachel. In any case, his wife's barely cold in the ground.

I went over the stuff about Evie as well – the attempted abduction – just in case she'd forgotten.

'She's very unstable,' I said. 'You might think I'm overreacting, but I can't take any risks where my family is concerned.'

'Not at all,' she said. 'Thank you very much for contacting me. If you see anything else that you consider suspicious, let me know.'

I've no idea what they'll do about her – perhaps just warn her off? It'll help, in any case, if we do start looking into things like restraining orders. Hopefully, for Tom's sake, it won't come to that.

After Tom leaves for work, I take Evie to the park, we play on the swings and the little wooden rocking horses, and when I put her back into her buggy she falls asleep almost immediately, which is my cue to go shopping. We cut through the back streets towards the big Sainsbury's. It's a bit of a roundabout way of getting there, but it's quiet, with very little traffic, and in any case we get to pass number thirty-four, Cranham Street.

It gives me a little frisson even now, walking past that house – butterflies suddenly swarm in my stomach, and a smile comes to my lips and colour to my cheeks. I remember hurrying up the front steps, hoping none of the neighbours would see me letting myself in, getting myself ready in the bathroom, putting on perfume, the kind of underwear you put on just to be taken off. Then I'd get a text message and he'd be at the door, and we'd have an hour or two in the bedroom upstairs.

He'd tell Rachel he was with a client, or meeting friends for a beer. 'Aren't you worried she'll check up on you?' I'd ask him, and he'd shake his head, dismissing the idea. 'I'm a good liar,' he told me once with a grin. Once, he said, 'Even if she did check, the thing with Rachel is, she won't remember what happened tomorrow anyway.' That's when I started to realize just how bad things were for him.

It wipes the smile off my face, though, thinking about those conversations. Thinking about Tom laughing conspiratorially, while he traced his fingers lower over my belly, smiling up at me, saying, 'I'm a good liar.' He *is* a good liar, a natural. I've seen him doing it: convincing check-in staff that we were honeymooners, for example, or talking his way out of extra hours at work by claiming a family emergency. Everyone does it, of course they do, only when Tom does it, you believe him.

I think about breakfast this morning – but the

point is that I caught him in the lie, and he admitted it straight away. I don't have anything to worry about. He isn't seeing Rachel behind my back! The idea is ridiculous. She might have been attractive once – she was quite striking when he met her, I've seen pictures: all huge dark eyes and generous curves – but now she's just run to fat. And in any case, he would never go back to her, not after everything she did to him, to us – all the harassment, all those late-night phone calls, hang-ups, text messages.

I'm standing in the tinned goods aisle, Evie still mercifully sleeping in the buggy and I start thinking about those phone calls, and about the time – or was it times? – when I woke up and the bathroom light was on. I could hear his voice, low and gentle, behind the closed door. He was calming her down, I know he was. He told me that sometimes she'd be so angry she'd threaten to come round to the house, go to his work, throw herself in front of a train. He might be a very good liar, but I know when he's telling the truth. He doesn't fool me.

Evening

Only, thinking about it, he *did* fool me, didn't he? When he told me that he'd spoken to Rachel on the phone, that she sounded fine, better, happy almost, I didn't doubt him for a moment. And when he came home on Monday night and I asked him about his day and he talked to me about a really tiresome meeting that morning, I

288

listened sympathetically, not once suspecting that there was no meeting, that all the while he was in a coffee shop in Ashbury with his ex-wife.

This is what I'm thinking about while I'm unloading the dishwasher, with great care and precision, because Evie is napping and the clatter of cutlery against crockery might wake her up. He *does* fool me. I know he's not always one hundred per cent honest about everything. I think about that story about his parents – how he invited them to the wedding but they refused to come because they were so angry with him for leaving Rachel. I always thought that was odd, because on the two occasions when I've spoken to his mum she sounded so pleased to be talking to me. She was kind, interested in me, in Evie.

'I do hope we'll be able to see her soon,' she said, but when I told Tom about it he dismissed it.

'She's trying to get me to invite them round,' he said, 'just so she can refuse. Power games.' She didn't sound like a woman playing power games to me, but I didn't press the point. The workings of other people's families are always so impenetrable. He'll have his reasons for keeping them at arm's length, I know he will, and they'll be centred on protecting me and Evie.

So why am I wondering now whether that was true? It's this house, this situation, all the things that have been going on here – they're making me doubt myself, doubt us. If I'm not careful they'll drive me crazy, and I'll end up like her. Like Rachel.

I'm just sitting here, waiting to take the sheets out of the tumble dryer. I think about turning on the television and seeing if there's an episode of *Friends* on that I haven't watched three hundred times, I think about doing my yoga stretches, and I think about the novel on my bedside table, which I've read twelve pages of in the past two weeks. I think about Tom's laptop, which is on the coffee table in the living room.

And then I do the things I never thought I would. I grab the bottle of red which we opened last night with dinner and I pour myself a glass. Then I fetch his laptop, power it up and start trying to guess the password.

I'm doing the things she did: drinking alone and snooping on him. The things she did and he hated. But recently – as recently as this morning – things have shifted. If he's going to lie, then I'm going to check up on him. That's a fair deal, isn't it? I feel I'm owed a bit of fairness. So I try to crack the password. I try names in different combinations: mine and his, his and Evie's, mine and Evie's, all three of us together, forwards and backwards. Our birthdays, in various combinations. Anniversaries: the first time we saw each other, the first time we had sex. Number thirty-four, for Cranham Street; number twenty-three – this house. I try to think outside the box – most men use football teams as passwords, I think, but Tom isn't into football; he quite likes cricket, so I try Boycott and Botham and Ashes. I don't know the names of any of the recent ones. I drain my glass and pour another half. I'm actually rather enjoying myself, trying to solve the puzzle. I think of bands he likes, films he enjoys, actresses he fancies. I type 'password'; I type '1234'.

There's an awful screeching outside as the London train stops at the signal, like nails on a chalkboard. I clench my teeth and take another long swig of wine, and as I do, I notice the time – Jesus, it's almost seven and Evie's still sleeping and he'll be home in a minute, and I'm literally thinking that he'll be home in a minute when I hear the rattle of the key in the door and my heart stops.

I snap the laptop shut and jump to my feet, knocking my chair over with a clatter. Evie wakes and starts to cry. I put the computer back on the table before he gets into the room, but he knows something's up and he just stares at me and says, 'What's going on?' I tell him, 'Nothing, nothing, I knocked over a chair by mistake.' He picks Evie up out of her pram to give her a cuddle and I catch sight of myself in the hallway mirror, my face pale and my lips stained dark red with wine.

RACHEL

Thursday, 15 August 2013

Morning

Cathy has got me a job interview. A friend of hers has set up her own public relations firm and she needs an assistant. It's basically a glorified secretarial job and it pays next to nothing, but I don't care. This woman is prepared to see me without references – Cathy's told her some story about me having a breakdown but being fully recovered now. The interview's tomorrow afternoon at this woman's home – she runs her business from one of those office sheds in the back garden – which just happens to be in Witney. So I was supposed to be spending the day polishing up my CV and my interviewing skills. I was – only Scott phoned me.

'I was hoping we could talk,' he said.

'We don't need... I mean, you don't need to say anything. It was ... we both know it was a mistake.'

'I know,' he said, and he sounded so sad, not like the angry Scott of my nightmares, more the broken one that sat on my bed and told me about his dead child. 'But I really want to talk to you.'

'Of course,' I said. 'Of course we can talk.'

'In person?'

'Oh,' I said. The last thing I wanted was to have to go back to that house. 'I'm sorry, I can't today.'

'Please, Rachel? It's important.' He sounded desperate and, despite myself, I felt bad for him. I was trying to think of an excuse when he said it again. 'Please?' So I said yes, and I regretted it the second the word came out of my mouth.

There's a story about Megan's child – her first dead child – in the newspapers. Well, it's about the child's father, actually. They tracked him down. His name's Craig McKenzie, and he died of a heroin overdose in Spain four years ago. So that rules him out. It never sounded to me like a likely motive in any case – if someone wanted to punish her for what she'd done back then, they'd have done it years ago.

So who does that leave? It leaves the usual suspects: the husband, the lover. Scott, Kamal. Or some random man who snatched her from the street – a serial killer just starting out? Will she be the first of a series, a Wilma McCann, a Pauline Reade? And who said, after all, that the killer had to be a man? She was a small woman, Megan Hipwell. Tiny, birdlike. It wouldn't take much force to take her down.

Afternoon

The first thing I notice when he opens the door is the smell. Sweat and beer, rank and sour, and under that something else, something worse. Something rotting. He's wearing tracksuit bottoms and a stained grey T-shirt, his hair is greasy, his skin slick, as though with fever.

'Are you all right?' I ask him, and he grins at me. He's been drinking.

'I'm fine, come in, come in.' I don't want to, but I do.

The curtains on the street side of the house are closed, and the living room is cast in a reddish hue which seems to suit the heat and the smell.

Scott wanders into the kitchen, opens the fridge and takes a beer out.

'Come and sit down,' he says. 'Have a drink.' The grin on his face is fixed, joyless, grim. There's something unkind about the set of his face. The contempt that I saw on Saturday morning, after we slept together, it's still there.

'I can't stay long,' I tell him. 'I have a job interview tomorrow, I need to prepare.'

'Really?' He raises his eyebrows. He sits down and kicks a chair out towards me. 'Sit down and have a drink,' he says, an order not an invitation. I sit down opposite him and he pushes the beer bottle towards me. I pick it up and take a sip. Outside, I can hear shrieking – children playing in a back garden somewhere – and beyond that, the faint and familiar rumble of the train.

'They got the DNA results yesterday,' Scott says to me. 'Detective Sergeant Riley came to see me last night.' He waits for me to say something, but I'm frightened of saying the wrong thing, so I stay silent. 'It's not mine. It wasn't mine. The funny thing is, it wasn't Kamal's either.' He laughs. 'So she'd someone else on the go. Can you believe it?' He's smiling that horrible smile. 'You didn't know anything about that, did you? About another bloke? She didn't *confide* in you about another man, did she?' The smile is slipping from his face and I'm getting a bad feeling about this, a very bad feeling. I get to my feet and take a step towards the door, but he's there in front of me, his hands gripping my arms, and he pushes me back into the chair.

'Sit the fuck down.' He grabs my handbag from my shoulder and throws it into the corner of the room.

'Scott, I don't know what's going on–'

'Come on!' he shouts, leaning over me. 'You and Megan were such good friends! You must have known about all her lovers!'

He knows. And as the thought comes to me, he must see it in my face because he leans in closer, his breath rancid in my face, and says, 'Come on, Rachel. Tell me.'

I shake my head and he swings a hand out, catching the beer bottle in front of me. It rolls off the table and smashes on the tiled floor.

'You never even fucking met her!' he yells. 'Everything you said to me – everything was a lie'

Ducking my head, I get to my feet, mumbling, 'I'm sorry, I'm sorry.' I'm trying to get round the table, to retrieve my handbag, my phone, but he grabs my arm again.

'Why did you do this?' he asks. 'What made you do this? What is wrong with you?'

He's looking at me, his eyes locked on mine, and I'm terrified of him, but at the same time I know that his question isn't unreasonable. I owe him an explanation. So I don't pull my arm away, I let his fingers dig into my flesh, and I try to speak clearly and calmly. I try not to cry. I try not to panic.

'I wanted you to know about Kamal,' I tell him. 'I saw them together, like I told you, but you wouldn't have taken me seriously if I'd just been some girl on the train. I needed–'

'You *needed!*' He lets go of me, turning away. 'You're telling me what you *needed...*' His voice is softer, he's calming down. I breathe deeply, trying to slow my heart.

'I wanted to help you,' I say. 'I knew that the police always suspect the husband, and I wanted you to know – to know there was someone else.'

'So you made up a story about knowing my wife? Do you have any idea how insane you sound?'

'I do.'

I walk over to the kitchen counter to pick up a

295

dishcloth, then get down on my hands and knees and clean up the spilled beer. Scott sits, elbows on knees, head hanging down. 'She wasn't who I thought she was,' he says. 'I have no idea who she was.'

I wring the cloth out over the sink and run cold water over my hands. My handbag is a couple of feet away, in the corner of the room. I make a move towards it, but Scott looks up at me, so I stop. I stand there, my back to the counter, my hands gripping the edge for stability. For comfort.

'Detective Sergeant Riley told me,' he says. 'She was asking me about you. Whether I was in a relationship with you.' He laughs. 'A *relationship* with you! Jesus. I asked her, have you seen what my wife looked like? Standards haven't fallen that fast.' My face is hot, there is cold sweat under my armpits and at the base of my spine. 'Apparently Anna's been complaining about you. She's seen you hanging around. So that's how it all came out. I said, we're not in a relationship, she's just an old friend of Megan's, she's helping me out...' He laughs again, low and mirthless. 'She said, she doesn't know Megan. She's just a sad little liar with no life.' The smile faded from his face. 'You're all liars. Every last one of you.'

My phone beeps. I take a step towards the bag, but Scott gets there before me.

'Hang on a minute,' he says, picking it up. 'We're not finished yet.' He tips the contents of my handbag on to the table: phone, purse, keys, lipstick, Tampax, credit-card receipts. 'I want to know exactly how much of what you told me was total bullshit.' Idly, he picks up the phone and looks at the screen. He raises his eyes to mine and they are suddenly cold. He reads aloud: "'This is to confirm your appointment with Dr Abdic at 4.30pm on Monday 19 August. If you are unable to make this appointment, please be advised that we require 24 hours' notice.'"

'Scott...'

'What the hell is going on?' he asks, his voice little more than a rasp. 'What have you been doing? What have you been saying to him?'

'I haven't been saying anything...' He's dropped the phone on the table and is coming towards me, his hands balled into fists. I'm backing away into the corner of the room, pressing myself between the wall and the glass door. 'I was trying to find out... I was trying to help.' He raises his hand and I cringe, ducking my head, waiting for the pain, and in that moment I know that I've done this before, felt this before, but I can't remember when and I don't have time to think about it now, because although he hasn't hit me, he's placed his hands on my shoulders and he's gripping them tightly, his thumbs digging into my clavicles, and it hurts so much I cry out.

'All this time,' he says through gritted teeth, 'all this time I thought you were on my side, but you were working against me. You were giving him information, weren't you? Telling him things about me, about Megs. It was you, trying to make the police come after me. It was you–'

'No. Please don't. It wasn't like that. I wanted to help you.' His right hand slides up, he grabs hold of my hair at the nape of my neck and he twists. 'Scott, please don't. Please. You're hurting me. Please.' He's dragging me now, towards the front door. I'm flooded with relief. He's going to throw me out into the street. Thank God.

Only he doesn't throw me out, he keeps dragging me, spitting and cursing. He's taking me upstairs and I'm trying to resist, but he's so strong, I can't. I'm crying, 'Please don't. Please,' and I know that something terrible is about to happen. I try to scream, but I can't, the noise won't come.

I'm blind with tears and terror. He shoves me into a room and slams the door behind me. The key twists in the lock. Hot bile rises to my throat and I throw up on to the carpet. I wait, I listen. Nothing happens, and no one comes.

I'm in the spare room. In my house, this room used to be Tom's study. Now it's their baby's nursery, the room with the soft pink blind. Here, it's a box room, filled with papers and files, a fold-up treadmill and an ancient Apple Mac. There is a box of papers lined with figures – accounts, perhaps from Scott's business – and another filled with old postcards – blank ones, with bits of Blutack on the back, as though they were once stuck on to a wall: the roofs of Paris, children skateboarding in an alley, old railway sleepers covered in moss, a view of the sea from inside a cave. I delve through the postcards – I don't know why or what I'm looking for, I'm just trying to keep panic at bay. I'm trying not to think about that news report, Megan's body being dragged out of the mud. I'm trying not to think of her injuries, of how frightened she must have been when she saw it coming.

I'm scrabbling around in the postcards and then

something bites me and I rock back on my heels with a yelp. The tip of my forefinger is sliced neatly across the top, and blood is dripping on to my jeans. I stop the blood with the hem of my T-shirt and sort more carefully through the cards. I spot the culprit immediately: a framed picture, smashed, with a piece of glass missing from the top, the exposed edge smeared with my blood.

It's not a photo I've seen before. It's a picture of Megan and Scott together, their faces close to the camera. She's laughing and he's looking at her adoringly. Jealously? The glass is shattered in a star radiating from the corner of Scott's eye, so it's difficult to read his expression. I sit there on the floor with the picture in front of me and think about how things get broken all the time by accident, and how sometimes you just don't get round to getting them fixed. I think about all the plates that were smashed when I fought with Tom, about that hole in the plaster in the corridor upstairs.

Somewhere on the other side of the locked door, I can hear Scott laughing and my entire body goes cold. I scrabble to my feet and go to the window, open it and lean right out, then with just the very tips of my toes on the floor, I cry out for help. I call out for Tom. It's hopeless. Pathetic. Even if he was, by some chance, out in the garden a few doors down, he wouldn't hear me, it's too far away. I look down and lose my balance, then pull myself back inside, bowels loosening, sobs catching in my throat.

'Please, Scott!' I call out. 'Please...' I hate the sound of my voice, the wheedling note, the desperation. I look down at my bloodstained T-shirt and I'm reminded that I am not without options. I pick up the photo frame and tip it over on to the carpet. I select the longest of the glass shards and slip it carefully into my back pocket.

I can hear footsteps coming up the stairs. I back myself up against the wall opposite the door. The key turns in the lock. Scott has my handbag in one hand and tosses it at my feet. In the other hand he is holding a scrap of paper. 'Well, if it isn't Nancy Drew!' he says with a smile. He puts on a girly voice and reads aloud: *Megan has run off with her boyfriend, who from here on in, I shall refer to as B.* He snickers. '*B has harmed her... Scott has harmed her...*' He crumples up the paper and throws it at my feet. 'Jesus Christ. You really are pathetic, aren't you?' He looks around, taking in the puke on the floor, the blood on my T-shirt. 'Fucking hell, what have you been doing? Trying to top yourself? Going to do my job for me?' He laughs again. 'I should break your fucking neck, but you know what, you're just not worth the hassle.' He stands to one side. 'Get out of my house.'

I grab my bag and make for the door, but just as I do, he steps out in front of me with a boxer's feint, and for a moment I think he's going to stop me, put his hands on me again. There must be terror in my eyes because he starts to laugh, he roars with laughter. I can still hear him when I slam the front door behind me.

Friday, 16 August 2013

Morning

I've barely slept. I drank a bottle and a half of wine in an attempt to get off to sleep, to stop my hands shaking, to quieten my startle reflex, but it didn't really work. Every time I started to drop off, I'd jolt awake. I felt sure I could feel him in the room with me. I turned the light on and sat there, listening to the sounds of the street outside, to people moving around in the building. It was only when it started to get light that I relaxed enough to sleep. I dreamed I was in the woods again. Tom was with me but still I felt afraid.

I left Tom a note last night. After I left Scott's, I ran down to number twenty-three and banged on the door. I was in such a panic I didn't even care whether Anna was there, whether she'd be pissed off with me for showing up. No one came to the door, so I scribbled a note on a scrap of paper and shoved it through the letter box. I don't care if she sees it – I think a part of me actually wants her to see it. I kept the note vague – I told him we needed to talk about the other day. I didn't mention Scott by name, because I didn't want Tom to go round there and confront him – God knows what might happen.

I rang the police almost as soon as I got home. I had a couple of glasses of wine first, to calm me down. I asked to speak to Detective Inspector Gaskill, but they said he wasn't available, so I ended up talking to Riley. It wasn't what I wanted – I know Gaskill would have been kinder.

'He imprisoned me in his home,' I told her. 'He threatened me.' She asked how long I was 'imprisoned' for. I could hear the air quotes over the line.

'I don't know,' I said. 'Half an hour, maybe.'

There was a long silence.

'And he threatened you. Can you tell me the exact nature of the threat?'

'He said he'd break my neck. He said ... he said he ought to break my neck...'

'He ought to break your neck?'

'He said that he would if he could be bothered.'

Silence. Then, 'Did he hit you? Did he injure you in any way?'

'Bruising. Just bruising.'

'He hit you?'

'No, he grabbed me.'

More silence.

Then: 'Ms Watson, why were you in Scott Hipwell's house?'

'He asked me to go to see him. He said he needed to talk to me.'

She gave a long sigh. 'You were warned to stay out of this. You've been lying to him, telling him you were a friend of his wife's, you've been telling all sorts of stories and – let me finish – this is a person who, at best, is under a great deal of strain and is extremely distressed. At best. At worst, he might be dangerous.'

'He *is* dangerous, that's what I'm telling you, for God's sake.'

'This is not helpful – you going round there, lying to him, provoking him. We're in the middle of a murder investigation here. You need to understand that. You could jeopardize our progress, you could–'

'What progress?' I snapped. 'You haven't made any bloody progress. He killed his wife, I'm telling you. There's a picture, a photograph of the two of them – it's smashed. He's angry, he's unstable–'

'Yes, we saw the photograph. The house has been searched. It's hardly evidence of murder.'

'So you're not going to arrest him?'

She gave a long sigh. 'Come to the station tomorrow. Make a statement. We'll take it from there. And Ms Watson? Stay away from Scott Hipwell.'

Cathy came home and found me drinking. She wasn't happy. What could I tell her? There was no way to explain it. I just said I was sorry and went upstairs to my room, like a teenager in a sulk. And then I lay awake, trying to sleep, waiting for Tom to call. He didn't.

I wake early, check my phone (no calls), wash my hair and dress for my interview, hands trembling, stomach in knots. I'm leaving early because I have to stop off at the police station first, to give them my statement. Not that I'm expecting it to do any good. They never took me seriously and they certainly aren't going to start now. I wonder what it would take for them to see me as anything other than a fantasist.

On the way to the station I can't stop looking over my shoulder; the sudden scream of a police siren has me literally leaping into the air in fright. On the station platform I walk as close to the railings as I can, my fingers trailing against the iron fence, just in case I need to hold on tight. I realize it's ridiculous, but I feel so horribly vulnerable now that I've seen what he is; now that there are no secrets between us.

Afternoon

The matter should be closed for me now. All this time, I've been thinking that there was something to remember, something I was missing. But there isn't. I didn't see anything important or do anything terrible. I just happened to be on the same street. I know this now, courtesy of the red-haired man. And yet there's an itch at the back of my brain that I just can't scratch.

Neither Gaskill nor Riley was at the police station; I gave my statement to a bored-looking uniformed officer. It will be filed and forgotten about, I assume, unless I turn up dead in a ditch somewhere. My interview was on the opposite side of town to where Scott lives, but I took a taxi from the police station. I'm not taking any chances. It went as well as it could: the job itself is utterly beneath me, but then *I* seem to have become beneath me over the past year or two. I need to reset the scale. The big drawback (other than the crappy pay and the lowliness of the job itself) will be having to come to Witney all the time, to walk these streets and risk running into Scott or Anna and her child.

Because bumping into people is all I seem to do in this neck of the woods. It's one of the things I used to like about the place: the village-on-the-

304

edge-of-London feel. You might not know everyone, but faces are familiar.

I'm almost at the station, just passing the Crown when I feel a hand on my arm and I wheel around, slipping off the pavement and into the road.

'Hey, hey, I'm sorry. I'm sorry.' It's him again, the red-haired man, pint in one hand, the other raised in supplication. 'You're jumpy, aren't you?' he grins. I must look really frightened, because the grin fades. 'Are you all right? I didn't mean to scare you...'

He's knocked off early, he says, and invites me to have a drink with him. I say no, and then I change my mind.

'I owe you an apology,' I say, when he – Andy, as it turns out – brings me my gin and tonic, 'for the way I behaved on the train. Last time, I mean. I was having a bad day.'

'S'all right,' Andy says. His smile is slow and lazy, I don't think this is his first pint. We're sitting opposite each other in the beer garden at the back of the pub; it feels safer here than on the street side. Perhaps it's the safe feeling that emboldens me. I take my chance.

'I wanted to ask you about what happened,' I say. 'The night that I met you. The night that Meg– The night that woman disappeared.'

'Oh. Right. Why? What d'you mean?'

I take a deep breath. I can feel my face reddening. No matter how many times you have to admit this, it's always embarrassing, it always makes you cringe. 'I was very drunk and I don't remember. There are some things I need to sort out. I just want to know if you saw anything, if

305

you saw me talking to anyone else, anything like that...' I'm staring down at the table, I can't meet his eye.

He nudges my foot with his. 'It's all right, you didn't do anything bad.' I look up and he's smiling. 'I was pissed, too. We had a bit of a chat on the train, I can't remember what about. Then we both got off here, at Witney, and you were a bit unsteady on your feet. You slipped on the steps. You remember? I helped you up and you were all embarrassed, blushing like you are now.' He laughs. 'We walked out together, and I asked you if you wanted to go to the pub. But you said you had to go and meet your husband.'

'That's it?'

'No. Do you really not remember? It was a while later – I don't know, half an hour, maybe? I'd been to the Crown, but a mate rang and said he was drinking in a bar over on the other side of the railway track, so I was heading down to the underpass. You'd fallen over. You were in a bit of a mess then. You'd cut yourself. I was a bit worried, I said I'd see you home if you wanted, but you wouldn't hear of it. You were ... well, you were very upset. I think there'd been a row with your bloke. He was heading off down the street, and I said I'd go after him if you wanted me to, but you said not to. He drove off somewhere after that. He was ... er ... he was with someone.'

'A woman?'

He nods, ducks his head a bit. 'Yeah, they got into a car together. I assumed that was what the argument was about.'

'And then?'

'Then you walked off. You seemed a little ... confused or something, and you walked off. You kept saying you didn't need any help. As I said, I was a bit wasted myself, so I just left it. I went down through the underpass and met my mate in the pub. That was it.'

Climbing the stairs to the apartment, I feel sure that I can see shadows above me, hear footsteps ahead. Someone waiting on the landing above. There's no one there, of course, and the flat is empty, too: it feels untouched, it smells empty, but that doesn't stop me checking every room – under my bed and under Cathy's, in the wardrobes and the closet in the kitchen that couldn't conceal a child.

Finally, after about three tours of the flat, I can stop. I go upstairs and sit on the bed and think about the conversation I had with Andy, the fact that it tallies with what I remember. There is no great revelation: Tom and I argued in the street, I slipped and hurt myself, he stormed off and got into his car with Anna. Later he came back looking for me, but I'd already gone. I got into a taxi, I assume, or back on to the train.

I sit on my bed looking out of the window and wonder why I don't feel better. Perhaps it's simply because I still don't have any answers. Perhaps it's because although what I remember tallies with what other people remember, something still feels off. Then it strikes me: Anna. It's not just that Tom never mentioned going anywhere in the car with her, it's the fact that when I saw her, walking away, getting into the car, she wasn't carrying the baby. Where was Evie while all this was going on?

Saturday, 17 August 2013

Evening

I need to speak to Tom, to get things straight in my head, because the more I go over it, the less sense it makes, and I can't stop going over it. I'm worried, in any case, because it's two days since I left him that note and he hasn't got back to me. He didn't answer his phone last night, he's not been answering it all day. Something's not right, and I can't shake the feeling that it has to do with Anna.

I know that he'll want to talk to me, too, after he hears about what happened with Scott. I know that he'll want to help. I can't stop thinking about the way he was that day in the car, about how things felt between us. So I pick up the phone and dial his number, butterflies in my stomach, just the way it always used to be, the anticipation of hearing his voice as acute now as it was years ago.

'Yeah?'

'Tom, it's me.'

'Yes.'

Anna must be there with him, he doesn't want to say my name. I wait for a moment, to give him time to move to another room, to get away from her. I hear him sigh. 'What is it?'

'Um, I wanted to talk to you... As I said in my note, I–'

'What?' He sounds irritated.

'I left you a note a couple of days ago. I thought we should talk...'

'I didn't get a note.' Another heavier sigh. 'Fuck's sake. That's why she's pissed off with me.' Anna must have taken it, she didn't give it him. 'What do you need?'

I want to hang up, dial again, start over. Tell him how good it was to see him on Monday, when we went to the lake.

'I just wanted to ask you something.'

'What?' he snaps. He sounds really annoyed.

'Is everything OK?'

'What do you want, Rachel?' It's gone, all the tenderness that was there a week ago. I curse myself for leaving that note, I've obviously got him into trouble at home.

'I wanted to ask you about that night – the night Megan Hipwell went missing.'

'Oh, Jesus. We've talked about this – you can't have forgotten already.'

'I just–'

'You were drunk,' he says, his voice loud, harsh. 'I told you to go home. You wouldn't listen. You wandered off. I drove around looking for you, but I couldn't find you.'

'Where was Anna?'

'She was at home'

'With the baby?'

'With Evie, yes.'

'She wasn't in the car with you?'

'No.'

'But–'

'Oh for God's sake. She was supposed to be going out, I was going to babysit. Then you came along, so she came and cancelled her plans. And I wasted yet more hours of my life running around after you.'

I wish I hadn't called. To have my hopes raised and dashed again, it's like cold steel twisting in my gut.

'OK,' I say. 'It's just, I remember it differently... Tom, when you saw me, was I hurt? Was I... Did I have a cut on my head?'

Another heavy sigh. 'I'm surprised you remember anything at all, Rachel. You were blind drunk. Filthy, stinking drunk. Staggering all over the place.' My throat starts to close up, hearing him say these words. I've heard him say these sorts of things before, in the bad old days, the very worst days, when he was tired of me, sick of me, disgusted by me. Wearily, he goes on. 'You'd fallen over in the street, you were crying, you were a total mess. Why is this important?' I can't find the words right away, I take too long to answer. He goes on: 'Look, I have to go. Don't call any more, please. We've been through this. How many times do I have to ask you? Don't call, don't leave notes, don't come here. It upsets Anna. All right?'

The phone goes dead.

Sunday, 18 August 2013

Early morning

I've been downstairs in the living room all night, with the television on for company, fear ebbing and flowing. Strength ebbing and flowing. It feels a bit like I've gone back in time, the wound he made years ago ripped open again, new and

310

fresh. It's silly, I know. I was an idiot to think that I had a chance with him again, just on the basis of one conversation, a few moments which I took for tenderness and which were probably nothing more than sentimentality and guilt. Still, it hurts. And I've just got to let myself feel the pain, because if I don't, if I keep numbing it, it'll never really go away.

And I was an idiot to let myself think that there was a connection between me and Scott, that I could help him. So, I'm an idiot. I'm used to that. I don't have to continue to be one, do I? Not any longer. I lay here all night and I promised myself that I'll get a handle on things. I'll move away from here, far away. I'll get a new job. I'll go back to my maiden name, sever ties with Tom, make it harder for anyone to find me. Should anyone come looking.

I haven't had much sleep. Lying here on the sofa, making plans, every time I started drifting off to sleep I heard Tom's voice in my head, as clear as if he were right there, right next to me, his lips against my ear – *You were blind drunk. Filthy, stinking drunk* – and I jolted awake, shame washing over me like a wave. Shame, but also the strongest sense of déjà vu, because I've heard those words before, those exact words.

And then I couldn't stop running the scenes through my head: waking with blood on the pillow, the inside of my mouth hurting, as though I'd bitten my cheek, fingernails dirty, terrible head, Tom coming out of the bathroom, that expression he wore – half hurt, half angry – dread rising in me like floodwater.

311

'What happened?'

Tom, showing me the bruises on his arm, on his chest, where I'd hit him.

'I don't believe it, Tom. I'd never hit you. I've never hit anyone in my life.'

'You were blind drunk, Rachel. Do you remember anything you did last night? Anything you said?' And then he'd tell me, and I still couldn't believe it, because nothing he said sounded like me, none of it. And the thing with the golf club, that hole in the plaster, grey and blank like a blinded eye trained on me every time I passed it, and I couldn't reconcile the violence that he talked about with the fear that I remembered.

Or thought that I remembered. After a while I learned not to ask what I had done, or to argue when he volunteered the information, because I didn't want to know the details, I didn't want to hear the worst of it, the things I said and did when I was like that, filthy, stinking drunk. Sometimes he threatened to record me, he told me he'd play it back for me. He never did. Small mercies.

After a while, I learned that when you wake up like that, you don't ask what happened, you just say that you're sorry: you're sorry for what you did and who you are and you're never, ever going to behave like that again.

And now I'm not, I'm really not. I can be thankful to Scott for this: I'm too afraid, now, to go out in the middle of the night to buy booze. I'm too afraid to let myself slip, because that's when I make myself vulnerable.

I'm going to have to be strong, that's all there is to it.

My eyelids start to feel heavy again and my head nods against my chest. I turn the TV down so there's almost no sound at all, roll over so that I'm facing the sofa back, snuggle down and pull the duvet over me, and I'm drifting off, I can feel it, I'm going to sleep, and then – bang, the ground is rushing up at me and I jerk upright, my heart in my throat. I saw it. I saw it.

I was in the underpass and he was coming towards me, one slap across the mouth and then his fist raised, keys in his hand, searing pain as the serrated metal smashed down against my skull.

ANNA

Saturday, 17 August 2013

Evening

I hate myself for crying, it's so pathetic. But I feel exhausted, these past few weeks have been so hard on me. And Tom and I have had another row about – inevitably – Rachel.

It's been brewing I suppose. I've been torturing myself about the note, about the fact that he lied to me about them meeting up. I keep telling myself it's completely stupid, but I can't fight the feeling that there is something going on between them. I've been going round and round: after everything she did to him – to us – how could he? How could he even contemplate being with her

313

again? I mean, if you look at the two of us, side by side, there isn't a man on earth who would pick her over me. And that's without even going into all her issues.

But then I think, this happens sometimes, doesn't it? People you have a history with, they won't let you go, and as hard as you might try, you can't disentangle yourself, can't set yourself free. Maybe after a while you just stop trying.

She came by on Thursday, banging on the door and calling out for Tom. I was furious, but I didn't dare open up. Having a child with you makes you vulnerable, it makes you weak. If I'd been on my own I would have confronted her, I'd have had no problems sorting her out. But with Evie here, I just couldn't risk it. I've no idea what she might do.

I know why she came. She was pissed off that I'd talked to the police about her. I bet she came crying to Tom to tell me to leave her alone. She left a note – 'We need to talk, please call me as soon as possible, it's *important*' ('important' underlined three times) – which I threw straight into the bin. Later, I fished it out and put it in my bedside drawer, along with the printout of that vicious email she sent and the log I've been keeping of all the calls and all the sightings. The harassment log. My evidence, should I need it. I called Detective Sergeant Riley and left a message saying that Rachel had been round again. She still hasn't rung back.

I should have mentioned the note to Tom, I know I should have, but I didn't want him to get annoyed with me about talking to the police, so I just shoved it in that drawer and hoped that she'd forget about it. She didn't, of course. She rang him tonight. He was fuming when he got off the phone with her.

'What the fuck is all this about a note?' he snapped.

I told him I'd thrown it away. 'I didn't realize that you'd want to read it,' I said. 'I thought you wanted her out of our lives as much as I do.'

He rolled his eyes. 'That's not the point and you know it. Of course I want Rachel gone. What I don't want is for you to start listening to my phone calls and throwing away my mail. You're...' he sighed.

'I'm what?'

'Nothing. It's just – it's the sort of thing *she* used to do.'

It was a punch in the gut, a low blow. Ridiculously, I burst into tears and ran upstairs to the bathroom. I waited for him to come up to soothe me, to kiss and make up like he usually does, but after about half an hour he called out to me, 'I'm going to the gym for a couple of hours,' and before I could reply I heard the front door slam.

And now I find myself behaving exactly like she used to: polishing off the half-bottle of red left over from dinner last night and snooping around on his computer. It's easier to understand her behaviour when you feel like I feel right now. There's nothing so painful, so corrosive, as suspicion.

I cracked the laptop password eventually: it's Blenheim. As innocuous and boring as that – the name of the road we live on. I've found no incriminating emails, no sordid pictures or passionate letters. I spend half an hour reading through work

315

emails so mind-numbing that they dull even the pain of jealousy, then I shut down the laptop and put it away. I'm feeling really quite jolly, thanks to the wine and the tedious contents of Tom's computer. I've reassured myself I was just being silly.

I go upstairs to brush my teeth – I don't want him to know that I've been at the wine again – and then I decide that I'll strip the bed and put on fresh sheets, I'll spray a bit of Acqua di Parma on the pillows and put on that black silk teddy he got me for my birthday last year, and when he comes back, I'll make it up to him.

As I'm pulling the sheets off the bed I almost trip over a black bag shoved under the bed: his gym bag. He's forgotten his gym bag. He's been gone an hour, and he hasn't been back for it. My stomach flips. Maybe he just thought, sod it, and decided to go to the pub instead. Maybe he has some spare stuff in his locker at the gym. Maybe he's in bed with her right now.

I feel sick. I get down on my knees and rummage through the bag. All his stuff is there, washed and ready to go, his iPod Shuffle, the only trainers he runs in. And something else: a mobile phone. A phone I've never seen before.

I sit down on the bed, the phone in my hand, my heart hammering. I'm going to turn it on, there's no way I'll be able to resist, and yet I'm sure that when I do, I'll regret it, because this can only mean something bad. You don't keep spare mobile phones tucked away in gym bags unless you're hiding something. There's a voice in my head saying, *just put it back, just forget about it*, but I can't. I press my finger down hard on the power

316

button and wait for the screen to light up. And wait. And wait. It's dead. Relief floods my system like morphine.

I'm relieved because now I can't know, but I'm also relieved because a dead phone suggests an unused phone, an unwanted phone, not the phone of a man involved in a passionate affair. That man would want his phone on him at all times. Perhaps it's an old one of his, perhaps it's been in his gym bag for months and he just hasn't got around to throwing it away. Perhaps it isn't even his: maybe he found it at the gym and meant to hand it in at the desk and he forgot?

I leave the bed half-stripped and go downstairs to the living room. The coffee table has a couple of drawers underneath it filled with the kind of domestic junk which accumulates over time: rolls of Sellotape, plug adaptors for foreign travel, tape measures, sewing kits, old mobile-phone chargers. I grab all three of the chargers; the second one I try fits. I plug it in on my side of the bed, phone and charger hidden behind the bedside table. Then I wait.

Times and dates, mostly. Not dates. Days. *Monday at 3? Friday, 4.30.* Sometimes, a refusal. *Can't tomorrow. Not Weds.* There's nothing else: no declarations of love, no explicit suggestions. Just text messages, about a dozen of them, all from a withheld number. There are no contacts in the phone book and the call log has been erased.

I don't need dates, because the phone records them. The meetings go back months. They go back almost a year. When I realized this, when I saw that the first one was from September last year, a hard

317

lump formed in my throat. September! Evie was six months old. I was still fat, exhausted, raw, off sex. But then I start to laugh, because this is just ridiculous, it can't be true. We were blissfully happy in September, in love with each other and with our new baby. There is no way he was sneaking around with her, no way in hell that he's been seeing her all this time. I would have known. It can't be true. The phone isn't his.

Still. I get my harassment log from the bedside table and look at the calls, comparing them with the meetings arranged on the phone. Some of them coincide. Some calls are a day or two before, some a day or two after. Some don't correlate at all.

Could he really have been seeing her all this time, telling me that she was hassling him, harassing him, when in reality they were making plans to meet up, to sneak around behind my back? But why would she be calling him on the landline if she had this phone to call? It doesn't make sense. Unless she *wanted* me to know. Unless she was trying to provoke trouble between us?

Tom has been gone almost two hours now, he'll be back soon from wherever he's been. I make the bed, put the log and the phone back in the bedside table, go downstairs, pour myself one final glass of wine and drink it quickly. I could call her. I could confront her. But what would I say? There's no moral high ground for me to take. And I'm not sure I could bear it, the delight she would take in telling me that all this time, *I've* been the fool. If he does it with you, he'll do it to you.

I hear footsteps on the pavement outside and I

318

know it's him, I know his gait. I shove the wine glass into the sink and I stand there, leaning against the kitchen counter, the blood pounding in my ears.

'Hello,' he says when he sees me. He looks sheepish, he's weaving just a little.

'They serve beer at the gym now, do they?'

He grins. 'I forgot my stuff. I went to the pub.'

Just as I thought. Or just as he thought I would think?

He comes a little closer. 'What have you been up to?' he asks me, a smile on his lips. 'You look guilty.' He slips his arms around my waist and pulls me close. I can smell the beer on his breath. 'Have you been up to no good?'

'Tom...'

'Shhh,' he says and he kisses my mouth, starts unbuttoning my jeans. He turns me around. I don't want to, but I don't know how to say no, so I close my eyes and try not to think of him with her, I try to think of the early days, running round to the empty house on Cranham Street, breathless, desperate, hungry.

Sunday, 18 August 2013

Early morning

I wake with a fright; it's still dark. I think I can hear Evie crying, but when I go through to check on her, she's sleeping deeply, her blanket clutched tightly between closed fists. I go back to bed, but I can't fall asleep again. All I can think about is the

319

phone in the bedside drawer. I glance over at Tom, lying with his left arm flung out, his head thrown back. I can tell from the cadence of his breathing that he's far from consciousness. I slip out of bed, open the drawer and take out the phone.

Downstairs in the kitchen, I turn the phone over and over in my hand, preparing myself. I want to know, but I don't. I want to be sure, but I want so desperately to be wrong. I turn it on. I press 'one' and hold it, I hear the voicemail welcome. I hear that I have no new messages and no saved messages. Would I like to change my greeting? I end the call, but am suddenly gripped by the completely irrational fear that the phone could ring, that Tom would hear it from upstairs, so I slide the French doors open and step outside.

The grass is damp beneath my feet, the air cool, heavy with the scent of rain and roses. I can hear a train in the distance, a slow growl, it's a long way off. I walk almost as far as the fence before I dial the voicemail again: would I like to change my greeting? Yes, I would. There's a beep and a pause and then I hear her voice. Her voice, not his. *Hi, it's me, leave a message.*

My heart has stopped beating.

It's not his phone, it's hers.

I play it again.

Hi, it's me, leave a message.

It's *her* voice.

I can't move, can't breathe. I play it again, and again. My throat is closed, I feel as though I'm going to faint, and then the light comes on upstairs.

RACHEL

Early morning

One piece of the memory led to the next. It's as though I'd been blundering about in the dark for days, weeks, months, then finally caught hold of something. Like running my hand along a wall to find my way from one room to the next. Shifting shadows started at last to coalesce and after a while my eyes became accustomed to the gloom, and I could see.

Not at first. At first, although it felt like a memory, I thought it must be a dream. I sat there, on the sofa, almost paralysed with shock, telling myself that it wouldn't be the first time I'd mis-remembered something, wouldn't be the first time that I'd thought things went a certain way when in fact they had played out differently.

Like that time we went to a party thrown by a colleague of Tom's, and I was very drunk, but we'd had a good night. I remember kissing Clara goodbye. Clara was the colleague's wife, a lovely woman, warm and kind. I remember her saying that we should get together again; I remember her holding my hand in hers.

I remembered that so clearly, but it wasn't true. I knew it wasn't true the next morning when Tom

321

turned his back on me when I tried to speak to him. I know it isn't true because he told me how disappointed and embarrassed he was, that I'd accused Clara of flirting with him, that I'd been hysterical and abusive.

When I closed my eyes I could feel her hand, warm against my skin, but that didn't actually happen. What really happened is that Tom had to half-carry me out of the house, me crying and shouting all the way, while poor Clara cowered in the kitchen.

So when I closed my eyes, when I drifted into a half-dream and found myself in that underpass, I may have been able to feel the cold and smell the rank, stale air, I may have been able to see a figure walking towards me, spitting rage, fist raised, but it wasn't true. The terror I felt wasn't real. And when the shadow struck, leaving me there on the ground, crying and bleeding, that wasn't real either.

Only it was, and I saw it. It's so shocking that I can scarcely believe it, but as I watch the sun rise it feels like mist lifting. What he told me was a lie. I didn't imagine him hitting me. I remember it. Just like I remember saying goodbye to Clara after that party and her hand holding mine. Just like I remember the fear when I found myself on the floor next to that golf club – and I know now, I know for sure that I wasn't the one swinging it.

I don't know what to do. I run upstairs, pull on a pair of jeans and some trainers, run back downstairs. I dial their number, the landline, and let it ring a couple of times, then I hang up. I don't know what to do. I make coffee, let it go cold, dial

Detective Sergeant Riley's number then hang up straight away. She won't believe me. I know she won't.

I head out to the station. It's a Sunday service, the first train isn't for half an hour, so there's nothing to do but sit there on a bench, going round and round, from disbelief to desperation and back again.

Everything is a lie. I didn't imagine him hitting me. I didn't imagine him walking away from me quickly, his fists clenched. I saw him turn, shout. I saw him walking down the road with a woman, I saw him getting into the car with her. I didn't imagine it. And I realize then that it's all very simple, so very simple. I *do* remember, it's just that I had confused two memories. I'd inserted the image of Anna, walking away from me in her blue dress, into another scenario: Tom and a woman getting into a car. Because of course that woman wasn't wearing a blue dress, she was wearing jeans and a red T-shirt. She was Megan.

ANNA

Sunday, 18 August 2013

Early morning

I hurl the phone over the fence, as far as I can; it lands somewhere on the edge of the scree at the top of the embankment. I think I can hear it rolling down towards the track. I think I can still hear her voice. *Hi. It's me. Leave a message.* I think I might be hearing her voice for a long time to come.

He's at the bottom of the stairs by the time I get back to the house. He's watching me, blinking, bleary-eyed, struggling out of sleep.

'What's going on?'

'Nothing,' I say, but I can hear the tremor in my voice.

'What were you doing outside?'

'I thought I heard someone,' I tell him. 'Something woke me. I couldn't get back to sleep.'

'The phone rang,' he says, rubbing his eyes.

I clasp my hands together to stop them shaking. 'What? What phone?'

'The phone.' He's looking at me as though I'm insane. 'The phone rang. Someone called and hung up.'

'Oh. I don't know. I don't know who that was.'

He laughs. 'Of course you don't. Are you all

324

right?' He comes across to me and puts his arms around my waist. 'You're being weird.' He holds me for a bit, his head bowed against my chest. 'You should've woken me if you heard something,' he says. 'You shouldn't be going out there on your own. That's my job.'

'I'm fine,' I say, but I have to clench my jaw to stop my teeth from chattering. He kisses my lips, pushes his tongue into my mouth.

'Let's go back to bed,' he says.

'I think I'm going to have a coffee,' I say, trying to pull away from him.

He's not letting me go. His arms are tight around me, his hand gripping the back of my neck.

'Come on,' he says. 'Come with me. I'm not taking no for an answer.'

RACHEL

Sunday, 18 August 2013

Morning

I'm not really sure what to do, so I just ring the doorbell. I wonder whether I should have called first. It's not polite to turn up early on a Sunday morning without calling, is it? I start to giggle. I feel slightly hysterical. I don't really know what I'm doing.

No one comes to the door. The hysterical feeling grows as I walk round the side of the house,

325

down the little passageway. I have the strongest feeling of déjà vu. That morning, when I came to the house, when I took the little girl. I never meant her any harm. I'm sure of that now.

I can hear her chattering as I make my way along the path in the cool shadow of the house, and I wonder whether I'm imagining things. But no, there she is, and Anna too, sitting on the patio. I call out to her and hoist myself over the fence. She looks at me. I expect shock, or anger, but she barely even looks surprised.

'Hello, Rachel,' she says. She gets to her feet, taking her child by the hand, drawing her to her side. She looks at me, unsmiling, calm. Her eyes are red, her face pale, scrubbed, devoid of make-up.

'What do you want?' she asks.

'I rang the doorbell,' I tell her.

'I didn't hear it,' she says, hoisting the child up on to her hip. She half turns away from me, as though she's about to go into the house, but then she just stops. I don't understand why she's not yelling at me.

'Where's Tom, Anna?'

'He went out. Army boys' get-together.'

'We need to go, Anna,' I say and she starts to laugh.

ANNA

Sunday, 18 August 2013

Morning

For some reason, the whole thing seems very funny all of a sudden. Poor fat Rachel standing in my garden, all red and sweaty, telling me we need to go. *We* need to go.

'Where are we going?' I ask her when I stop laughing, and she just looks at me, blank, lost for words. 'I'm not going anywhere with you.' Evie squirms and complains and I put her back down. My skin still feels hot and tender from where I scrubbed myself in the shower this morning; the inside of my mouth, my cheeks, my tongue, they feel bitten.

'When will he be back?' she asks me.

'Not for a while yet, I shouldn't think.'

I've no idea when he'll be back, in fact. Sometimes he can spend whole days at the climbing wall. Or I thought he spent whole days at the climbing wall. Now I don't know.

I do know that he's taken the gym bag; it can't be long before he discovers that the phone is gone.

I was thinking of taking Evie and going to my sister's for a while, but the phone is troubling me. What if someone finds it? There are workers on

327

this stretch of track all the time: one of them might find it and hand it in to the police. It has my fingerprints on it.

Then I was thinking that perhaps it wouldn't be all that difficult to get it back, but I'd have to wait until night time so no one would see me.

I'm aware that Rachel is still talking, she's asking me questions. I haven't been listening to her. I feel so tired.

'Anna,' she says, coming closer to me, those intense dark eyes searching mine. 'Have you ever met any of them?'

'Met who?'

'His friends from the army? Have you ever actually been introduced to any of them?' I shake my head. 'Do you not think that's odd?' It strikes me then that what's really odd is her showing up in my garden first thing on a Sunday morning.

'Not really,' I say. 'They're part of another life. Another of his lives. Like you are. Like you were supposed to be, anyway, but we can't seem to get rid of you.' She flinches, wounded. 'What are you doing here, Rachel?'

'You know why I'm here,' she says. 'You know that something … something has been going on.' She has this earnest look on her face, as though she's concerned about me. Under different circumstances, it might be touching.

'Would you like a cup of coffee?' I say, and she nods.

I make the coffee and we sit side by side on the patio in silence that feels almost companionable. 'What were you suggesting?' I ask her. 'That Tom's friends from the army don't really exist?

That he made them up? That he's actually off with some other woman?'

'I don't know,' she says.

'Rachel?' She looks at me then and I can see in her eyes that she's afraid. 'Is there something you want to tell me?'

'Have you ever met Tom's family?' she asks me. 'His parents.'

'No. They're not talking. They stopped talking to him when he ran off with me.'

She shakes her head. 'That isn't true,' she says. 'I've never met them either. They don't even know me, so why would they care about him leaving me?'

There's darkness in my head, right at the back of my skull. I've been trying to keep it at bay ever since I heard her voice on the phone, but now it starts to swell, it blooms.

'I don't believe you,' I say. 'Why would he lie about that?'

'Because he lies about everything.'

I get to my feet and walk away from her. I feel annoyed with her for telling me this. I feel annoyed with myself, because I think I do believe her. I think I've always known that Tom lies. It's just that in the past, his lies tended to suit me.

'He is a good liar,' I say to her. 'You were totally clueless for ages, weren't you? All those months we were meeting up, fucking each other's brains out in that house on Cranham Street, and you never suspected a thing.'

She swallows, bites her lip hard. 'Megan,' she says. 'What about Megan?'

'I know. They had an affair.' The words sound

strange to me – this is the first time that I've said them out loud. He cheated on me. He cheated on *me*. 'I'm sure that amuses you,' I say to her, 'but she's gone now, so it doesn't matter, does it?'

'Anna...'

The darkness gets bigger; it's pushing at the edges of my skull, clouding my vision. I grab Evie by the hand and start to drag her inside. She protests vociferously.

'Anna...'

'They had an affair. That's it. Nothing else. It doesn't necessarily mean–'

'That he killed her?'

'Don't say that!' I find myself yelling at her. 'Don't say that in front of my child.'

I give Evie her mid-morning snack, which she eats without complaint for the first time in weeks. It's almost as though she knows that I have other things to worry about, and I adore her for it. I feel immeasurably calmer when we go back outside, even if Rachel is still there, standing down at the bottom of the garden by the fence, watching one of the trains go past. After a while, when she realizes that I'm back outside, she walks towards me.

'You like them, don't you?' I say. 'The trains. I hate them. Absolutely bloody loathe them.'

She gives me a half-smile. I notice that she has a deep dimple on the left side of her face. I've never seen that before. I suppose I haven't seen her smile very often. Ever.

'Another thing he lied about,' she says. 'He told me you loved this house, loved everything about it, even the trains. He told me that you wouldn't dream of finding a new place, that you wanted to move in here with him, even if I had been here first.'

I shake my head. 'Why on earth would he tell you that?' I ask her. 'It's utter bullshit. I've been trying to get him to sell this house for two years.'

She shrugs. 'Because he lies, Anna. All the time.'

The darkness blossoms. I pull Evie on to my lap and she sits there quite contentedly, she's getting sleepy in the sunshine. 'So all those phone calls...' I say. It's only really starting to make sense now. 'They weren't from you? I mean, I know some of them were, but some–'

'Were from Megan? Yes, I imagine so.'

It's odd, because I know now that all this time I've been hating the wrong woman, and yet knowing this doesn't make me dislike Rachel any less. If anything, seeing her like this, calm, concerned, sober, I'm starting to see what she once was, and I resent her more, because I'm starting to see what he must have seen in her. What he must have loved.

I glance down at my watch. It's after eleven. He left around eight, I think. It might even have been earlier. He must know about the phone by now. He must have known for quite some time. Perhaps he thinks it fell out of the bag. Perhaps he imagines it's under the bed upstairs.

'How long have you known?' I ask her. 'About the affair.'

'I didn't,' she says. 'Until today. I mean I don't know what was going on. I just know–' Thankfully she falls silent, because I'm not sure I can stand hearing her talk about my husband's infidelity. The thought that she and I – fat, sad Rachel and I – are now in the same boat is unbearable.

'Do you think it was his?' she asks me. 'Do you think the baby was his?'

I'm looking at her, but I'm not really seeing her, not seeing anything but darkness, not hearing anything but a roaring in my ears, like the sea, or a plane right overhead.

'What did you say?'

'The... I'm sorry.' She's red in the face, flustered. 'I shouldn't have... She was pregnant when she died. Megan was pregnant. I'm so sorry.'

But she's not sorry at all, I'm sure of it, and I don't want to go to pieces in front of her. But I look down then, I look down at Evie, and I feel a sadness unlike anything I've ever felt before crashing over me like a wave, crushing the breath right out of me. Evie's brother, Evie's sister. Gone. Rachel sits at my side and puts her arm around my shoulders.

'I'm sorry,' she says again, and I want to hit her. The feeling of her skin against mine makes my flesh crawl. I want to push her away, I want to scream at her, but I can't. She lets me cry for a while and then she says in a clear, determined voice, 'Anna, I think we should go. I think you should pack some things, for you and Evie, and then we should go. You can come to my place for now. Until ... until we sort all this out.'

I dry my eyes and pull away from her. 'I'm not leaving him, Rachel. He had an affair, he... It's not the first time, is it?' I start to laugh, and Evie laughs too.

Rachel sighs and gets to her feet. 'You know this isn't just about an affair, Anna. I know that you know.'

'We don't know anything,' I say, and it comes out in a whisper.

'She got into the car with him. That night. I saw her. I didn't remember it– I thought at first it was you,' she says. 'But I remember. I remember now.'

'No.' Evie's sticky little hand presses against my mouth.

'We have to speak to the police, Anna.' She takes a step towards me. 'Please. You can't stay here with him.'

Despite the sun, I'm shivering. I'm trying to think of the last time Megan came to the house, the look on his face when she said that she couldn't work for us any longer. I'm trying to remember whether he looked pleased, or disappointed. Unbidden, a different image comes into my head: one of the first times she came to look after Evie. I was supposed to be going out to meet the girls, but I was so tired, so I went upstairs to sleep. Tom must have come home while I was up there, because they were together when I came downstairs. She was leaning against the counter, and he was standing a bit too close to her. Evie was in the high chair, she was crying and neither of them were looking at her.

I feel very cold. Did I know then that he wanted her? Megan was blonde and beautiful – she was like me. So yes, I probably knew that he wanted her, just like I know when I walk down the street that there are married men with their wives at their sides and their children in their arms who look at me and think about it. So perhaps I did know. He wanted her, he took her. But not this.

He couldn't do this.

Not Tom. A lover, husband twice over. A father. A good father, an uncomplaining provider.

'You loved him,' I remind her. 'You still love him, don't you?'

She shakes her head, but there's no conviction there.

'You do. And you know ... you know that this isn't possible.'

I stand up, hauling Evie up with me, and move closer to her. 'He couldn't have, Rachel. You know he couldn't have done this. You couldn't love a man who would do that, could you?'

'But I did,' she says. 'We both did.' There are tears on her cheeks. She wipes them away and as she does so something in her expression changes and her face loses all colour. She's not looking at me, but over my shoulder, and as I turn around to follow her gaze, I see him at the kitchen window, watching us.

MEGAN

Friday, 12 July 2013

Morning

She's forced my hand. Or maybe he has. My gut tells me she. Or my heart tells me so, I don't know. I can feel her, the way I could before, curled up, a seed within a pod, only this seed's smiling.

Biding her time. I can't hate her. And I can't get rid of her. I can't. I thought I would be able to, I thought I would be desperate to scrape her out, but when I think about her, all I can see is Libby's face, her dark eyes. I can smell her skin. I can feel how cold she was at the end. I can't get rid of her. I don't want to. I want to love her.

I can't hate her, but she scares me. I'm afraid of what she'll do to me, or what I'll do to her. It's that fear that woke me just after five this morning, soaked in sweat despite the open windows and the fact that I'm alone. Scott's at a conference, somewhere in Hertfordshire or Essex or somewhere. He's back tonight.

What is it with me, that I'm desperate to be alone when he's here, and when he's gone I can't bear it? I can't stand the silence. I have to talk out loud just to make it go away. In bed this morning I kept thinking what if it happens again? What's going to happen when I'm alone with her? What's going to happen if he won't have me, won't have us? What happens if he guesses that she isn't his?

She might be, of course. I don't know, but I just feel that she isn't. Same way I feel that she's a she. But even if she isn't, how would he know? He won't. He can't. I'm being stupid. He'll be so happy. He'll be mental with joy when I tell him. The thought that she might not be his won't even cross his mind. Telling him would be cruel, it would break his heart, and I don't want to hurt him. I've never wanted to hurt him.

I can't help the way I am.

'You can help what you do, though.' That's what Kamal says.

I called Kamal just after six. The silence was right on top of me and I was starting to panic. I thought about ringing Tara – I knew she'd come running – but I didn't think I could stand it, she'd be all clingy and over-protective. Kamal was the only person I could think of. I called him at home. I told him I was in trouble, I didn't know what to do, I was freaking out. He came over right away. Not quite without question, but almost. Perhaps I made things sound worse than they are. Perhaps he was afraid I was going to Do Something Stupid.

We're in the kitchen. It's still early, just after seven thirty. He has to leave soon if he's going to make his first appointment. I look at him, sitting there across from me at our kitchen table, his hands folded together neatly in front of him, his deep doe eyes on mine, and I feel love. I do. He's been so good to me, despite the crap way I've behaved.

Everything that went before, he's forgiven, just like I hoped he would. He wiped everything away, all my sins. He told me that unless I forgave myself this would go on and on and I would never be able to stop running. And I can't run any more, can I? Not now she's here.

'I'm scared,' I tell him. 'What if I do it all wrong again? What if there's something wrong with me? What if things go wrong with Scott? What if I end up on my own again? I don't know if I can do it, I'm so afraid of being on my own again – I mean, on my own with a child…'

He leans forward and puts his hand over mine. 'You won't do anything wrong. You won't. You're not some grieving, lost child any longer. You're a completely different person. You're stronger. You're an adult now. You don't have to be afraid of being alone. It's not the worst thing, is it?'

I don't say anything, but I can't help wondering whether it is, because if I close my eyes I can conjure up the feeling that comes to me when I'm on the edge of sleep, which jolts me back into wakefulness. It's the feeling of being alone in a dark house, listening for her cries, waiting to hear Mac's footfall on the wooden floors downstairs and knowing that they're never going to come.

'I can't tell you what to do about Scott. Your relationship with him... Well, I've expressed my concerns, but you have to decide what to do for yourself. Decide whether you trust him, whether you *want* him to take care of you and your child. That must be your decision. But I think you can trust yourself, Megan. You can trust yourself to do the right thing.'

Outside, on the lawn, he brings me a cup of coffee. I put it down and put my arms around him, pulling him closer. Behind us a train is rumbling up to the signal. The noise is like a barrier, a wall surrounding us, and I feel as though we are truly alone. He puts his arms around me and kisses me.

'Thank you,' I say. 'Thank you for coming, for being here.'

He smiles, drawing back from me, and rubs his thumb across my cheekbone. 'You'll be fine, Megan.'

'Couldn't I just run away with you? You and I ... couldn't we just run away together?'

He laughs. 'You don't need me. And you don't

need to keep running. You'll be fine. You and your baby will be fine.'

Morning

I know what I have to do. I thought about it all day yesterday, and all night, too. I hardly slept at all. Scott came home exhausted and in a shitty mood; all he wanted to do was eat, fuck and sleep, no time for anything else. It certainly wasn't the right time to talk about this.

I lay awake most of the night, with him hot and restless at my side, and I made my decision. I'm going to do the right thing. I'm going to do everything right. If I do everything right, then nothing can go wrong. Or if it does, it cannot be my fault. I will love this child and raise her knowing that I did the right thing from the start. All right, perhaps not from the very start, but from the moment when I knew she was coming. I owe it to this baby, and I owe it to Libby. I owe it to her to do everything differently this time.

I lay there and I thought of what that teacher said, and of all the things I'd been: child, rebellious teenager, runaway, whore, lover, bad mother, bad wife. I'm not sure if I can remake myself as a good wife, but a good mother – that I have to try.

It's going to be hard. It might be the hardest thing I've ever had to do, but I'm going to tell the truth. No more lies, no more hiding, no more running, no more bullshit. I'm going to put everything out in the open, and then we'll see. If he can't love me then, so be it.

Evening

My hand is against his chest and I'm pushing as hard as I can, but I can't breathe and he's so much stronger than I am. His forearm presses against my windpipe, I can feel the blood pulsing at my temples, my eyes blurring. I try to cry out, my back to the wall. I snatch a handful of his T-shirt and he lets go. He turns away from me and I slide down the wall on to the kitchen floor.

I cough and spit, tears running down my face. He's standing a few feet from me, and when he turns back to me my hand instinctively goes to my throat to protect it. I see the shame on his face and want to tell him that it's OK. I'm OK. I open my mouth but the words won't come, just more coughing. The pain is unbelievable. He's saying something to me but I can't hear, it's as though we're under water, the sound muffled, reaching me in blurry waves. I can't make anything out.

I think he's saying that he's sorry.

I haul myself to my feet, push past him and run up the stairs, then slam the bedroom door behind me and lock it. I sit down on the bed and wait, listening for him, but he doesn't come. I get to my feet and grab my overnight bag from under the bed, go over to the chest to grab some clothes and catch sight of myself in the mirror. I bring my hand up to my face: it looks startlingly white against my reddened skin, my purple lips, my bloodshot eyes.

Part of me is shocked, because he's never laid a hand on me like that before. But there's another part of me that expected this. Somewhere inside I always knew that this was a possibility that this was where we were headed. Where I was leading him. Slowly, I start pulling things out of the drawers – underwear, a couple of T-shirts; I stuff them into the bag.

I haven't even told him anything yet. I'd just started. I wanted to tell him about the bad stuff first, before we got to the good news. I couldn't tell him about the baby and then say that there was a possibility it wasn't his. That would be too cruel.

We were outside on the patio. He was talking about work and he caught me not-quite-listening.

'Am I boring you?' he asked.

'No. Well, maybe a bit.' He didn't laugh. 'No, I'm just distracted. Because there's something I need to tell you. There are a few things I need to tell you, actually, some of which you're not going to like, but some–'

'What am I not going to like?'

I should have known then that it wasn't the time, his mood was off. He was immediately suspicious, searching my face for clues. I should have known then that this was all a terrible idea. I suppose I did, but it was too late to go back then. And in any case, I had made my decision. To do the right thing.

I sat down next to him on the edge of the paving and slipped my hand into his.

'What aren't I going to like?' he asked again,

but he didn't let go of my hand.

I told him I loved him and I felt every muscle in his body tense, as if he knew what was coming and was bracing himself for it. You do, don't you, when someone tells you they love you like that. I love you, I do, but... *But.*

I told him that I'd made some mistakes and he let go of my hand. He got to his feet and walked a few yards in the direction of the track before turning to look at me. 'What sort of mistakes?' he asked. His voice was even, but I could hear that it was a strain to keep it so.

'Come and sit with me,' I said. 'Please?'

He shook his head. 'What sort of mistakes, Megan?' Louder that time.

'There was ... it's finished now, but there was ... someone else.' I kept my eyes lowered, I couldn't look at him.

He spat something under his breath but I couldn't hear it. I looked up then but he'd turned away and was facing the track again, his hands up at his temples. I got to my feet and went to him, stood behind him and placed my hands on his hips, but he leaped away from me. He turned to go into the house and without looking at me, spat, 'Don't touch me, you little whore.'

I should have let him go then, given him time to get his head around it, but I couldn't. I wanted to get over the bad stuff so that I could get to the good, so I followed him into the house.

'Scott, please, just listen, it's not as awful as you think. It's over now. It's completely over, please listen, please–'

He grabbed the photograph of the two of us that

he loves – the one I had framed as a gift for our second wedding anniversary – and threw it as hard as he could at my head. As it smashed against the wall behind me, he lunged, grabbing me by the tops of my arms and wrestling me across the room, throwing me against the opposite wall. My head rocked back, my skull hitting plaster. Then he leaned in, his forearm across my throat, he leaned harder, harder, saying nothing. He closed his eyes so that he didn't have to watch me choke.

As soon as my bag is packed, I start unpacking again, stuffing everything back into the drawers. If I try to walk out of here with a bag, he won't let me go. I have to leave empty handed, with nothing but a handbag and a phone. Then I change my mind again and start stuffing everything back into the bag. I don't know where I'm going, but I know I can't be here. I close my eyes and can feel his hands around my throat.

I know what I decided – no more running, no more hiding – but I can't stay here tonight. I hear footsteps on the stairs, slow, leaden. It takes forever for him to get to the top – usually he bounds, but today he's a man ascending the scaffold. I just don't know whether he's the condemned man or the executioner.

'Megan?' He doesn't try to open the door. 'Megan, I'm sorry I hurt you. I'm so sorry that I hurt you.' I can hear tears in his voice. It makes me angry, it makes me want to fly out there and scratch his face. *Don't you bloody dare cry, not after what you just did.* I'm furious with him, I want to scream at him, tell him to get the hell away from the door, away from me, but I bite my tongue, because I'm not stupid. He has reason to be angry. And I have to think rationally, I have to think clearly. I'm thinking for two now. This confrontation has given me strength, it's made me more determined. I can hear him outside the door, begging for forgiveness, but I can't think about that now. Right now, I have other things to do.

At the very back of the wardrobe, in the bottom of three rows of carefully labelled shoe boxes, there is a dark-grey box marked 'red wedge boots', and in that box there is an old mobile phone, a pay-as-you-go relic I bought years ago and hung on to just in case. I haven't used it for a while, but today's the day. I'm going to be honest. I'm going to put everything out in the open. No more lies, no more hiding. It's time for Daddy to face up to his responsibilities.

I sit on the bed and switch the phone on, praying that it still has some charge. It lights up and I can feel the adrenaline in my blood, it's making me dizzy, a little bit sick, and it's making me buzz, as though I'm high. I'm starting to enjoy myself, enjoy the anticipation of putting everything out there, confronting him – all of them – with what we are and where we're going. By the end of the day, everyone is going to know where they stand.

I call his number. Predictably, it goes straight to voicemail. I hang up and send a text: *I need to talk to you. URGENT. Call me back.* Then I sit there, and I wait.

I look at the call log. The last time I used this phone was April. A lot of calls, all of them unanswered, in early April and late March. I called and called and called, and he ignored me, he didn't even respond to the threats I made – I'd come to the house, I'd talk to his wife. I think he'll listen to me now, though. I'm going to make him listen to me now.

When we started all this, it was just a game. A distraction. I used to see him from time to time. He'd pop by the gallery and smile and flirt, and it was harmless – there were plenty of men who came by the gallery and smiled and flirted. But then the gallery closed and I was here at home all the time, bored and restless. I just needed something else, something different. Then one day, when Scott was away, I bumped into him in the street, we started talking and I invited him in for coffee. The way he looked at me, I could see exactly what was going through his mind and so it just happened. And then it happened again, and I never meant for it to go anywhere, I didn't want it to go anywhere. I just enjoyed feeling wanted; I liked the feeling of control. It was as simple and stupid as that. I didn't want him to leave his wife; I just wanted him to *want* to leave her. To want me that much.

I don't remember when I started believing that it could be more, that we should be more, that we were right for each other. But the moment I did, I could feel him start to pull away. He stopped texting, stopped answering my calls, and I've never felt rejection like that before, never. I hated it. So then it became something else: an obsession. I can see that now. In the end I really thought I could just walk away from it, a little bruised, but no real harm done. But it's not that simple any longer.

Scott is still outside the door. I can't hear him, but I can feel him. I go into the bathroom and dial the number again. I get voicemail again, so I hang up and dial again, and again. I whisper a message. 'Pick up the phone, or I'm coming round there. I mean it this time. I have to talk to you. You can't just ignore me.'

I stand in the bathroom for a while, the phone on the edge of the sink. Willing it to ring. The screen stays stubbornly grey and blank. I brush my hair and my teeth, put on some make-up. My colour is returning to normal. My eyes are still red, my throat still hurts, but I look all right. I start counting. If the phone doesn't ring before I get to fifty, I'm just going to go down there and knock on the door. The phone doesn't ring.

I stuff the phone into my jeans pocket, walk quickly through the bedroom and open the door. Scott is sitting on the landing, his arms around his knees, his head down. He doesn't look up at me, so I walk past him and start to run downstairs, my breath catching in my throat. I'm afraid that he'll grab me from behind and push me. I can hear him getting to his feet and he calls, 'Megan! Where are you going? Are you going to him?'

At the bottom of the stairs, I turn. 'There is no *him*, OK? It's over.'

'Please wait, Megan. Please don't go.'

I don't want to hear him beg, don't want to listen to the whine in his voice, the self-pity. Not when my throat still feels like someone's poured acid down it.

'Don't follow me,' I croak at him. 'If you follow

345

me, I'll never come back. Do you understand? If I turn around and see you behind me, that'll be the last time you ever see my face.'

I can hear him calling my name as I slam the door behind me.

I wait on the pavement outside for a few moments to make sure he isn't following me, then I walk, quickly at first, then slower, and slower, along Blenheim Road. I get to number twenty-three and it's then that I lose my nerve. I'm not ready for this scene yet. I need a minute to collect myself. A few minutes. I walk on, past the house, past the underpass, past the station. I keep going until I get to the park and then I dial his number one more time.

I tell him that I'm in the park, that I'll wait for him there, but if he doesn't come, that's it, I'm coming round to the house. This is his last chance.

It's a lovely evening, a little after seven but still warm and light. A bunch of kids are still playing on the swings and the slide, their parents standing off to one side, chatting animatedly. It looks nice, normal, and as I watch them I have a sickening feeling that Scott and I will not bring our daughter here to play. I just can't see us, happy and relaxed like that. Not now. Not after what I've just done.

I was so convinced this morning that getting everything out in the open would be the best way – not just the best way, the only way. No more lying, no more hiding. And then when he hurt me, it only made me all the more sure. But now, sitting here on my own, with Scott not just furious but heartbroken, I don't think it was the right thing at all. I wasn't being strong, I was being reckless, and there's no telling how much damage I've done.

Maybe the courage I need has nothing to do with telling the truth and everything to do with walking away. It's not just restlessness – this is more than that. For her sake and mine, now is the time to go, to walk away from them both, from all of it. Maybe running and hiding is exactly what I need to do.

I get to my feet and walk round the park just once. I'm half willing the phone to ring and half dreading it ringing, but in the end I'm pleased when it stays silent. I'll take it as a sign. I head back the way I came, towards home.

I've just passed the station when I see him. He's walking quickly, striding out of the underpass, his shoulders hunched over and his fists clenched, and before I can stop myself, I call out.

He turns to face me. 'Megan! What the hell...' The expression on his face is pure rage, but he beckons me to go to him.

'Come on,' he says, when I get closer. 'We can't talk here. The car's over there.'

'I just need–'

'We can't talk here!' he snaps. 'Come on.' He tugs at my arm. Then, more gently, 'We'll drive somewhere quiet, OK? Somewhere we can talk.'

As I get into the car, I glance over my shoulder, back the way he came. The underpass is dark, but I feel as though I can see someone in there, in the shadows – someone watching us go.

RACHEL

Sunday, 18 August 2013

Afternoon

Anna turns on her heel and runs into the house the second she sees him. My heart hammering against my ribs, I follow cautiously, stopping just short of the sliding doors. Inside, they are embracing, his arms enveloping her, the child between them. Anna's head is bent, her shoulders shaking. His mouth is pressed to the top of her scalp, but his eyes are on me.

'What's going on here then?' he asks, the trace of a smile on his lips. 'I have to say that finding you two ladies gossiping in the garden when I got home was not what I expected.'

His tone is light, but he's not fooling me. He's not fooling me any more. I open my mouth to speak, but I find that I don't have the words. I have nowhere to start.

'Rachel? Are you going to tell me what's going on?' He relinquishes Anna from his grasp and takes a step towards me. I take a step back, and he starts to laugh.

'What on earth's wrong with you? Are you drunk?' he asks, but I can see in his eyes that he knows I'm sober and I'm betting that for once he wishes I wasn't. I slip my hand into the back

348

pocket of my jeans – my phone is there, hard and compact and comforting, only I wish I'd had the sense to make the call already. No matter whether they believed me or not, if I'd told them I was with Anna and her child, the police would have come.

Tom is now just a couple of feet away from me – he's just inside the door and I'm just outside it.

'I saw you,' I say at last, and I feel euphoria, fleeting but unmistakeable, when I say the words out loud. 'You think I don't remember anything, but I do. I saw you. After you hit me, you left me there, in the underpass...'

He starts to laugh, but I can see it now and I wonder how I never read him this easily before. There's panic in his eyes. He shoots a glance at Anna, but she doesn't meet his eye.

'What are you talking about?'

'In the underpass. On the day Megan Hipwell went missing...'

'Oh, bullshit,' he says, waving a hand at me. 'I did not hit you. You fell.' He reaches for Anna's hand and pulls her closer to him. 'Darling, is this why you're so upset? Don't listen to her, she's talking absolute rubbish. I didn't hit her. I've never laid a hand on her in my life. Not like that.' He puts his arm around Anna's shoulders and pulls her closer still. 'Come on. I've told you how she is. She doesn't know what happens when she drinks, she makes up the most–'

'You got into the car with her. I watched you go.' He's still smiling, but there's no longer any conviction there, and I don't know whether I'm imagining it, but he looks a little paler to me now.

349

He relaxes his grip on Anna, releasing her once again. She sits down at the table, her back to her husband, her daughter squirming on her lap.

Tom passes his hand over his mouth and leans back against the kitchen counter, folding his arms across his chest. 'You saw me get into the car with who?'

'With Megan.'

'Oh, right!' He starts laughing again, a loud, forced roar. 'Last time we talked about this, you told me you saw me get into the car with Anna. Now it's Megan, is it? Who's it going to be next week? Princess Diana?'

Anna looks up at me. I can see the doubt, the hope, flash across her face. 'You're not sure?' she asks.

Tom drops to his knees at her side. 'Of course she isn't sure. She's making this up – she does it all the time. Sweetheart, please. Why don't you go upstairs for a bit, OK? I'll talk this through with Rachel. And this time–' he glances up at me, 'I promise I'll make sure she won't bother us any more.'

Anna's wavering, I can see it – the way she's looking at him, searching his face for the truth, his eyes intently on hers. 'Anna!' I call out, trying to bring her back to me. 'You *know*. You *know* he's lying. You know that he was sleeping with her.'

For a second, no one says a thing. Anna looks from Tom to me and back again. She opens her mouth to say something, but no words come.

'Anna! What does she mean? There's ... there was nothing between me and Megan Hipwell.'

'I found the phone, Tom,' she says, her voice so

small she's almost inaudible. 'So please, don't. Don't lie. Just don't lie to me.'

The child starts to grizzle and moan. Very gently, Tom takes her from Anna's arms. He walks across to the window, rocking his daughter from side to side, murmuring to her all the while. I can't hear what he's saying. Anna's head is bowed, tears dripping from her chin on to the kitchen table.

'Where is it?' Tom says, turning to face us, the laughter gone from his face. 'The phone, Anna. Did you give it to her?' He jerks his head in my direction. 'Do you have it?'

'I don't know anything about a phone,' I tell him, wishing that Anna had mentioned this earlier.

Tom ignores me. 'Anna? Did you give it to her?'

Anna shakes her head.

'Where is it?'

'I threw it away,' she says. 'Over the fence. By the track.'

'Good girl. Good girl,' he says distractedly. He's trying to figure things out, work out where to go from here. He glances at me and then looks away. For just a moment, he looks beaten.

He turns to Anna. 'You were so tired all the time,' he says. 'You just weren't interested. Everything was about the baby. Isn't that right? It was all about you, wasn't it? All about you!' And just like that, he's on top again, perked up, pulling faces at his daughter, tickling her tummy, making her smile. 'And Megan was so ... well, she was available.'

'At first, it was over at her place,' he says. 'But she was so paranoid about Scott finding out. So we started meeting at the Swan. It was... Well, you remember what it was like, don't you, Anna? At the beginning, when we used to go to that house on Cranham Street. You understand.' He glances back over his shoulder at me and winks. That's where Anna and I used to meet, back in the good old days.'

He shifts his daughter from one arm to the other, allowing her to rest against his shoulder. 'You think I'm being cruel, but I'm not. I'm telling the truth. That's what you want, isn't it, Anna? You asked me not to lie.'

Anna doesn't look up. Her hands are gripping the edge of the table, her entire body rigid.

Tom gives a loud sigh. 'It's a relief, if I'm honest.' He's talking to me, looking at me directly. 'You have no idea how exhausting it is, coping with people like you. And, fuck, I tried. I tried so hard to help you. To help both of you. You're both... I mean, I loved you both, I really did, but you can both be incredibly weak.'

'Fuck you, Tom,' Anna says, getting up from the table. 'Don't you lump me in with *her.*'

I look at her and realize how well suited they are, Anna and Tom. She's a much better match than I am, because this is what bothers her: not that her husband is a liar and a killer, but that he's just compared her to me.

Tom goes to her side and says soothingly, 'I'm sorry, darling. That was unfair of me.' She brushes him away and he looks over at me. 'I did my best, you know. I was a good husband to you, Rach. I put up with a lot – your drinking and your depression. I put up with all that for a long time before I

352

threw in the towel.'

'You lied to me,' I say, and he turns to face me, surprised. 'You told me everything was my fault. You made me believe that I was worthless. You watched me suffer, you–'

He shrugs. 'Do you have any idea how boring you became, Rachel? How ugly? Too sad to get out of bed in the morning, too tired to take a shower or wash your fucking hair? Jesus. It's no wonder I lost patience, is it? It's no wonder I had to look for ways to amuse myself. You've no one to blame but yourself.'

His expression changes from contempt to concern as he turns to talk to his wife. 'Anna, it was different with you, I swear. That thing with Megan, it was just … just a bit of fun. That's what it was meant to be. I'll admit it wasn't my finest hour, but I just needed a release. That's all. It was never going to last. It was never going to interfere with us, with our family. You must understand that.'

'You…' Anna is trying to say something, but she can't get the words out.

Tom puts his hand on her shoulder and squeezes it. 'What, love?'

'You had her looking after Evie,' she spits. 'Were you screwing her while she was working here? While she was looking after our child?'

He removes his hand, his face a picture of contrition, of deep shame. 'That was terrible. I thought... I thought it would be... Honestly, I don't know what I thought. I'm not sure I was thinking at all. It was wrong. It was terribly wrong of me.' And the mask changes again – now he's

353

wide-eyed innocence, pleading with her: 'I didn't know then, Anna. You have to believe that I didn't know what she was. I didn't know about the baby she killed. I would never have let her look after Evie if I'd known that. You have to believe me.'

Without warning, Anna jumps to her feet, pushing her chair back – it clatters on to the kitchen floor, waking their daughter. 'Give her to me,' Anna says, holding her arms out. Tom backs away a little. 'Now, Tom, give her to me. *Give her to me.*'

But he doesn't, he walks away from her, rocking the child, whispering to her again, coaxing her back to sleep, and then Anna starts to scream. At first she's repeating *give her to me, give her to me,* but then it's just an indistinguishable howl of fury and anguish. The child is screaming, too. Tom is trying to quieten her, he's ignoring Anna, so it falls to me to take hold of her. I drag her outside and talk to her, low and urgent.

'You have to calm down, Anna. Do you understand me? I need you to calm down. I need you to talk to him, to distract him for a moment while I ring the police? All right?'

She's shaking her head – she's shaking all over. She grabs hold of my arms, her fingernails digging into my flesh. 'How could he do this?'

'Anna! Listen to me. You need to keep him busy for a moment'

Finally, she looks at me, really looks at me, and nods. 'All right.'

'Just... I don't know. Get him away from this door, try to keep him occupied for a bit.'

She goes back inside. I take a deep breath, then turn and take a few steps away from the sliding door. Not too far, just on to the lawn. I turn and look back. They're still in the kitchen. I walk slightly further away. The wind is getting up now: the heat is about to break. Swifts are swooping low in the sky, and I can smell the rain coming. I love that smell.

I slip my hand into my back pocket and take out my phone. Hands trembling, I fail to unlock the keypad once, twice – I get it on the third time. For a moment I think about calling Detective Sergeant Riley, someone who knows me. I scroll through my call log but can't find her number, so I give up – I'll just dial 999. I'm on the second nine when I feel his foot punch the base of my spine and I go sprawling forward on to the grass, the wind knocked out of me. The phone flies from my grasp – he has it in his hand before I can raise myself to my knees, before I can take a breath.

'Now, now, Rach,' he says, grabbing my arm and hoisting me to my feet effortlessly. 'Let's not do anything stupid.'

He leads me back into the house, and I let him, because I know there's no point fighting now, I won't get away from him here. He shoves me through the doorway, sliding the glass door closed behind us and locking it. He tosses the key on to the kitchen table. Anna is standing there. She gives me a small smile and I wonder, then, whether she told him that I was about to call the police.

Anna sets about making lunch for her daughter, and puts the kettle on to make the rest of us a cup of tea. In this utterly bizarre facsimile of reality, I feel as though I could just politely bid them both goodbye, walk across the room and out into the safety of the street. It's so tempting, I actually take a few steps in that direction, but Tom blocks my path. He puts a hand on my shoulder, then runs his fingers under my throat, applying just the slightest pressure.

'What am I going to do with you, Rach?'

MEGAN

Saturday, 13 July 2013

Evening

It's not until we get into the car that I notice he has blood on his hand.

'You've cut yourself,' I say.

He doesn't reply; his knuckles are white on the steering wheel.

'Tom, I needed to talk to you,' I say. I'm trying to be conciliatory, trying to be grown-up about this, but I suppose it's a little late for that. 'I'm sorry about hassling you, but for God's sake! You just cut me off. You–'

'It's OK,' he says, his voice soft. 'I'm not... I'm pissed off about something else. It's not you.' He turns his head and tries to smile at me, but fails. 'Problems with the ex,' he says. 'You know how it is.'

'What happened to your hand?' I ask him.

'Problems with the ex,' he says again, and

there's a nasty edge to his voice. We drive the rest of the way to Corly Wood in silence.

We drive into the car park, right up to the very end. It's a place we've been before. There's never anyone much around in the evenings – sometimes a few teenagers with cans of beer, but that's about it. Tonight we're alone.

Tom turns off the engine and turns to me. 'Right. What is it you wanted to talk about?' The anger is still there, but its simmering now, no longer boiling over. Still, after what's just happened I don't feel like being in an enclosed space with an angry man, so I suggest we walk a bit. He rolls his eyes and sighs heavily, but he agrees.

It's still warm; there are clouds of midges under the trees and the sunshine is streaming through the leaves, bathing the path in an oddly subterranean light. Above our heads, magpies chatter angrily.

We walk a little way in silence, me in front, Tom a few paces behind. I'm trying to think of what to say, how to put this. I don't want to make things worse. I have to keep reminding myself that I'm trying to do the right thing.

I stop walking and turn to face him – he's standing very close to me.

He puts his hands on my hips. 'Here?' he asks. 'Is this what you want?' He looks bored.

'No,' I say, pulling away from him. 'Not that.'

The path descends a little here. I slow down, but he matches my stride.

'What then?'

Deep breath. My throat still hurts. 'I'm pregnant.'

There's no reaction at all – his face is completely blank. I could be telling him that I need to go to Sainsbury's on the way home, or that I've got a dentist's appointment.

'Congratulations,' he says eventually.

Another deep breath. 'Tom, I'm telling you this because ... well, because there's a possibility that the child could be yours.'

He stares at me for a few moments, then laughs. 'Oh? Lucky me. So what – we're going to run away, the three of us? You, me and the baby? Where was it we were going? Spain?'

'I thought you should know, because–'

'Have an abortion,' he says. 'I mean, if it's your husband's, do what you want. But if it's mine, get rid of it. Seriously, let's not be stupid about this. I don't want another kid.' He runs his fingers down the side of my face. 'And I'm sorry, but I don't think you're really motherhood material, are you, Megs?'

'You can be as involved as you like–'

'Did you hear what I just said?' he snaps, turning his back on me and striding back up the path towards the car. 'You'd be a terrible mother, Megan. Just get rid of it.'

I go after him, walking quickly at first and then running, and when I get close enough I shove him in the back. I'm yelling at him, screaming, trying to scratch his fucking smug face and he's laughing, fending me off with ease. I start saying the worst things I can think of. I insult his manhood, his boring wife, his ugly child.

I don't even know why I'm so angry, because what did I expect? Anger, maybe, worry, upset.

Not this. It's not even rejection, it's *dismissal*. All he wants is for me to go away – me and my child – and so I tell him, I scream at him, *I'm not going away. I am going to make you pay for this. For the rest of your bloody life you're going to be paying for this.*

He's not laughing any more.

He's coming towards me. He has something in his hand.

I've fallen. I must have slipped. Hit my head on something. I think I'm going to be sick. Everything is red. I can't get up.

One for sorrow, two for joy, three for a girl. Three for a girl. I'm stuck on three, I just can't get any further. My head is thick with sounds, my mouth thick with blood. Three for a girl. I can hear the magpies – they're laughing, mocking me, a raucous cackling. A tiding. Bad tidings. I can see them now, black against the sun. Not the birds, something else. Someone's coming. Someone is speaking to me. *Now look. Now look what you made me do.*

RACHEL

Sunday, 18 August 2013

Afternoon

In the living room, we sit in a little triangle: Tom on the sofa, the adoring father and dutiful husband, daughter on his lap, wife at his side. And the ex-wife opposite, sipping her tea. Very civilized. I'm sitting in the leather armchair that we bought from Heal's just after we got married – it was the first piece of furniture we got as a married couple: soft tan buttery leather, expensive, luxurious. I remember how excited I was when it was delivered. I remember curling up in it, feeling safe and happy, thinking *this is what marriage is – safe, warm, comfortable.*

Tom is watching me, his brow knitted. He's working out what to do, how to fix things. He's not worried about Anna, I can see that. I'm the problem.

'She was a bit like you,' he says all of a sudden. He leans back on the sofa, shifting his daughter to a more comfortable position on his lap. 'Well, she was and she wasn't. She had that thing ... messy, you know. I can't resist that.' He grins at me. 'Knight in shining armour, me.'

'You're no one's knight,' I say quietly.

'Ah, Rach, don't be like that. Don't you remem-

360

ber? You all sad, because Daddy's died, and just wanting someone to come home to, someone to love you? I gave you all that. I made you feel safe. Then you decided to piss it all away, but you can't blame me for that.'

'I can blame you for a lot of things, Tom.'

'No, no.' He wags a finger at me. 'Let's not start rewriting history. I was good to you. Sometimes ... well, sometimes you forced my hand. But I was good to you. I took care of you,' he says, and it's only then that it really registers: he lies to himself the way he lies to me. He *believes* this. He actually believes that he was good to me.

The child starts to wail suddenly and loudly, and Anna gets abruptly to her feet.

'I need to change her,' she says.

'Not now.'

'She's wet, Tom. She needs changing. Don't be cruel.'

He looks at Anna sharply, but he hands the crying child to her. I try to catch her eye, but she won't look at me. My heart rises into my throat as she turns to go upstairs, but it sinks again just as fast, because Tom is on his feet, his hand on her arm. 'Do it here,' he says. 'You can do it here.'

Anna goes across into the kitchen and changes the child's nappy on the table. The smell of shit fills the room, it turns my stomach.

'Are you going to tell us why?' I ask him. Anna stops what she's doing and looks across at us. The room is still, quiet, save for the babbling of the child.

Tom shakes his head, almost in disbelief him-

361

self. 'She could be very like you, Rach. She wouldn't let things go. She didn't know when she was over. She just ... she wouldn't *listen*. Remember how you always argued with me, how you always wanted the last word? Megan was like that. She wouldn't listen.'

He shifts in his seat and leans forward, his elbows on his knees, as if he's telling me a story. 'When we started, it was just fun, just fucking. She led me to believe that was what she was into. But then she changed her mind. I don't know why. She was all over the place, that girl. She'd have a bad day with Scott, or she'd just be a bit bored, and she'd start talking about us going away together, starting over, about me leaving Anna and Evie. As if I would! And if I wasn't there on demand when she wanted me, she'd be furious, calling here, threatening me, telling me she was going to come round, that she was going to tell Anna about us.

'But then it stopped. I was so relieved. I thought she'd finally managed to get it into her head that I wasn't interested any longer. But then that Saturday she called, saying she needed to talk, that she had something important to tell me. I ignored her, so she started making threats again – she was going to come to the house, that sort of thing. I wasn't too worried at first, because Anna was going out. You remember, darling? You were supposed to be going out to dinner with the girls, and I was going to babysit. I thought perhaps it wouldn't be such a bad thing – she would come round and I'd have it out with her. I'd make her understand. But then you came along, Rachel, and fucked everything up.'

He leans back on the sofa, his legs spread wide apart, the big man, taking up space. 'It was your fault. The whole thing was actually *your* fault, Rachel. Anna didn't end up having dinner with her friends – she was back here after five minutes, upset and angry because *you* were out there, pissed as usual, stumbling around with some bloke outside the station. She was worried that you were going to head over here. She was worried about Evie.

'So instead of sorting things out with Megan, I had to go out and deal with you.' His lip curls. 'God, the state of you. Looking like shit, stinking of wine ... you tried to kiss me, do you remember?' He pretends to gag, then starts laughing. Anna laughs, too, and I can't tell whether she finds it funny or whether she's trying to appease him.

'I needed to make you understand that I didn't want you anywhere near me – near us. So I took you back up the road into the underpass so that you wouldn't be making a scene in the street. And I told you to stay away. And you cried and whined, so I gave you a smack to shut you up, and you cried and whined some more.' He's talking through gritted teeth; I can see the muscle tensing in his jaw. 'I was so pissed off, I just wanted you to go away and leave us alone, you *and* Megan. I have my family. I have a good life.' He glances over at Anna, who is trying to get the child to sit down in the high chair. Her face is completely expressionless. 'I've made a good life for myself, despite you, despite Megan – despite everything.

'It was after I'd seen you that Megan came

along. She was heading down towards Blenheim Road. I couldn't let her go to the house. I couldn't let her talk to Anna, could I? I told her that we could go somewhere and talk, and I meant it – that was all I was going to do. So we got into the car and drove to Corly, to the wood. It was a place we sometimes used to go, if we hadn't got a room. Do it in the car.'

From my seat on the sofa, I can feel Anna flinch.

'You have to believe me, Anna, I didn't intend for things to go the way they did.' Tom looks at her, then hunches over, looking down at the palms of his hands. 'She started going on about the baby – she didn't know if it was mine or his. She wanted everything out in the open, and if it was mine she'd be OK with me seeing it... I was saying, I'm not interested in your baby, it's got nothing to do with me.' He shakes his head. 'She got all upset, but when Megan gets upset ... she's not like Rachel. There's no crying and whining. She was screaming at me, swearing, saying all sorts of shit, telling me she'd go straight to Anna, she wasn't going to be ignored, her child wasn't going to be neglected... Christ, she just wouldn't fucking shut up. So ... I don't know, I just needed her to stop. So I picked up a rock...' – he stares down at his right hand, as though he can see it now – 'and I just...' He closes his eyes and sighs deeply. 'It was just one hit, but she was...' He puffs out his cheeks, exhales slowly. 'I didn't mean for this. I just wanted her to stop. She was bleeding a lot. She was crying, making a horrible noise. She tried to crawl away from me. There was nothing I could do. I had to finish it.'

The sun is gone, the room is dark. It's quiet, save for the sound of Tom's breathing, ragged and shallow. There's no street noise. I can't remember the last time I heard a train.

'I put her in the boot of the car,' he says. 'I drove a bit further into the wood, off the road. There was no one around. I had to dig...' His breathing is shallower still, quickening. 'I had to dig with my bare hands. I was afraid.' He looks up at me, his pupils huge. 'Afraid that someone would come. And it was painful, my fingernails ripped in the soil. It took a long time. I had to stop to phone Anna, to tell her I was out looking for you.'

He clears his throat. 'The ground was actually quite soft, but I still couldn't go down as deep as I wanted. I was so afraid that someone would come. I thought there would be a chance to go back, later on, when things had all died down. I thought I would be able to move her, put her somewhere ... better. But then it started raining and I never got the chance.'

He looks up at me with a frown. 'I was almost sure that the police would go for Scott. She told me how paranoid he was about her screwing around, that he used to read her emails, check up on her. I thought ... well, I was planning to put her phone in his house at some point. I don't know. I thought I might go round there for a beer or something, a friendly neighbour kind of thing. I don't know. I didn't have a plan. I hadn't thought it all through. It wasn't like a premeditated thing. It was just a terrible accident.'

But then his demeanour changes again. It's like

365

clouds scudding across the sky, now dark, now light. He gets to his feet and walks slowly over to the kitchen, where Anna is now sitting at the table, feeding Evie. He kisses her on the top of the head, then lifts his daughter out of the chair.

'Tom...' Anna starts to protest.

'It's OK,' He smiles at his wife. 'I just want a cuddle. Don't I, darling?' He goes over to the fridge with his daughter in his arms and pulls out a beer. He looks over at me. 'You want one?'

I shake my head.

'No, best not, I suppose.'

I hardly hear him. I'm calculating whether I can reach the front door from here before he can get hold of me. If it's just on the latch, I reckon I could make it. If he's locked it, then I'd be in trouble. I pitch myself forward and run. I get into the hallway – my hand is almost on the door handle when I feel the bottle hit the back of my skull. There's an explosion of pain, white before my eyes, and I crumple to my knees. His fingers twist into my hair as he grabs a fistful and pulls, dragging me back into the living room, where he lets go. He stands above me, straddling me, one foot on either side of my hips. His daughter is still in his arms but Anna is at his side, tugging at her.

'Give her to me, Tom, please. You're going to hurt her. Please, give her to me.'

He hands the wailing Evie over to Anna.

I can hear Tom talking, but it seems like he's a long way away, or as though I'm hearing him through water. I can make out the words but they somehow don't seem to apply to me, to what's happening to me. Everything is happening at one remove.

'Go upstairs,' he says. 'Go into the bedroom and shut the door. You mustn't call anyone, OK? I mean it, Anna. You don't want to call anyone. Not with Evie here. We don't want things to turn nasty.' Anna doesn't look down at me. She clutches the child to her chest, steps over me and hurries away.

Tom bends down, slips his hands into the waistband of my jeans, grabs hold of them and drags me along the floor into the kitchen. I'm kicking out with my legs, trying to get a hold of something, but I can't. I can't see properly – tears are stinging my eyes, everything is a blur. The pain in my head is excruciating as I bump along the floor and I feel a wave of nausea come over me. There's hot, white pain as something connects with my temple. Then nothing.

ANNA

Sunday, 18 August 2013

Evening

She's on the floor in the kitchen. She's bleeding, but I don't think it's serious. He hasn't finished it. I'm not really sure what he's waiting for. I suppose it's not easy for him. He did love her, once.

I was upstairs, putting Evie down, and I was

thinking that this is what I wanted, isn't it? Rachel will be gone at last, once and for all, never to return. This is what I dreamed about happening. Well, not exactly this, obviously. But I did want her gone. I dreamed of a life without Rachel, and now I could have one. It would be just the three of us, me and Tom and Evie, like it should be.

For just a moment, I let myself enjoy the fantasy, but then I looked down at my sleeping daughter and I knew that was all it was. A fantasy. I kissed my finger and touched it to her perfect lips and I knew that we would never be safe. *I* would never be safe, because I know, and he won't be able to trust me. And who's to say another Megan won't come along? Or – worse – another Anna, another me?

I went back downstairs and he was sitting at the kitchen table, drinking a beer. I couldn't see her at first, but then I noticed her feet, and I thought at first that it was done, but he said she was all right.

'Just a little knock,' he said. He won't be able to call this one an accident.

So we waited. I got myself a beer too, and we drank them together. He told me he was really sorry about Megan, about the affair. He kissed me, he told me he'd make it up to me, that we'd be OK, that everything would be all right.

'We'll move away from here, just like you've always wanted. We'll go anywhere you want. Anywhere.' He asked me if I could forgive him, and I said that I could, given time, and he believed me. I think he believed me.

The storm has started, just like they said it

would. The rumble of thunder wakes her, brings her to. She starts to make a noise, to move around on the floor.

'You should go,' he says to me. 'Go back upstairs.'

I kiss him on the lips and I leave him, but I don't go back upstairs. Instead I pick up the phone in the hallway, sit on the bottom stair and listen, the handset in my hand, waiting for the right moment.

I can hear him talking to her, soft and low, and then I hear her. I think she's crying.

RACHEL

Sunday, 18 August 2013

Evening

I can hear something, a hissing sound. There's a flash of light and I realize it's the rain, pouring down. It's dark outside, there's a storm. Lightning. I don't remember when it got dark. The pain in my head brings me back to myself, my heart crawls into my throat. I'm on the floor. In the kitchen. With difficulty, I manage to lift my head and raise myself on to one elbow. He's sitting at the kitchen table, looking out at the storm, a beer bottle between his hands.

'What am I going to do, Rach?' he asks when he sees me raise my head. 'I've been sitting here for

... almost half an hour now, just asking myself that question. What am I supposed to do with you? What choice are you giving me?' He takes a long draught of beer and regards me thoughtfully. I pull myself up to a sitting position, my back to the kitchen cupboards. My head swims, my mouth floods with saliva. I feel as though I'm going to throw up. I bite my lip and dig my fingernails into my palms. I need to bring myself out of this stupor, I can't afford to be weak. I can't rely on anyone else. I know that. Anna isn't going to call the police. She isn't going to risk her daughter's safety for me.

'You have to admit it,' Tom is saying. 'You've brought this upon yourself. Think about it: if you'd just left us alone, you'd never be in this situation. *I* wouldn't be in this situation. None of us would. If you hadn't been there that night, if Anna hadn't come running back here after she saw you at the station, then I'd probably have just been able to sort things out with Megan. I wouldn't have been so ... riled up. I wouldn't have lost my temper. I wouldn't have hurt her. None of this would have happened.'

I can feel a sob building in the back of my throat, but I swallow it down. This is what he does – this is what he always does. He's a master at it, making me feel as though everything is my fault, making me feel worthless.

He finishes his beer and rolls the empty bottle across the table. With a sad shake of his head, he gets to his feet, comes over to me and holds out his hands. 'Come on,' he says. 'Grab hold. Come on, Rach, up you come.'

I let him pull me to my feet. My back is to the kitchen counter, he is standing in front of me, against me, his hips pressing against mine. He reaches up to my face, wipes the tears off my cheekbones with his thumb. 'What am I supposed to do with you, Rach? What do you think I should do?'

'You don't have to do anything,' I say to him, and I try to smile. 'You know that I love you. I still do. You know that I wouldn't tell anyone ... I couldn't do that to you.'

He smiles – that wide, beautiful smile that used to make me melt – and I start to sob. I can't believe it, can't believe we are brought to this, that the greatest happiness I have ever known – my life with him – was an illusion.

He lets me cry for a while, but it must bore him, because the dazzling smile disappears and now his lip is twisted into a sneer.

'Come on, Rach, that's enough,' he says. 'Stop snivelling.' He steps away and grabs a handful of Kleenex from a box on the kitchen table. 'Blow your nose,' he says, and I do what I'm told.

He watches me, his face a study in contempt. 'That day when we went to the lake,' he says. 'You thought you had a chance, didn't you?' He starts to laugh. 'You did, didn't you? Looking up at me, all doe-eyed and pleading... I could have had you, couldn't I? You're so easy.' I bite down hard on my lip. He steps closer to me again. 'You're like one of those dogs, the unwanted ones that have been mistreated all their lives. You can kick them and kick them, but they'll still come back to you, cringing and wagging their tails. Begging. Hoping that this time it'll be different, that this time they'll do something right and you'll love them. You're just like that, aren't you, Rach? You're a dog.' He slips his hand around my waist and puts his mouth on mine. I let his tongue slip between my lips and press my hips against his. I can feel him getting hard.

I don't know if everything's in the same place that it was when I lived here. I don't know whether Anna rearranged the cupboards, put the spaghetti in a different jar, moved the weighing scales from bottom left to bottom right. I don't know. I just hope, as I slip my hand into the drawer behind me, that she didn't.

'You could be right, you know,' I say when the kiss breaks. I tilt my face up to his. 'Maybe if I hadn't come to Blenheim Road that night, Megan would still be alive.'

He nods and my right hand closes around a familiar object. I smile and lean in to him, closer, closer, snaking my left hand around his waist. I whisper into his ear, 'But do you honestly think, given you're the one who smashed her skull, that I'm responsible?'

He jerks his head away from me and it's then that I lunge forward, pressing all my weight against him, throwing him off balance so that he stumbles back against the kitchen table. I raise my foot and stamp down on his as hard as I can, and as he pitches forward in pain, I grab a fistful of hair at the back of his head and pull him towards me, while at the same time driving my knee up into his face. I feel a crunch of cartilage as he cries out. I push him to the floor, grab the keys from the kitchen table and am out of the French doors before he's able to get to his knees.

I head for the fence, but I slip in the mud and lose my footing, and he's on top of me before I get there, dragging me backwards, pulling my hair, clawing at my face, spitting curses through blood – *you stupid, stupid bitch, why can't you stay away from us? Why can't you leave me alone?* I get away from him again, but there's nowhere to go. I won't make it back through the house and I won't make it over the fence. I cry out, but no one's going to hear me, not over the rain and the thunder and the sound of the approaching train. I run to the bottom of the garden, down towards the tracks. Dead end. I stand on the spot where, a year or more ago, I stood with his child in my arms. I turn, my back to the fence, and watch him striding purposefully towards me. He wipes his mouth with his forearm, spitting blood to the ground. I can feel the vibrations from the tracks in the fence behind me – the train is almost upon us, its sound like a scream. Tom's lips are moving he's saying something to me, but I can't hear him. I watch him come, I watch him, and I don't move until he's almost upon me, and then I swing. I jam the vicious twist of the corkscrew into his neck.

His eyes widen as he falls without a sound. He raises his hands to his throat, his eyes on mine. He looks as though he's crying. I watch until I can't look any longer, then I turn my back on him. As the train goes past I can see faces in brightly lit windows, heads bent over books and phones, travellers warm and safe on their way home.

Tuesday, 10 September 2013

Morning

You can feel it: it's like the hum of electric lights, the change in atmosphere as the train pulls up to the red signal. I'm not the only one who looks now. I don't suppose I ever was. I suppose that everyone does it – looks out at the houses they pass – only we all see them differently. All *saw* them differently. Now, everyone else is seeing the same thing. Sometimes you can hear people talk about it.

'There, it's that one. No, no, that one, on the left – there. With the roses by the fence. That's where it happened.'

The houses themselves are empty, number fifteen and number twenty-three. They don't look it – the blinds are up and the doors open, but I know that's because they're being shown. They're both on the market now, though it may be a while before either gets a serious buyer. I imagine the estate agents mostly escorting ghouls around those rooms, rubberneckers desperate to see it up close, the place where he fell and his blood soaked the earth.

It hurts to think of them walking through the house – my house, where I once had hope. I try not to think about what came after. I try not to think about that night. I try and I fail.

Side by side, drenched in his blood, we sat on the sofa, Anna and I. The wives, waiting for the ambulance. Anna called them – she called the police, she did everything. She took care of everything. The paramedics arrived, too late for Tom, and on their heels came uniformed police, then the detectives, Gaskill and Riley. Their mouths literally fell open when they saw us. They asked questions but I couldn't make out their words. I could barely move, barely breathe. Anna spoke, calm and assured.

'It was self-defence,' she told them. 'I saw the whole thing. From the window. He went for her with the corkscrew. He would have killed her. She had no choice. I tried...' It was the only time she faltered, the only time I saw her cry. 'I tried to stop the bleeding, but I couldn't. I couldn't.'

One of the uniformed police fetched Evie, who miraculously had slept soundly through the whole thing, and they took us all to the police station. They sat Anna and me in separate rooms and asked yet more questions that I don't remember. I struggled to answer, to concentrate. I struggled to form words at all. I told them he attacked me, hit me with a bottle. I said that he came at me with the corkscrew. I said that I managed to take the weapon from him, that I used it to defend myself. They examined me: they looked at the wound on my head, at my hands, at my fingernails.

'Not much in the way of defensive wounds,' Riley said doubtfully. They went away and left me there, with a uniformed officer – the one with the neck acne who came to Cathy's flat in Ashbury a lifetime ago – standing at the door, avoiding my eye. Later, Riley came back. 'Mrs Watson confirms your story, Rachel,' she said. 'You can go now.' She couldn't meet my gaze either. A uniformed policeman took me to the hospital, where they stitched up the wound on my scalp.

There's been a lot of stuff about Tom in the papers. I found out that he was never in the army. He tried to get in, but he was rejected twice. The story about his father was a lie, too – he'd twisted it all round. He took his parents' savings and lost it all. They forgave him, but he cut all ties with them when his father declined to remortgage their house in order to lend him more money. He lied all the time, about everything. Even when he didn't need to, even when there was no point.

I have the clearest memory of Scott talking about Megan, saying *I don't even know who she was,* and I feel exactly the same way. Tom's whole life was constructed on lies – falsehoods and half-truths told to make him look better, stronger, more interesting than he was. And I bought them, I fell for them all. Anna, too. We loved him. I wonder whether we would have loved the weaker, flawed, unembellished version. I think that I would. I would have forgiven his mistakes and his failures. I have committed enough of my own.

Evening

I'm at a hotel in a little town on the Norfolk coast. Tomorrow, I go further north. Edinburgh, maybe, perhaps further still. I haven't made my mind up yet. I just want to make sure I put plenty of distance behind me. I have some money. Mum was quite generous when she discovered everything I'd been through, so I don't have to worry. Not for a while.

I hired a car and drove to Holkham this afternoon. There's a church just outside the village where Megan's ashes are buried, next to the bones of her daughter, Libby. I read about it in the papers. There was some controversy over the burial, because of Megan's supposed role in the child's death. But it was allowed, in the end, and it seems right that it was. Whatever she did, she's been punished enough.

It was just starting to rain when I got there, with not a soul in sight, but I parked the car and walked around the graveyard anyway. I found her grave right in the furthermost corner, almost hidden under a line of firs. You would never know that she was there, unless you knew to go looking. The headstone marker bears her name and the dates of her life – no loving memory, no beloved wife, or daughter, or mother. Her child's stone just says 'Libby'. At least now her grave is properly marked; she's not all alone by the train tracks.

The rain started to fall harder, and when I went back through the churchyard I saw a man standing in the doorway of the chapel, and for just a second I imagined that he was Scott. My heart in my mouth, I wiped the rain from my eyes and looked again, and saw that it was a priest. He raised a hand to me in greeting.

I half ran back to the car, feeling needlessly afraid. I was thinking of the violence of my last meeting with Scott, of the way he was at the end – wild and paranoiac, on the edge of madness. There'll be no peace for him now. How can there be? I think about that, and the way he used to be – the way *they* used to be, the way I imagined them to be – and I feel bereft. I feel their loss, too.

I sent an email to Scott, apologizing for all the lies I told him. I wanted to say sorry about Tom, too, because I should have known. If I'd been sober all those years, would I have known? Maybe there will be no peace for me, either.

He didn't reply to my message. I didn't expect him to.

I return the car, make my way to the hotel and check in, and to stop myself thinking about how nice it would be to sit in a leather armchair in their cosy, low-lit bar with a glass of wine in my hand, I go for a walk out to the harbour instead.

I can imagine exactly how good I would feel halfway through my first drink. To push away the feeling, I count the days since I last had a drink: twenty. Twenty-one, if you include today. Three weeks exactly: my longest dry spell in years.

It was Cathy, oddly enough, who served me my last drink. When the police brought me home, grimly pale and bloody, and told her what happened, she fetched a bottle of Jack Daniel's from her room and poured us each a large measure. She couldn't stop crying, saying how sorry she was, as though it was in some way her fault. I drank the whisky and then I vomited it straight back up; I haven't touched a drop since. Doesn't stop me wanting to.

When I reach the harbour, I turn left and walk around its edge towards the stretch of beach along which I could walk, if I wanted to, all the way back to Holkham. It's almost dark now, and cold down by the water, but I keep going. I want to walk until I'm exhausted, until I'm so tired I can't think, and maybe then I will be able to sleep.

The beach is deserted, and it's so cold I have to clench my jaw to stop my teeth chattering. I walk quickly along the shingle, past the beach huts, so pretty in daylight but now sinister, each one of them a hiding place. When the wind picks up they come alive, their wooden boards creaking against each other, and under the sound of the sea there are murmurs of movement someone or something, coming closer.

I turn back, I start to run.

I know there's nothing out here, there's nothing to be afraid of, but it doesn't stop the fear rising from my stomach to my chest and into my throat. I run as fast as I can. I don't stop until I'm back on the harbour, in bright streetlight.

Back in my room I sit on my bed, sitting on my hands until they stop shaking. I open the minibar and take out the bottled water and the macadamia nuts. I leave the wine and the little bottles of gin, even though they would help me sleep, even though they would let me slide, warm and loose, into oblivion. Even though they would let me forget, for a while, the look on his face when I turned back to watch him die.

The train had passed. I heard a noise behind me, and saw Anna coming out of the house. She walked quickly towards us, and reaching his side, she fell to her knees and put her hands on his throat.

He had this look on his face of shock, of hurt. I wanted to say to her, *It's no good, you won't be able to help him now,* but then I realized she wasn't trying to stop the bleeding. She was making sure.

Twisting the corkscrew in, further and further, ripping into his throat, and all the time she was talking to him, softly, softly. I couldn't hear what she was saying.

The last time I saw her was in the police station, when they took us to give our statements. She was led to one room and I to another, but just before she parted, she touched my arm. 'You take care of yourself, Rachel,' she said, and there was something about the way she said it that made it feel like a warning. We are tied together, forever bound by the stories we told: that I had no choice but to stab him in the neck; that Anna tried her best to save him.

I get into bed and turn the lights out. I won't be able to sleep, but I have to try. Eventually, I suppose, the nightmares will stop and I'll stop replaying it over and over and over in my head, but right now I know that there's a long night ahead. And I have to get up early tomorrow morning, to catch the train.

ACKNOWLEDGEMENTS

Many people have helped in the writing of this book, but none more than my agent, Lizzy Kremer, who is wonderful and wise. Huge thanks also to Harriet Moore, Alice Howe, Emma Jamison, Chiara Natalucci and everyone at David Higham, as well as to Tine Neilsen and Stella Giatrakou.

I am very grateful to my brilliant editors on both sides of the Atlantic: Sarah Adams, Sarah McGrath and Nita Pronovost. My thanks also to Alison Barrow, Katy Loftus, Bill Scott-Kerr, Helen Edwards, Kate Samano and the fantastic team at Transworld – there are too many of you to mention.

Thank you Kate Neil, Jamie Wilding, Mum, Dad and Rich for all your support and encouragement.

Finally, thank you to the commuters of London, who provided that little spark of inspiration.

The publishers hope that this book has given you enjoyable reading. Large Print Books are especially designed to be as easy to see and hold as possible. If you wish a complete list of our books please ask at your local library or write directly to:

Magna Large Print Books
Magna House, Long Preston,
Skipton, North Yorkshire.
BD23 4ND

This Large Print Book for the partially sighted, who cannot read normal print, is published under the auspices of

THE ULVERSCROFT FOUNDATION

THE ULVERSCROFT FOUNDATION

... we hope that you have enjoyed this Large Print Book. Please think for a moment about those people who have worse eyesight problems than you ... and are unable to even read or enjoy Large Print, without great difficulty.

You can help them by sending a donation, large or small to:

The Ulverscroft Foundation, 1, The Green, Bradgate Road, Anstey, Leicestershire, LE7 7FU, England.
or request a copy of our brochure for more details.

The Foundation will use all your help to assist those people who are handicapped by various sight problems and need special attention.

Thank you very much for your help.